Mary

Mary

Sholem Asch

Translated by Leo Steinberg

CARROLL & GRAF PUBLISHERS, INC.
New York

First Carroll & Graf edition 1985

Carroll & Graf Publishers, Inc.
260 Fifth Avenue
New York, NY 10001

ISBN: 0-88184-141-2

Manufactured in the United States of America

PART ONE

CHAPTER I

Every dawn renews the Beginning, and to behold the earth struggling out of the formless void, out of the night, is to witness the act of creation.

The night hung low over the chine of the hills; but the concave of heaven, inlaid with innumerable brightness, diffused a shower of starlight that lent transparency to the night air. In the limpid darkness of the valley small houses nestled against one another in drowsy hamlets, where cypresses and olive groves shielded them on all sides. And on the hills each leaf of grass could be distinguished as it trembled under the fresh dew, swaying in the breeze as in mute prayer, and irradiated by the selfsame glow with which it had been charged in the first hours of Genesis.

Over the dew-blown hills rode a young traveler, clothed in a cowled white mantle to protect him from the damp of the night. He had given the ass rein to pick its way among the yews, wild rosebushes, and laurel shrubs that covered the hillsides, while he gave himself up to his thoughts. He considered the goal of his journey which was taking him to new people in an unfamiliar place. Would God prosper his way and help him to find favor with his kinsmen in Nazareth, to whom he was now turning, as Jacob had turned to Laban, to take a wife from their midst?

For the traveler was of noble family, the most high-born in Israel, the House of David, and it was no simple matter for one descended from the royal line to find a fitting wife for himself.

The noble families in Israel showed a relentless zeal in preserving the purity of their lineage and required every member to marry only with such families as equalled his own in rank and station. Nothing in a Jewish home was more tenderly guarded than the ancestral register, handed down from generation to generation as the most highly prized of heirlooms. And if a man married beneath his station, his kinsmen foregathered at the marketplace, called their children from their several homes and, with appropriate solemnity, distributing nuts and sweetmeats, told the children that "such-and-such a member of our house has taken an unworthy woman to wife, and we fear lest his offspring mix with ours. Remember, then, for all time, that this man's children shall not marry among us." And the children, having received their share of nuts and honey-wafers, responded: "Let this man be no more a member of our house."

If ordinary gentlefolk were so anxious to maintain the purity of their line, how much more zealous were those few who traced their lineage to the royal House of David, and from whose loins, in days to come, would spring the Messiah.

The traveler came from an impoverished branch of this mighty family. A joiner by trade, the son of parents whose entire fortune had been confiscated by Herod, he could not hope to be accepted as son-in-law in one of the rich families of the House of David—those who had made their peace with Herod and who, in consequence, could maintain winter palaces in Jerusalem and summer homes among the date gardens of Jericho. He had heard, however, that in the remote town of Nazareth, set in the mountains that surround the Valley of Jezreel, on a rarely frequented road that connects the Bay of Acco with Damascus, there lived a widow and her daughter who were descendants of the House of David. The father, who had died a short while since, had lived as a poor farmer and a God-fearing man. An elder daughter, Mariama, the wife of an artisan, was living in the town, helping the widow and her younger daughter Miriam to cultivate the family plot in Nazareth.

The traveler had chosen to make his journey by night, partly to avoid the heat of the day, and partly because he wished to keep his wandering thoughts close to his God. For his spirit was heavy and his heart filled with anxiety, and he knew that nothing brought him nearer to the face of God than being alone in the silence of the night.

He felt like a lamb, brought forth in an open field and abandoned to God's mercy. From early childhood he had been forced to support himself by his labor. Never had he been able to go up to Jerusalem to sit at the feet of the great rabbis and sages. His schooling had not progressed beyond what he had learned as a child; but it had served to quicken the hunger in his soul for God, for His Law and the justice of His ways. His guides, in the absence of father and kinsmen, had been the snatches of learning he recalled from his schooldays—a few quotations from the Prophets, the Psalms he could recite by rote, the prayers which fell fluent from his lips. For just as, from his earliest youth, he had supported his body with the work of his hands, so he had fed his spirit on the treasures stored in his heart. He did not think these treasures very rich, but he was a man satisfied with his portion and, as he never grumbled at the modest livelihood which his trade yielded, so he rested content with his smattering of Holy Writ. Greatest among his spiritual treasures was his possession of the Psalms, which he constantly repeated to himself, as he did now, riding his little ass across the hills under the starlit sky.

The recital of King David's verses did not prevent him from pursuing his meditations. If only God would help him to find favor and good fortune with his kinsmen in Nazareth and with the widowed mother and the girl Miriam who was to be his betrothed!

As he gave himself up to thoughts of his bride, he recalled how he had once met a man from Jerusalem, who had repeated to him the sayings he had heard a famous rabbin deliver in the forecourt of the Temple. Forty days before a man is born—the rabbin had taught—there is heard a heavenly voice, calling: The daughter of such-and-such is hereby bestowed upon this or that man! Perhaps just such a voice had called out for him, saying that Miriam, daughter of Hanan, would be his, Joseph ben Jacob's wife. If so, she was already his affianced bride, appointed by the Lord to help him build his house in Israel.

He shivered at the thought, as though he had touched on something ineffable and holy, as though he held his own soul in the palms of his hands.

Joseph halted his ass, slipped from the saddle, and poured off the water from the leather bottle which he carried with him for

3

the ceremony of the washing of the hands. Then he knelt on the moist earth and, like Jacob at Bethel, lifted his arms to the sky, while his lips murmured the prayer that had ripened in his heart:

"Lord of the world, God of Abraham, Isaac, and Jacob, who didst preserve the father of my house, Thy beloved servant David, in all his ways! Prosper my enterprise and make me walk in Thy true path. And when I reach the place to which Thou leadest me, let me find favor in her eyes whom Thou hast appointed for my wife, and in the eyes of her kinsmen and friends, that I may wed her in holiness and purity according to Thy Law, and build with her my house in Israel."

When Joseph rose again from the damp ground he saw a milky mist, like a woolen sheet, over the plain that stretched itself at the foot of the hills. Housetops and cypress trees were beginning to pierce it, tearing it into patches of cloud.

Perched high above the mist Joseph felt like one suspended in air. And looking to the horizon he saw a glorious whiteness, as from an unseen source, spread a thin sheen of light across the sky. Little by little the world carved itself out of the nameless darkness which had held heaven and earth in one embrace, and, as on the first day of creation, the firmament once more divided from the land.

And at his feet, hugged in a mountain dale as between the humps of a camel, Joseph caught sight of the small humble town of Nazareth. Bathed in dew, the little close-clinging town, within its green girdle of cypress groves, rose from the surrounding green of the country, lifting itself through the mist that still covered the land.

Joseph reined his ass to the path that led to the town.

Not wishing to take the widow and her daughter unawares, he resolved to call first on an uncle of the girl's, her father's brother, one Reb Elimelech. Reb Elimelech was of his own kin. Like the girl's deceased father, he was a near cousin on his father's side, and, like himself, earned his bread as a joiner. For in most families in Israel the ancestral calling was passed on from father to son through the generations. Joseph determined, therefore, to guide his first steps in the town to Reb Elimelech's house, and to reveal to him, as to the orphan's nearest kinsman, the nature of his suit, that the old man might bring his cause before the girl and her mother.

And Joseph with his ass, both soaked in the night's dew which lay upon his cloak, his hair, and his bare feet, and on the ass's skin, waded through the rank growth of oleander and laurel shrubs that lined the path to the town.

The daughters of the town, with pitchers mounted on their heads, were strolling out toward the common well. Plumes of smoke issued from open doors. Day-laborers were readying their tools and going to work with spades and axes on their shoulders. The air filled with the braying, mooing, and lowing of asses and kine, the clang of hammers, and the shouting of children. Flocks of sheep and goats going to pasture raised clouds of dust behind them.

Joseph guided his ass through the narrow, awakening streets and, turning to the women who sat with handmills in their laps in the thresholds of their houses, asked where among them lodged Reb Elimelech, the joiner.

The household of Hannah, Hanan's widow, had risen with the rest of the town to its daily tasks. It was not a large house. Situated at the outskirts of Nazareth, it adjoined the olive grove which filled the vale between the mountain and the village. The grove was the common; it belonged to the town, and every man had a right to its fruit. The house itself was enclosed on three sides by a hedge of wild-growing willow branches to separate it from the common. A small hill loomed before it on which their animals grazed. And like every house in Israel it had a vegetable garden, carefully tended to ensure that the diverse kinds did not mix in the same furrow. Thus, wherever one vegetable had been planted, it was severely fenced off from the neighboring beds. A grapevine ran along a trellised bower, and an orchard was there with a few olive and fig trees and a handful of pomegranates. The scanty herd of animals consisted of some ten sheep and their young, and an ass who toiled both as a beast of burden and before the plow. This small flock, scrupulously segregated from the family's living quarters, was housed in a few stalls which were covered at the top

5

with a matting of twigs. At the back of the house, beyond the vegetable garden, was the cistern, shaded by cypress trees, carefully enclosed with stones and clay and, in accordance with the law, protected by a sturdy fence—that there might be no accident to man or beast.

The dwelling itself was low and small. Plain limestone walls contained a long narrow room whose center was occupied by a stone fireplace and tripod. A hole cut in the ceiling served as an outlet for the smoke. For windows there were open gaps in the walls, while another larger opening, hung with a heavy woven cloth, served as the door.

The roof was low and heavy, and beams of cypress wood ran its entire length. These were crossed with bamboo stems and—between them—a thick layer of palm sprigs. In one corner only, at the room's eastern end, which pointed to Jerusalem, the roof was reinforced with more platted bamboo, for here, above the ceiling, was a small attic, open to the sky and approached by a ladder. It served the family as a place of rest and prayer and was used also for the drying of fruit and cheese.

The furnishing of this east corner of the room was rudimentary —a low-legged table flanked by a wall seat padded with cushions and shawls. But here stood the family shrine, the chest with the family treasures. It contained two scrolls of the Law, which had come down through many generations; a parchment of the Book of Isaiah, the songs of David, and the sacred histories, which told the life of the great king from whom their tribe had sprung; the Book of Ruth, first mother of their house; and, finally, the critical family document, the register of births, which traced, through fathers and sons, their descent from King David, and which the family cherished and preserved as though it were its very life.

While the head of the household was living, all solemn rites of Sabbath and festival were performed in this corner. At this table, each Friday night, the father had ushered in and sanctified the Sabbath with a cup of wine. The homely feats which accompanied these ceremonies were conducted in this corner, as was the reading of the Holy Writ before the assembled family each morning and evening, at dawn and at dusk, that there might be fulfilled the commandment: "And thou shalt ponder it by day and by

6

night." The widow had upheld this custom despite her husband's death; each day began, and each day closed, with a verse from the Book, from which she read aloud in her child's hearing.

As in every Jewish home, so there were in Hannah's house separate quarters, partitioned off by hanging curtains, for men and for women. Though no menfolk remained in the house, and the widow, ever since the elder Mariama had joined her husband's family, was left living alone with her younger daughter, she yet retained the partitions as in her husband's time. Within her own curtained chamber the mistress of the house could abide undisturbed whenever she wished to be alone. It was her personal refuge and, besides her pallet, an earthen jar, and a chest of clothes, contained her written marriage contract but for whose possession she could not have lived lawfully with her husband. And like the matron of the house, so the daughter came to have her personal retreat as soon as she had come of age. In it stood the loom on which Hannah had woven her own and her husband's garments.

The first breath a Jew draws on awakening from a night's sleep belongs to God; thus, too, in the house of the widow Hannah. Stepping out of their separate chambers after the first cry of the cock, mother and daughter washed their hands and eyes and pronounced the morning's blessing. The girl found her mother already seated in her husband's place by the table at the east end of the room, a position she occupied only when fulfilling one of her husband's sacramental duties. Hannah withdrew a parchment from the chest and read out the first chapter of the Book of Ruth, her favorite reading. Ruth was of her kin; Ruth, no less than the great King himself, was the pride of all who looked upon themselves as scions of the House of David. And Ruth was the most cherished idol of the women in the family. The book which bore her name in the Scriptures was reverently read and re-read by them times without end. For Ruth had sprung from an alien people and yet, thanks to her loyalty, had attained the highest grace to which a mother in Israel could aspire—to be the founding matriarch of the royal and Messianic line.

After the reading of the first chapter the two women said the *Sh'ma Yisroel*—"Hear, O Israel." The Law, it is true, did not

7

exact this observance from their sex, but pious women continued in the recitation of the prayer and the sages did not stay them. Only when the prayer was done did mother and daughter turn to their household tasks.

The second daily duty in a Jewish home, after due praise had been offered to God, was to provide feed and water for the animals. Man must not sit down to his morning meal before the hunger of his animals is stilled. Thus, as the mother attended to the work indoors, the daughter went forth to cater to the herd.

Outside, the mist that weighted the atmosphere was beginning to lift. Loose shreds of cloud, like floating veils, stole through the air, catching on branches and roofs. The mist was decomposing into drops of dew that shone again from every leaf and petal. The girl's feet soaked up the damp, and pearly drops settled on the thick black locks that strayed from her kerchief. Her frail throat, showing above a homespun tunic, shivered at the freshness of the early morning. But she felt neither the damp nor the cold, eager air which had surged forward to embrace her as she stepped outdoors. Her mind was occupied still with the images conjured by her mother's reading—Hebrew word-images translated for her into the colloquial Aramaic—the story of Naomi and her two daughters-in-law returning to Bethlehem. It was often she had heard the tale, but each time it seemed as new. She was one with Naomi and Ruth on the road to Bethlehem. She heard the voice of Ruth, saying: "Whither thou goest I will go, and where thou lodgest I will lodge." How inscrutable were the ways of the Lord to elect this foreign woman, sprung from an alien people and an alien god, to be one of the holy Jewish mothers, even as Sarah and Rebecca! No, she was like Rachel herself. Hers was the grace to bring forth the Messiah. Was not this proof that the King-Messiah would come for all men and all nations, seeing that all nations were children of the Lord, as told by the Prophets? An alien people had cradled the mother of David's tribe in order that all nations might have a share in the inheritance, in the King-Messiah, the shoot of the House of David.

The girl reached the sheep's pen. The flock was waiting for her, listening for her footfall. Moist, slavering muzzles stretched toward her, snuggled against her, wetted her hands with slick

8

tongues and eyes. Miriam had a name for each sheep as each came up in turn to fetch its share of tenderness. One she caressed over the eyes and called him "Moonlight"; another was lent a finger to lick. One presented its ears to be stroked, another its nostrils. Small suckling kids and lambkins she took up in her arms, rested her cheek against theirs, shared the commingling heat of their bodies, and drew her fingers through their shaggy wool. The guiltless pulse of their animal life beat against her arms and breast and sent a shudder down her own young body, as though she felt the doom of every kid and lamb that was appointed for a taintless sacrifice to God.

Miriam opened the fold and led the animals to the trough, where she opened the drain that ran down from the cistern. Last came the ass, waiting with a donkey's resignation for his portion of love. Miriam tickled the adam's apple under his straggling whiskers, and the ass acknowledged the favor with a soft bray of satisfaction while Miriam led him to water and finally threw him a bundle of hay.

The earth was dry under her feet when she returned to the house. The sun had sent a rich bright blaze across the sky; like fervent tongues, its rays lapped up the dew from grass and twigs and dried the damp on the girl's hair and her bare arms and feet. Sunlight was playing on the faded blue of her tunic, lending it some of the hue and radiance of the sky. She walked in a tremulous haze of light which sparkled again in her eyes and showed up the blue veins that formed a tracery under the translucent skin of her temples. The kiss of the sun's heat on her skin made her blood quicken and sent a flush to her face. She inclined her head, and with the flat of her hand covered her eyes.

Before re-crossing her mother's threshold she remembered that there was a friend waiting for her, and she guided her steps back to the cistern at the far corner of the yard. Making her way through heavy clumps of cypresses and oleander, she reached the edge of the well where she found the young doe and fawn that came each morning to drink from its water. Miriam had come upon them once and gained their trust with a handful of grass. Thus had their friendship begun, and from that day, each morning, as soon as the household animals had been watered and fed,

Miriam plucked fresh leaves from beet or carrot plants in her garden and brought them to regale her guests, who continued to come down daily from the wooded hills, finding their own way into the yard. Miriam could not spare them much of her time. In the beginning, when their friendship was young, she could not do enough for these strange visitors; there was never an end to the stroking, hugging, and tousling of fur. But they were old friends now and there was not time every day for such indulgences; mother was waiting for her in the house, and her work for the day had only just begun. Miriam had to content herself with one fleeting caress of the doe's delicate head and a lick of the fawn's tongue. Then mother and young munched hurriedly at the fresh vegetable leaves she had brought, or the occasional armful of hay, which came out of the ass's allowance, until Miriam suddenly turned on her heels and, like another doe, fled back to the house. For her mother's voice was now coming from the distance:

"Miriam, Miriam, where are you?"

"I am coming!" she called back and, turning in her stride to the wildcat that had come down from the mountains looking for company, "You'd better go back to your hills. I have nothing for you. Go find your own."

Back in the house Miriam hoisted two pitchers and sortied out again, this time to the town well to draw water for the family's use; the animals, for the time being, could make do with the cistern water, the spring rains having but recently passed.

Thus, each day went by in a round of duties—indoors, out in the garden, in the fields. For the household in the main was self-sufficient—with a few exceptions. Thus Miriam would lead the sheep to the meadow between the olive yard and the foot of the stone mountain, a common pasture ground where a hired shepherd, maintained by the community, tended the sheep, goats, and cattle of the inhabitants. Before nightfall the shepherd drove her little flock back to the house, a light task this, since Miriam's sheep knew their way blind and, upon reaching the opening in the low willow hedge, entered without being coaxed.

Certain other tasks, too, were performed by hired day-laborers —such as shearing the sheep and washing and carding their wool, these being regarded as purely masculine employments. Miriam then looked after the vegetable garden and the flower beds, which were planted to yield incense for the women; for every woman in Israel, no matter how poor, kept a store of incense oils. It was for Miriam also to press oils for the lamps, since it was traditionally the woman's part to provide them for her husband's house out of her own earnings, or with the labor of her hands.

All this Miriam had learned, like every Jewish daughter, in her girlhood, that she might know how later to perform the duties of her husband's house. She must know how to use pestle and mortar for the pressing of oils and the pounding of spices. She must be deft with the spindle and the loom, gather brushwood and dry kindling from the olive grove to heat the oven, prepare the pallets, keep the house tidy, set the table, and wash her own linen. Beyond all this Miriam had to cultivate the small field that adjoined their house.

All day was filled out with work, leaving only a few odd moments here and there, brief respites between one task and another, which might be used to visit a sick neighbor with a ladle of hot soup, or else were spent at the loom, weaving some fabric to take up to Jerusalem as an offering for a Temple hanging or a holy vestment for an aspirant priest.

During the hot summer days, following the midday meal, the women took a hurried siesta in the cool shade of the house. But throughout the year the proper time for rest was after sunset. Then the widow would tell Miriam pious legends of the lives of the Patriarchs and their womenfolk and read from the Scriptures, returning nightly with especial reverence to those Prophets who spoke of mankind's hope, the King-Messiah, for whose coming Israel waited day by day.

That night after dusk, when, by the light of the oil lamp, the widow and her daughter had eaten their main meal of the day, when the dishes were cleared away and the lamp was back on the table so that the day might end as it had begun with the reading of God's word as delivered by His Prophets, that night there was a knocking at the widow's doorpost, where the *Mezuzah* hung—three knocks to signify a visitor. The women exchanged wondering glances; who could be calling on them in midweek?

Visits were paid only on the Sabbath or on festival days. And they turned to face the entering form of the uncle, the tall Reb Elimelech, whose long, tapering beard lent nobility to his features even at a distance, even in the semi-darkness which reigned in the room.

Widow and daughter rose from their places and came forward to hail their guest and return his greeting, *"Shalom aleichem"*— "Peace be with you." After the family custom they welcomed their kinsman with a kiss on cheek and hand and led him to the place of honor, the master's seat at the table.

The girl Miriam made haste to place refreshments before the visitor; a bowl of nuts, almonds, and dried grapes. Reb Elimelech pronounced the blessing before tasting of the proffered fruit, then introduced his errand with a verse from the Scripture: "King Solomon, peace be with him, has said: 'Cast thy bread upon the waters, for thou shalt find it after many days.' This has even now come to pass. My cousin Jacob who, as you remember, was kinsman to your husband, once lived here with us. Many years ago he forsook this town and journeyed to the hills of Judah to hide from the kingdom of evil. I never heard from him to this day, nor saw him all these years. For many years passed and I feared lest his branch of our family had been cut off and lost in Israel. This day the bread that was cast upon the waters has returned unto us. At daybreak a stranger knocked at my door, and when I asked him for his name, he said, 'I am your kinsman; my father, peace be with him, was your second cousin. His name was called Mar Jacob of the House of David. And I am called Joseph.'"

"Yes, I remember how we accompanied Reb Jacob out of the town," the widow interrupted. "My husband went with him two miles of the way."

As she spoke, Hannah laid a toil-worn hand over her bloodshot eyes to shut out the light of the lamp.

Reb Elimelech resumed: "The bread that we then cast upon the waters we have found again. Reb Jacob was gathered to his people, but his son, who is strong and God-fearing, has returned to his father's homestead."

"And what is the young man's purpose? Will he stay here with us?"

"Yes, for he has brought with him the skill of his hands, our family trade. He, too, is a joiner." And Reb Elimelech nodded knowingly at the widow, who was not slow to catch his meaning. Turning to her daughter, she said:

"The animals must be fed betimes tomorrow and the hour grows late. Go, my child, to your room. I will yet sit a while with your uncle to speak with him another word or two."

Miriam, bowing to her mother and uncle, retired to her chamber. Reb Elimelech waited until she had gone and then continued.

"When my brother, your husband, Reb Hanan, fell into a sickness and knew that he would soon be gathered to his people, he called me to his bedside and took my oath that I would see his youngest daughter, Miriam, marry only with such a family as made a fitting peer to ours, which is of the House of David. For he loved his youngest child above his life, because she gladdened his old age."

"Indeed, I know," interjected the widow. "My husband had always longed and hoped for a son to build his house in Israel after his passing. But for my sins God withheld His grace from me and I bore him no son. And when I was delivered of this youngest child, and he found her, too, to be a daughter, he said to me— I remember it as though it were yesterday—'Be not troubled, my wife, for she is dearer to me than ten sons.' And so she became like a son in his eyes, and he raised her up as though she were a boy. He taught her to read and study the Law, and when she came of age he sent her to Jerusalem that she might be near the Temple of the Lord. . . ."

"And now the Lord has given it into my hand to redeem my promise to your husband," said Reb Elimelech quickly, before the widow could continue. "Know then, Hannah, daughter of Jochebeth, that the young man who this day crossed my threshold springs, as do we, from the pure and holy line of our father David and his grandam Ruth. Now this is the purpose of his coming to our town: if it find favor in your eyes, and in the eyes of your maiden daughter, he is ready to take her to wife and build his house in Israel with us in our town.

"When I heard this I resolved in my heart that I would come tonight to bring his cause before the maiden's mother. For this man has found favor in my eyes. He fears the Lord and, though the Law is not strong in his hand, he has the temper of the Patriarchs. He is pious and God-fearing and walks humbly in the ways of his fathers."

"Then the Lord has heard the widow's prayer!" Hannah cried out, locking her hands and raising them above her head. "For in my old age this alone troubled my heart—how I should see my daughter wed to one of our kin, being so poor. But this is joyful news, more fitting for the Sabbath. That day bring you the lad to our house that he may see our maiden. And if the young folk find favor in each other's eyes, we shall, with God's help, see them betrothed before the month of Adar is out."

Here, for a time, the matter rested. Taking the oil lamp from the table, the widow escorted her guest over the threshold. And since he was alone, she placed the lamp into his hand to light his way. Then she withdrew into the house where the girl Miriam lay sleepless on her pallet, gazing with wide eyes at the stars that shone in through the open window.

CHAPTER II

ON THE following Sabbath Reb Elimelech presented his kinsman Joseph ben Jacob to the assembled congregation in the synagogue of Nazareth. The citizenry of the small town consisted for the most part of a few outstanding families; there was the family of Reb Hanan and Reb Elimelech, descended from the House of David, and there were the sons of Pinhas, a family of common priests, who traced their lineage to Aaron, first high priest of Israel; there were families, too, of the tribe of Issachar and representatives of Zadok's house.

Each family had its own trade. The sons of David, as has been said, were joiners and carpenters; those of Issachar were sandal makers and driers of fruit, and they grew nuts and dates and supplied wood to the town from the surrounding hills. As for the sons of Pinhas, their rank entitled them to live on the priestly portion of the people's tithes; but since, as common priests, they had few opportunities to serve in the Temple at Jerusalem, they eked out their livelihood as potters, taking their wares to market in the commercial center of Sepphoris and the towns of the Jezreel plain. For the people of Nazareth were far too poor to support their own priestly caste.

Repeated intermarriages had rendered Nazareth a close-knit community, where all men knew each other for generations back. It was no wonder, therefore, that the young Joseph was readily accepted by those of his kin. In welcoming the son they hailed the return of Jacob's house to Nazareth, and their welcome was the heartier when they learned that the young man had come to wed one of their daughters and build his house in Israel in their midst. For the matter of his projected marriage was not kept secret. On the contrary, it was broadcast by both parties, both by Reb Elimelech, who regarded himself as the suitor's closest kinsman, and by the maiden's mother. It was necessary for the entire town to know that a certain man was seeking to take a girl to wife, so that if, God forbid, any man objected to the marriage, or wished to make an evil report against bridegroom or bride, he could stand forth and speak before it was too late. And so the whole town knew that on this Sabbath, the bride would sit through the day in her mother's house to receive the visits of relatives and friends, and that on the fourth day of the coming week, to wit, on Wednesday next, the contract of betrothal would be written according to the law of Israel.

Joseph, then, was accepted as one of the community. The town rabbi, Reb Jochanan of the sons of Zadok of Jerusalem, called on him to mount the steps that led up to the ark of the Torah. Joseph obeyed. He was wearing a white, freshly-laundered, sleeveless tunic, his festive dress. His dark hair was parted in the middle and combed down smoothly to frame his head and neck. His lean face, tapering to a small pointed beard, bore a youthful dignity as he marched up the aisle, and only his eyes looked fearful and shy.

He was called to the reading of the Torah; and when, after the reading, he raised the heavy scroll with both arms, holding it high

15

for all the people to see, the rabbi rose from his seat and, with two judges of the court at his side, took his stand next to Joseph so as to face the congregation and called out:

"This our brother in Israel, the bachelor Joseph, Reb Jacob's son, who is of the family of David the King, has returned to our town, which is the town of his parents, and desires to wed Miriam, daughter of Reb Hanan, who is of like descent; and he desires further to settle among us to build his house in Israel in our midst. Let him who has aught to bring against him come forth now and speak."

For a long while the congregation kept silent—though there was a restive stir among the young men at the back, and chiefly among those who were of the bride's family and who had nurtured secret hopes to take the place now occupied by the stranger. But when several minutes had passed and no man had dared protest against the newcomer in the face of his protector, the venerable Reb Elimelech, the rabbi, turning to Joseph, called out in a loud voice:

"Blessed be your coming; a brother you shall be to us!"

His words were promptly echoed by the congregation. Even some of the young men, though their eyes were pinched with jealousy, mounted the rostrum after their elders to greet the stranger with the formula of benediction: "Blessed be your coming among us, our brother!"

In this manner was Joseph accepted a citizen of Nazareth.

Throughout that Sabbath day the bride sat on a wooden bench in her mother's house. Her braids were loosened and her hair fell free over her nape and back—a symbol of her maidenhood for all to see and remember. As a maiden she was entitled in her marriage contract to no less than two hundred silver dinars, to be paid by her husband in case of divorce. It was important, therefore, lest future evidence were needed, that the townspeople see her sit through the day with disheveled hair. Children would be handed honeycakes and almonds the better to remember the occasion. And for the adult guests the tables would be set with earthen dishes, filled with slices of melon and dried figs, and raisins, nuts and plums, and apricots and cuts of pomegranates dipped in wine, and cooling liquids, such as the kingly juice of

16

the asparagus, to help sustain the midday heat. And, in addition, the women would prepare dates and cakes kneaded in honey—named honey-wafers for the desert's manna—and pastries soaked in milk. And there would be no want of visitors to eat the proffered things, from the closing of the service in the synagogue to the setting of the sun.

First to arrive were the bride's friends, the neighbors' daughters. They came with wreaths of fresh forget-me-nots and marguerites to adorn the bride's head and shoulders. Then they grouped themselves two-deep on either side of the room—the comely girls behind the bride, the homely ones in front; the nobly-born at the back, the others before. Thus the bride's gentle birth and beauty would shine forth freely without rivalry, and the groom would not be tempted to cast his eye on others.

Next to arrive, in accordance with custom, were the townsmen, and after them their womenfolk and children; and before long the little house was filled with genial visitors. But suddenly, the curtain in the doorway was rudely brushed aside to admit the big-boned solemn form of Reb Hanina ben Safra, the local priest of the house of Pinhas. He entered broadly, followed by his six grown sons who at once planted themselves behind him like a stockade of cypress trees.

The priest remained standing, despite Reb Elimelech's and the widow Hannah's invitation to seat himself at the head of the table by the rabbi's side, despite the obvious movement of the humbler townsfolk at the table to make room for him. He stood squarely in the middle of the room, his eyes dark and stern under a pair of grizzled eyebrows, his heavily ringed fingers stuck in the purple belt that bound his long white mantle. And fixing his gaze—the haughty gaze of practiced priesthood—on the pale face of the groom who sat on a separate stool at the bride's side, he said in a voice edged with rancor:

"And what inquiries have been made to ascertain the origin of this young lad, who came here from we know not where and now lays claim to the noblest-born of our daughters?"

There was immediate silence in the room. It was common knowledge that Reb Hanina ben Safra regarded himself as a sage and that he was the most voluble speaker at all public gatherings. And it was known that he was remotely related to the bride on her mother's side, so that he would look upon himself as her kinsman, with a kinsman's prerogatives. But it was notorious also that Reb Hanina had hoped to see the young orphan, daughter of a noble house, married to one of his own sons, so that his present show of solicitude might well be actuated by self-seeking. The company, therefore, tried to ignore his speech, so as not to disturb the joyfulness of the occasion and cause pain to the bride. Even more they felt for the young stranger whose blood the priest was shedding before so large a company. At length one of the guests tried to relieve the tension by turning to the children present with more fruits and nuts and saying to them:

"Now you, little ones, remember when you grow up that you witnessed the betrothal of this maiden, Miriam, to Joseph ben Jacob of the House of David, and that you had your nuts and almonds as a token of her maidenhood."

But the priest was not so easily distracted.

"It is an open truth before the Maker of Light that I pose my question not in my own interest, nor for the honor of my house, but solely for the honor of this orphan who is of royal blood, even of the House of David the King, Israel's minstrel. And even though differences existed between Hanan and me, her mother is my kinswoman. As her kinsman, then, I demand to know what inquiries have been made, and what precautions taken, regarding this young man."

"Why, we all know the house from which he springs," said Reb Elimelech softly, without looking at the priest. "His father was one of us, and do not all of us remember Mar Jacob of the House of David? His son Joseph has come home to marry one of his own kin, for he is kinsman to the bride, as Boaz was to Ruth. If the questioner has anything to bring against the groom, why did he hold his peace this morning in the synagogue when the match was announced? For it is not meet to shed the young man's blood here where we are gathered to rejoice with the young couple."

"The synagogue is no place for such business," retorted the priest. "This matter should have been probed by the bride's kin before spreading it abroad. Now, as a kinsman of the bride, I demand to know what amount the groom will subscribe in the marriage contract, and whether he has a field and oxen, and what his inheritance is in Israel. . . . Yes, we all know that Mar Jacob once lived among us, but it is many years since he forsook our town. And there are several eligible bachelors in Nazareth whose descent from the house of Aaron gives them a better title to the bride than this young stranger who arrived but yesterday—and now, with unseemly haste, proposes to inherit a field and a house in addition to the noble daughter of one of our most respected families."

The company now understood the drift of his intention, and a smile flickered across the faces of the men as they winked knowingly at one another.

At this point the rabbi, Reb Jochanan, rose to put an end to the matter.

"We are all children of God," he quoted gravely, "and it is not our way in Israel to distinguish between newcomers and old-time residents. 'Thou shalt love the stranger within thy gate, for ye were all strangers in the land of Egypt,' says the Scripture. I must, therefore, with all the respect I bear our priest, put a stop to this altercation, seeing that it profits no man but rather spills the blood of an innocent. The lad Joseph ben Jacob has a full right to this match and we are not assembled here to try his merits but to rejoice in his good fortune. Therefore, I say, let us sing to the young folk—to the groom Joseph who is king today, and to Miriam, the queen-bride."

But the matter did not rest here, for they were bitter men, these Galileans. They were wont to stand on their rights and rarely shrank from a fight—"quick to anger and hard to conciliate" as the saying goes. And the next day, in the market, Hanina ben Safra doggedly pursued his point:

"And even if the young man's family has been investigated, this will not suffice for me. As kinsman to the bride I have a right to insist that the investigation satisfy me as well as the next man. Therefore, I question the rabbi's judgment. The kinsmen should have been consulted first."

His persistence finally aroused more of the bride's kin to a sense of injury. Cleophas, the artisan who had married the bride's elder sister, Mariama, suddenly recalled that he too had been rudely by-passed in the marriage preparations. And other families joined in the dispute; men who but the day before had extended friendly welcome to the stranger now came to look at him askance, as on one who had willfully invaded their province to carry off the noblest of their daughters.

The town of Nazareth, they argued, was none too rich, and it was hard enough for old inhabitants to make ends meet. They did not need another joiner in the town to vie with them for every crust of bread.

And it must be admitted that there was a certain justice in their complaint. The town lay on the Galilean-Syrian highway, and the joiners supported themselves largely by mending the wagons of passing travelers. This source of livelihood was of necessity limited. As for the soil of Nazareth, though it could not be called arid, it certainly could not compete with the rich dark earth on the Sea of Genesaret—to say nothing of the richer soil of the Jezreel valley. The fruit crops of Nazareth—the figs, dates, and almonds—matured too late in the season, and most of the local wine, produced by small growers, was too thin to sustain the competition of such celebrated vineyards as Sichna—whose products were sold as far south as Jerusalem for use in Temple services. The best of Nazarene wines only just qualified for export from the tollhouse at K'far Nahum, whence they were shipped to the Greek cities of Decapolis on the farther side of the Lake, where prices for imported Galilean crops stood higher than at home. But this applied to the wines only; the poor quality of other crops restricted them to the home markets where prices were perennially low and rarely yielded enough for the high taxes which the government imposed. Thus many of the farmers of Galilee were compelled to seek the bulk of their livelihood as artisans—in pottery, carpentry, and allied trades.

For all these reasons opposition to a newcomer like Joseph was easily fomented, particularly among the bride's near and distant kin who shared his profession.

"Has anyone seen the camels bowed down with precious gifts which this new Eliezer has brought the brothers of his bride?" sneered one of the relatives.

"Empty-handed as he is, he expects us to adopt him as a brother," said a second.

"But who said he came empty-handed? Did he not bring with him the skill of his hands?"

"Then he brought sand to the seashore," laughed another. "Is there a want of carpenters in Nazareth?"

Thus, so soon after his arrival, there grew up an estrangement, almost a hostility, between the newcomer and his bride's family. Fortunately for Joseph he stood under the protection of Reb Elimelech, the head of David's house in Nazareth. Under the old man's roof, Joseph settled in the town, to all appearances a brother of the sons of David. But the priest Hanina and his family nursed the rancor in their hearts and bided their time.

CHAPTER III

IT WAS the dream of every girl in Israel to go up to Jerusalem and there to do her share of service in the workshops of the Temple—weaving vestments for the priests and curtains to drape the countless halls and chambers of the Sanctuary. For daughters of noble or affluent houses it was an easy wish to gratify, since their families usually had influential kinsmen living in the capital. For those that came from indigent families in Galilee, it was a distant dream beyond attainment in this life.

Although there was a town in Galilee where draperies were woven for the Temple, Reb Hanan had felt that his younger daughter, Miriam, should go up to Jerusalem like the best of her people. Thus, when his wife's kinsman, Zachariah, a son of Aaron of the division of Abijah, was appointed to the sacred service in the inner Temple, he sent Miriam to Elisheva, the priest's wife, under whose spiritual guidance Miriam was to spend her days in the holy city.

The Law had been sparing in the sacred obligations it had laid on Jewish daughters. Women were valued not for themselves, but as complements to their men. Woman's highest service was to bear children, her proudest state, not wifehood nor virginity, but motherhood. And every Jewish daughter had this one overriding ambition—to be married to an honest man and bear him sons in Israel. The female child, therefore, was of little standing, and one did not even trouble to name it for some favorite kinswoman. Daughters were named simply after a Matriarch or some other heroine who had won renown in Israel. Thus Miriam, the sister of Moses, was well loved in Jewish memory and her name was frequently bestowed on new-born girls, even though it might be borne already by other daughters of the house. So it had come to pass that Hanan's daughters both bore the name of Miriam, and were called, for distinction's sake, "the elder" and "the younger." In time the elder of the two came to be called, after the current Aramaic fashion, Mariama.

But while all this was true, it must be admitted also that for a long time past, certain individual women had been mainstays of the imaginative life of the people. Their names assumed high rank in Israel's hierarchy and quickened the creative fantasy of the myth makers. The Matriarchs of Israel were canonized by the people and placed, beside their men, on the uppermost rungs of Jacob's heavenly ladder. The matron Sarah became a prime factor in the founding of the nation, even as Abraham himself. Isaac, father of Israel, was her issue and could have been no other woman's. And what was true of Sarah applied equally to her successors who shared the Patriarchs' Tomb in the cave of Machpelah. Similarly those later heroines—Miriam, Deborah, or Hannah, Samuel's mother—had captured a firm hold on the devotion of the people. Nor was this devotion reserved only for women born in Israel; Pharaoh's daughter, for having found the infant Moses in the bulrushes and adopting him for a son, was gratefully remembered and accorded an honored place in Eden—to say nothing of the stranger Ruth whom the Lord had favored more highly than any Israelite, seeing that she became the ancestress of David's house to which were tied all Jewry's hopes of salvation.

But of all mothers in Israel none was loved more deeply than Rachel, Jacob's bride-elect. For her the youthful Jacob had toiled twice seven years, and still she was an outcast in the holy matriarchy. In pain and agony she had born Israel a son, and had died bearing him another. And she alone among the Matriarchs was not laid in the ancestral sepulchre, to share the shade of Abraham and Isaac and her doting husband Jacob—as did her rival, Leah. She, Rachel, was hastily interred on the road to Ephrath, which is Bethlehem, like some worthless stone that one thrusts out of one's way. Yet, surely, there was providence even in this. For she was buried on the highway down which, in years to come, Nebuzaradan would lead Jewry into exile. The ruthless Babylonian would be scourging them past Rachel's grave, and she, a sentinel by the roadside, would arise from her tomb and come before the Lord with bitter weeping for her children's sake. And God would sustain her with words of comfort, saying:

"Refrain thy voice from weeping, and thine eyes from tears; for thy work shall be rewarded, saith the Lord, and thy children shall return to their own borders."

Thus Rachel's name was woven into legend; she became Israel's grieving mother, who bore on her frail shoulders all the sorrow of the people. Her stature as an intercessor began to rise beyond that of her peers. When all the Patriarchs, when even Moses, could not sway the will of God, Rachel came before the Presence with her tears and her wild grief and showed the Lord her broken heart, and the Lord dried her tears with words of consolation.

For the girl Miriam, Rachel had long been the chosen patroness, a guardian angel watching over her. Many times she saw her, not only in her dreams at night, but in broad daylight, seeing with inward eyes. The mother Rachel would appear to her, swathed in a dusky veil. At times her features were uncovered to reveal large dark eyes, reddened and moist, and heavy with grief and compassion, as though the anguish of all Israel were stored in them. And from those eyes Miriam felt the anguish radiating into her own heart as if the mother Rachel wished to make the girl a part of her and bind her to herself in a community of love and grief. To the girl Miriam the thought of Rachel was like the immanence of heaven.

The courts of the Temple, flanked by vaulted colonnades, gave access to innumerable halls and chambers, some open, others closed against the public stare. Among the pilgrims who thronged into these courts rumors were rife of secret labyrinths and subterranean passages, said to lie deep below the Temple's cellar and excavated in King Solomon's days, if not before.

Each of these passages had its separate name, such as the Cave of Elijah, or Jeremiah's Pit. Other stories spoke of forbidden passages whose trails led to the upper regions of the world. One such was said to lead to the Garden of Eden, another to the Patriarchs' Tomb; for it was fabled that a secret corridor linked the Temple with the sepulchre in Hebron. Yet another subterranean chamber in the Temple was reputed to be the abode of the holy mothers of Israel.

Like every pious pilgrim, the girl Miriam accepted the reality of these underground passages with perfect faith. She believed, too, that there was direct access from the abode of the Matriarchs to Rachel's grave on the Bethlehem road, and that Rachel, like the Patriarchs and Prophets, rested in the mystic shade of the Temple.

Once, as she knelt in the Court of the Women, transported in the ecstasy of prayer, the form of Rachel appeared before her eyes. It approached and touched her hand and Miriam heard a voice, saying: "Come with me, child." And Miriam, following, beheld one of the secret caves, the Hall of the Patriarchs, on which no human eyes had gazed before.

On Sabbath and feast days, Miriam stood with her cousin Elisheva in the Court of the Women, watching the Levites, harp in hand, ranged on the stairs that led into the inner sanctum and listening to their Song of Ascents. On these occasions the courts of the Temple overflowed with pilgrims drawn from every corner of the Holy Land and every quarter of the Empire. Most of them were kneeling or lying prostrate on the ground, while within, inside the inner Temple, the priests were kindling the day's offerings. Deeply stirred, Miriam would close her eyes and see the Holy One of Israel, attended by seraphs and angels, and seated in the Holy of Holies on the throne of Glory, which her vision painted as a fiery flame, with wheels of burning fire. This innermost sanctuary of the Temple, this Holy of Holies—in her fancy it was transmuted into the highest field of heaven, upon which

24

He, the Lord of all, had bestowed His Presence to make His glory shine in Israel's midst during the season of the festal pilgrimage.

The images came to her inward eye against her will, against her better knowledge, for she knew it was sin to visualize the Holy One of Israel in whatsoever form. But then—it was not Him she tried to see, only the pillaring clouds that hid His Presence, the clouds that had once rested on Mount Sinai. She knew herself unworthy to glimpse even the shadow of His Presence. Her mind fled from the vision and, to escape the great transgression of idolatry, tried to fasten upon the Son of Man of Daniel's prophetic dream, on him who rode the clouds of heaven to come before the Ancient of Days.

Elisheva initiated Miriam into the mysteries of the Messiah and introduced her to a sisterhood of holy women who formed her intimate circle. Sitting at evening in her upper chamber, open to the skies, they would read from the visionary Book of Enoch: "The Son of Man, clothed in the raiments of justice, shall drive the princes of the earth, the usurpers of power, from their dominions and the men of violence from their throne; and he shall undo the fetters which hold the nation bound and draw the teeth of them that practise evil."

Among the women who thus congregated on the roof of Elisheva's house were many ancient crones, with gray sunken eyes wedged deep between jutting cheekbones, and younger women with high vaulting eyebrows and inhumanly pale faces. These were the women who thronged the forecourt of the Sanctuary— daughters of priests, daughters of noble families, drawn from every province of the land and from as far as Babylon, to labor in the workshops of the Temple, spinning the finest flax, weaving and embroidering the curtains of the Temple and holy vestments for the officiating priests and Levites.

Many of them, through their own exultation, were condemned to permanent residence within the Temple walls. They were intoxicated by the chant of the Levites, the majestic ritual of the sacred service, the vast resplendent aggregation of Jewish pilgrims from Asia Minor, from Alexandria and Ethiopia, from the Greek islands and the rivers of Babylon. There, on Elisheva's roof, during the hot, heady nights, under the showering glitter of the stars, they revealed their visions to each other—their nightly dreams and voices, or the ecstatic revelations undergone by day in the Court of the Women—and how all these mysterious signs pointed to the imminence of redemption. The approaching tread of the Messiah's feet was almost audible to them, for the pain and sorrow of the world had overflowed the measure of endurance; the monstrous government of Herod had outrun its course, had passed its apogee. Jerusalem was heavy with iniquity; and the brood of tax-farmers, informers, sheriffs, police agents, and spies had turned God's Holy City into a nest of vipers. But even now their days were numbered; he who wore the mantle of God's glory would come before long to consummate their destruction. In his hands was the rod of power, and in the breath of his mouth the evil-doers would quail and perish, for he would fling wide the gates of the prisons in which the men of violence had pent the meek.

The women squatted and knelt in a circle, their heads cowled under black veils, and at their feet lay the prostrate form of the seeress Hannah, daughter of Phanuel, her face turned up to the night sky, her desiccated lips emitting words of ecstasy:

"I see the heavens yawn, and lo, the million feet of the angelic host tread upon burning fire, and they are clothed in white, and their faces are like whirling flames of snow. . . . I see Him who is called the Ancient of Days, His visage like the white shearings of lamb's wool. . . . And with Him is another, and His countenance is like the face of man and nobly featured like the holy seraphs. . . . And I questioned the angel who walked by my side, and he revealed to me the hidden things that pertain to the Son of Man—who He may be and whence He cometh and why He abideth with the Ancient of Days. And thus saith the angel: 'Behold, He is the Son of Man; His is the judgment and He dwelleth in righteousness, and in Him shall ancient mysteries be unsealed, for Him alone the King of Spirits hath elected. And His place is before the King of Spirits in the ultimate justice at the end of time. . . .'"

Miriam of the house of Hanan cherished the secret longing of many a Jewish woman that the awaited King-Messiah issue from her womb. The image of the Son of Man, so vividly delineated by the Prophet, haunted the young girl's mind. Sometimes the Prophet's vision took on physical contours and stood before her embodied in the reality of flesh. She looked upon his pallid face and yearned to share with him the weight of his trials. If she could not be a part of him, she could at least partake of his sorrow and put her loyalty to proof.

Accordingly, she renounced all the jollity and diversion which the life of the Temple could offer a young girl of her standing. Vainly her friends urged her to join their outings in the orchards of Jerusalem. Thus, for instance, after the close of the annual Day of Atonement service, when the High Priest had been borne home with pomp and circumstance, it was customary for the daughters of Jerusalem to foregather in the orchards nearby, where they were followed by the young men of the city and by those country visitors who had made the pilgrimage.

Each suitor here would choose a match for himself from among the girls, who lined up in successive rows, calling out to the young men: "Look not for wealth or beauty; choose rather one who is well-born!"

Alone in the old woman's company Miriam would weave her thoughts of the Messiah, until of a sudden she would be struck by the presumption of her meditations. In shame and contrition she would ask herself if she was not being led astray by a proud and overbearing spirit. Who was she, and what was her father's house that it should cradle the anointed one of Israel? True, the Messiah would be a shoot of David's house, but other, more important branches of the family had a far better title to the glory than the forgotten, orphaned house of her father. Only one thing —that the Messiah would come—was beyond question. Perhaps he had been born already and was even now walking unrecognized in their midst, or, more likely, sitting among the learned and the expounders of the Law, the rabbis who spread God's word among the children of Israel, the men who abode in the Holy City, close to the Presence of the Lord.

Her father's house was in the humble town of Nazareth, as barren of the word of God as a stone cast away in a flowering field. Then who was she to share the King-Messiah's ordeal?

She was as the twig of an old withered tree among the cedars of Lebanon.

In these moments of dejection the young girl turned her prayer to God and asked for the boon of humility, for the deliverance of her soul from false ambitions.

But the rejected dream returned. Deep within herself she saw the Messiah's image, nourished it with her tears throughout the long nights in Jerusalem, and felt her soul swoon in the longing to behold him with her eyes.

And at those times, kneeling perhaps in the women's court of the Temple, she cast her face down on the ground, not in a prayer for special grace, but only to relieve her overflowing heart. Forgetting where she was, or the order of the ceremony, she intoned with the Psalmist: "As the hart panteth after the water brooks, so panteth my soul after thee, O God. My soul thirsteth for God, for the living God. When shall I come and appear before God?"

Whenever she raised herself from the ground after one of these trances, her eyes shone with feverish intensity and her face was suffused with a hectic glow. Chance passersby would shun her path, taking her for one of the possessed who roamed the courts of the Temple.

Once, when she was caught up in mystic ecstasy, she was approached by Old Hannah, who had something of a Sibylline reputation among the women of Jerusalem. She was an ancient widowed crone, who rarely stirred beyond the precincts of the Temple. She could sustain a fast for weeks on end. Her parched, emaciated limbs seemed like long sticks sheathed in a wrinkled hide, and in her face one saw only the eyes, interred in deep black sockets. There were many stories current about her. Some said she was a reincarnation of the prophetess Deborah, returned to earth to redeem Jewry and bring nearer the day of salvation with penitential fasts and prayers. Others would have her possessed of a spirit that spoke through her mouth. But all agreed in paying her the utmost respect and holding her in reverential awe.

For some time Old Hannah had been watching Miriam in the Court of the Women. Then, in her old woman's wheedling voice, she said, pointing a skeletal finger at the girl:

28

"Mark her well, you women; she is a daughter of the House of David and from her womb shall Israel's Redeemer come."

Miriam caught her words and started, then blushed with shame and hurried back to her loom in the Temple's weaving shop. . . .

About this time a strange affliction befell the Priest Zachariah, in whose house she lived in Jerusalem. The old man was executing the priest's office in the order of his division, while the multitude of the pilgrims waited in the outer court. But when his task, which was to burn incense at the altar, was completed, he failed to emerge from the sanctuary. The people, waiting in the court outside, marveled that he overstayed his time so long; and they continued there with mounting impatience until at length they saw the aged Zachariah staggering out of the Temple supported by two brother priests, and it appeared that he had lost the power of speech. The people said that he said seen a vision, but no one knew what it was he had seen.

That same day the form of Rachel appeared to Miriam. Standing in a crowd of praying women, Miriam heard her voice: "Go home, daughter, to your mother's house in Nazareth, for behold, the time has come."

CHAPTER IV

Custom in Israel required that a maiden's contract of betrothal be written on a Wednesday, a widow's on a Thursday; and this in the middle of the month, with the full moon shining for good luck. Accordingly, the nearest Wednesday in the month of Adar was appointed for the betrothal of the young Joseph ben Jacob and the maiden Miriam.

A happy month was Adar, and the proverb had it that "when Adar comes Israel reaps gladness." For Adar brought the joyous holiday of Purim and, in its train, the holy Passover feast.

It brought also the finest season of the year, when all the fields in the vicinity of Nazareth were sprayed with poppy blossoms;

when the vines were sprouting with young fruit that dragged their twisted stems to earth; when pomegranates were in full bloom, and in the fertile Valley of Jezreel cornfields and flower beds, vineyards and olive groves were bursting into color. Galilee in Adar looked like God's own garden, and in this garden were the "Tents of Jacob" pitched, the little Jewish towns and villages that studded the countryside as far east as Mount Tabor, over whose sides a thousand cypress trees spread a rich somber green until they reached its naked crest that bore the curse of David.

The widow Hannah took one of the large earthen vessels that stood at the entrance of the house—the same vessels which stored newly-pressed wine over the winter and, during the rest of the year, served as tubs for the Sabbath ablutions—and carried it into her daughter's chamber. There, having filled it with fresh water from the well, she helped to bathe the bride. Shortly thereafter came the bride's friends and dressed her in white linen and twined for her a wreath of poppies and olive leaves to make a fillet for her head. With more fresh flowers from gardens and fields—cyclamen, irises, and lilies— they decked the widow's walls and ceiling, and placed olive boughs beside the benches that lined the walls in readiness for the guests. Then came the matrons of the town to help the widow prepare the food. They kneaded the bread and baked it in the open air on improvised clay ovens. Honey-wafers were made for the children, for whom also dried fruits and nuts were provided. Dishes and plates were filled with honey, and the larder was emptied of its store of black olives which had been kept in salt and vinegar to prevent their spoiling. Pasties of dried figs were sliced and spread on earthen trays. Gourds of precious date-wine emerged from their hiding place to honor the guests, and cool country ale, brewed from grain, was there to quench the thirst when the good wine should be exhausted.

Nor did the neighbors come with empty hands. From their own gardens they had plucked the freshest greens; vegetables that satisfy like meat, such as tubers of artichoke, which one could eat both seethed and raw; others that whet the appetite and heat the blood, such as the pungent dill and onion; and the tongue-stinging anise and royal asparagus, the taste of which brightens the eye and which is served only to gentlefolk and children. For the rest the tables were set with jugs of milk and curds and dried cheeses and, here and there, a dash of butter rolled in honey.

No fleshmeats were used. They were too poor, the farmers of Nazareth, to afford the slaughter of a kid or lamb, even for so rare an occasion as the betrothal of a daughter. Furthermore, the use of meat was circumscribed by complex rules of sacrifice and ritual slaughter. Animal flesh was a luxury reserved for those who lived in Jerusalem where meat could be had in abundance. Country people rarely saw meat from one Passover to the next when they journeyed up to the Holy City to sacrifice the paschal lamb. And similarly the eating of fish was a rare indulgence. The little fishes that were caught in the Genesaret Sea and salted in the harbor towns of K'far Nahum and Sidon never reached out-of-the-way settlements like Nazareth. They were found only in the major population centers, such as Sepphoris, Na'in, and Cana. Thus, the farmers of Nazareth had to make do with greens and dairy products, supplemented on Sabbath days and festivals with eggs or even fowl—that is, if a scholar could be found who knew the rules of slaughter.

The feast in the widow Hannah's house began, as usual, at night. The farmers and artisans of Nazareth could not have spared their daylight hours for idle celebrations; they were, most of them, day-laborers, and only the evenings were their own. And as the evening approached the hostess placed lamps on the tables—earthenware bowls in which the flaxen wicks glowed dim amid small pools of oil. A larger lamp, which burned only the finest olive oil, was placed near the seats of honor—those of the elders and the groom and bride—that its fragrance might be pleasing to their nostrils. Outside the door a torch of rushes soaked in pitch was fastened to the wall, and next to it a white pennant to proclaim the happy revelry within and invite passing strangers to enter and partake of the night's hospitality.

The guests began to arrive after sunset, most of them coming with their children. The learned and the elders of the town were dressed in ceremonial robes—loose black mantles not unlike Roman togas—and their heads were covered as a mark of their social

31

distinction. The simpler townspeople, bare-headed and unsandaled, wore multicolored sleeveless tunics, girt with rope or, in the cases of the well-to-do, with linen belts. Before crossing the widow's threshold they washed hands and feet with water from the jugs that stood ready at the door.

The heads and beards of the patrician visitors glistened with freshly-applied olive oil; rings sparkled on their fingers, and tiers of ornamental pendants hung about their necks. But of them there were few—only the town rabbi and some of the sons of Pinhas, the priests headed by Hanina ben Safra, who had come for the betrothal ceremony despite his earlier vexation.

The sons of Issachar, on the other hand, were of the poor artisan class and, though sandal sewing was one of their trades, most of them came barefoot. However, to honor the occasion, they too had rubbed unguents of oil into their hair and beards.

None came without bringing a present. Thus, Reb Elimelech's shepherd boy preceded his master with two ewes and their newborn lambs—a gift for the bride from the groom's first kinsman—wherewith the couple might found a herd of their own. The widow Hannah herself presented Joseph with a prayer shawl, with ritual fringes at the four corners, each tassel consisting of eight threads to make a combined total of thirty-two, the numerological value of the Hebrew word "heart." Only Cleophas, Miriam's brother-in-law, bore no presents: his kinship to the bride placed him, he felt, in the role of a recipient, rather than a donor of gifts.

On entering the festive room each guest considered it his duty first to step before the bride—who sat by Joseph's side at the head of the table—and praise her beauty to the groom and the assembled company, for it was considered a gracious thing in a guest to extol the bride in her groom's hearing, and the more praise he gave, the richer the blessing he called down on his own head.

"The bride's eyes are lovelier than the eyes of doves, washed with milk and fitly set," began Reb Tudrus, chief of the sons of Issachar, smiling broadly through his thick black beard and depositing at Miriam's feet a pair of delicate embroidered sandals.

"Beauty in a bride is her chief treasure," added Jochanan, the wheelwright, a neighbor of long standing. And he smiled good-humoredly at the groom though, as one of the rich Hanina's sons who might have been himself a candidate for Miriam's hand, he could well have grudged Joseph his good fortune.

But the great Hanina ben Safra himself seemed in a forgiving mood. Entering with his usual ponderous gait, a white priest's mantle thrown over his shoulders, and his graying hair glossy with oil, he detached a money pouch from his belt and held it up to one eye as though to inspect its contents. Then, inserting two fleshy fingers, he withdrew from it several silver dinars—some of which he allowed to drop back, deciding at last, after evident deliberation, that two dinars would suffice—and threw the coins with a loud clang on a tray that stood near the head of the table. Finally, speaking without irony, he addressed these words to Joseph:

"Find a wife and you find good fortune; so said the wisest of men."

In this and like manner each guest delivered his present and his praise until the floor space near the bride was covered with household utensils, articles of apparel, bales of cloth and skeins of wool and flax—all given with their donors' blessings.

At length, when the company had found seats, the time came for the writing of the contract of betrothal, and all turned to the groom to hear him announce the extent of the contribution he was making to the family. And it transpired that the groom had by no means come so shorn and empty-handed as his opponents had assumed. To begin with, he had brought the two hundred dinars which the laws of marriage required him to inscribe in his wife's name if she was a maiden. And, to the general surprise, Joseph produced a newly-sewn linen purse and laid it shyly before the rabbi; he had sold his share in the paternal estate to produce the money. Next he opened a small bag and withdrew from it a silver ring which he handed as a gift to Cleophas, the brother-in-law. For the bride's mother he had fine woolen cloth for a garment, and for the bride herself, a belt woven of lamb's wool, purple, and ending in a buckle wrought of pure silver and embossed with the form of a lion, the heraldic device of the House of David. And he had with him also a skein of gossamer Sidonian flax, fit for the bride's wedding dress.

33

At this point the rabbi rose and asked the groom for some token object—Joseph handed him his girdle—and the rabbi, before witnesses, placed it in the bride's hands, this being the time-honored ritual symbol for every concluded covenant or transaction.

Then the scribe was called to pen the conditions of the contract, and the completed document was stamped and sealed by two witnesses. And almost simultaneously the children were rallied to receive honeyrolls and nuts that they might fix it in their memories—lest there be any litigation in the future—that on the day of this espousal the bride was not a widow but a maiden, as had been shown by her sitting in her mother's house with loosened and disheveled hair.

Lastly, the groom produced a thin veil and placed it over the bride's head so as to cover her face, and all present turned to Joseph ben Jacob and cried out:

"May she be to you as Rachel and Leah who built the House of Israel."

And the guests stayed and ate of the good things before them and drained the flagons and offered praise to God in songs and benedictions until half the night had passed.

That night Miriam could not sleep. She lay waking on her pallet of wood and straw, her large eyes open and staring into the dark. She thought of her stay in Jerusalem, of the Levites, posted with harps and psalteries on the steps that led into the inner Temple. All the strange things that had befallen her crowded back into her memory. She recalled her cousin Zachariah and the apparition, for such it must have been, that had struck him dumb at the altar of incense. She remembered the old seeress Hannah, mumbling fearful prophecies in the Court of the Women. And she thought of her own mystic vision, of her whom she called Mother Rachel, and who had told her to be ready without staying to unfold her meaning.

Whenever she recalled her vision she thought of the King-Messiah and of Isaiah's prophecies that heralded his coming. For a brief span she fancied she could see him, the Messiah, walking beyond the darkness, walking in silence. Not knowing how or why, she yet felt a mystic kinship with him, felt him near and felt the unknown, unseen light of him pierce and penetrate her heart. Was there not an ancient prophecy that a virgin would conceive and give birth to a son? She had heard it spoken of, or perhaps had read it; but what was it to her? She was betrothed to Joseph, shortly to be wed, like any other girl, according to the Law of Moses. She was now his, appointed to fulfill those wifely duties which were the charge of every Jewish daughter—to bear a man-child to her husband and build his house in Israel.

It was all over, then. The judgment had been passed.

And suddenly she felt herself seized in an agony of rebellion. Her nature revolted against her sentence. In the flash of a moment she felt that she would never be able to do as they asked, that it was not in her power to perform what was required of all others.

"But then, why did I hold my peace? Why did I deceive this congregation and this guileless youth who came for me from afar? Shall I shame a man who is better than I and who walks with the Lord? . . . I will speak with him. I will tell him of my resolve, that I have sanctified my life to the Lord even as Hannah sanctified Samuel, her only child, to God. He will hear me and understand, and he will leave me to the Lord. His face is my assurance that he will not betray me, for his eyes are clear and look with mildness and humility. Surely, he will understand and offer me no injury.

"But who am I that I should lift up my heart above all others? What is my life that the Lord should deem it worthy to take me for a sacrifice? My heart is a nest of vipers and I am filled with pride and self-deception. My eyes look upon things they should not see and my mouth utters language that should be left unspoken. Father in heaven, have pity on me! Take from me my delusions and my proud speech. Make me worthy to be as one of Thy lowliest creatures. Bind my heart to Thy will and subject me to Thy intention, and let all things fare with me even as Thou wilt. . . ."

Early next morning Miriam rose with a calm spirit and quietly set about her daily tasks. The proud ambitions had fallen from her and she desired only to do the will of God.

35

Outside, the day was breaking. The young dawning sun had not yet set its full dominion over heaven and earth, and only the earth's brink was marvelously radiant. The fields of the Valley of Jezreel were basking under streams of light, but the hills of Nazareth were drowsing still, awakening darkly under their dew-laden covering of cypress grove and copse. And though the sky was a clear limpid blue, the earth was resting still in its own light; it seemed as though the meadows and the flower beds about the house were lighted by an inner glow. Their colors, fresh and fragrant and replete with splendor, made one feel nature was young again, magnificent as on the first of days.

The girl Miriam was turning over the soil of a bed of sweet peas which touched the wall of the house just below the window of her chamber. Against the dampness of the early morning she wore a tunic of heavy blue wool; her feet were sandaled, and over her shoulders was thrown a woolen kerchief of her mother's, an old piece from which the color had long faded. Her head was bare, and drops of dew, dripping from branches overhead, fell on her thick, dark tresses. She crouched against the wall and marveled at the delicate tints of her slender-stemmed plants, the purple, salmon, and white of their blossoms and the feathery spray of their leaves. Lightly between her fingers she held the fragile flowers, gazing with love and wonder at the fine filigree of every petal on which some dew drops lingered like tears upon an infant's cheek.

"O Lord, how manifold are Thy works," she thought. "The earth is full of Thy riches!"

A sudden shudder wrenched her body. Something was happening to her, for her heart was pounding at her throat. She knew not why, but she raised her head and looked about and it seemed to her that a deep weight of silence had settled upon all the living; as though time and the very course of creation had come to a standstill. Flowers and leaves, branches and shrubs, houses and trees, the cattle grazing in the fields, the laborers—each and all had grown still, their motion arrested, their lives suspended in one breathless, timeless moment.

In the full light and color of the day every creature of God stood and waited upon God's word. And Miriam waited, tensed for something which could not be far off, which she knew must occur, which was occurring even now.

A sudden fear came over her, a flutter of fright over a deep sea of joy which filled her darkest being; fear and joy and the sudden consciousness of a vast inner richness at the thought of what was now coming to pass.

Once more she looked about her and her glance fell upon the clay wall of her chamber where, below the roof, a hole served as a window. Something beckoned from the chamber, though no voice was audible, no form apparent to the eye. And yet she knew someone to be within, and someone called to her to enter and becked insistently with unseen sign and invisible finger.

With bowed head Miriam left the garden and, walking through the house, entered her room.

The stillness here was even deeper, as if this were the core and center of the silence. Yet nothing in the room had stirred from its place, everything stood as she had left it: near the wall the straw pallet on the wooden bench was covered with a green cloth; the loom nearby was strung with a fine warp of flaxen threads, her bridegroom's gift—mother, it seemed, had started on her wedding dress; through the small window showed a few pink and blue-eyed sweet-pea blossoms, rearing themselves on slender stems that had outclimbed their fellows; in a corner, the wooden box with her psalter and inscribed parchments of the Holy Writ; and, hanging from a wooden peg, her blue woolen Sabbath dress with its white veil of homespun flax, which she had worn in the court of the Temple.

Miriam halted in the middle of the chamber; her hands hung limp and useless, not knowing what to do. The stillness here was dense and palpable; only her heart pounded on in fear while cold drops of perspiration glistened on her forehead and her face burned as in a fever. Surely, someone was in her chamber; she could not see him, only feel the weight and extension of his presence. For one moment she felt the noiseless shadow of two mighty wings quivering above her head. The fear rose in her throat, and in its train the joy and the richness. What should she do; how break this endless, timeless silence? And suddenly a clear unearthly light, not of the sun, strayed in through the small

37

window, coming to rest upon the plaited bamboo mat, her prayer rug, that straddled the ground next to her pallet. With her hands shielding her face Miriam fell upon the rug, toward the light; no words rose from her lips, only her heart cried out in prayer. . . .

When Miriam lifted up her eyes again she was no longer alone, and there was no astonishment in her when she saw her chamber shared by an angel. His tall form, from crest to heel, was concealed behind powerful wings, only the massive head protruding. It bore the face of a young man, of a young priest perhaps, such as she had seen in the courts of the Temple—but graver still, more radiant and untouchable. The face looked down at her with an air of wistful compassion in the smile of its lips, its large eyes looking serious and kind.

Girl and angel stood for a while facing each other. Their glances met, the girl's glance, like the angel's, weighted with sadness and pity. Her lips, too, were tightly closed; only her eyes spoke and laid the sorrow of mankind before the angel. She stood in his sight without flinching, piercing his gaze despite the persistent drumming in her breast; and the veins at her neck stood out taut and tensed and pulsated with her heart's rhythm.

As Jacob wrestled with the nameless man at Peniel, thus Miriam's glance strove with the angel's. And it was he, the seraph, who at length lowered his head upon his wings, unable to withstand the mortal grief in the girl's eyes. Then, in a still small voice that seemed to have been born a whisper at the far end of distant spaces but, coming close, had gathered strength and volume until now, in the room, it sounded with a human ring:

"Peace be with you, daughter of Hanan, for the Lord is with you!"

Only then, when Miriam heard the angel hail her in a human tongue, did she once more grow conscious of her earthly nature. She understood that the angel had come to her, had saluted her and none other. Once more the fright welled up in her, and she became again a humble young girl trembling, with a heart that hammered against the walls of her body and caused her mother's faded shawl to flutter on her chest. Miriam's eyes sank as if to bury themselves in the ground. Wisps of her hair clung to her

38

damp brow and neck; her face grew ashen and her hands began to shake.

The seraph's lips curled faintly, and his strangely distant voice sounded again: "Fear not, Miriam, for you have found favor with God. And, behold, you shall conceive and bring forth a son and you shall call his name Yeshua. And he shall be great and shall be called the son of the Highest; and the Lord God shall give unto him the throne of his father David. And he shall reign over the House of Jacob for ever, and of his kingdom there shall be no end."

Miriam's eyes remained cast down as she listened to the angel's speech in silence. But at his last word she lifted up her head and gazed at him again with her grief-darkened eyes, saying softly:

"How shall this be, seeing I know not my husband?"

And the angel answered:

"The Holy Ghost will come upon you, and the power of the Highest will overshadow you. And therefore the holy thing which will be born of you shall be called the Son of God."

Miriam stood long without speaking. Her eyes were closed. But the color had returned to her face and her cheeks burned with a glow of sacred fire.

"I am the handmaid of the Lord," she said at last; "be it with me according to your word."

And when she opened her eyes again she saw the angel departing from her.

CHAPTER V

IT WAS considered in poor taste for groom and bride to show themselves together more often than was necessary; and even for married couples good form dictated a certain restraint in the frequency of their public appearances. From these considerations Joseph had taken up his quarters in the house of his kinsman, Reb Elimelech, where he proposed to spend the months that still separated him from his wedding. By day he went to the established carpenters of the town and hired himself out as a day-laborer. At night, after the work was done, he called on his bride and helped her till the field or garden, or else prepared his joiner's workshop in the widow's house where he was to live after the marriage. Thus there was scant leisure left for intimate communion.

Only on Sabbath and feast days was the rule broken; then Joseph spent all day in Miriam's house, and sometimes, every now and then, snatched a fugitive moment alone with his bride—as when they went outdoors to tend the garden and Miriam proudly showed him the drooping bean-filled pods, the sturdy heads of the artichoke, the white and yellow umbels of dill—or when, for a minute or two, they watched the widow's little herd of sheep milling about the courtyard waiting for the trough to be filled. At such moments Joseph, not daring to look at his bride, would say softly:

"If it please God and we build our house together—you, Miriam, shall have an equal part with me in everything the Lord may give. Your mouth shall rule over my house and your hand shall nourish it, for truly, a woman of valor has God given me for a wife."

Miriam then would lower her head and make no answer.

Once, in the evening, after the passing of the Sabbath, he sat by her side in the widow's house. The faltering light of an oil lamp barely reached to their corner. The widow Hannah was busying herself in the pantry at the opposite end of the room, assembling cheeses and dried fruit which she had fetched down from the roof to bring to market next day in the large town of Sepphoris.

The preparations for her daughter's wedding required large expenditures; untold quantities of wine had to be readied, even though the groom was expected to provide it. But what of the oil, the olives, and the dried fruit, to say nothing of the bread and chicken meat, of which so much was eaten at a wedding, seeing that the guests were many? It was a heavy load for the widow to carry and she was beginning in good time to prepare the provisions by selling her surplus fruit, greens, and dairy produce in the market towns nearby.

And her problems were not alone financial; though herself of priestly descent she never knew her way certain through the legal intricacies of tithe payment. Did one or did one not pay the Levites' tithe on mint and hops? Must she tax her artichokes and precious asparagus? And how should she remember from what beds the firstlings had already been taken, seeing that many plants matured at different seasons? And so Hannah waited for Hanina ben Safra, the town priest, who could tell by previous markings, which of the beds were yet untithed. Before long she heard his heavy tread behind the door and saw, through the chinks of the doorposts, the light of his lamp. A moment later she heard his staff pounding impatiently on the threshold—for the priest had little time to spare; this same evening he was due to make the round of many more Nazarene farmers to tell them which of their crops they could safely take to market and what others were yet to be tithed. And Hannah did not keep him waiting but hurried out to him, leaving Joseph and her daughter alone in the house.

Joseph let a moment pass and then, shifting closer to his bride, whispered in her ear:

"If it be God's will and you are sanctified to me after the Law of Moses and Israel, you shall be to me as Rachel was to Jacob, for my soul languishes for you."

Again Miriam said nothing, and the ensuing silence was broken once more by Joseph: "And if, God willing, you bear me sons in Israel, we will raise them to be rich in learning and good deeds."

But when Joseph had uttered these words Miriam slowly raised her head and looked at her bridegroom. And despite the gathering darkness Joseph, overawed, saw a mysterious light shining in her eyes. Unconsciously he edged away from her and stammered out in a voice tremulous with sudden fear:

"What has happened to you, Miriam? I do not recognize you."

"To me? Why, what could have happened to me?"

"I do not know, but—I fear you, Miriam."

She looked at him again and her mouth smiled faintly.

"Why fear me, Joseph? You are my bridegroom and have known me many days."

41

"But you have changed. You were not always so sad."

"I am not sad, Joseph; my heart is like a ripe pomegranate, filled with joy."

"And like a pomegranate will the Lord bless the fruit of your womb."

"When God has had his will with me, the fruit of my womb shall be consecrated to Him," Miriam said with sudden firmness.

The words silenced Joseph and the color ebbed from his face. What he had heard was a solemn vow and it had come upon him without warning. He was unprepared for such a sacrifice—to relinquish his first-born to God's service, for this he took to be the meaning of her words. He pondered for a while, trying to grasp the full import of the vow, and his heart grieved for his unborn son who was even now deprived of his inheritance in Israel.

Once more he turned to look at Miriam's face, hoping perhaps to remonstrate with her. But the darkness in the room had deepened and made the unearthly light of her eyes shine with redoubled luster. Joseph lost heart again and, lowering his head, said with humility:

"You have vowed it, Miriam. As Hannah dedicated Samuel, so you have given up your son to the Lord. The Lord's he shall be."

There was a break in his voice which made the girl turn quickly and say, as though to console him:

"But Joseph, you know that whatever comes from God, belongs to God."

Joseph did not understand, but he clenched his mouth in silence.

Just then the widow Hannah reentered, followed by the priest. Hanina cast a glowering look at the young couple sitting close together in the darkest corner of the room and, raising his stick in their direction, waved it back and forth as one waves a disapproving finger.

"Is it the way in Israel for a bride and groom to consort privately together before they are joined by the Law of Moses?"

Joseph leapt up from his seat, his pale face reddening with mortification. Miriam remained motionless, her eyes fixed on the ground.

"Those who are pure, are pure in all their deeds," interjected the widow, trying to soothe the hurt inflicted by the priest's reproof. "And, after all, their wedding day is almost at the door."

The priest turned his bulk toward her: "Your daughter's high birth confers certain responsibilities on her," he said. "Conduct such as this is unseemly in one of her station." And with that, shaking his head like a man painfully disappointed, he left the widow's house.

It was not long before all Nazareth spoke of the change that had come over Miriam. Instead of being merry with her friends and rejoicing in her bridal state, the girl was often observed to slink into quiet corners and to show an unaccountable predilection for solitude and darkness. And yet her melancholy was not of the kind that enervates and depresses the beholder. It emanated from her like the strains of a song, filling men's hearts with a strange exultation. People felt happier and comelier in her presence. Nevertheless, her company was felt somehow to be a disquieting experience. It was thought better not to look into her eyes, and her own mother, when she saw the girl in the mornings emerging from her chamber, would feel strangely disturbed. At such times the girl seemed to be veiled in light, and her eyes shone with a radiance that was more than a reflection from the lights of this world.

Seeing her thus one morning, the widow Hannah caught her breath and in a quivering voice asked of her daughter: "Miriam, my own daughter, you are like a stranger to me. What, in the name of the Lord, has happened?"

"I know not what you mean, mother."

"Do you not, Miriam? You look as though an angel hovered over you. I almost hear the beat of his wings."

Miriam answered in a simple, unconstrained tone: "God has let His grace descend on me, mother."

Hannah looked sharply at her daughter. "God's grace is upon us all, I think."

"I know it, mother. But He has chosen me to bring comfort and hope to the oppressed. Israel's mother has He appointed me."

"Miriam, my heart trembles at your words! Something has come over you, I know not what. But this I know: you must not

43

let such words fall on strangers' ears. Evil tongues will speak ill of you."

"What evil can they do me when He stands over me like a pillar of fire? Whom shall I fear seeing that He has chosen me to bear the hope of Israel?"

Hannah blanched with terror.

"Pray God that you put no shame on me, Miriam," she said. "And may He grant that everything go well." And she took her daughter's hand and led her back into her curtained chamber, saying:

"Hide yourself between these walls. I fear your going among people lest they hear your speech."

But the people did hear. Often, in broad daylight, while working in her field or garden, Miriam would fall to her knees. Sometimes, alone on the roof of her house, she stood erect, staring at the stars, or dropped to her knees with her hands outspread to the sky, while she intoned the Psalms of David, or verses of her own composing whose source and drift no one could comprehend. The words were not those of a prophetess, but rather the exultant paeans of a priestess. She chanted songs of praise and magnificats to the Lord for miracles that had been wrought in her. She sang of promises fulfilled, of pledges made of old to the Patriarchs, of the approach of salvation and the great redemption that was at hand.

"Open wide the gates of glory for the Holy One of Israel!" she sang. "The captive and the thirsty abide his coming! Sing all the earth unto the Lord . . . !"

From these raptures the widow Hannah would awaken her, raise her up, and help her down the ladder into the privacy of her house. She did not want the gossip of the town to feed on her daughter's distress.

But rumors, nonetheless, spread like a forest fire: a new prophetess, it was said, had arisen in Israel—none other than the daughter of the widow Hannah and the late joiner Hanan, the same Miriam who but the other day had been espoused to the newcomer Joseph. Stories circulated of visions she had seen, and surely a spirit had possessed the girl. It was this spirit—and who knew what manner of spirit it might be?—that spoke through her when

44

she opened her mouth. Was it the spirit of God or, Heaven forbid, of Satan?

And once the daughters of the town heard Miriam's spirit at first hand.

Miriam had continued to draw water each morning at the communal well behind the town. Hannah let her go, much against her inclination, only because it was so natural a thing to have one's daughter go to the town well that no other course seemed conceivable.

Now the town well was the women's forum, the hub from which all news, gossip, and scandal radiated. Here, in the early mornings, amid much whispering and husky cachinnation, the girls and women exchanged confidences and told one another the events of the previous day, and what was lately being said of this man or that woman. Needless to say, Miriam's conduct had become a rich source of gossip for the chattering women, and each morning Miriam's neighbors would come running up breathlessly to tell their cronies in a panting voice what the girl had lately been heard singing from her mother's rooftop—that she of all daughters in Jewry had been elected to bring hope to Israel.

On one of these mornings, as Miriam approached with her pitcher mounted on her head, she noticed the women and girls standing in a cluster by the well, whispering together. Their eyes, without exception, were fixed on herself, so that the subject of their conversation could not well be doubted. As Miriam reached the mouth of the well, the women backed away to give her room, though her turn was not yet. But no sooner had she filled her pitcher and had turned, ready to go home, than she found herself surrounded on all sides by women who would block her path. One of them, with a face swarthied by the sun and a brassy ringlet dangling from her nose—they called her "Avihu of the Evil Tongue"—strutted before Miriam with her arms akimbo, saying:

"So you're the one that's been picked to bring hope to the Jews and become Israel's mother?"

"Doesn't she look like a Matriarch now," taunted another, "just like Rachel and Leah?"

"I have been chosen to be the handmaid of the Lord," said Miriam, as if the questions had been posed in good faith.

45

"How do you know?" they asked again. "If you have not been with a man, how do you know these things will come your way? Perhaps the Lord will lock your womb with seven bolts."

"Who knows? Pilfered fruit, they say, tastes sweetest," threw in old Tamar, a grass-widow of long standing; and she let out a whiffling chuckle from her ruined mouth that looked like a broken-in window.

Miriam glanced about her. The women stood their ground in a closed circle, their faces dark with hate and malice. The girl felt a chill of fear upon her spine and, letting go of her pitcher, sank to her knees and raised her folded hands. She said nothing, but her lips trembled and the hectic rose so quickly to her face that the women backed away and almost fell over each other. From a distance they continued to stare at the kneeling girl and held their breath, listening to a soliloquy which fell from Miriam's lips like the chant of a psalm that one has learned by rote:

"Mighty acts has the Lord shown unto me. As an eagle did he come into my chamber and as a raven did he lift me up upon his wings to carry me into the clouds. Not among the cedars of Lebanon, nor among the mountains of Judah did he build his nest, but planted it among the tender reeds of Galilee. And in my father's humbled house he chose the lowliest of his handmaids to bear within her womb the hope of Israel. From her loins shall issue succor and salvation which shall know no bounds, nor cease until the end of time to fill the earth and the vault of heaven! ..."

"Did you hear that? Did you hear what she said?" cried one of the women in a shrill, hysterical voice.

"She said herself she was pregnant with the hope of Israel!"

And the women turned and rushed wildly home to spread the fearsome tidings in the town: "A virgin has conceived in Israel!"

CHAPTER VI

WITHIN a short time the occurrence at the well had become the talk of the town. Wherever Miriam went, to the well or the market, young girls and matrons alike strained their eyes for the scandalous virgin—shyly or expertly, depending on their status—seeking to confirm the suspicions which the girl's words had aroused.

"Why, you fools! Her belly's mounting to her teeth and you're still looking for signs!" laughed a widow who pretended to some knowledge of midwifery.

"The new joiner likes stealing the figs before they're ripe," suggested another.

It was not long before the rumors came to the attention of the authorities, and the rabbi, with the judges of the court, decided that the matter called for an official investigation.

Now, from a strictly legalistic point of view, the act of cohabitation between bridegroom and bride was no offense. In fact, it was one of the three recognized modes of concluding a marriage covenant; but it must be added that its legality in no way mitigated its unseemliness, since intercourse with an unmarried bride was viewed as a brutal violation of decorum and a permanent stain on the good name of the bride's family. The act itself, however, was not punishable, provided that the groom confessed himself its perpetrator and declared openly that he had chosen this method whereby to consummate his marriage. But if, God forbid, the groom denied his part in the affair, then the guilt of infidelity fell squarely on the shoulders of the bride and she was branded an adulteress. And for the crime of adultery the Mosaic Law countenanced but one punishment—death by stoning. With this threat in mind, the authorities were loath to mortify a daughter in Israel by charging her with a capital offense. They decided, therefore, to begin by questioning the bridegroom. Should he confess to the deed, the case would be dismissed out of hand.

As might have been expected, Joseph was wholly unaware of the rumors that agitated the town, even though they had thrown

47

a cloud of gloom over his nearest family. There was ceaseless whispering about him, and the faces of his kinsmen wore a surly look whenever he was present, yet Joseph barely noticed the change and certainly was far from suspecting its true cause. He was too much absorbed in ordering his coming wedding, was carefully saving his meager earnings so that he would be able to buy presents for the bride's family and purchase the wine which it was his part to furnish at the marriage feast. He knew the custom which honored a marrying man in proportion to the bumpers of wine drained at his wedding.

Joseph was so engrossed in these preparations, and entered into them with such full heart, that he even failed to notice the changed aspect of his kinsman and former well-wisher Reb Elimelech. The old man had grown estranged from him, had almost ceased to return his greeting. And things were worse, if possible, in the bride's family, whose members murmured bitterly against the young invader of their peace. Miriam's mother herself retired to a corner of her house when Joseph called of an evening to see his bride.

In the synagogue Joseph suddenly found himself shunned. Men ignored his salutations as they avoided his pew, and Joseph saw them glowering at him with looks of scorn and contempt. He was bewildered by this treatment, unable to find guilt in himself. At the same time, he would have vehemently rejected the suggestion that this general hostility, which pressed upon him like a deadly load, had anything to do with his bride, let alone with his bride's chastity. He would have silenced any man that dared impugn the honor of a daughter of Israel. Thus he remained in ignorance, oblivious to the mordant abuse that was hurled at him from all sides.

It was therefore with genuine and profound shock that he received the summons to appear before the court of Nazareth.

"Joseph ben Jacob!" the rabbi began, swaying back and forth like a man praying, and clutching at the silky white strains of his beard. "Information has reached us concerning the maiden Miriam whom you have lately espoused. The matter troubles our hearts and cries aloud for clarification. . . ." He paused, and the sway of his lean body seemed almost lost in the voluminous black

48

folds of his gown. "For even if such things have occurred in the past—as we know from previous instances that have come to our ears—yet it is not our way in Galilee. But the act of which I speak is permissible only if the bridegroom admits to having performed the deed in the order of marriage; but if not, not. Now therefore, I call on you, Joseph ben Jacob, to tell this court whether or not you have married your bride, the said Miriam, in the order of cohabitation, and whether the child under her heart is of your begetting."

Joseph returned no answer. His face turned ashen; he closed his eyes that had bulged forward, and his long chin dropped on his chest in a gesture of shame and despondence. He did not see the angry glances of his brother-in-law, Cleophas, and the priest Hanina who occupied the side benches reserved for the bride's kin. He did not notice the wan, haggard features of Reb Elimelech whose lined face seemed to have grown more deeply furrowed during these last days. He forgot the presence of the rabbi and his assistants and the head of the synagogue, the venerable Reb Jochanan of the sons of Issachar, who was a member of the court. He did not even hear the suppressed muttering of the congregation which occupied the rear benches of the court and thronged in at the doorway. Nor did he see the faces of the women and young girls that looked in through the open casements of the courtroom. He seemed to have collapsed under the unexpected blow; his very body suddenly seemed pinched and shrunken, as if the life blood had been drained from it; and he said nothing.

For several minutes the entire court, crowded as it was, joined in the silence. Every man stopped his breath to hear how the young stranger would meet the accusation made against him. But Joseph still said nothing.

"Silence is tantamount to confession," Reb Elimelech said at last, anxious to put an end to the painful tension. But the rabbi persisted:

"This matter is too grave to be dismissed on a mere confession-by-silence," he said. "Joseph ben Jacob, I call on you a second time, in the name of this just court, to declare before us whether or not you have consummated your marriage by cohabitation, or whether, God forbid, you are innocent in this matter and have not

49

sired the child which your bride Miriam has under her heart."

The rabbi's words echoed away and left a deeper silence. Their full import settled on the consciousness of every man present, and fear crept through the hall as if the still air of the courtroom had been stirred by the wings of the angel of death. All knew what it would mean if Joseph were to deny his part in the affair, and all were tensed for his answer.

A long moan rent the silence and Joseph, sobbing, cried aloud: "Father in heaven, wilt Thou stand by to see the humbling of an innocent daughter in Israel!"

"What did he say? What did he say?" came the hushed whispering of the people.

"Explain your meaning, Joseph ben Jacob," said the rabbi.

"My meaning," said Joseph, "is this: what man or woman has poured this vile slander on my bride?"

For a moment the rabbi and his fellow judges sat stunned, as though the young man's accusation had been aimed at their heads. Then the bride's kinsmen rose in an uproar; Cleophas shot up like a man stung and shook a threatening fist at the defendant; close behind him was the priest Hanina, gesticulating wildly. The murmur at the door swelled into a riot of confused, irate voices. But the rabbi raised his hand to silence the crowd and resumed in a quavering tone:

"Joseph ben Jacob! The Lord is witness that it was not from this court that the charge issued against your bride. Before we summoned you in this cause we received information which agitated our hearts. But we did not, God forbid, rest content with such information, for we took pains to search the matter out and heard witnesses of unimpeachable integrity—many matrons and young girls who heard your bride, the maiden Miriam, confess herself with child. She called upon the Holy Name and offered thanks to God for the grace He had bestowed on her. Nor was she heard to say this only once or twice, but many times. At the well where she draws water in the mornings, and again after dusk, she has confided in her friends. And still we delayed proceedings until we had questioned women who are versed in these matters, and who declared before us that your bride, the maiden Miriam, was with child beyond the possibility of error. We see no cause to doubt the testimony of these witnesses. We therefore ask you for the third time to state publicly, before this assembled congregation, whether or not the child which your bride, Miriam, carries in her womb is of your seed. If, God forbid, some other man fathered the child, you know the doom that hangs over your bride, over her mother's house, and over all of us in this sacred congregation. Joseph ben Jacob, cleanse the name of a daughter of David; soothe the troubled hearts of this community in Israel; I beg for your confession!"

The congregation had averted their faces from Joseph. Every man kept his eyes fixed on the ground as though the danger to the life of Joseph's bride were their common peril. Joseph did not answer at once. Then, after an eternity of breathless waiting, he lifted up his head and, looking full at the rabbi, said in a loud ringing voice:

"I declare before this sacred congregation that my bride Miriam, the daughter of Hanan, is chaste and without taint. She is innocent of all blame, for the guilt is mine. . . . Deal with me now according to the Law."

His words broke the tension. The company relaxed as he ceased speaking and clenched fists were brandished at him from all sides. Behind him voices rose in anger and, above the general tumult, Cleophas, beside himself with rage, was heard to shriek:

"I'll have reparation from him! For the whole family I'll get damages from him!"

"What did I tell you?" shouted the priest. "Was there a want of bachelors in our town that we had to abandon the orphaned Miriam to this stranger who puts our noblest families to shame?"

Once more the rabbi silenced the crowd. He was breathing with relief, knowing that a terrible doom had passed over his congregation, and he turned in the direction of the bride's kinsmen, saying: "Our young friend Joseph ben Jacob has just told us that he has taken his bride to wife in a manner sanctified by the Torah and the Law of Moses and Israel. He has brought no shame upon the family and no one can claim satisfaction from him. From this day Miriam, Hanan's daughter, is his lawful wife and—" here he turned to Joseph—"I pray your union will be blessed with joy and happiness." With that the rabbi stepped down to the bewildered

Joseph and held out his hand to him. Lastly, he turned to the company and concluded with these words: "People of Nazareth! A new house has been built in Israel. Let us wish them good fortune without end."

Next to approach Joseph was Reb Elimelech: "As you know, Joseph, this has not been our way in Israel, and I had hoped my brother's daughter had deserved the marriage canopy. But with God's help your marriage will be blessed, and your wife will bear you sons to raise to learning and good deeds." And the old man turned homeward and left Joseph standing alone in the court-room.

Few words passed between Joseph and Miriam when they sat together on the roof of her house later that night. Joseph's head lay motionless in his hands and his eyes were rigid on the ground. He did not see that Miriam was looking at him with that over-flowing compassion of which her eyes were capable, as though her glances could wash away the stains of misery that darkened his young face from which the mark of youth seemed to have fled.

"Say one word to me, Miriam," Joseph whispered at last. "Tell me that they are wrong who accuse you. I will believe; I know your heart is without sin."

"They spoke the truth, Joseph."

"Who?"

"They who said I bore the world's hope under my heart."

"Miriam, I do not understand."

"I have conceived a child."

A shudder ran through Joseph's body and he released his head and rose heavily from his seat.

"Miriam, I know that there can be no wickedness in you," he said. "May God protect you always, wherever you go."

He bowed low before his wife and left her alone in the darkness. Miriam's eyes followed his form as he staggered across the garden and vanished among the lighted houses of the town.

On reaching the small workshop of Reb Elimelech Joseph threw himself upon his couch and began pondering what to do next. He felt no resentment against Miriam, for he knew in his heart that he could not charge her with faithlessness. He was certain there was something she had wished to tell him, but had left unsaid. Her eyes had spoken to him with an articulateness of their own, so that only the grossness of his understanding had prevented him from grasping their meaning. Her eyes had pleaded with him, had beseeched him to withhold his judgment . . . No, God forbid that he should judge her! He had but newly come from a distance—who could tell what tribulations she had undergone before their meeting? Who could know the sorrow in her heart, whereof her eyes showed but a faint glimmer? . . . But was it really sorrow he had seen in her glance? Surely there was singing in her eyes, and happiness and bliss without end. The hope of the world was in her womb, she had said. He had not understood—and did not now—but the deathless joy of her eyes had confirmed her words, placed them beyond the reach of questioning and prying doubt. With such radiance no sin could be mingled; it did not call for pity—only for a sharing of joy.

But there was no place for him in her happiness. There had been someone else—someone she had found worthier. Was he not then a stumbling block in her way, a living token or reproof? He did not wish to reprove her. His part was done. He had taken upon himself all there was of responsibility, had publicly confessed himself the author of whatever shame had been committed. Miriam was safe from the Law; nothing could touch her now. And as for him, the only thing remaining was to retire from her sight and retrace his steps that had brought him to Nazareth. Of course, he could not go without the curses of the town at his back. They would say that he had married a poor orphan only to forsake her, and it was a grievous thing, no doubt, to leave a sullied name behind! But there was no help for it. Later, from a distance, he would be able to send a bill of divorcement as prescribed by the Law of Israel. His heaviest burden was the pain he would be causing his good kinsman, Reb Elimelech. From the moment of his arrival, until these recent days, the old man had shown him every kindness, lent him all the protection in his power. It turned Joseph's heart to know that Elimelech would be thinking evil of him the rest of his days. But even this he would bear. He would willingly pay any price to spare Miriam the shame and distress of his presence, that she might stand immaculate and guiltless before her family and the people of Nazareth.

It would not take him long to leave the town. His kit was light —a small bag to be hung to a staff and the ass to carry him away. There were some hours yet before the crack of dawn. Until then he would rest, for his eyes were heavy and the harrowing of the day had exhausted his body. He felt his limbs grown dull with drowsiness. His lids fell shut; his weary mind, drained of its consciousness, became a lulling void, a hollow cradling shell of sleep. And Joseph saw his couch stir, rockingly at first, then sway and lift itself and soar with him beyond the reach of clouds. He felt himself carried up into measureless heights and plunged upward into a sea of light. It was too luminous for human eyes and Joseph saw nothing but the blinding brightness of it, nothing but a face, fulgent and infinite, a sun of suns. The face bent over him and Joseph felt the timid pressure of an all-pervading softness and saw the shade of two limitless wings falling about his couch. He thought he lay like Jacob in the arms of a seraph and heard a voice speaking to him:

"Joseph ben Jacob, fear not to take your bride Miriam to wife, for that which is conceived in her is of the Holy Ghost. She will bear a son and you shall call his name Yeshua, for he will save his people from their sins. And lo, all this was done that the word of the Prophet might be fulfilled: 'Behold, a virgin shall be with child and shall bring forth a son; and they shall call his name Emmanuel.' "

Joseph awoke with his heart beating wildly. Sweat trickled from his forehead and his limbs shook uncontrollably. He was afraid of his vision, and yet he felt a gush of happiness within his body. The bitter recollection of the previous day was gone. The world around was bright and shadowless, and Joseph's heart leapt for joy:

"I submit, Father in heaven, I submit," he kept repeating and at last threw himself to the ground and buried his face in the bare earth that was the floor of Reb Elimelech's workshop. "How shall I thank Thee, O my God, my heavenly Father, that Thou hast found me worthy to be a guardian to her."

Then he raised himself up and hurried to the widow Hannah's house.

But his steps slackened as he came nearer: the house lay under a mist of dew that hung about it like a shielding cloud. Joseph by-passed the house and on reaching the vegetable garden at the rear caught sight of his wife Miriam standing within the haze of dew.

Without daring to go farther he bowed his head before Miriam, whispering with flying breath as in a fever, while tears ran down his cheeks and daubed his lips:

"Have mercy on me, sinner that I am. Forgive me that I thought evil of you—I know now that you are God's chosen one, that the child must be born of a virgin, in fulfillment of the prophecy."

Miriam came forward, her feet and lower body still screened in a mist of vapor, so that it seemed a wind was wafting her toward him. And Joseph's heart sank as she approached, for the fear of God had fallen on him.

"O Miriam, holy one," he cried, "where shall I hide from the wrath of God, I, who stretched forth my hand to snatch the fire from His altar!"

"Be easy in your heart, Joseph. The words of the Prophet must be fulfilled; yet a father on earth you shall be to the son of promise."

CHAPTER VII

EVEN though Joseph ben Jacob was descended from the House of David, he had long despaired of seeing the monstrous government of Herod driven from the throne by one of his own house. Like all good men in Israel, Joseph waited for a saviour greater than a king; he waited for the fulfillment of the Messianic hope.

The time had passed when the Messianic ideal could be constrained in the Procrustean mold of a Jewish king. Since the prophetic age of the Babylonian exile, it had swelled to the proportions of a national obsession, burst through the narrow limitations of Jewish kingship, and demanded nothing less than the government of the world under a new universal order.

No matter how far the Messianic hope had been debased in Ezra's and Nehemiah's time to the level of mere nationalist aspirations, the very attainment of these aspirations by the Maccabees sufficed to rouse the scribes and the common people from their purblind state, teaching them that any purely political solution to their national ambitions—by means of independence under a Jewish king—would fall painfully short of the celestial splendor envisioned for the age of the Messiah, for which alone it was worth suffering and waiting.

The later Hasmoneans, the Hellenized descendants of the Maccabees, perverted the Messianic dream of Jewish kingship into a fratricidal wrangle over the inheritance of power. Under their rule not one of the prophetic postulates for the Messianic state was fulfilled. Instead, the land was torn to shreds by petty tyrants whose goals were set only by personal ambitions.

Little by little the old dream returned, the Messianic vision of a world redemption which could have nothing whatsoever in common with narrow nationalist aspirations. Once more Jewry looked to the vision of the Prophets concerning the sublimation of mankind through a universal saviour, one who would rule not with the legions of this world but with the spirit of God, a dual personality—angel and man in one—who would come with the clouds of heaven, as Daniel had foretold, not to deliver the Jews only, but the whole human species, and erect a new world order on the ruins of the old.

Among the people voices were heard which once more echoed the visionary strains sounded by the Prophets on behalf of the world. Writings circulated in town and country which founded their authority on ancient, sainted names. To win Jewry's regard these spurious tracts would claim the authorship of legendary, mystic figures, such as old father Enoch, the pre-diluvial Patriarch, or of King Solomon; wrapped in Moses's mantle, they would bring a new gospel from the mouth of Jacob, the beloved Patriarch, purporting to be the testament of his twelve sons, the tribal ancestors of Israel; or, playing on the strings of David's harp, they would offer a new psalter to express the highest hopes and yearnings of the Jews.

"Then shall the Lord appoint a new priest, to whom shall be revealed all wisdom and all words of God, and he shall bring true judgment over all the earth when his time cometh. . . . He shall open wide the gates of Eden and abolish the sword to frighten man no more. And he shall feed his saints with the fruit of the tree of life, and the Holy Ghost shall be with him. . . . And he shall bind the Prince of Darkness and strengthen the hand of his children to rout the spirits of evil. And the Lord will rejoice in His children and their mouths shall praise and magnify the Eternal."

In the free Judaea, in the delivered Holy City of Jerusalem, in the shadow of the stately Temple built by Herod, everywhere within the far-flung borders of the new Palestine, Israel's yearning was not for a national hero, but for a universal saviour. The Jewish Messiah had outgrown the narrow confines of his country and the beggar rags of a paltry local despot; he demanded the world for his footstool, the heavens for his seat of majesty.

What could a Herod with his gaudy Temple offer Israel, when even his Temple was overtopped by the Antonia fortress from whence the Roman centurion cast his shadow into the innermost court of the Sanctuary? True, Jewish national ambitions had never reached such full realization as under the despotic government of Herod the Great. No other Jewish monarch could have likened himself to King Solomon, who symbolized the golden age in Israel's past. Like Solomon, Herod had pushed out the frontiers of Palestine, and he surpassed his predecessor in the extent and volume of his trade in the world. If he had not accomplished this, as Solomon had done, with David's sword, he had succeeded, nonetheless, in his own way, the only way which in his time could lead to territorial aggrandizement—shrewd diplomacy and abject flattery offered before the throne of the Caesars. Like Solomon, the cunning Herod had truly estimated the potential value of a national center in Jerusalem and had reared the most opulent, the most spectacularly sumptuous edifice Jewry could boast throughout its history—the Second Temple. Herod knew the importance of the Temple as a lodestone for the allegiance of those countless Jews in the Diaspora, already scattered across the seven seas. For apart from the revenue, which thus flowed into the coffers of the Temple, he knew how to evaluate the influence of Jews in the Diaspora for the extension of his commerce over the entire ancient world.

Apart from his role as a tyrant in which, be it said in passing, he was no exception among the great and lesser rulers of his time, Herod achieved the highest material prosperity for his country, though he gained it at the expense of the poor peasantry whom he bled white with heavy taxes. He acquired dignity, respect, and importance, not for himself alone, but for his state and people, by the munificent gifts he showered upon every important city in the Roman Empire with which he wished to enter into trade negotiations, presenting them with colonnaded temples, stadia, baths, and public parks. In the interest of commerce, too, he equipped Israel with the splendid port of Caesarea—and with pagan temples dedicated to the worship of Augustus Caesar. He dredged and widened the obsolete harbors of Jaffa and Acco, enabling them to compete with the old-established ports of Gaza and Ascalon, Tyre and Sidon.

One may say that the Jews in his time were transformed from a poor farming community into a prosperous mercantile nation. Herod broke through the window that opened to the world. He set up theaters and gymnasiums and introduced pageants and public games, wrestling tournaments and races. The modern stadium he built in the old city of Sichem, with sweeping colonnades, marbled pergolas, and arena, was accounted one of the largest in the Empire; here many cities congregated to perform their chariot races and watch the sport of man-murdering beasts. If one were to judge him by the scope of his political and economic vision, by his pomp and the pageantry of his buildings, Herod would stand as one of the great Jewish kings.

But Herod's realm was of the empire of Satan; he could not lure the love of the Jews by gorging and glutting their national appetites, by advancing the borders of their country, uncovering new sources of income, flattering their cities with marble and precious stones, paving the streets of Jerusalem with gold and silver, as Solomon had done; nor even by erecting a magnificent Temple to the Lord to attract the Jews of the Diaspora and foreign sight-seers in endless procession.

Israel was waiting for another, for the Messiah, son of David, and waiting with all Israel was Joseph ben Jacob.

At this time the House of David was a political factor no longer. Fallen from its princely status it stood, humbled and impoverished, among the patrician families of Israel.

In even worse plight was the royal House of the Hasmoneans, whose very name had once sounded with a Messianic ring. After Herod had assassinated the aged Hyrcanos, last of the Hasmonean kings, and had killed by drowning the last High Priest of the Maccabean dynasty, the handsome young Jochanan Aristobolus, both offices, that of king and high priest, came gradually to lose their Messianic connotations. The high priesthood as such remained, of course, supremely venerable, but the personality of the priest sank steadily in the regard of the people. No longer was he a grandson of the glorious Maccabees. He was more likely now to be the father of one of Herod's concubines. Nor was even he likely to hold his post for long, since this highest office in the land was shuffled, like a profitable sinecure, from hand to hand. As for the families of David's house, those who accepted the Herodian regime and served it loyally were tolerated and sometimes permitted to retain their wealth. The others, if they gave the king the least cause to suspect their loyalty, were mercilessly rooted out to the last man.

Many of David's house submerged among the people to escape Herod's wrath. They turned their backs on the large cities and retired to the provinces, to the smallest villages and the remotest hamlets, where they could mix with the country people without fear of discovery by the ubiquitous agents of the king. And among the descendants of the House of David who had thus faded into the people to escape Herod's spite, was the family of Joseph ben Jacob. Reb Jacob, Joseph's father, had gone at first to Nazareth in Galilee, where he lived inconspicuously as a joiner, while his ancestral holdings were being confiscated by King Herod in a general expropriation of dynastic families. Several years later, when Herod's spies had smelled him out in this small Galilean town, he took to the hills of Judaea, the immemorial sanctuary of men who had incurred the displeasure of tyrant kings. Their innumerable valleys, gullies, and ravines rendered them an ideal refuge. Countless settlements of varying sizes animated the hills. Villages nestled inside mountain gorges, their flat plaster roofs undistinguishable against the chalky whiteness of the surrounding rock. By day, the presence of these settlements was betrayed only by the herds of sheep and cattle which clung to the steep slopes of the mountains looking for grass among laurel and oleander shrubs. At night, dim curling plumes of smoke might be seen to ascend from the mouths of the ravines, acknowledging the presence of some human habitation.

In these hills Reb Jacob found a mountain hamlet and there raised his sons in the trade he had mastered during his exile in Nazareth. Joseph was the youngest of his sons, too young to remember the good days in Bethlehem and Jericho, when the family had lived in ease and plenty. He had grown up with poverty a familiar guest at the family table. His father and older brothers— particularly the hot-headed Asher—resented bitterly the turn of their fortunes; they hankered after their former status and hoped one day to retrieve their property and play once more their old patrician role, meanwhile waiting doggedly for the downfall of the Herodian regime, to hasten which Asher had even joined an insurrectionary band. Joseph alone had made peace with his condition. More than that, he found a genuine pleasure in the environment of hardship in which his family was forced to live. Not only had he, like others of his kinsmen, abandoned every hope of seeing David's house reinstated on the throne of Israel, he had actually relinquished his pride as the descendant of a king for the greater dignity of belonging to a family that would sire the redeemer of Israel and mankind. How this would come about, and what connection there would be between the descendants of David and the Messiah who would come riding with the clouds of heaven to set up a celestial empire on earth, Joseph did not know and did not trouble his mind to discover. This was one of the mysteries of which the sages said: "Seek not to uncover that which is hidden from you"—like the forbidden mysteries of heaven, or the state of the world prior to Genesis. Joseph accordingly refrained from pondering this aspect of the Messiah, and merely waited with a humble spirit for his inevitable coming.

In the meantime the humdrum everyday life of his family was perfectly fitted to his disposition, and he could not have felt more at home among the simple villagers of his environment had he been born among them. As for the carpenter's skill which he acquired together with his brothers, Joseph found it an indestructible source of pleasure and valued it, not so much for the honest crust of bread it yielded him, as for giving him a secure hold on life and rooting him in the community of men. It was his trade that made him a full citizen of whatever place he occupied. His trade bound him to his people instead of keeping him apart in the chill climate of the aristocracy. In the humblest of ways, he felt, it made him a partner to the act of creation, since it enabled him to contribute his mite to the sum of works that constituted God's world. And so he loved his labor with a wholeness of heart, and enjoyed a mystic fellowship with the peasant who furrowed the earth with a wooden plowshare of his making. The bread he saw kneaded in his troughs became as much his gift as the sower's, the reaper's, or the thresher's. Joseph regularly blessed the tools that issued from his shop. His heart swelled joyfully over every completed bowl or cask destined to hold the scant food and drink which the peasant in the sweat of his brow wrung from the unwilling soil.

Joseph was one with the poverty-pinched villagers of his community. He knew their troubles and saw their want and helpless isolation. He saw the state gnawing away the little flesh that still cleaved to their parched, haggard bodies after the heavy tithes and taxes exacted by the law had been yielded up. For the earth was poor among these mountains. The rains swept every precious grain of soil that lingered in the rocky crevices into the valleys. Food-bearing soil had to be dug in fistfuls from cracks in the stone and secured on hanging terraces against the pillage of the rains. Truly, every span of earth owned by these mountain farmers was painfully, laboriously wrested from chaos. And the niggardly crops they reaped from their small holdings had to feed many mouths, and many more whose hands had no share in the labor. The Judaean farmer was toiling, in fact, to maintain Herod's fabulous expenditures—the building of theaters, stadia, arenas, temples, and baths with which Herod decked foreign as well as his own cities. Not a few times the young Joseph witnessed deeds of violence practised on defenseless peasants by the king's tax-gatherers or publicans.

The hills were bordered by a fertile plain which stretched along the sea and threw a girdle of green around the mountains. This coastal belt, formerly Philistine territory, was now part of Judaea. The soil here was fat and generous to man, and the coastline was punctuated by ancient harbor towns, all of which had felt Herod's modernizing zeal. With the single exception of Ascalon, an enclave of Philistine remnants within a solid Jewish population, the entire coastline was Jewish-held—from the old harbor town of Gaza in the south to the gaudy, bustling new port of Caesarea in the northern portion of the plain of Sharon, where Herod had settled a mixed population of Jews and Greeks. And ships of all nations ferried the renowned wheat and spelt of Ephraim, the rich wines and honeys and refined oils from the olive groves of the Shephela to the marts of Tyre and Sidon and, farther still, to the ship-surfeited world port of Tarsus.

Great market towns studded the fertile plain, and here the mountain farmers sold the meager produce of their lands. To one of these, Lydda, the jewel of the plain, came the craftsmen as well as the farmers of the mountain settlements, bringing their finished wares. Joseph, too, often descended into Lydda, traveling in a caravan of artisans and farmers and leading by the halter an ass packed high with the products of his labor—carved wooden yokes, spinning wheels and looms, and casks.

The market was under the supervision of a special officer, known as the *agoranome*. Needless to say, the office was commonly held by someone with connections at court or by a member of a family of fortune. For it was a highly coveted post, offering limitless possibilities for graft. On occasion the state traded it, for a fat return, to some private contractor who would move into the job with a host of duns, tax-farmers, and toll clerks. Every artisan and peasant who wished to bring his goods to market was made to cross a narrow bridge which led straight to the toll-gate where he unstrapped his packwares to pass the tollmaster's inspection. The corn, the fruit, the greens, and every cruse of oil or honey were hauled down from the ass's back to be weighed and measured and paid for on the spot. The wealthy farmers, those who were able to pay in cash down to the last groat, escaped by defraying the official duty stipulated for each product. But from the indigent peasants, who were not blessed with ready money, the tax was taken in kind—and here the tollmaster was free to make his own assessments; and he mulcted his victims at once on the state's behalf, the agoranome's, and his own.

The same procedure was applied to the artisans. The rich paid cash; the others were despoiled of so many pairs of sandals, so many lengths of dyed wool, so many earthen pitchers, and as many benches and tables as the toll station could conveniently accommodate. Again and again Joseph saw the neighbors of his villages—those who had come with him to market—compelled to sell their donkeys in return for some raw wool and dye with which to pursue their trade. In such case the peasant or the artisan would do his ass's work, dragging his raw materials up the mountainous trails that led to home.

Taxes, as a rule, were doubly paid—once by the producer and again by the buyer. For in addition to the duties which the seller paid upon reaching the market, the customer was taxed for every item in his purchase. To this end the market place was set swarming with watchful toll clerks, each man with a brazen badge on his bare chest and a club in his fist—the insignia of his office. They kept their eye on every booth and exacted tribute for every article as it changed hands.

But it was not the government alone that pressed yoke-like upon the necks of the Judaean peasantry. The Jewish farmers, laborers, and artisans of Palestine were caught between two millstones—the government on the one hand and, on the other, the learned scribes and doctors who brandished the Law over their heads, and kept them pent in a prison which held their souls together with their bodies captive. They pried in every nook and corner, peered under the lid of every cruse of oil or honey to ascertain whether the said oil or honey be ritually clean or no. However salutary such Laws of Moses as the prohibition against sowing the same furrow with diverse seeds may have been in their time—and in this instance the intent was certainly the improvement of the country's flora—the interpreters of the Law, with their unshakable severity and legalistic involutions, turned the commandments into an intolerable burden for the peasant who was frequently beside himself with fear lest he inadvertently mix flax with cotton. Poor country folk, too ignorant to grope their way safely through the forbidding labyrinth of statutes, regulations, and commandments, would find themselves, at every turn, in head-on conflict with the Law.

Joseph could not forget how the poor farmers of his native province cursed their ill fate whenever the season required them to sow their wretched fields. They were in a perpetual agony lest some law had been violated, in which case all the toil sunk into the earth would be vain, for then the local scholar, the rabbi, or his deputy, would condemn his crop, pronounce it unclean, order him to pluck out the vegetables, destroy the fruit, and burn the wheat before it could mature.

As a devout Jew and a child of the Torah, Joseph bore gladly the yoke of the Law which the rabbis had laid across his shoulders. These same rabbis, after all, and in particular the Pharisees, were revered by the people. The authority to whom Israel looked for guidance was not the depraved House of Herod, nor the corrupt clique of the High Priest, but these very scholars, the sages, rabbis, Pharisees. Joseph knew, as did every Jew in the country, that their laws and regulations served but one object—to protect Jewry as by an iron wall from the incursions of paganism and the abominations which abounded throughout the Gentile world. But they had spread the mantle of holiness over too small a section of the people, over those few only who were armed with knowledge of the Law. And they had shut out a great mass of Jewry, placed them beyond the pale of sanctity, because they were not competent to understand the many accessory statutes and superadded regulations with which the rabbis had fenced in the Mosaic Law.

For many years the doubts had gnawed like cankers at Joseph's peace of mind. Not that he challenged the authority of the scribes to interpret the Law and pass judgment on transgressors—this

64

would have been unthinkable; but he could not make peace with the notion that the Father of all living things, the God of compassion, He who loved the oppressed and to whom none was closer than the humblest spirit, that He, who bore pity for all creatures, should watch with Argus-eyes whether or not His poorest peasant planted his seeds in segregated furrows, as enjoined by the Law. He could not find it in his heart to justify the wrongs that were daily perpetrated by the scholars against an entire class of the population—the poorest and most honest of the people, who won the bread they ate in the sweat of their brow and by the toil of their hands. These very people the scholars branded ignorant, denied them the protection of an incomprehensible code, and almost banished them from the community of Israel. Surely the scholars had done strange things with the Lord. He of whom Israel's minstrel had sung that He loved the broken, contrite heart; of whom the Prophets said that He required nothing of men but that they walk in righteousness—in the mouths of the scholars He became a sullen and capricious tyrant who had proclaimed as unclean all His works, and all mankind who were His children, so that the contact of their hands defiled and the glance of their eyes soiled and contaminated, as though the very current of creation were charged with fiends and unclean spirits who poisoned the atmosphere in which man was condemned to walk; and His own chosen people He had bound and fettered with a thousand knotted coils which none but the scholars might untangle.

In such circumstances, where the scholars kept aloof from the unlettered countrymen, while aristocrats and civil servants gaped only for private increment, the population inevitably fell into castes. Political associations and religious sects mushroomed and decayed with surprising rapidity, all of them equally indifferent to the entirety of Israel and concerned only with their own salvation.

At that time Joseph's family, too, fell apart. Some of his older brothers, whose hearts still smouldered with the ancient hope of seeing David's house regain its kingship, enrolled in secret revolutionary groups that had their nests in every part of the country. Others enlisted with followers of the Galilean rebel chief, Yehuda; they hid in mountainous retreats, raided the highways, and sortied

65

against towns and villages, determined to break the yoke of Herod and his Roman overlords by violence and open insurrection.

But Joseph was no warrior by nature. There was too much of gentleness and humility in his disposition, and his naïve trustfulness was such as almost to warrant the name of simpleton by which his older brothers sometimes called him. He sought out those whom all others had foresworn, who were relegated to the lowest rung in Israel's hierarchy—the illiterate peasant population.

He did not scruple to enter their mud cabins, to drink with them from the same bowl, to squat with them on the bare earth and dip his hand in the communal earthen dish, from which they ate with blackened grime-encrusted fingers. At night he lay with them on strawen pallets, in conscious violation of the explicit ban of the rabbis. Like them he donned a habit of sackcloth, bound with a rope, and shared their hatred for those learned favorites who had taken sole possession of the Lord and tied up His Torah in their purses. Joseph endeavored to console them. Though his scholarship was scant, he could read the Hebrew Scriptures, and the words of the Prophets were familiar to his memory. And so, at night, he would repeat to them the songs of Israel's minstrel, translating them into the current Aramaic idiom, or tell them of the saviour whose coming was foretold by Isaiah, whose mission was the deliverance of Israel from foreign and domestic yokes, who, with God's word, would change the order of the universe, promulgate a new law, and close a new covenant between humanity and God; who would break down the walls that separated man from man and nation from nation and unite all the peoples of the earth in Zion; a prophet, a redeemer would he be, anointed by the Lord to preach good tidings to the meek, to bind up the brokenhearted and proclaim liberty to prisoners.

For such a deliverer Joseph had waited many years, and without troubling himself to penetrate the mysteries of his advent. This only he knew; that the Messiah would not be a king, nor a hero of war, nor yet a prophet like the ancient seers who had been his heralds. He would be God's chosen Messiah, for whom all Jewry waited with a thirsting soul. And now, suddenly, he himself, Joseph ben Jacob, was to become a part in the miracle of the Messiah's coming. It was more than his waking mind could comprehend. Joseph strayed through the streets of Nazareth as though gripped in a dream, like a man drunken with sweet wine.

CHAPTER VIII

JOSEPH'S kinsmen in Nazareth avoided his house, and even his old friend Reb Elimelech shrank from his company. All the bitterness and anger over the shame heaped on the family were trained on him. He could not slip through an alley of the town without starting at sneering voices behind him, followed usually by peals of raucous laughter; "There he goes, the lad who eats his grapes unripened."

She, Miriam, was spared; she was treated as an innocent victim and allowed to go about her business. There seemed to be nothing in her life which would have marked her off from any other girl in her condition. She attended to her household tasks and served her husband as would any other wife. Her mother, indeed, wondered at the separation of their beds—Miriam passed the nights alone in her chamber while the son-in-law slept in the new annex he had built for his workshop. But this she attributed to a modesty born of remorse and thought it best to say no more about it.

Often, when the day's work was complete, the newlyweds sat side by side in the main room, neither of them caring to speak. For there was always silence around Miriam; her own reticence, that seemed so demure at a distance, was at close quarters so authoritative that Joseph would have thought it a desecration to rend the stillness by so much as one thoughtless word. Thus they would sit together without speaking, Miriam sometimes turning to show a smile over her shoulder—at which Joseph would cast down his eyes.

Ever since his dream, since the seraphic voice had sounded in his ear, he had looked upon his wife as a mysterious being, whom he not only did not understand but whom, from some religious inhibition in his soul, he did not wish to understand. He won-

67

dered that she should be at his side, she whom he had coveted for his body before he was aware of God's design, before he knew that she was God's elected mother. And now her womb was big with Israel's hope, fructified by God's Holy Spirit to conceive the redemption of mankind. And upon him had fallen the lot to be her guardian and protector; she and her offspring were his sacred trust. Whenever in his reveries he returned to this, his own part in the miracle, he felt his thoughts recoil in despair at his insufficiency and he would seek recourse in voiceless prayer—"Father in heaven, purge my heart and fit me for my task; open my eyes to Your teaching and make me worthy to abide in her presence."

At such times it seemed to Joseph that Miriam had divined his thoughts, for she would reach out for his hand and make him look into her smiling eyes as she said:

"Joseph, you are my arm and shield, and the protector of my child."

On hearing such words and feeling the cool touch of her hand, Joseph would think his prayer miraculously answered, as though some of her sanctity, outflowing through her fingers, had in one moment made him worthy of her nearness.

One morning they were both working in the vegetable garden. Joseph was digging ditches to irrigate the greens. Miriam, behind him and a few paces distant, was kneeling on the ground, weeding the bed of sweet peas. Suddenly Joseph was startled by the sound of her singing. He turned round and saw Miriam, still kneeling, softly humming to herself in prayer. She had let her kerchief fall over her face as if to shut out all distractions. Joseph at once left off digging and, carefully unbending, walked to a distance, hoping only that God would open his understanding and make him receptive to Miriam's unspoken desires. And when he had stood awhile at the far end of the garden, with his eyes closed and the height of his body curved with humility, he suddenly felt Miriam's hand on his shoulder.

"Miriam!" he cried anxiously, seeing the tears in her eyes, "what has made you unhappy?"

"Joseph, I am not weeping with unhappiness. Good tidings have reached my ears and it is joy which puts tears in my eyes."

"What tidings, Miriam?"

"That God has granted consolation to my cousin Elisheva. In her old age He has opened her barren womb. And even now Elisheva is far gone with child. I beg you, Joseph, take me to her that I may be comforted in the grace God has vouchsafed her."

Joseph did not hesitate; he bowed his head still deeper and answered: "Even as you say, Miriam, I shall do."

No one in Nazareth knew for certain why the young couple left their nest so soon after their marriage to set out upon so long a journey. But the gossipers made free with conjectures, concluding finally that the young wife was too deeply smitten with shame over her husband's wantonness to show her face among such as knew her history; and surely she had every cause to leave the scene of her degradation and seek refuge in the sheltered seclusion of the Judaean wilderness where she could stay with her kinsman, the old priest Zachariah, until the matter had blown over. Miriam's old mother—who in the past few weeks had aged beyond her years, and who eschewed all company in the knowledge that her children were the butt of every idle prattler in the neighborhood—she, the old lonely widow, was glad to see her daughter go, at least for a while, until the girls and matrons of the town could find another juicier morsel to meet the nine measures of scurrility and tittle-tattle allotted to the daughters of Eve. The rest of Miriam's family likewise had few regrets when they learned of her departure.

Even Joseph, Miriam's own guide, could not fully account for his wife's eagerness to take so arduous a journey in the midst of her pregnancy, merely to join her relatives in the southern desert. He nevertheless obeyed her wish, convinced that Miriam's every desire was backed by a divine intent.

Miriam did have good cause for the journey—though she did not reveal it to her husband. To her, the old priest and his wife Elisheva who had reared her as a child were spiritual parents. And Miriam had need of someone to strengthen her hands. It was not that she doubted the words of the angel who had told her of her election—and yet, throughout the journey her heart was uneasy. Her cousin's motherhood was a rare blessing, to be sure, but there were precedents for it and people could accept the report without overtaxing their credulity. Had not the same grace been shown to the aged Sarah, and to Hannah when she bore Samuel, the Prophet? But when, in human memory, had a virgin conceived, being overshadowed by the Holy Spirit of God? Her own experience was to be accepted on faith alone. Her virgin pregnancy was the first test of faith in the Messiah. Would she find such faith in her old cousin; in the old priest who caviled with the voice of his angel, so that he was struck dumb in punishment and deprived of his holy office? To this day she had found but one man in all the world—including even her nearest family—who believed in her with perfect faith. And he had borne grief and humiliation on her behalf, without once opening his mouth to bewail his condition. Miriam had been apprised of his stand in the court, and knew the contumely he had met as his reward. She knew of the derisive looks, the tittering behind his back, the fists clenched in anger by his kinsmen. She marveled at his uncomplaining joyousness of heart. And while the donkey under her stepped gingerly over the rocky trail, she rested her hand on Joseph's shoulder as he, with his staff and bundle, kept pace with the ass, and she said:

"Joseph, what grief and shame I have brought on your head! Yet like a sponge you drink up the sorrow and never say a word."

"O Miriam, is it not enough that God has placed you in my care to convert all my suffering into joy? Is it not sufficient grace for me to go with you like your own shadow? Can a man ask more than to be chosen guardian of the holy thing in your womb? The tread of your feet, Miriam, is dear to me as the beat of my heart, and the air I breathe in your presence purifies my being, for you, Miriam, are holy and lend of your sanctity to all that come near."

Miriam listened in happy silence and said at last: "Joseph, I thank God every day for entrusting me into your hands."

Joseph conducted his young wife over the stony trail that joined their little town with the Plain of Jordan and then proceeded due south with the river valley as far as Jericho. To avoid the towns of the Samaritans, who sat astride the roads that linked Galilee with Judaea, Joseph, like all lone travelers when they made the pilgrimage to Jerusalem, spurned the Sichem-Ephraim highway, preferring to sustain the greater rigors of the mountainous Jordan route.

It was a long journey that took almost a full week. But it was late spring, the kindest season to travelers. The fields were blanketed with an abundance of varied greens, and men and women were tending the vegetable gardens with which the Plain of Jordan was so thickly planted. Now and then the travelers inhaled a fragrance, zephyr-borne, of lotus, cinnamon, and flowering ginger. Some of the fields around were sown with flax, cotton, and hemp, and there the women could be seen spinning and weaving out-of-doors, while the young girls combed the yarn ready for the spindle, bleached linen, or twisted rope. The fields teemed with activity, for they were potent with ripe fruit and ready for harvest. On all sides, wherever fell the random glance of the travelers, they saw the sparkling multi-colored pattern of beets, radishes, and artichokes, and fat Egyptian gourds and melons and herbs and flowering shrubs and spices.

The riches of the fields overflowed the paths along the river banks where Joseph's donkey walked with dainty steps, its belly tickled by luxuriating poppy blossoms, while others bent under the crush of its hoofs. Overhead the white and red flower clusters of the oleander filtered and strained the vivid shafts of the sun, spreading a mottled shade over the rider and her guide.

At noon they found shelter from the midday sun with the mowers and reapers of the adjoining cornfields, for the latter, obeying Jewish custom, rarely failed to invite the travelers to share with them their vegetables and fresh water. When evening fell they sought cover in some garden bower or in a fisherman's tent by the river, and sometimes in one of the night watchmen's huts, of which there were large numbers studding the vineyards— unless a farmer offered them the protection of his house or barn.

Joseph took care to by-pass the houses of wealthier countrymen; he did not choose to burden their hospitality. He would see Miriam safely into the shelter he had found for her, while he himself seated himself outside, the ass's halter in his hand so that the animal could eat the grass that bordered on the path and not

71

trespass into private plantations. Thus every night he watched over his wife and grudged himself each quarter hour of involuntary sleep.

The Jordan is not everywhere so lenient to men. The river meanders through the valley, winds in and out with a serpentine motion, sealing off sometimes whole tracts of land. Only a little way upstream it seemed to flow blithely through gardens and meadows, cajoling fishermen and farmers to its shores—then suddenly it turns abruptly off and, before veering back farther downstream, bequeaths to the fisherman a half-circle of inaccessible marshland, overgrown with writhing waterplants in fulsome profusion. Stumps of dead trees and fallen trunks and branches bar every access to the river bank. These captive areas within the river's course are fitly called the "pride of the Jordan" —they are the Jordan's arrogance, its inapproachability, its Olympian disregard of mortal needs. They are areas of real danger, and the most practised travelers—not to mention the pilgrims journeying to Jerusalem—avoid their treacherous undergrowth and choose detours that take them through the settlements at the foot of the hills. For there are savage animals that lurk in the thickets; wildcats leap from the branches, boars show their hard, bristling snouts, and with the fall of night comes the cry of the jackal.

Joseph was unfamiliar with this region, and at one point, leading the donkey along the river bank which he had taken for his guide, he lost the hackneyed path which had abandoned Jordan for the security of the hills.

The night was falling fast, as is the way in the land of Israel. Joseph and Miriam found themselves deep in an island-wilderness encoiled by the river, and Joseph did not know the peril into which he had guided his ward.

Both of them were accustomed, from their childhood, to sleep in the open—this they had learned whenever they had pilgrimaged to Jerusalem. Thus Miriam alighted from the ass and Joseph chose the moss at the foot of a sycamore and its dense foliage overhead for her bed and canopy. He stripped the shawls and blankets from the donkey's back and spread them on the ground. For a few moments he sat by Miriam's side while they consumed

72

their bread and a handful of olives and drank fresh water from Joseph's leather bottle. Then they blessed God for His bounty and Miriam stretched herself and was soon asleep, for she was wearied by the day's long traveling under the beating sun.

Joseph sat down a short distance away keeping an eye on the donkey and prepared, as he was every night, to remain awake in order to guard his wife from all danger.

But the sky had no sooner darkened than the wild disconsolate wail of the jackals pealed through the stillness. At once the thickets came alive with the growls and snorts of unseen animals, and the smooth waters of the Jordan were churned by swamp vermin that added their hiss to the general howl of dissonance. Joseph felt a chilling clutch on his heart and spun around to see, beneath the undergrowth, the icy glitter of a pair of animal eyes focused on him. He turned back and back, and wherever he turned he saw the same cold sparks—saw them within the thickets, in the branches overhead, below the gnarled and twisted roots of trees. And about him, in the dark, among the shrubs and rushes, he heard the shuffling and scuffing of animal feet coming close.

The little ass sniffed the air with flying nostrils, then brayed in wild panic and began kicking into the void of darkness.

The uproar was still filling the air when Joseph suddenly started to a piercing scream. It did not fade, but rather swelled to deafening intensity and, in one flash of horror, it seemed to Joseph not like the shriek of any living beast. His eyes froze in their sockets as though to arrest the fiendish dancing shadows of the night, the cat-clawed demons, horned like beasts and visaged like the sons of men, spawned by the darkness from the seed of his own terror-stricken brain. He saw them closing in, casting unholy shadows over Miriam's slumbering body, enwheeling him in the green scintillating phosphorescence of a thousand eyes, strangling his breath like a choking noose; and though the pandemonium would not let him hear, he sensed the oncoming of lynx-like feet, the gnashing of bared teeth, the tensing of monstrous claws and talons. Every second tightened the ring about his little camp, and Joseph, in shame and despair at his own help-

73

lessness, threw up his head and cried—"Lord God, save the mother and her child! . . ."

He had barely uttered his cry when he felt strangely relieved. The uproar was as violent as before; the gleam of hostile eyes still shone from every bush and shrub; he could still see the flicker of animal shapes stalking his camp; but he suddenly knew Miriam safe, and with Miriam, himself and his donkey, as though a magic circle of protection had been thrown around all three. The reality of this circle was to him so palpable that he thought it must be a ring of living bodies which he could not see, of which he saw only the shadows falling. And though he saw no wings he felt upon his cheek the cooling breath of air stirred by their flutter. Joseph wiped the cold sweat from his brow and his face relaxed. He felt safer and more invulnerable than he could have felt in the mightiest citadel and, for the first time in many nights, he slept.

When he awoke the sun had risen and Joseph saw his wife looking at him with clear smiling eyes. Miriam was well rested, having slept in deep oblivion of the peril through which they had passed.

Joseph did not wish to frighten her by speaking of the night's visitation. But he knew thenceforth that his young wife and the load of her womb were not under his protection only, and he resumed his march with confidence and with joy in his heart. And thus he brought her safely into the date groves of Jericho.

A stony waste is the Wilderness of Judah; no desert of untrodden sand but a vast ruin of extinguished towns and cities, of halfsunken temples, colonnades, and terraced palaces, tumbled in heap upon heap of ruins.

Southward from Jericho the little ass that bore the weight of Miriam was forced to climb and clamber over rolling masses of stone, the sunken ghosts of ancient cities that once barred Joshua's way into the Promised Land. With wary steps, as though it knew the nature of its burden, the donkey picked a path between sharp razing crags and headlong chasms, digging its hoofs into the rocky groove it had chosen to follow and conscious of the yawning gorge that opened a few feet away. Joseph did not for a moment leave its side, feeling Miriam's hand on his shoulder and ready any moment to help if the donkey should misjudge its step.

Above them, the rocks reared their points against the sky. Here and there, among the piles of stone, Joseph thought he distinguished the remains of some heathen temple, strewn with the shattered images of bestial gods and idols. On every hand the jagged precipices of the mountains recalled the façades and crumbled colonnades of long-forgotten palaces—the wreckage at their feet, the huge flagstones of ancient marts and arenas—dwellings, these, of an extinct race of giants, obscene sons of Asmodeus who raised an impious revolt against the Lord, reared towers to ascend to heaven, and presumed to dethrone the Almighty power who, in righteous vengeance, scattered their towns like chaff before the wind, leaving only the beetling summits of the rocks to monument their insubordination.

A stillness as of extinction reigned among these stones. No man or animal or habitation, as far as the eye could reach—nothing but the colossal bulk of stone and precipice falling off steeply into wadies of pulverized rock whose mounting dust seemed like the steam of cauldrons stirred by a witch's brood. Never the sound of running water; never a glimpse of a tree; only the grueling cry of the hyena pursued by a bird of prey that circled overhead biding its victim's exhaustion. The vulture's flitting shadow was the only sign of life in this wilderness, and sometimes, very rarely, the form of a fugitive gazelle, perched for a moment on a mountain peak to disappear as quickly as it had come.

Since ancient times the Judaean wilderness had served as refuge for men who sought to escape persecution. In the caves of these rocks, David and his men hid from the wrath of Saul. To these mountains fled the Prophet Elijah when the Baal-worshipping Jezebel threatened his life. And hither came the priest Zachariah to hide the shame of his dumbness; for he was still awed by the vision he had seen in the Temple and by the ire of the angel whose word concerning Elisheva's opened womb he had dared to question. He had taken his wife and wandered with her into this wilderness, here to await the fulfillment of the angel's promise of a son and, with it, release of his captive tongue.

There were several scattered oases in the Wilderness of Judah; between the sheer stone walls of the mountains the winds, over the years, had deposited layer upon layer of earth-dust which, being watered by attendant mountain springs—of these there were not a few in the area—gradually turned into narrow swaths of arable soil. Around such pitifully small oases gathered groups of men who had personal or public reasons for embracing solitude. They pitched tents in the rocky crevices, sowed what they needed for subsistence, and perhaps planted a date palm or two to supplement the handful of fruit trees that grew wild near the spring. With the years, some of these oases developed into small settlements, known as the "mountain towns." In one of these towns—consisting almost wholly of tents and rudely improvised sheds, made of heaped stones and covered with palm sprigs and mats of rushes—in one of these forsaken settlements the aged priest and his wife had settled to await the future.

Twilight was falling when Joseph, still leading Miriam's ass, caught sight of the tents and stone cabins, wedged high above eye level in the folds of the rock. He knew that this must be his destination and goaded the exhausted animal to a last spurt of effort to climb the rough-hewn terraced steps that led up to the settlement. At last they reached the mountain town—a small square with a well to hold the spring water and a few scattered palms. The dwellings, some twenty in all, were concealed within the face of the rock at various levels.

A man, evidently a hermit of long standing, sat alone by the well-curb, and from him Joseph asked the whereabouts of the priest Zachariah. The stranger pointed mutely to one of the sheer mountain walls where Joseph now saw what seemed like a cavern, sheltered against the sun by a matting of coarse goat's hair. Joseph found a rock-hewn stairway that ran up to the lodgment and, placing his foot on the first step, called:

"Zachariah, Zachariah, come forth to welcome your guests!"

His call faded away without answer, as though the all-devouring silence of the dusk had snatched it from his lips and drawn it to itself. In the distance the mountain cliffs were fretted with the glim-gilt light of the declining sun; here, on the plateau, below the steep walls of the surrounding rocks whose lengthening shadows crept over the wilderness, the gloom was almost complete. But it was only a few seconds, which seemed longer

76

in the solemn stillness, before the mat of Zachariah's cave was moved aside from within to reveal the tall frame of the priest. His white gown still showed clearly in the darkness and Joseph followed its sway as the priest descended the steps. Then Joseph saw the man of whom Miriam had often told him on the road; recognized from her description his long tapering white beard and clear blue eyes. And, with joy written over his old face, the priest stretched out his arms toward Joseph and embraced him and all the while motioned upward with his hands toward the cave.

Down the stone steps now came another figure—as thin and almost as tall as the priest's. It was the aged Elisheva, her dress of dark sackcloth taut over a bulging belly, a lighted earthenware lamp in her hand. Still from afar she recognized who sat on Joseph's ass, for she suddenly speeded her steps and ran the last part of the way, oblivious to the gesticulations and the muted groans of the priest with which he tried to restrain her pace.

Miriam slipped down from her saddle and at once buried her face in the old woman's breast, and Elisheva laid her cheek against Miriam's and stroked her hair and held her close as though she would not let her go. Then she turned to Joseph and finally, without relinquishing Miriam's hand, lighted the way up to her mountain dwelling, while the priest and Joseph followed with the ass.

And when they had sat down on the hempen rugs inside the cave, Miriam turned once more to her old cousin and began to speak.

"I have made this long journey, cousin Elisheva, to rejoice with you in the gift God has bestowed on you."

As Elisheva heard these words the blood rushed to her head and her face colored crimson like a skin of wine. Her sunken eyes, that were wont to look at the world with a mat shimmer as of unpolished gems, suddenly kindled like bright fires. She rose briskly to her full length, so that the high dome of her head almost touched the ceiling. Strands of her hair trembled under her black kerchief and, for a moment, she stared at Miriam with mixed terror and exultation before dropping heavily to her knees and crying loudly:

"I see what I see!"

With that she prostrated herself before her young ward and stretched toward her a pair of long, wrinkled hands, saying:

"Blessed are you among women, and blessed is the fruit of your womb. . . . For no sooner had your greeting reached my ears but the babe in my womb leapt for joy!"

Joseph did not stir; he kept his eyes cast down as was his wont. But the old priest suddenly raised himself up and stood motionless against the rocky wall so that even the fine hairs of his beard seemed frozen into immobility. For a moment his eyes gaped wildly at the two women and an inarticulate moan wrung itself from his chest. Then he, too, lowered his eyes as though to see were to trespass, and both men held their breath, for it seemed to them that the air of the cave was charged with the substance of another world, all mankind, disembodied, gathered under the palm roof and paying homage to the virgin seated by the wall, an infinity of unfleshed souls—the generations of the living, the dead, and the unborn.

Then Miriam rose, her face so radiant one would have said the sun had set behind the whiteness of her skin, and she opened her lips in a song of praise, singing for sky and earth, for man and angel, for the quick and the dead, singing to all the ends of the earth from the day of creation to the end of time.

"My soul doth magnify the Lord," she sang.

"My heart rejoiceth for in Him is my succor.

"He hath seen the lowliness of His handmaid, and behold, from this day all generations shall call me blessed, for the Mighty One hath done great things in me.

"Holy is His name, and His mercy shall endure everlastingly for such as fear Him.

"Miracles hath He wrought by the strength of His arm.

"The princes of the earth He hath driven from their thrones.

"And the pride of the wicked He hath humbled.

"The poor He hath raised up out of the dust and the hungry He hath filled with good things. But the rich He hath sent empty away.

"He hath holpen Israel, His suffering servant, and hath remembered in mercy the people of His covenant, Abraham his seed for ever and ever."

Miriam stopped, but none of her companions dared to break in on her silence. They feared to move lest their gross flesh impinge on the invisible convocation of souls by which they felt themselves surrounded. But as Miriam continued standing in the center of the room, they dropped to their knees and the first sound to be heard was Elisheva's joyful sobbing. Joseph, too, wept, still without saying a word. Only the priest, in a sudden spasm of uncontrollable exultation, tore himself loose from his wall, ripped down the curtain at the mouth of the cave, and bellowed across to the mountains, into the night, the inhuman cry of the dumb.

It faded, inarticulate and echo-borne, from range to range—the first annunciation to the world of the Messiah's coming.

CHAPTER IX

LEAVING his young wife to Elisheva's care in the Wilderness of Judah, Joseph retraced his steps to Nazareth, there to establish himself in his new home and workshop.

He continued living in the widow Hannah's house against which he had built his shop, for as her son-in-law he was now part of the late Hanan's household, as was Cleophas, the Nazarene who had married the elder Miriam, called Mariama. And indeed, the two men, though they were not friends, often tilled the widow's earth together, sharing both its toil and its produce. To Joseph, coming from the heights of Judaea, the land seemed fruitful in these Galilean hills. And he saw to it that the small plot under his care yielded enough fruit and vegetables for the widow's table where these were the staple foods. This diet, supplemented with a dash of goat's milk, might well have sufficed their needs had it not been for high taxes claimed by the government and the financial needs of the municipal administration, which also were met out of the private fortunes of the citizens. Joseph, accordingly, eked out the family income with the proceeds of his labor in the joiner's shop.

Joseph worked for the poor. The squalid peasants who were his neighbors brought him their broken shares to mend, sometimes a riven shaft or axle, a flail, a wooden bowl or trough; but in the main his occupation was to carve yokes for the oxen that plowed their dwarfish holdings.

He was well content. The town, though it was scarcely known in Israel and often slighted by its neighbors, was not so isolated as most people who had heard its name believed. True, it lay neither on the pilgrims' highway to Jerusalem nor on the royal road that led from the shores of the great sea—from the great port of Caesarea—to Damascus, a road used for travel by all Roman officials and by the bulk of the Arabian trade; yet it was reasonably close to the large town of Sepphoris through which the merchant caravans had to pass. Sometimes the cohort of a Roman legion strayed from the highway to find itself in Nazareth, and instantly the men would plunge into excesses of debauchery unheard-of in the major towns where they were checked by the severity of military discipline. Women then had to hide in ditches outside the town. Some of them even were concealed in wells lest they be strumpeted by the soldiers. The Roman grazed his horses in the little vegetable gardens of the town, looted the homes for wine and oil, slaughtered the last sheep in a family's possession. But in return, as it were, he brought to Nazareth a breath of the great world that lay beyond the sea, where the Roman eagle was reared highest to cast its straddling shadow over all known lands. Thanks to these periodic assaults the Nazarenes learned to know their official masters.

But such invasions did not as a rule last long. After a few days, the men would answer their centurion's call and leave the town. And in the lull they left behind, the citizens would gradually regain their peace and composure.

So much for the Nazarenes' contact with the Empire; their sense of community with Israel was due almost entirely to their proximity to Sepphoris. For Sepphoris was a city of sages and scholars. Apart from its numerous synagogues, it boasted several academies where distinguished men of the Torah taught before large numbers of disciples. The citizens themselves were pious Jews who jealously guarded the Law and made frequent pilgrimages to Jerusalem—not the men only, but the women too, a practice which had given rise to a jest about Sepphorite women visiting Jerusalem every Friday in the month. And if this was an unkind exaggeration, it was true nonetheless that Jerusalem, like an enormous sponge, drew to itself the sap of Galilee as well as Judah. For every city in Israel considered itself merely an appendage to Jerusalem, a halfway house, as it were, to the Temple. Sepphoris thus was well furnished with news from the capital. Its scribes and doctors of the Law knew every amendment to the *Halacha* or *Agada* promulgated in the academies of Hillel or of Shammai; they followed every argument and controversy fought by these rival schools. Nor did they fail to take sides, but debated the matter heatedly in their own institutions. Similarly the revolutionists and rebel spirits of Sepphoris learned of every new disturbance in the capital which aimed at the suppression of the House of Herod, or threw a challenge to the government of Rome. Sepphoris was a hotbed of mutiny and its young men were constantly inciting the town to declare open insurrection and march on Jerusalem.

All of these voices—whether of rebel or of preacher—found a rumbling echo in the out-of-the-way town of Nazareth. Farmers returning from the Sepphoris market brought back the latest news, and occasionally a scholar from the big town made a temporary stop in Nazareth. He would lecture in the synagogue and expatiate on some abstruse point of the Law, acquainting the elders of the town with recent innovations introduced by the school of Hillel or his perennial opponent. And when he left, the elders and the learned men of Nazareth continued for weeks to discuss his revelations, took sides among themselves, and carried on the controversy generated in the Holy City. But the interest aroused by such visits was as nothing compared to the excitement of the town when a deputy of the Pharisees, straight from the capital, arrived to check on general conditions and press for contributions to the schools of learning. At such times, while the nuncio lingered in the town, Nazareth basked in the pride of being among the mother cities of Israel, a member of the sacred congregation of the chosen people.

There were yet other sources of contact with the outside world. Merchants from the maritime cities of the Phoenician north were wont to scour the area for wool to feed the looms of Tyre—as also for frankincense and myrrh, ginger and cinnamon, which were known to thrive well in the Nazarene hills. They introduced into the town the picturesqueness and the godless levity of Gentile living. Leather-shod and dressed in multi-colored tunics, their unctuous locks held down by golden circlets, with broad silken sashes wound thrice about their bellies and sagging on one side from the weight of their purses—with all this bravery of attire, they differed markedly from the indigenous population which, for the most part, dressed in burlap shirts, their loins girded with a hempen rope, their feet naked or tied to wooden soles. The Tyrian merchants came and went—and left behind a legacy of sin, a lust for riches and indulgence. Now and then, you actually saw one of the wealthier citizens strutting about the town in mid-week with a beard combed and curled in Tyrian fashion and a head beslimed with olive oil. Some of the women, too, took to aping Tyrian modes, showed themselves in purple or vermilion fabrics, with painted cheeks and eyebrows, their heads shamelessly bared, exuding lewd odors of perfume, enticements to lust.

It was plain that these men and women had been misled by transient Sybarites, and the town rabbi with the elders of the synagogue lost no time to guide such erring Jews back to the ways of Israel, preaching to the entire congregation each Sabbath after the reading of the Torah.

But then again it happened that a runaway bondsman from the slaveships of Tyre or Sidon found his way into Nazareth. And then the town heard a different tale of life in the great foreign cities—a tale of toil beyond endurance and necessity, a tale of men and women and young children chained to insatiable looms and toiling there till their lives faded out.

Joseph became acquainted with his neighbors before he had been long returned to Nazareth. The house which he now shared with the widow Hannah stood almost at the brink of the town, close to the communal well. Not far distant, outside the town proper, there lived a tanner. He lived in almost total isolation, since the law required all tan-yards to be set up in open country, the tanner's trade being regarded as a noisome occupation and a sufficient reason even for a wife to divorce her husband—if he had not given her to understand in time that she would have to bear the foul effluvia of his body.

The man had built both his hut and tannery in a gutter formed by the drainage of the well, so that he could be near his house when soaking his sheepskins. His dwelling was damp the year round; its walls of platted rushes, putrid with moisture; the earth that was its floor, constantly under water; these conditions had, over the years, induced a paralysis in his wife, as well as dropsy in some of his children, who walked their swollen bellies on thin spindling legs, crippled for life.

Taddi the tanner, though he had misery enough in his bed-ridden wife and ailing children, had been born to a genial and happy disposition which made him shrug off every calamity with a stock phrase—"It is all for the best." Overworked as he was, what with laboring at his trade and nursing his entire household, he had not been heard to complain within anybody's memory. He was a small man, stockily built, whose face was almost drowned under a thick black mane of hair and equally unruly beard. Dressed—if such it could be called—in a few shreds of burlap, steeped in the noxious exhalations of his soaking hides, with animal hairs cleaving everywhere to his bare skin, he would quietly come from his trough of tannin to serve a hot soup to his family. He spoonfed his wife, who had long lost the use of her arms, and satisfied his children, and still found leisure, three times daily, to recite the "Hear, O Israel"—as he found leisure also to attend the reading of the Torah three times a week including Sabbath at the synagogue, where he huddled in the doorway with the rest of the poor. But the most remarkable trait of the tanner was the surprising store of learning he had managed to accumulate. He knew no end of Psalms by heart and would mutter them to himself in an undertone as he limed or unhaired his skins. Furthermore, he not only recalled his childhood training in the Prophets and the writings of the Scripture, but all the talks and sermons he had heard delivered by the sages in the academies; all this he remembered—like a flawless vessel that will not yield one drop of what it was meant to contain.

One late afternoon, shortly before the fall of night, Joseph passed the tannery and stopped, astonished at the sight of a half-naked, raven-haired Jew, bespattered head to heel with fetid tannin, standing between drums and troughs of soaking hides, standing motionless and absorbed in the *Sh'ma*.

Joseph waited for the tanner to complete his service, and then approached and greeted him:

"*Shalom aleichem*. I am your neighbor," he said, bowing low, "I have long desired your acquaintance but feared that you might scruple to consort with a man of such lowly occupation as mine, for I am a carpenter." Knowing the repute in which the tanner's trade was held, Joseph purposely discredited his own.

"A lowly occupation—carpentry? And you say this to a tanner? My friend, you are a mocker of the poor." But there was no offense in the tanner's words and he grinned broadly as he spoke. "It is I who dared to come under your roof, for you know how people's noses wrinkle when they smell a tanner from afar. But, as our wise men say—'Better to skin a carcass in the street than to depend on humankind.' But God sees a man's heart under any dress, and whatsoever He has made He has made for the best; for it is written—after every creation God saw that it was good; not 'beautiful,' mark you, but 'good.' It follows then that whatsoever is useful and good must needs be beautiful."

"You teach well, master," said Joseph, bowing again. "Your words are full of learning and wisdom and I am much in your debt. But, rabbi, teach me one more thing: How comes it that you, who are surely of the Essenes, say the 'Hear, O Israel' in your workaday garments?"

The tanner grinned again and replied: "First I must beg you, young man, not to call me rabbi or master, seeing that I am neither the one nor the other. I am a simple Jew who has rolled a little in the dust of the sages—as little as my work permits, which work I hold in very high regard since it feeds those of my house. As for the Essenes, I have never been their member, for when you belong to one group you shut the door on all others.

84

It is enough for me to belong to the Congregation of Israel. Now you reprove me for praying unwashed in my working clothes, but, as I remember, the Prophet speaks only of purging one's heart before entering God's house, not of washing one's clothes. I come before God in the garments He gave me."

"You have forbidden me to call you rabbi, but your words flow as from a spring of learning," Joseph said. "Let me do a little thing in return for the great thing you have done for me; your bucket there is leaky; it needs mending, and what else is a cooper good for?"

"Ah, the rich man goes to market and takes what buckets he may need, whether his purse be filled or no, for he can pay later. But the poor man can buy only when his cash is ready."

"You have already more than paid me with your generous teaching," Joseph replied. "In my shop is a piece of hardwood which will do very well to wedge your bucket." And with that Joseph hoisted the vessel to his shoulders and went off to forestall further argument. And when he had walked a dozen paces the tanner's voice came after him:

"Mend my bucket and you shall have leather for new sandals!"

Thus began Joseph's friendship with the tanner. With his other neighbor, the Edomite planter of incense, it began in this wise:

Joseph, one day, was standing in his workshop which he had built of four oaken posts driven into the earth and strung with plaited mats, when he heard a voice outside:

"Joiner, come out, I have business for you!"

Joseph went out and found his neighbor, Yekatiel, a tall Edomite, standing off at a respectful distance. Joseph had seen him before, working on his aromatic gums and spices on the farther side of the hill. Now he stood before Joseph with a broken mortar in his hand.

"Why do you trouble me to step out when the doorway of my shop is wide open to every man?" Joseph began.

"Shall I come into your house? I am unclean; I am an Edomite, a Gentile."

Joseph pondered a moment; he recalled his unclean peasant friends of the Judaean hills:

"No man is unclean," he said. "We were all made in the image

85

of God. Come in—and may your entering under my roof be blessed."

The Edomite looked incredulous.

"Are not you one of the Jews?" he asked.

"Indeed, I am."

"And you invite me into your house?"

"In my house every man is a welcome guest."

"Even I?"

For answer Joseph guided him into the shop. He placed him at his table and, having set a bowl before him, filled it with fresh water. But the Edomite made no move to drink.

"You would do better to insure that your brothers do not see me in your house, seated at your table and drinking from your cup, for they will pronounce your house unclean."

"They cannot make unclean what God has made pure," Joseph said, motioning the Edomite to drink from the bowl. "But tell me, what has brought you here?"

"I am a mixer of oils and perfumes. I press them from the incense plants in my garden which is on the farther side of your hill. Now there are certain noble plants—like saffron and the king's rose—which one should pound only in a wooden mortar carved from the finest fragrant cedar wood. For the scents of cedar and saffron make a pleasing blend, but a mortar of stone dulls the aroma. This was my mortar, which, as you see, broke in the pounding. And more's the pity, for I had it from my father who taught me my trade. And now no Israelite joiner will mend it for me or make me another, since they suspect me of mixing incense for the merchants of Tyre to kindle in the temples of Baal."

"Is this true?" asked Joseph.

"I have mortgaged my field to a Tyrian merchant; so I must sell to him. I cannot know for what use he sells it—for the women or the temples."

"But do you burn your incense before false gods?"

"I use my perfumes to purchase my bread—and little enough it is."

Joseph meanwhile had been turning the mortar in his hands, shaking his head in a gesture of deprecation.

"False gods do not exist," he said. "There is only the one living

86

God who is Father to all men. What profit could there be in burning incense to gods that never were? And as for your mortar—this one is beyond repair. You will need another; and I shall need a piece of cedar wood to carve it from. Wait till the coming Monday when I return from Sepphoris. I can buy cedar wood in the bazaar and I will make you a new mortar—for incense, but not for any idols."

"My good man, I work only that I may live," said the Edomite, evasively.

"So long as you serve human needs," Joseph replied and conducted his guest out of his shop.

It did not take Joseph long to discover that Galilee was very different from his native Judaean hills. The land was richer and the soil itself more fruitful. And even though Ephraim in the south was rightly celebrated for the rich straw made by its long stalks of wheat, the grain of the Jezreel valley headed more fully and yielded greater quantities of meal. Bread was more abundant in Galilee than in the poor Judaea, to say nothing of the many fruits and vegetables which Judaea never saw except by import—the melons, gourds, and pumpkins, the chicory and artichokes, the succulent shoots of asparagus, and the many kinds of nuts and almonds which yielded precious oils under the grinding pestle; the wild-growing figs and pomegranates, apples, peaches, lotus fruit. The land was heavy with abundance. Every acre of soil was cultivated. Even the animals and fowls were fatter here than in Judaea. The cattle fed on juicier grasses and their milk oozed from distended udders. The farmers of the valley—and most of the local inhabitants were small landowners—were hardworking men, who rose with the sun and returned late from their tilling. It is true that the Galilean farmers were an ignorant lot and unversed in the Law; they were constantly transgressing the statutes of the rabbis—not only in regard to sowing and planting, but also in the rites of purification, whether of house, vessel, or body. But they failed not from negligence, and certainly not from disdain of the Law; on the contrary, they were guileless and simple-minded men, and deeply imbued with their faith. No other Jews made the Jerusalem pilgrimage more frequently than they—and not only the wealthier farmers for whom the pilgrimage was a small burden; the most indigent among them made the long trek on foot, not alone on the three prescribed occasions—the feasts of Passover, Pentecost, and Tabernacles—but at every opportunity that offered a pretext to their religious ardor. In certain rituals, moreover, they were, if anything, more orthodox than their Judaean brothers. Thus they celebrated the eve of Passover—or the eve of the Day of Atonement—as though it were the feast itself. Nor was any Jew more jealous of Israel's liberty. The Galilean peasant was ever the first to join an insurrection or a secret society against Herod or Rome. But this same freedom-loving nature of his rendered it difficult for him to stay clamped in the vise of separateness and seclusion enjoined by the rabbis who would not have a man pollute himself by contagion with unclean things. The Galilean cared less for purity than the Judaean, and for this laxity incurred the contempt of the Jerusalemite, who dismissed him flatly as an ignoramus.

Two other factors helped to distinguish the men of Galilee from those of the south; first, Galilee had never been wholly Israelite; many races had mingled here during centuries of miscegenation. And even though the king Jannaeus, following his annexation of Galilee a century before, had compelled the aboriginal Gentiles of his newly-conquered territory to adopt Israel's faith on pain of death, so that they would no longer constitute a threat to Jewish independence, yet Judaism had struck no deep roots in their hearts. The Jews were too esoteric in their religious endowment and too aloof in their ways of living to assimilate alien races. For appearance's sake various Edomites, Moabites, and even Canaanite immigrants from Tyre and Sidon submitted to circumcision, but for which they could not have dwelled in any Jewish province. They adopted the less onerous of Jewish ritual obligations and made a show of observing the seven cardinal laws which Judaism laid on all sons of Noah; thus they did not eat the flesh of cadavers, abstained from incest, and, to some extent, succumbed to the observance of the Sabbath as a day of rest. But in their hearts they remained strangers and pagans. They ignored the major part of the Mosaic code, chiefly the laws of cleanliness. And indeed, most of them sooner or later betrayed their professed faith, and returned to the heathen idols which they had never truly abjured. Secretly at first, and openly after Herod's usurpation of power, they reinstated the heathen worship of Astarte, goddess of fertility.

The little goddess, imaged as a naked woman with a lasciviously flaunted belly, pressing a dove to her bare breasts or clutching her paps in the manner of squeezed udders, had long bewitched the Gentile nations of the Orient and had at times presumed to compete even with the God of Israel. In Galilee not all Jews were indifferent to her spell, in particular the women who allowed her the power of sterility and fruitfulness. Certainly every Gentile home concealed, or brazenly displayed, the goddess's likeness—in large or in little, according to the worshipper's resources—a statue barbaric in design and rudely cast in bronze or baked from the fat loam of Galilee. Often her odious image stood tucked away on a small shelf which served as her altar. And on the proper occasions—before the farmer sallied out to sow his field, before the mating of heifer and bull, or when the woman of the house was in travail, incense was burned upon her altar and it was strewn with flowers, or else the fleshbud of her belly was smeared with honey and rose water. Larger occasions—as when the matron of the house offered a special prayer for man-children to her goddess—called for the slaughter of a white dove, whose body, incense-laden, was burned before the idol.

But these were the practices of the indigenous Gentiles, those who could rightly be called "strangers within the gate" and whom the Jew owed the utmost consideration to accord with the explicit ordinance of Moses: "And thou shalt love thy stranger, for ye were all strangers in the land of Egypt." The province of Galilee, however, harbored many alien Gentiles who had come from neighboring countries to enjoy its better soil. Among them were numbers of Greek immigrants from the Decapolis, the ten Hellenic cities on the far side of Jordan—from Gadara, Philadelphia, and Capitolias. These immigrants indulged their idolatry with unrestrained abandon. They, together with the Canaanite slaves whom they brought down from the bazaars of Tyre and Sidon, were a truly unassimilable element in Israel. And more alien still were the Hellenized Arabs who filtered in from Damas-

89

cus in the north and Petra in the south, the rock city on the brink of Arabia Deserta. Their excesses threatened seriously to undermine the moral resistance of the people and the integrity of Jewish family life. If one admits that the Greeks of the Decapolis at least paid lip service to certain ethical philosophies—and some of them had gone through the disciplinarian training of the Stoics—no such restraining influences could be argued for the Hellenized riffraff of Araby who had ignored the philosophic findings of the Greeks to seize merely on the surface temptations of Greek life—the worship of many gods, the frivolous, luxurious living, the cult of nudity, the sexual perversion, and erotic license. Their men and women set no bounds to lechery, reviving the abominations of Sodom and Gomorrah to pander to their lust.

Confronted with such influences, the elders of Israel made the utmost efforts to maintain among the people the high moral and ethical standards inculcated by the Jewish faith and exacted from its followers. And if they could not, or perhaps did not sufficiently attempt, to draw the foreign elements under the wings of Judaism and assimilate them to the religious culture of the Jews, they tried the harder to rescue Jewry from submersion in the Gentile sea, which they sought to accomplish by keeping Israel divided from the nations of the earth, and shackling it with the fetters of the Law. A Jew was made to watch himself with scrupulous circumspection lest he defile himself by contact with a Gentile. And he was kept like a snail at home lest he see too much of the goings-on of the world. For not only was the Gentile's body unclean, but everything that had felt the touch of his fingers was by that touch polluted. His hands that served the graven image, his flesh befouled in sexual abominations—every particle of him carried the sperm of corruption. The puritanical obsession was driven *ad absurdum* until a network of protective moats separated the Jews not only from the Gentiles but from one another. Sects and castes sprang into being, all equally zealous to keep within their borders. The Pharisee distinguished between comrade and outsider, between the common and the ascetic Pharisee. Within the Essene brotherhood an older member felt that he had forfeited some jot of purity if a younger brother so much as touched his body. Indeed, the overwrought insistence on absolute purity—which the

Jews had brought back from their captivity in Persian Babylon—did much to undermine the democratic foundations laid for all Israel by the Law of Moses and the Prophets. The nation splintered into groups that vied with one another in the excessiveness of their ablutions. There was a certain justice in the wry comment of the Sadducees about their Pharisaic rivals—"If they but could, they would have washed the sun and moon itself."

In Judaea the rabbis succeeded, to their greater or lesser satisfaction, in throwing up physical and spiritual barriers between Gentile and Jew, between the urban scholar and the uneducated countryman; in polyglot Galilee they failed almost entirely, particularly in the country, where there was no close-knit Jewish community life to enforce ritual segregation. Here the Jews lived cheek by jowl with foreign-born strangers, and a thousand reasons might render daily contact unavoidable.

And since Galilee was essentially a land of small farmers, who tended less than their Judaean brothers to concentrate in cities, the rabbinic discipline of segregation could not be very well upheld, and mingling with Gentiles was rampant throughout the province. For which reason the rabbis declared Galilee's farming population to be unclean—thus pouring away the child with the soiled water, as the saying goes.

Joseph felt that the plight of Galilee was worse, if possible, than that of his native hills. In the latter region—as in other parts of Israel—the disdain of unclean illiterates was meted out to individuals only, however great their number; here, in Galilee, he was faced with the virtual ostracism of the entire peasant class, reduced almost to the level of unbelievers. To the learned aristocrats of Jerusalem all Galilee was an object for disregard and isolation.

Now more than ever Joseph longed for the fulfillment of the Messianic hope. He waited for the master potter who would reassemble the scattered shards of Israel, the world redeemer who would level the walls that separated man from man and fill the moats that kept nation from nation.

That night, after he had met the Edomite idolator, Joseph unrolled the family scroll of Isaiah's prophecies and turned to his favorite chapter—"Comfort ye my people."

"A voice crieth in the wilderness," he read. "Prepare ye the way of the Lord. Make straight in the desert a highway for our God. Every valley shall be exalted, and every mountain and hill shall be made low; and the crooked shall be made straight, and the rough places plain. And the glory of the Lord shall be revealed, and all flesh shall see it together; for the mouth of the Lord hath spoken it."

CHAPTER X

THREE months Miriam stayed with her cousin Elisheva in the Wilderness of Judah. Then Joseph came for her and brought her safely home to Nazareth. Her pregnancy by this time was well in evidence. But, though it was noticed by all, it was rarely commented upon; Nazareth had come to accept her condition as the normal state of a woman who had been married several months. She tended her little vegetable garden, looked to the small herd of sheep, plied the spinning wheel, and wove on the family loom the fabrics needed for their dress; she ground meal in the hand mill to provide bread for the household, refined oil for the lamps, brought water from the well in the mornings and, in the evenings, prepared her husband's pallet on one of the benches in the main room.

Indeed, Miriam looked after her new household as would any other Jewish woman who had been brought up to know her duties and station. The visions and ecstasies of her maidenhood had ceased. No more was she inspired to intone unknown psalms and utter prophecies at night on her mother's roof. At the well and at the market she conducted herself with the modesty and reserve expected from a woman in her condition. And yet, though there was nothing demonstrative in her conduct, there was something inexplicably strange in her effect upon the neighbors. In speaking with her, or merely being in her presence, men and women alike felt an onrush of joy within their hearts which at once silenced their chatter and deafened them to the world out-side, in the manner of expectant mothers who will suddenly turn their senses inward to feel the child stir in the womb.

Miriam carried her child over all fields—those that bore grain for human sustenance and those that lay fallow and neglected, overgrown with thistles and thorns. She wanted her child's senses to experience, through her, every sight, sound, and taste, to touch equally the good and the malignant plants, to smell sweet as well as fetid odors. But now she noticed, curiously, that flowers, plants, or men and women no longer appeared to her as they appeared to other people—or as they had seemed to herself before her pregnancy. They now seemed of another substance as though the men and things in question had suddenly revealed themselves in their true light.

Even odors were transmuted. Thus Miriam often went to the tanner Taddi, to help him with his household, tend his ailing wife, and bring food to his hungry children. Whenever she had done this in the past she was greeted from afar by the sting of heavy pungent odors in her nostrils—the stench of soaking animal hides and newly-tanned leather. Miriam would hold her breath and pant shortly through her open mouth, unable to endure the vile smell that surrounded the unhappy family.

Now, since carrying the child, the odor was not the same. Whenever she approached the tanner's yard she was refreshed by a clear scent, sweeter than acacia, softer than aloes and myrrh. And again, whenever the tanner himself, with his matted beard and his stained body, dressed in rotting shreds of burlap, came to-ward her, Miriam's nostrils dilated pleasantly, as though the tan-ner had been soaking his skins in sweet-smelling oils. In Miriam's presence, a fragrance of rare incense seemed to surround the tanner.

The very opposite occurred whenever Miriam passed the garden of the Edomite incense planter. She had sought out the little hill on which the garden lay that the child in her womb might smell the sweetness of his herbs; but as she started to ascend the slope she was hit by the acrid stench of burning brimstone, which caused her to retrace her steps in haste.

One would have said the blessed load of Miriam's womb was

93

righting human errors. Upon approaching the coarse tanner's shack, she smelled the kindled incense of the temple—as though the Jewish tanner had turned his humble occupation into a form of sacred service for the living God; and by the same reversal of false human values, the garden of the Gentile oil and incense mixer exuded nauseous fumes of sulphur and corruption reeking up from the altars of Moloch and Astarte.

Plants, too, revealed themselves to Miriam in an unexpected light. If Miriam chose to tread a path ordinarily shunned for its thorny growth, the spurned plants would seem to stretch toward her and extend their prickly spines as if they craved for Miriam's beatifying touch. They spread themselves at her feet, clung to the hem of her dress, coiled around her knees and ankles. And Miriam never felt their heat or sting—on the contrary, she felt the touch of nettles like the caress of some fluffy down or the softness of moss. Grasses did not singe her skin; cactuses did not prick her as she walked by in her bare feet. But then there were times when Miriam shuddered at a seemingly innocent plant as if she sensed in it an exhalation of uncleanliness.

Once Miriam had occasion to pass the Edomite planter's house on the other side of the hill. Walking barefoot as usual, she had just come unscathed through a cactus grove and was entering upon a field of irises—splendid deep blue flowers past their prime and touched with purple. Miriam had been walking with a light step past the threatening spurs of giant cactuses, but now, amidst these handsome flowers she suddenly felt suffocated by dense choking fumes. She quickened her step to put the field behind her, but the more she hurried the farther it seemed to extend itself in every direction. Miriam knew the hill from childhood, knew it as intimately as the very walls of her chamber, but she could not recall ever seeing this field of irises before. The field was like an alien blanket drawn over her familiar haunts. It now stretched boundlessly away and she stopped to look about her. Nothing within her horizon was recognizable, as if she had strayed into some foreign land. The very earth beneath her seemed of a different color; gone were the calm fields of her home town, the cypress-capped hills with their flocks of grazing sheep; gone were the familiar olive groves and vineyards. Blue irises swarmed like

94

locusts over the face of the earth, teeming in violet and indigo, throttling the green of the land under a darkling carpet of oppressive blue. The sky itself lost its azure light and, reflecting the livid color of the flowering sea below, hung heavy and opaque over the frightened woman. And a pestilential stench rose from the plants as from a well of rotting fungus, befouling the air and choking Miriam's throat with putrescence. And then a powerful gust of wind broke from within the flowers, whirling and wheeling about her body in a tightening circle. Miriam tried this way and that, but the winds danced about her like demented fiends, blowing the fetid odors of decomposition into her face and barring all escape.

Miriam cast her eyes about in terror, searching for a saving miracle. And suddenly she saw before her the figure of a woman, tall and strong, with large heavy bones and prehensile arms. Her feet, too, were of inhuman size, the toes like the gnarled roots of ancient olive trees. She seemed too big to be merely a human being, as though she hailed from another, mightier race of men, the extinct giant race of the sons of Anak who once trod the shrinking soil of Canaan. Her vast face was dark, ancient, and furrowed like the earth, and her coarse hair fell about her head like stalks of yellow wheat ready for harvest. The woman took Miriam up in her mighty arms and bore her through the irises and their mephitic exhalations, her giant feet crushing the flowers in her stride.

"Who are you?" asked Miriam. "And where is your home?—for I never saw you in these parts before."

"I am the mother of many nations, for whom your womb carries the blessing of salvation. The powers of darkness massed themselves against you and came to capture you in this field where incense for idolatrous usage grows before God. Here the Lord's earth is leased to alien gods and their incense rules the atmosphere. But God in His compassion for the nations of the world has delegated me to lead you out of the idolators' domain. Come, I will show you the peoples who await the salvation."

At first Miriam saw nothing. About her was a white gas filling all the air. Slowly it thinned, then dappled into shreds of fog that wafted to and fro like cloudlets before the wind. Below, a stretch

95

of green emerged from the mist. Smoke veils ascended from it as they ascend from the land at early dawn when the earth frees itself from night's embrace. Crests of trees came into view and, at their feet, green meadows, veined with rivulets and brooks; and between clusters of trees small lakes lay dark and still. And suddenly Miriam caught the strains of a song arising from this foreign earth. It was not the chant of angels; it was a human song, a song of old and young men and of children. And there were white sheep grazing on the hills that flanked the meadows, and mothers nursed their babes-in-arms, and fathers plowed the fields. The vision changed and she saw other lands where trees sank and decayed in mire and men lived in the shade of somber forests; and lands covered with eternal snow, where winds and hurricanes blew without cease and carried heaps of snow from place to place. And even here there were men living; Miriam saw them dressed in the pelts of beasts, crawling like animals out of their caves. And she saw lands that rode the chine of giant mountains—and they too were peopled with men. And she saw peaceful green fields and silent valleys sprinkled with branch-plaited dwellings. And she saw pointing cliffs inhabited by storms that never spent their fury, and sunny verdant hills where men abode in the shade of palm trees. And waste deserts she saw, swept by hot wind and sand, and coastal lands whose people dwell in ships.

And Miriam heard voices singing. The song was charged with painful, prayerful anxiety. And a fragrance of aromatic gums and flowers arose from the melody, the noble scent climbing with the song like incense kindled for the pregnant mother. And suddenly Miriam felt herself lifted up beyond all heights and she felt the child stir in her womb.

"These are the peoples of the world," the strange woman said, "and this is the cry of their yearning for the salvation you bear in their behalf. For by the fruit of your womb shall they be united in one kindred before God."

Then Miriam felt herself put down again on solid earth, and she recognized once more her own family plot with its small peaceful house and the few sheep grazing in the faltering sunlight of the afternoon.

CHAPTER XI

I N Jerusalem they found an inn near the Pool of Siloam in the
lowest part of the city, not far from David's wall where ass-
drivers and cameleers were wont to pass the night. On the
short road that led from Jerusalem southward to Bethlehem—or
rather Ephrath, since Joseph and Miriam preferred to call the
town by its ancient patriarchal name—they made a lengthy stop
at Rachel's sepulchre. Joseph was impatient, anxious to reach Bethlehem before nightfall. But Miriam tarried at the tomb as though
her presence there could reassure Israel's grieving mother that the
time of redemption was near.

Miriam was well aware why her husband was taking her to
Bethlehem. It was not only on account of the census proclaimed
by Cyrenius, the Hegemon of Syria, who had ordered the entire
population to proceed to their places of origin to register for taxation in their home towns. The order required Joseph, as a descendant of the House of David, to go to Bethlehem.

There was a weightier reason for the journey. It had long been
said among those who awaited the Messiah that His birthplace
would be in Bethlehem, for had not the Prophet Micah spoken in
the Lord's name, saying: "But thou, Bethlehem—Ephrath—,
though thou be little among the thousands of Judah, yet out of
thee shall he come forth unto me that is to be ruler in Israel,
whose origin is from of old, from everlasting."

How close had God brought her to the fulfillment: "Out of
Bethlehem shall come a Governor to rule God's people Israel,
and his origin shall be from the first days, from the beginnings of
the world." He would not date his descent from David, nor even
from Abraham, but from the first beginnings. Whom could the
Prophet have meant but the Messiah? And what he had foretold,
she was about to fulfill: she was even now journeying to Bethlehem to bear the saviour of Israel. Should she not be rejoicing
then? But Miriam's joy was shadowed with anxiety. She waited
joyously for the holy hour of the Messiah's birth, but as the time
drew close she felt increasing pain and terror for the fate of her

child. If the words of Micah were about to be fulfilled, then surely there would be fulfillment also for those other prophecies, those fearsome oracles of Isaiah which dinned in her ears, though she would press her fists against her head to shut them out. Isaiah's words returned, in daylight hours and at night, dreaming and waking, words that told of the Messiah's sorrows, of the sins of the many which he would bear in his flesh, going at last "like a sheep to the slaughter." Truly, it were better not to recall such words!

How near was Rachel to her now! Miriam closed her eyes before the ancient sepulchre and fancied she saw Rachel, in the form in which she had appeared to her so often, rising from her tomb and taking her stand at the road whose gravel was stamped by the feet of countless Jews, trudging into exile under the lash of Nebuzaradan, the Babylonian. And then she saw Rachel alone, standing by the roadside, the pathway into night. And the dust had not yet settled on the road, for Israel was not long out of sight; the imprint of their wounded feet was still fresh on the ground; the gutter was still strewn with the remains of mangled and dismembered infants, the flayed corpses of old men, the bodies of women thrown to the bloodhounds. And bundles of treasured household goods littered the road, and shreds of sacred inscribed parchment bearing with God's word the stamp of Jewish blood, and tattered prayer shawls whose rents bore violent witness that they were not willingly abandoned. A pathway into the night, into eternal exile, was this road, the beginning of an endless journey that would take numberless generations of the sons of Jacob past Rachel's tomb, while she, the mother of them all, stretched out her hands in helpless pity for her weary children.

Then suddenly Miriam saw herself standing with Rachel by the roadside. Her hands also were uplifted after those whom the lash had newly driven past the tomb. But new processions of hapless sufferers were following after, and newly-spilled blood slaked the dust of the road. And the grief Rachel bore for Israel was hers to bear for all the world; they were two mothers weeping for Israel and for mankind.

But why were they weeping? Miriam asked herself. Was not she carrying salvation for all the painful wanderers who trod the Bethlehem road? Was she not bringing the deliverer, God's pledge to the sufferers of the earth? Was not the end of pain and evil within sight, the healing of all sickness? Even now she felt the Messiah's heartbeat in her womb and even now she was bound for Ephrath, Bethlehem, to redeem God's promise and bear the saviour who would put an end to all exile and dry all mortal tears.

"Rachel, be comforted. I am the mother of the hope, come to bear the saviour. Behold, I walk the road to Bethlehem whence Israel's ruler shall arise. Be comforted, Rachel; there is a reward for thy tears: thy exiled children shall return unto their homes."

As the Lord set a limit to the sea, so He set limits to the desert. For the desert, or wilderness, of Judah is like an ocean petrified in a moment of arrogance by a curse of God. Its rocks plunge headlong from the heights of Judah into the nether world of the Dead Sea, beyond which the hills of Moab—timeless monuments to Sodom and Gomorrah—gleam like heaped dust of gold and silver under a blazing sun. To the west the ascent of the stony wilderness is abruptly halted as by divine command to check encroachment upon the Judaean plateau.

On this plateau, which spreads in an extended strip over the crest of Judah, lies the small town of Bethlehem; it sits, like its sister towns and villages, in a green belt of fruitful undulating land that stretches from Jerusalem to Hebron, and in the west inclines toward the coastal plain of Ascalon and Gaza, the land of the Philistines by the shore of the great sea.

In summer and autumn the country here is densely bedded with vineyards. The reddish, newly-tilled soil sprouts everywhere with thick-stemmed vine, twisted like the gnarled fingers of a toil-worn hand. Weighted and weary with clusters of fat grapes, the vine strains up the sides of the hills. And over the hills, and in the valleys below, flocks of sheep, like flakes of falling snow seen from a distance, feed on the fatness of the fields. The white sheep lolling in dark-fruited vineyards bespeak the power of Jacob's dying blessing when he told Judah that his sons' teeth would be white with milk, that they should wash their garments in the blood of grapes.

Now, in the depth of winter, the vineyards lay waste and desolate. Stripped skeletons of grapevines rose above a chilled and naked soil. In hill and hollow the wintry grass grew niggardly, and small forlorn flocks, led by fur-clad shepherds, searched among thorns and thistles for some stray nettle-grass that had escaped the sickle, or for a muzzleful of clover which might have shot more recently from the damp ground, while their disconsolate bleating carried a message of sharpened famine from hill to hill.

A milky fog hung over the landscape as Joseph led the ass toward the gates of Bethlehem. It hung motionless over the town until, suddenly, it broke before the last oblique rays of the sun. The mist cleared for a little, and the travelers caught a last evening glimpse of the surrounding hills, capped with thin, freshly fallen snow.

As they drew nearer to the city walls, the traffic thickened on the road. Others, in increasing numbers, were trying to clear the gates before the fall of night. Many were moving in caravans of camels and mules, the latter loaded with packwares, the former with the portly supine forms of important travelers and wealthy merchants, at ease in their upholstered saddles. Men and women thronged down the road—the women veiled or with bared faces, wearing crescents and headtires of sparkling stones, their necks hung with golden chains, their arms with heavy bracelets. The rich moved under escorts of slaves and freedmen, and some were preceded by announcers who strutted before their masters and with long staves made gangways through the crowd, calling out in a continuous sing-song drawl: "Make way! Make way for the distinguished Reb Zavda bar Kafda who nourishes the poor in times of famine!" Or—"Make room for a scion of the House of David who comes home to the town of his fathers!"

Sometimes you saw a worthy from Jericho carried all the way to Bethlehem in a private litter after the Roman fashion. Aping the Roman patricians, he was accompanied by a group of freedmen, and while his bearers jerked their heads to and fro to shake the running sweat from their faces, the worthy, wrapped in a modish Roman toga, held gracious converse with his clients. He, too, commonly followed the lane beaten by his crier who proclaimed loudly his master's pedigree and record of good deeds. Others within the caravans carried themselves more modestly, riding by on asses and ox-carts. They were for the most part natives of Bethlehem or former inhabitants of the town who came from their new domiciles, like Joseph and Miriam, to attend the population census conducted by the administration.

At the town walls, Joseph found a large concourse of men and animals besieging the gates—asses and camels heavily laden, ox-carts piled high with merchandise, foot-travelers with bundles on their backs. Each man and animal had to pass the inspection of the toll clerks within the gate who gave priority to the caravans of the rich, from whom they levied a head-tax for each member in their suite and for each camel in their caravan, taxing even the provisions carried. It took hours, sometimes, for the officers to weigh every cruse of oil and cask of wine and every basket of dates or sack of refined flour; to assess the myrrh and spikenard and the oils, salves, and perfumes which anoint the body and lend gloss to the beard. And meanwhile the short winter day was fast sinking and there were many in the line waiting to enter the town. Joseph and Miriam slipped through the gates a brief minute before they were closed in the face of a crowd of footsore wanderers.

Bethlehem lay too far from the nearest trade routes to have become a commercial center. It had remained a small provincial town, poised on the edge of the Judaean wilderness. The town nevertheless enjoyed a measure of renown beyond its actual importance. Israel looked to it with a sentimental attachment, partly for its antiquity—since even the Patriarchs had known of Bethlehem—and partly because it was here that Samuel had anointed the young David, because within its gates had dwelled the well-beloved Ruth with her adopted mother Naomi. For those who claimed descent from the House of David, the town had a special meaning; it was the birthplace of their ancestor, the founder of the Messianic dynasty. No matter where their destinies might take them, they liked to dwell on that moment in David's life when he, as king of Israel, was laying siege to his native town then held by the Philistines, and, giving way to a thoughtless whim, exclaimed—"Oh, that one would give me drink of the water of the well of Bethlehem!" Whereupon three of the king's men broke through the ranks of the Philistines and, having drawn fresh water from the well by the gate, brought it to David—who would not drink thereof but poured it out unto the Lord, saying, "Is not this the blood of the men that went in jeopardy of their lives?"

Thus the name of Bethlehem was dear to every Jewish heart. But as a town it played a very minor role in the economy of Judaea. The bulk of the population were shepherds who reared their flocks in the green hills about the town—and brought fat ewes and lambs to the Sheep Gate at Jerusalem where the demand was high for sheep to offer in the Temple.

In addition, the town was kept moderately busy catering to travelers who passed the night here on their way to Hebron and the coastal plain. During the summer months the strangers stayed in the market place or in the colonnade of a mansion. In winter they found dearer accommodation in the town's single inn hard by the gate.

Like most houses in Bethlehem the inn consisted of a building, whose entrance faced the street, and a courtyard that merged into a field at the rear. The structure itself was in three parts; nearest the entrance was the tavern where the perspiring landlord hovered over a tripod, roasting slices of lamb's meat, while the hostler-wife served the guests with bread and viands, wine, and beer brewed from pearl barley or cheap poppy seeds. An upper story contained the sleeping quarters—the larger, airier, part for the men, the other for women. But this accommodation was for the wealthier clients only. For the rest the inn provided a stable at the far end of the yard close by the well. It consisted of walls of heaped stones, open to the sky. Here the muleteers could provide their animals with water and shade and tether them to the mangers that were nailed to the walls; and here the men and animals spent the nights sleeping side by side.

This stable, though technically a part of the inn, was in a larger sense common ground. Every inn in Israel provided such stables not only for the animals of its guests, but equally for the use of transient muleteers who wished to quarter their stock for a night. Moreover, it served all passing wayfarers and the poor generally, whose habit and appearance precluded their stay within doors. In the stables they found no protection from the rains, but these were a rare blessing in Judaea, and it was comfort enough for the poor to find shelter from nocturnal winds, and warmth in the breath of sleeping animals.

Though the night was bright, the moon in full orb and the snow melting on the ground in vivid puddles, Joseph nevertheless unfastened the oil lamp which he had dangling from the ass's panel, and lighted it to guide his way through the crooked, pitted lanes that led to the hostelry.

Turning into the street of the inn he heard from afar the confused bedlam of voices in the common room. A few more paces brought him into a medley of camels, asses, and mules, camping in the street before the gates of the inn. Evidently the stables at the rear failed to accommodate the many who had flocked into the town in compliance with the Governor's decree. Light and smoke and shouts and laughter came spilling out at the door like foam from the bung-hole of a cask.

Joseph helped his wife from the saddle and tethered the ass to a pole that stood free before the inn. Then he wrapped his own cloak around Miriam's shoulders and left her outside to watch the animal while he entered.

Pent-up fumes from the cooking tripod puffed at his face as he pushed open the door, and for a moment he felt deafened by a tumultuous roar of blustering voices and rough laughter. It took a while before his eyes could pierce the smoky blur to distinguish details.

On his right he recognized the worthy whose train had passed him on the road. Spread before him was a low stool and a cluster of good things upon it. The great man was lolling between cushions as though he had never moved from his earlier position in the divan seat of his camel. He was flanked on each side by a servant while two others darted back and forth through the crowd to bring their master steaming platters of food and to refill his cups.

Opposite him, against the left wall of the room, Joseph recognized the other baron of the road. Mistrusting perhaps the floors of the inn, he was still reclining in his modish Roman litter. He, too, looked down on a table spread with fare from his own stock; and he, too, gloried in the tireless exertions of his servants.

Clearly the two men were engaged in dogged rivalry as to which could outdo the other in ostentatious display—a rivalry which was vicariously played out by their servants. And before long, around the tripod where the innkeeper, in the thick of hot fumes, was barely visible, they fell to quarreling with one another, trying to snatch for their respective masters the side of lamb that happened to be roasting at the moment.

Between the two great men—two static poles of inertia—the room was strident with hungry diners. Cheek by jowl they sat crushed to each other, and through this human farrago the hostess, tall and plump, with painted brows and oily hair that straggled out from under a loose caul, threaded her way. The neckline of her dress, cut too low for decency, was fripped out with an edging of cheap bangles while her swelling front exuded a strong odor of myrrh. Every now and then her scarlet Sidonian tunic, donned especially for the occasion, flared through a chink in the crowd and vanished again behind the heaving mass of men. Within her blowzy arms she hugged the tankards of beer and wine which aspiring hands everywhere tried to wrench out of her grasp.

The rabbis did not hold these hostler-wives in high repute, these women who brushed constantly against male bodies. Some even suspected them of downright harlotry—as the hostess seemed to know, for she wore a diffident and pleading look before the wealthy customers who had come down from Jerusalem, Jericho, and Hebron to attend the census in the town of David. In placing a dish of eggs or a wine cup before her clients she smiled shyly in her painted eyes as if to beg their pardon not so much for her delay in coming as for her being there at all.

As if these interminable delays were not in themselves sufficient grounds for apology! Evidently the inn had not expected guests in such multitude, the fare being pitifully inadequate. The two newly-slaughtered lambs had long been eaten and still the company was dunning for more.

"Ho, mistress!" came a mocking voice from an assembly of young sparks at a corner table. "What say you to a breast of capon done the Ascalonian way—fried with calf's liver and stuck with cloves and soaked in a sauce of wine and honey?"

The theme was quickly taken up by his cronies.

"Ho, mistress! Let's see that asparagus juice I ordered an hour ago!"

A third, still taunting the obvious modesty of the establishment, called loudly for spiced wine: "I'll quaff no wine but spiced wine!" he cried.

"And you had better serve us on Sidonian platters! I'm damned if I'll eat off anything else!"

"And what would you have her serve you?" asked his friend with mock courtesy on behalf of the hostess.

"Why, let me see—olives from Bishni and wine of Cyprus in a Corinthian pitcher. And—yes—see that it comes with a Tyrian piper and a drove of dancing girls from Egypt to make me merry, for, mistress, I am damnably dejected and my heart's wore out and weary with waiting and languishing for your sorry cakes and weeping onions."

"Why not still your hunger with a filling glance from her eyes? And if you ask for the honeymilk of her smile she may yet quench your thirst."

"Oh, fie on you, adulterer! Would you have me covet my neighbor's wife?"

"God forbid! But have you not heard? The rabbis have enjoined all taverners to divorce their wives to make them accessible to the trade."

"May your foul mouth be stopped with adders and vipers for slandering the rabbis!" called out a thundering voice from the middle of the room.

"Was I slandering them?" the young man called back with a great show of indignation. "I say the rabbis are to be commended for such a salutary innovation."

The man in the middle of the room raised himself briskly above the crowd and pointed sharply at the little circle of scoffers:

"And these worldlings call themselves sons of David, and this is how they spend the night in their ancestor's town, whiling the hours away with coarse jests!"

Others joined in his protest.

"Our father David was content with roasted ears of corn, but you must needs have spiced capon and piping musicians!"

"Right! And a comely Abishag to warm my feet and more!"

"Do you hear him? Now he blasphemes against David the King!"

"Who? What did he say?"

"Over there, that milk-faced mocker!"

"He should have his belly ripped up like a fish!"

"No man shall vilify King David in this town and walk home with unbroken bones!"

"To David, King of Israel, may he live and endure!"

"Throw them out into the street!"

"The street's too good for them! Throw them to the crocodiles!"

And, with the crowd shouting David's name like a battle-cry, the gay young men were hustled out-of-doors.

Three times Joseph repeated his request to the innkeeper, while the latter, as though not he was meant, continued leaning over his tripod.

"Son of Abraham," Joseph began again, "show mercy to a daughter of Israel and lodge her in your inn, for she is in sore need."

The innkeeper was a short stocky man with a protruding paunch and an unkempt black beard. There was no knowing how long he had been standing over his tripod, for the sweat fairly gushed from his low forehead and trickled through his beard down to his fleshy chest which showed beneath his open tunic. Spear in hand, he was roasting chunks of meat over the flame, trying vainly to prevent their being snatched away before they were done. He gave Joseph no answer, but his face contracted in a grimace of impatient irritation. Once more Joseph reiterated his plea, his voice growing more insistent:

"Do you hear me? She is in dire need and must come under a roof."

"In dire need, eh?" the innkeeper said at last, without looking up from his spit. "What kind of need, young man?"

"She is near her confinement; she is due tonight."

"Near confinement, eh? And what business, pray, has she in

Bethlehem at a time like this when our greatest men are gathered
here for the census?"

"We also have come for the census."

"What, you too?" And, for the first time, the innkeeper measured Joseph with a cursory glance.

"Yes," Joseph repeated. "We are of David's seed and had
to come here for the registration according to the Hegemon's
decree."

"Of David's seed, eh?" said the innkeeper and with sudden
ferocity impaled another slab of meat on his spear. "In this town
we will not have the name of our king bandied about by the like
of you. You saw how we handled those young rascals a while
back. So get outside before we make you."

"But I do not make light of our king! We are his true descendants."

"I'll see your blooded camels and mules first and then judge
for myself of your descent."

"We travel according to our means. But, lest you worry yourself about payment, we have money enough for our lodging."

"The house is filled already with true descendants of the House
of David—honorable men from Jericho and princes from Jerusalem who travel with large retinues. For your like there is the
stable at the rear. This town is overrun with vagabonds who
would blame their origin on King David. Get your wife into the
stable—if you can squeeze her in."

"But she is near her time," Joseph urged in a last desperate
effort. "She must have a roof over her head!"

"Stand away, man! You hinder my labor! Can you not see I am
occupied?—Yes, Reb Zavda, it's coming up this moment. Hold off
there; this piece is for Reb Zavda, and so is that flagon. The cakes,
Reb Zavda, are on their way; we've sent for them.—Unhand me,
man; get yourself to the stables! The animals will keep you warm.
There's not a tramp in town but has to sleep at the inn. And at a
time like this, too."

Joseph walked out heavily and, finding Miriam still with the
ass, recounted his failure, and told her they would have to pass the
night with the mulemen and animals. Miriam looked up at him

and, seeing his dejection, smiled unconcernedly and said, quoting the Psalmist:

"He that dwells in the secret place of the most high, shall abide in the shadow of God."

And Joseph, his face brightened at once, replied with the next verse:

"And I will say of the Lord: He is my refuge and fortress; in Him will I trust."

He untethered the ass and, with Miriam at his side, left the inn for the cool open field. And as they reached the stable he heard his wife say:

"Perhaps it is God's will that my child see the light of the world among the humble and the poor."

CHAPTER XII

I T WAS a cold, crisp night, one of many such nights in Judaea. On the hilltops the thin snow of the last afternoon squall had frozen to a pearly crust of white, while in the sheltered valleys it was showing here and there as a dark stain of moisture from which the moon, a hard-rimmed circle of white fire, called up a dim reflection. The stars massed so closely in the sky, they seemed to be clanging against one another. Their blended light laid a white haze over lift and hollow, so that the ancient, gravid earth of Judah seemed to rest once again in its primal virginity, undarkened and unstained by mortal sweat, the curse of man's first disobedience.

It was a short path that led from the inn and through the courtyard to the field where the well and stable were situated. Joseph found the stable bright with moonlight, its stone walls clothed with a cool silky shimmer as though they had been draped in veils. No one was about—a strange circumstance this, since Joseph had expected to meet the horde of ass and camel drivers who had brought the notables from Jericho, Hebron, and Jerusalem. Only three large camels squatted on their bellies near the well by the stable gate, and Joseph noticed that the water in the trough that ran down from the well looked in the moonlight like a rivulet of molten silver. But it was strange that there were no cameleers about to guard such precious animals. For these camels loomed excessively large, as though accustomed to the weight of titans; and they were richly loaded and their heads adorned with crown-pieces and fronts of delicately wrought and burnished metal. The animals reared their haughty necks and turned solemnly toward Joseph and Miriam who, by this time, had come close enough to observe that the piled bales between their humps were covered with a film of dust, as though these camels had traveled a long way from foreign lands and winterless climes. And Joseph wondered whence such camels could have come and whom they had deposited before this stable.

He pushed the gate open and led his ass into the stall. Three shepherds were seated in the middle of the floor under the open night sky. They wore white shepherd's cloaks, and all were covered with dust—like the camels outside. The moonlight rendered their faces abnormally pale and made their forms stand out in sharp light-fretted silhouettes. One of them, the tallest, was hoary with age, and his long beard covered his chest. The face of the second was that of an adolescent with curly black hair and pensive features. Despite the nipping cold he wore a short shepherd's tunic which, but for the cloak, would have left his arms and legs bare. Tied to his back was a bundle of brushwood such as shepherds carry to kindle fires in the field. The third was a man of middle years, heavy-boned and deep-chested, with a skin coarsened and tanned by all weather. His hair and beard were black as pitch and hung from him in corkscrew curls like ringlets cast in iron. All three were powerfully built and, when they rose to greet the newcomers, seemed in their full height like the survivors of a race of giants.

"Blessed are they that come in the name of the Lord," they said, bowing to the young couple.

"May God cheer your hearts as you cheer ours," Joseph replied, bowing in his turn before the oldest of the three. "We found no shelter in the inn and so came here to rest for the night."

"Here as everywhere you will find God. Jacob slept in the open field and the Lord revealed Himself to him. Then let not your hearts grieve that you must pass the night in a stable among shepherds and sheep, seeing that our fathers were shepherds of yore."

"Your words bring peace to the heavy laden," said Joseph; "may God's blessing comfort you as you comfort us. My wife is in labor and may bear a child this night."

"David was called away from his flock to become king in Israel. Since you are of David's lineage, descended from a shepherd, you will not disdain to make this sheep's manger a cradle for the child. Come," he added, turning to his companions, "let us go forth and leave the mother to fulfill the promise of her womb."

"The night is cold and windy," Joseph warned.

"Shepherds are used to the cold of night. We shall betake ourselves outside and leave you with a shepherd's blessing for a shepherd child. Farewell."

Joseph and Miriam stared after them as they left the stable. Then Miriam said: "It is a good omen. Shepherds came to bless my child. The Patriarchs were shepherds, Joseph."

"See, Miriam, the things they left behind."

"What things?" asked Miriam.

"These bales of frankincense, and these oils and caskets. These are gifts for your child!"

Outside, the night was growing brighter—not with the light of day, nor yet with the starlight of the night; it was a novel brightness as though pearl-beams were being woven through the ether. The stars grew larger, multiplied, and seemed to wend toward the earth. They rained down rays of light which lent a virgin whiteness to the land they touched upon, rendering all things bright and transparent, so that one could not say whether the landscape was of solid substance or not rather a pattern of veiled, dancing chimeras. Hills, houses, valleys, and flocks of sheep revealed themselves for an instant and retired from sight. The greenness of the valleys became greener still, and from the darkness of the thickets rose a dewy mist that filled the air with an aroma of fresh pastures in full spring.

A thin white flurry of snow swept down from the heights, and the poor shepherds, who could not provide roofed cover for their flocks and who were pasturing them far from their homes, were trying bravely to keep the sheep warm in their own body heat, crowding them against each other as closely as possible. From a distance each flock seemed like a many-headed woolen fleece, strung out like a white rug over the dale. A vaporous mist went up from their damp shags and, mingling with their steaming breath, hung like a cloud over the herd.

The shivering shepherds were wrapped in sack-like coats, most of them soaked to the skin by windswept snow. Some had thatched themselves over with burlap rags, cloths of goat's hair, or crudely woven wool. And here and there they could be seen to crouch about a small brushwood fire.

For several hours past they had observed an unfamiliar radiance pouring down from the sky. It was not the unusual size and brightness of the stars, nor even their exceptional profusion on this night, that made the herdsmen raise their heads again and again as though the sky owed them an answer; it was their terrified realization that all the floating glimmer of the Milky Way was hanging over Bethlehem, that the white buoyant skyways, blown like drifting veils from the horizon, were straining to a stop over their slumbering town. Never had they seen the blended galaxy emitting a more radiant light, nor seen it strike such pearly iridescence from the snow on the hills. Never before had they seen stars so closely thronged that their flash and scintillation seemed like the sparking of metallic bodies in collision. And suddenly they saw their flocks disband, abandoning the woolen womb of warmth which their commingling bodies had posed against the cold. With flaring nostrils they sniffed fresh fatty vapor rising up from shrubs and pasture grasses and began scattering through the vales and even climbing the hills. The very landscape changed its aspect. A current of warmth swept through the atmosphere. Earth was shaking off the winter, breathing forth a waft of spring. Each bush and shrub exhaled a balm as of flowering blossoms, filling the world with a smell of youth and revival. And suddenly the shepherds saw their winter transfigured into spring. Every valley shone with the green of young grass, and on the hills fresh pastures showed through the retreating white, and the sheep grazed in the meadows and the pearly light fell upon them. A stillness settled over all creation.

Squatting on their haunches around their small fire, the shepherds remained motionless with terror and dared not speak a word. And in another moment they looked up fearfully, for they heard, above their heads, a suppressed whirr as of fanned air. The sound could not be placed; they saw only the veiled white trails of the eastern sky, stretched low like tenuous clouds and streaking toward Bethlehem.

Then suddenly the sky-veils parted and revealed a fiery flame, fluttering down toward the kneeling shepherds. And within the flame stood the form of an angel, and a voice said:

"Fear not: for, behold, I bring you good tidings of great joy which shall be to all people. For unto you is born this day in the city of David a Saviour, which is the Messiah. And this shall be a sign unto you: You shall find the babe wrapped in swaddling clothes, lying in a manger."

And when the shepherds lifted up their eyes to see who it was that spoke, they saw the angel surrounded by a multitude of the heavenly host, and they were praising the Lord:

"Glory to God in the highest, and on earth peace, good will toward men."

The song faded out, and with the song, the vision of the host. Then, when the shepherds had regained their speech, they turned to one another, saying:

"Why do we linger here? Let us hasten to Bethlehem and see with our own eyes what God has given us to know."

CHAPTER XIII

LIKE every other architectural enterprise of Herod's, his royal winter residence in Jericho was a conglomerate of massive buildings ranged about an inner garden square. The outer structures were for the most part army barracks that quartered the king's bodyguard, the notorious German auxiliary cohort and its horses. The inner buildings, surmounted by a watch tower, housed the king's retinue and administration and, in their subterranean vaults and dungeons, the more important prisoners who followed him from residence to residence. The royal palace itself lay at the heart of the pile in a splendidly set out palm and cypress garden where the king had his private swimming pool, flanked by a sweeping arcade of Ionian columns. And beyond the colonnade, approached by a wide straddling staircase, soared the high windowless keep which, within spacious walls of solid rock, contained King Herod's private chambers.

In a large, muted hall, an anteroom to the king's chambers, sat three of Herod's confidants: the Hellenized Jew, Nicolaus of Damascus, court historian, secretary, and personal adviser to the king; the treasurer Talamai; and Herod's sister, the infamous Shulamith.

The hall was a gloomy place, with no casement or embrasure opening to the outside; nothing but the severe, undecorated, cold stone walls supporting a massive cedar roof. The hall was lighted only by the oil burning in bowls of Corinthian bronze that stood upon rose-banded alabaster pillars; and even their light was dulled and dimmed by smoke that hung in stagnant clouds over the bowls. At the high doorway, whose open bronze gates hugged the walls, a few sparse beams of light filtered through hangings of costly Persian silk and design. The hangings were sprinkled with rose water and perfumes, and two Ethiopian slaves waved them rhythmically so that their cooling fragrance somewhat mitigated the heat and sultriness caused by the lamps.

The three occupants of the hall sat at a distance from each other and exchanged no words. Nicolaus of Damascus kept to himself with stoic immobility; wrapped in a Roman toga, he cast no glance on the fidgeting Shulamith, who was his closest rival for Herod's confidence. She, the red-haired Shulamith, was well aware that Nicolaus was not only the king's most intimate familiar, but that he had forever captured the king's heart by his toadeating history in which he had placed the word "Magnus"—"the Great"—after the king's name. In childish gratitude the ailing Herod had handed him the reins of power and was consulting him even now on whom to appoint heir to the throne in view of the rebellious defection of Antipater, his son. Shulamith knew only too well that the wily Nicolaus would maintain his hold equally on Archelaus, the new heir-apparent, and that it was to Nicolaus she would have to turn if she was to receive Caesar Augustus's endorsement of the inheritance willed her in Herod's final testament. With nervous gesturing she tried to catch the great man's eye and perhaps engage him in innocuous talk. But the exquisite Nicolaus was nauseously conscious of the ugly gray roots of Shulamith's raddled hair, which no dye in nature, no Antioch tincture or Alexandrian henna, could conceal. Unable to endure the rape thus perpetrated on his sensibilities, he kept his head averted and his eyes sunk in the documents he had brought for the king's attention.

The undersized Talamai, treasurer to the king and royally empowered farmer of taxes, had perched his shrinking body on a wide, ivory-inlaid chair from which his legs dangled limp and inadequate. He had puckered up his body out of a habitual craving for invisibility, and the only motion he allowed it was an obsequious fingering at his grizzled goatee. But for the sparkle of an absurdly large emerald seal on his hand he might indeed have escaped notice. Of all people he had perhaps the best reason to court obscurity, since, for all the immense fortune he had amassed during his tenure, he had never yet learned to dodge the sting of his weakling's conscience. He knew well that the very air of Judaea was charged with the accumulated bitterness of an oppressed people and that a storm of fury would descend on Herod's henchmen an hour after the king had closed his evil eyes forever. He knew, too, that he would be the choicest victim of an angry mob, he being foremost in the nation's hatred and second only to the king himself. But the wise Talamai had not delayed to make his preparations. His movable wealth, his hoard of ready money, stacked in sacks of gold denarii, in gold bars and precious stones, had recently been shipped to his business partner in Antioch, whither he himself was ready to follow any day. In Antioch he could wait until the people's wrath should settle in oblivion. And now, sitting in his stately decorated chair, he tried to estimate the span of life remaining to his sickly king. This very day, he concluded, he must determine Herod's likelihood of survival and lay his plans accordingly.

Thus was each of the three absorbed in his own thoughts until, suddenly, they heard a violent uproar within the king's innermost chambers, as though thunder had broken loose. There was a clatter of metallic objects on marble floors, a striking against walls and pillars, followed by a prolonged rumbling reverberation.

All eyes went to the heavy doors that gave to the royal suite, though no one dared to move in their direction. Two tall blond centurions of the German cohort, armored and buckled to the teeth, with naked broadswords at the ready, stood guard at the doors. And it was common knowledge that these guards were under orders to smite down any man or woman that approached without the king's behest, no matter whether it was the king's enemy or friend, or even blood relation.

"Ah, she has come again, the ghoul that plagues his spirit. So many years since she was killed and still she will not give him peace." It was Shulamith speaking, hissing with venom and anger through her clenched teeth.

Both Talamai and Nicolaus knew whom she meant. Shulamith's reference was to the king's wife, Mariamne the Hasmonean, whom Herod had turned over to the headsman with the remainder of her kin. Rumor had it that the king still doted on her like a callow schoolboy and that he was tormented by hallucinations during which the long-beheaded queen appeared again in living form. These sick imaginings had lately multiplied alarmingly.

"King Herod the Great, friend of the Caesar and of the people of Rome, does not indulge himself in the phantasms of a sickling," said Nicolaus in a severe tone, rising from his seat. "His is a healthy mind in a healthy body, and the reins of government are firm in his hand. Whoever says otherwise is guilty of high treason to the king, though he be never so near in flesh and blood."

Shulamith paled; even the hectic dye of her hair seemed, absurdly, to lose color. She became an old broken woman, cringing before a cruel master.

"Forgive me," she said. "The first of the king's servants speaks

115

true, as always. The king is well in mind and body and the reins of government are firm in his hand. Long live King Herod!"

"Long live the king!" echoed Talamai and leapt abruptly from his oversized chair to make a timely protestation of loyalty, for at that moment the doors behind the German guards flew open and a man, tall, bony, and past belief emaciated, reeled into the hall. His disease-bitten face, his entire body, looked haggard and cadaverous. His reddened, bloodshot eyes seemed like a pair of living wounds, and they strained madly into the void, dragging after them the man's unwilling body. It was the king. With one hand he was trailing a white toga which caught constantly between his legs, so that he stumbled and fell after each half-dozen steps. With the other hand outstretched, he kept grasping the air as if to choke some invisible object, while his scum-drooling mouth, spat slaver and wild ranting words:

"I know what you came for—to taunt me with Antipater's mutiny. Ha! I did well to sentence you and your depraved parents and—yes—your pretty-faced young brother. And if they came to life again, I, Herod, I myself, would throttle them with these bare hands; yes, you and your foul breed. Ha, do you think I did not see them leer, as I see you now, at the slave who set his heel on his master's house? Who was that slave, and who the master? What a wretched kingdom did I inherit from your paughty, your vainglorious sanctimonious Maccabees! What did they ever do for the state but fight like curs over little ribbons of dirtland which they did not know how to share? Their devout little ambitions—they make me laugh—to be a high priest or to monarchize over one paltry province! Where stood the boundaries of Israel during your father's reign, and where are they now, ha? I flung them farther than King David, farther than Solomon. Unto Damascus reach my frontiers, and eat into the heart of Egypt, for Augustus Caesar, my good friend, is kind to me. I made Jerusalem a world metropolis and Judaea a power to be reckoned with. The crops of my kingdom are chaffered over in every mart and bazaar of the world. I have starved the ports of Tyre and Sidon and opened gateways to the world in Caesarea, Acco, Jaffa, Gaza, Ascalon. And who was it made Jerusalem a center for the scattered Jews of the Diaspora? From every country of dispersed Jewry they

116

come to the Temple, to my Temple—Herod's Temple. But you! What did you do? You were busy intriguing, plotting sedition against me!

"Yes, I know why you hate me; because I had my gladiators give a fatal dousing to your pretty little brother—a handsome high priest he made, and drowned like a dead fish not fifty ells from here in my own swimming pool. You thought I killed him because the people cheered when he emerged safe from the Holiest on Atonement Day? You thought I could not bear to see the populace jubilant over another man? You thought me jealous of the vulgar rabble's love! Ah, Mariamne, little you know me. I spurn the people's love like the dung on my shoes! It is false and fickle, Mariamne—worse than the love of woman. No, not for the people's love did I kill him; for yours, Mariamne, for yours. . . ."

Outside was heard a blast of silver trumpets. They proclaimed that the king had issued from his private chambers, and Nicolaus feared lest some Roman officer see the king's deranged condition. As Herod's first minister he therefore mustered the courage to rouse the king from his delirium. He knew a certain means to bring Herod to his senses. Stepping before the mouthing king he intoned solemnly:

"The Lord of the Empire, Caesar of Rome, divine Augustus, sends greetings and inquires after the peace of his friend, King Herod the Great."

The words had a magic effect. Herod's movements froze of a sudden; he looked about in astonishment and recognized his secretary. Then he pulled up the end of his trailing toga and, flinging it over his shoulder, threw himself into the imperial posture, one hand laid across the chest.

"A missive from the Emperor?" he asked. "Read it, Nicolaus of Damascus." Saying which he mounted the dais nearby upon which stood a valanced throne, studded with adamant. He did not seat himself, but placed one hand upon the arm-rest of the throne while he stood listening to the Imperial text. (Roman messengers were not admitted to his presence, since Rome was to be kept in ignorance of his insanity.)

And Nicolaus read: "The Emperor expresses grief and sympathy for you over your misfortune in having faithless children. But his advice is to proceed with patience and caution and to search diligently for the truth before taking measures which cannot be undone. The Emperor is willing to ratify your death sentence against Antipater, trusting to your justice and your natural love for your own flesh and blood. But the Emperor is loth to do aught that may later cause you sorrows and regrets. Therefore, he urges once again that you search the matter out and trace every fact in the case, to ascertain beyond the shadow of doubt whether or not Antipater treasonably sought your death; which done, the Emperor will be glad to add his sanction to your verdict."

Herod reached for the script and ceremoniously pressed it to his heart, his eyes, and lips. Then he sat down, visibly exhausted. His long curls of hair that reached almost to his chest, despite their being dyed and oiled each day by his personal barber, had lost their black luster and fell about him in mat lifeless strands of gray.

"The Emperor shows his concern for me," he said tiredly, as though misdoubting his own words. "The Emperor declines to act hastily lest I come to grief over his action. The Emperor laments with me in my misfortune . . . Talamai!"

The weazened treasurer slouched forward with warped back and knees.

"Talamai, you will assign fifteen hundred slaves and as many talents of gold to the construction of a Temple which I shall dedicate to the divine Augustus. You will have it built in my palace in Sebaste and you will build it higher than my Augustus Temple in Caesarea."

"The king's will shall be done," said Talamai and shuffled awkwardly on his knees.

"And you, Nicolaus! Dispatch a letter to the Emperor. Tell him that we have ample proof in hand, that we have intercepted my son's traitorous correspondence with my brother, yes, with my own brother. Oh, shall there never be an end to my misfortune?" —and Herod broke down again and fell to sobbing in mawkish self-pity. "My very family plots after my life, first the children, and now my brother, too. Where shall I find me friends that can be trusted? Will no one stand by me? Must I for ever start at every shadow on the wall?"

In such moods the king was known to be dangerous since, as often as not, they would give way to a blind fury. There was a sensible fear in the hall and only Nicolaus kept his calm, being too well-bred in the Stoic school to forego his composure.

"Write to the Emperor Augustus," Herod continued, when he had recovered himself. "Write that I bow before his wisdom and that I am his faithful servitor unto the last breath of my life. His words, tell him, are to me as the waters of rejuvenation. But—" and here the king exploded in a sudden flurry of rage—"tell him that my own brother Pheroras joined with my son to conspire against my life. We are in possession of all their letters. And we have even tested the poison they had readied for my death. Tell him it killed my brother. Write it at once, Nicolaus, my good friend, to enlighten the Emperor; and, while we wait for his sanction, let a pound of flesh be burned out of my son's body—let it burn and heal, and burn and heal, and burn again!" And the king yelled hysterically, fanning his own rage. "And tell the physician that I shall hold his life as bail and surety for my son's. My son shall live that I may smell his scorching flesh. I say he shall live!"

"The king's will shall be done," said Nicolaus, bowing with dignity.

"And what else?" asked the king, somewhat calmed.

"There is the matter of Judah ben Sarifai and Mattathias ben Margalot, the two young zealot rabbis who incited their students to tear the Roman eagle from the Great Gate of the Temple. The king's order has been executed and they have both been brought to Jericho. The king expressed the wish to see and judge these men in person. Is it the king's pleasure to see them now?"

"It is. I am curious to see the madmen who durst raise their hands against the emblem of Rome. I am the friend of the people of Rome; Augustus himself conferred the title on me and I shall defend it against all comers. Have them brought in."

Nicolaus motioned to the German guards and within a short space two youths were dragged into the hall. Bloodied stripes covered their faces and half-naked bodies, and their beards and earlocks were caked with gore, ghastly evidence of the tortures they had undergone since their arrest. Yet they took their stance before the king with calculated arrogance, and looked him up and down as though they were his judges and he a tramp brought in for petty larceny. Such insolence was more than the sick king could bear; his sunken cheeks turned purple with rage and an attack of his gallstones made him wince with anguish so that he began reeling in his throne and would have fallen on his face but for one of the slaves behind him who caught him by the shoulders. The king settled his head against a pillow and for a while stared with pained, dolorous eyes at the young rebels. There was enough of hate and cruelty in these eyes, but more of misery, as though he were imploring his hangmen to behold his unhappy fate and show him mercy.

"It was you, then," he said at last, "it was you who incited the students to tear Rome's eagle from the gates of the Temple?"

Judah spoke: "There was no incitement, Herod. It was an order. We went forward and bade our students follow."

"By what authority, pray?"

"By the authority of the Torah, the Law of God, given to Israel by Moses, which forbids the making of graven images."

"Are you aware that you are guilty of treason to Caesar in Rome, and that the penalty is death?"

"That penalty Herod is wont to mete out on less provocation. The answer to your question is yes. Rome's lackeys will not fail to do their worst." And Judah smiled at the king with polite irony.

"Then you know what is in store for you. Yet you seem somewhat unconcerned."

Mattathias, the younger of the two, replied: "When we leave this earth, which you and your Roman masters have drenched in sin, the gates of heaven will be open to receive us. Why then should we be afraid?"

"Nicolaus," said the king, "do you hear them? They are quite sure that heaven only waits to reward them for their feat of arms against a golden eagle. Tell me, you men, has anyone come back from the other world to acquaint you with its methods of procedure?" he added, grinning wide so that his fleshless skin gathered in many folds within the sunken hollows of his cheeks.

120

"You too shall shortly discover what is in store for you," Mattathias answered.

"I?" asked the king.

"Yes, Herod, you—because there is a breath of ashes in your nostrils and the taste of dust is in your mouth. Before another month is out you shall see the portals of Gehenna gaping for you. . . ."

"Burn them alive!" shrieked the king at the shrill limit of his voice. He was shaking from head to foot and trying to get on his feet, and as the two young rabbis were led out of the hall he bellowed to the guards:

"Burn them alive!"

The fading chant of the rabbis came back in reply: "I rejoiced when they said unto me; into the house of the Lord let us go . . ."

"What makes those whipsters so merry, Nicolaus?" asked the king. "I send them to the stake and they sing and rejoice."

"It does not befit His Majesty, Herod the Great, to ponder over the notions of the enemies of Rome, or to trouble his royal heart with their babble," replied the secretary.

"Nicolaus, my counselor, my historian, you are right. You remind Herod the Great that Rome's enemies are his enemies and that it is not seemly in a friend of the Caesar to burden his mind with the delirious ravings of men about to die. . . . But why were they happy when they knew I would burn them alive? . . . Oh, of course! They were rejoicing in my death. Ashes in my mouth and nostrils, they said. And how gaily they foretold that I would bite the dust before the month was out. All Jerusalem longs for my death. What is it in me, Nicolaus, what have I done that every living soul awaits my end? Shall I have none but hired weepers at my burial? And to think that I built my gorgeous Temple for those ingrates! Did I not feed the people in the hunger years? Did I not give Cleopatra all my gold and silver in return for grain to nourish my people when the famine came? Why then do my people pray for my early death? What have I done to earn their curses, Nicolaus? What is it in me that I cannot warm any man's heart in friendship? But—I know what I shall do—" Herod ceased whining and his voice pitched to a strident scream—"in every street, nay, in every house, they shall hear the

121

wail of mourning women after my death!" He stopped and, looking about him with his sickly red eyes, relapsed feebly as he said: "But who is there that I can trust to execute my order when the time comes?"

Shulamith had kept safe in the background, but judging now that the moment was opportune, she emerged from the shadows and, throwing herself at Herod's feet, cried out:

"Three husbands I delivered to your justice when they failed you. And if you needed my own life, willingly would I place it in your hands!"

"Ah, my sister; you alone of all my family are faithful to me," and the king reached out to touch her head.

"You know, my Lord and King, that you can trust me with your orders. I will execute them!"

"Yes, Shulamith, you will, I know. Go therefore and assemble the most respected rabbis of Jerusalem, and of Hebron, and Jericho—wherever they may be. Take all who have standing as teachers and leaders of the people, and put them behind bars. And double the guards at the prison. Here is my ring. My trusted German cohort will blindly do your bidding if you but show this ring to their chief." At this point Herod tried to drop his voice before continuing, but his sickness and hysterical condition had left him with so little control over his body that he could no longer make his voice inaudible at will. "On the day of my death I want all the rabbis and all the leaders of the people beheaded. Will you promise it, sister?"

"I do promise it," said Shulamith reassuringly, in the tone one adopts with froward children.

Nicolaus said nothing and made no motion to suggest that he had overheard the king. But the crease between his eyebrows deepened and his thin lips grew white under clenched pressure.

Shulamith, encouraged by the king's demonstration of confidence, raised herself to her feet. She spread her arms theatrically and exclaimed:

"My Lord and King, terrible tidings have reached our ears. Your trusted secretary has withheld the news from you, and I myself was wavering whether or not to disturb your tranquillity by making you this revelation. But the time has come for you to know, else I would be failing in my duty as a loyal subject. You must know, so that your wisdom may direct our efforts to suppress the rumor which is now spreading among the people and which promises to become a serious threat to—"

"Speak your mind, woman," interrupted the king.

Shulamith hesitated a while longer, savoring the king's impatience—then blurted out:

"Rumor has it that the Messiah has been born."

"The Messiah!" cried the king, cowering as under the sharp impact of a blow and veering abruptly toward the door. "Who are they that say so?"

"It seems that shepherds first spread the tale in Bethlehem," Shulamith replied, with growing confidence. "I have ordered them brought into the palace that you may hear the slander from their own mouths."

"My Lord and King," said Nicolaus, stepping forward resolutely, "this matter is not worthy of your personal attention. We sent emissaries to Bethlehem as soon as ever we heard of this rumor. We know of every reputable member of the House of David who was in Bethlehem during the time of the census. Every man of them is your loyal, loving subject, who has no ambitions whatsoever for the restoration of his own House, or that of the Hasmoneans. On the night quoted by these foolish shepherds not one of these families had a child born. We are therefore safe in concluding that the whole matter is the childish fancy of illiterate herdsmen, engendered, no doubt, by the unusual brilliance of the night of which they speak."

"I will hear these shepherds, nevertheless," said the king.

A small group of shepherds was brought into the hall. They were old and young, and all were dressed in sheepskin rags, their feet wrapped in burlap for protection against the cold. They bowed awkwardly.

"Tell what you saw and what you heard during that night," said the king.

The eldest of the shepherds took a reluctant step forward and began: "My Lord King, we heard stars singing like angels and saw angels shining like stars. There were so many that we could not count them—the stars in the sky and the angels over the land

123

—and they all sang together in one voice: 'Glory to God in the Highest, and on earth peace, goodwill toward men.' "

"Goodwill toward men?" the king repeated after them, and gave a short, nervous laugh. "What does this mean? . . . Well, well, go on with your story."

"And then, my Lord King, there was one star—very big and bright it was—that went ahead of the others and stopped over Bethlehem, and then an angel appeared to us as we stood there watching and all of us trembling for fear, and he said: 'Have no fear, for behold, I bring you tidings of great joy for all the people. This night was a Saviour born, which is the Messiah of the House of David, and he shall rule—' "

"It is below the dignity of Herod the Great, the friend of the Caesar, the friend of the people of Rome, of whom his enemies live in perpetual terror, to incline his ear to the chatter of these stockish countrymen," called out Nicolaus with unusual warmth; and, with a crushing glance at Shulamith, he added: "And surely it is ill to disturb the king's spirit with the silly dreams of shepherds who went lunatic under the full moon!"

"My Lord King," threw in Shulamith hastily, fearing to lose her grip on the king, "the shepherds further maintain that they themselves saw the child."

"Yes, my Lord King," said one of the younger shepherds in the group, "we saw it just as the angel had said. For we got up and ran into Bethlehem after the big star and there we found a child lying in a manger and wrapped in swaddling clothes and the mother beside it, just as the angel had said."

"I have made full investigation," interrupted Nicolaus, growing visibly agitated. "And I declare once more that there was no child born on that night to any of the reputable families of David's House who were then in Bethlehem."

"But my Lord King," urged the young shepherd, "the man who was with the child's mother was a poor man whom no one had ever seen before. He had traveled a long way and nobody knew whence he had come. And the innkeeper would not admit him to the inn, he being known to none. And this is how the woman came to have the child in the stable."

Nicolaus threw up his hands in despair: "And such gibberish is brought before the king!"

Talamai, who had been standing well back, now risked a gleeful titter: "A tramp, a vagabond, an unknown loafer from the Lord knows where—and he should be the son of David?"

"But the Patriarchs themselves came to visit them," the young shepherd insisted. "Abraham, Isaac, and Jacob came to the stable to hail the child."

"The Patriarchs?"

"Why, yes. They were seen riding on three camels, such camels as were never seen by living men. And they were loaded heavily with bales of frankincense and oils and other costly gifts for the babe. And of the riders one was an old man with a broad white beard, and he was taller than any man living. And behind him was a youthful shepherd with bare legs, and behind the youth a dark-skinned man with a shepherd's crook in his hand. They were seen riding through Bethlehem to the inn where the child was born."

"Did you see them yourself? The Patriarchs, I mean?" asked Talamai, venturing closer.

"And what makes you say they were the Patriarchs?" Nicolaus queried, in a taunting voice.

"After we saw the child, we remembered the strange shepherds," replied the eldest of the group. "Who but the Patriarchs could they have been? Where else would you find shepherds looking like kings?"

"And you dare voice such folly before Herod!" exclaimed Nicolaus.

At this point Herod motioned to Nicolaus to have the shepherds removed. Then he said: "Nicolaus, despatch my best astrologers to Bethlehem to bring me knowledge about the signs and constellations on that night."

Then he clapped his hands three times, at which the doors opened and Hermanus, chief centurion of the German guard, who never stirred far from the king's presence, stepped before the throne.

"Hermanus," said the king—he was speaking with quiet resolution, without a trace of anger or anxiety—"Hermanus, you will take ten horsemen and ride them into Bethlehem and there kill every man-child born in the night before the census."

And the centurion, with outstretched palm, retreated.

Later, after the close of the audience with the king, Nicolaus sought out the centurion in the royal stables where his ten horsemen were being accoutered for the ride to Bethlehem.

"Hermanus," he said, "the king, may God speed his recovery, is not in the best health. This day he has issued two orders which Rome will never countenance—the killing of all Jewish rabbis on the day of his death and the slaughter of innocent children in Bethlehem. The Emperor, Hermanus, will take it favorably, as will the king's successor, if you desist from executing this command."

"I am here to take orders, not to argue them," the centurion replied, and turned scornfully away.

An hour later, the ten horsemen thundered into Bethlehem. But when they inquired after the children that were born in the days of the census, no one knew of any such. One male child only had been born the night before the census, and this child had vanished with its parents and left no trace behind.

PART TWO

CHAPTER I

MIRIAM sat before the door of her house in Nazareth, playing with the child in her lap.

It was early spring, the season of the latter rains. The earth smelled young and new, as though it had thrown off an old black garment. On every hand young shoots broke from the softened soil. They wore the same color as yesteryear's grasses and shrubs, but their green had the gloss of succulence, a cool-soft innocence like the young skin of Miriam's child, and the impulse of their growth was so bold and sure that where grassblades bent under the hoofs of romping lambs they rose again like released springs, impelled by their own momentum. The rains had cut deep channels in the earth and the wet slopes of the hills were honeycombed with rivulets that sent threads of water wriggling into gulch and gulley. And the new waters that swashed and splashed through the valleys changed the familiar face of the landscape, much as a horde of boisterous young visitors, returned from school, will change the look of an old house within a few brief moments.

The child in Miriam's arms would not stay still. His legs whipped back and forth, he rocked himself across his mother's knees, and his plump, chubby hands dabbled and paddled at her cheeks and neck. With bright astonished eyes he blinked and smiled and puffed in her face, and his little lips moved ceaselessly in a garrulous, unarticulated chatter as though he could not contain himself for amazement.

"What is it you are telling me, *tinoki?*" Miriam asked. "Will you tell me of your Father's house, and of the peace and light you left behind? Tell me all, my child, and your mother shall not weary of your tale."

And the better to convince him of her understanding she caught his tiny hands between her lips and sucked at his fingers.

In these playful moments which she spent sitting with her child before the door of her house, she would sometimes look about her and it would seem to her that the countryside was spreading itself at her feet to bring the child its happiness and voice its joy over the new-born. She fancied that every plant in the ground, every beast of the field and fowl of the air was preening itself before the infant to show its special virtue and the skill with which the Lord had fitted it. The small field on the hill before the house seemed to her unspeakably beautiful and breathed a scent of paradisal efflorescence such as no flowers in her ken exuded. At times the hillock was decked over with exotic blooms which she had never seen planted. One moment she saw all poppy blossoms, like those that teemed at this time of year in the Valley of Jezreel; but in another moment the field was dotted with unfamiliar gladiolas, whose red and blue hoods lilted merrily before the infant's eyes. To Miriam's enchanted mind it seemed that the world's flora was on parade before her child, as it had paraded before Adam at the birth of time.

And then again there were hours when birds and animals appeared to entertain the child; not only the few sheep of her own flock came up to rub their muzzles against her legs or lick the infant's feet, waiting for his restless hands to light in blessing on their shags; the doe, too, came from the forest and approached with timid steps, and Miriam would take the infant's hand in hers to pat the animal's head. At such times Joseph's little ass, who liked to stand guard over the mother and child, would, after the oratory of donkeys, bray loudly for attention. But more animals came from beyond their fields—sometimes an outlandish bird spread its wings to show the splendor of its plumage, and a canary found a roost directly overhead to perch on before bursting into melody.

But no bird or animal so delighted the child, or the mother, as the fledgling swallow whom, for his liveliness, Miriam had dubbed Poriah—vagabond.

Poriah was one of those common or garden swallows who flit all day about the doors of the stables and never tire of picking grains of corn and worms from the ground and flying them home to fill the yawning beaks of their young, while they announce their achievements with shrill proclamatory chirps. Since Poriah had no special excellence to display before the child—his plumage being a plain dun and his voice but so-so—he made up in mobility what he lacked in distinction. Without rest or respite he skipped about the mother and child, determined to hold their interest; he would vanish and reappear, flutter irrevocably away, veer sharply back to cut a caper and circle about their heads before dashing back to the stable where he picked up a mote of straw to deposit reverently at Miriam's feet.

The infant had long noticed Poriah and would follow his frisks with eager eyes.

"Look, *tinoki*," Miriam would say, "do you see what Poriah does for you? Here he has fetched you a grain of corn; he wants to rear you as he rears his own. And here he has brought as big a chip of straw as he could carry to build a nest for you. Bless him, *tinoki*."

And the child's hand would dart after the bird, which, for its part, would stop in its flight and return, skip on Miriam's lap, take off again and, like a harbinger of good news, make for the stable with an excited twitter that would start a merry hubbub among the other swallows.

Poriah was good for more than mere buffoonery. It came to pass one day, as mother and child were sitting in the sun in their usual place on the threshold of the house, that a small frog hopped out from the dense hedge of nettles and oleander shrubs that surrounded the vegetable garden. Behind it an adder crawled in close pursuit.

A few flying leaps brought the frog close to Miriam's feet, where it turned to face the approach of its pursuer. The serpent writhed forward in slow slithering coils and, coming near, raised its head like the striking knob of a cane, while its peppercorn eyes glinted coldly at the panting frog.

Slowly the adder drew up its tail for the lunge; from its jaws a needle-thin tongue shot out in lightning flickers, shot out and backed into the cleft with a merciless, teasing rhythm. Then—just before the mortal plunge—down lighted Poriah to take his stand

129

foursquare between the killer and the victim. He chirped and trilled and beat his wings and so confounded the snake that it leveled itself for a brief moment—and with one leap the little frog escaped to safety.

"Do you see, *tinoki,* how God sends help to each of His creatures? And His ministers are many; a young swallow—like this Poriah—may do His office."

The child's body wriggled lithely and his arms and legs kicked out in all directions. His hands collided in mid-air and settled in his mouth, whose prattle they could not inhibit.

"What is it, *tinoki,*" said Miriam bending over, "what is it you want to say?"

Miriam was nursing the child in the open when, on looking up, she saw a woman standing before her and looking down at the infant. She seemed familiar; Miriam had seen such a woman in her nightmare vision many months ago on the Gentile incense planter's hill. This woman too was large and bony, with an earth-blackened skin, as though her form had been hewn from the trunk of an oak.

"Who are you, and what do you want with me?" Miriam asked uncertainly, and her hands, involuntarily, tensed around her child.

"Do you not recognize me?" said the other. "I am Adamia, the wife of Yekatiel the incense planter, your neighbor."

Then Miriam recognized her. It was Adamia, certainly; she had been standing with her back to the sun so that Miriam, looking up, had seen only her silhouette, a massive, brooding shadow between her and the sun.

"What is your errand, Adamia?" Miriam said.

"I come to ask you for the loan of an earthenware dish to keep milk cool for my ailing child," Adamia answered, looking at her with a nervous glance.

"For your child you shall have the dish," Miriam replied. "But you must not use it for your idols, since for such purpose the Law will not let me lend it."

"It is for my child. For him alone will I borrow your dish." Adamia spoke with eyes obliquely averted, almost sullenly.

Miriam rose up with her child and brought back from the house an earthenware bowl. "Will you have some rubbing oil also, Adamia? My mother presses oil from nutmeg roots which makes a good salve for the sick."

"No, Miriam," said Adamia softly, "but if you will be generous, give me a twig or two of your incense . . . ."

"Why would you want our incense when you grow all kinds in your own garden?"

There was another sullen pause, then—

"Miriam, there is no comparing your incense with ours. There is a potency in yours; your kindled incense can confound an evil eye and keep malignant spirits from my ailing child."

"But this is blind superstition, Adamia. There is only one cure for all ills—faith in the lone God of Israel who is supreme in heaven. Pray to Him, Adamia, and your child shall be well. But if you want incense to make your sickroom fragrant, you shall have a sheaf of it." And Miriam returned once more into the house to fetch a bundle of wild thyme and myrrh. And while she was yet withindoors, Adamia called after her:

"The spirit of the gods shines on your son!"

"Not of the gods, Adamia," Miriam replied, emerging. "Of God!"

With the coming of the autumnal rains, the weather in the hills of Galilee changes abruptly. A winter night belies a summer dawn; the morning's sun becomes an improbable memory as clouds in rolling inky masses obliterate the sky.

The walls of Miriam's house shook with the storm; a drumming as of a million bony fingers beat against roof and walls, as though the winds were wailing for entry.

Miriam was watching her son as he lay sleeping in the wooden trough that served as his cradle. His lips were parted and his breath was even so that it barely stirred his coverlet. The faint motion of his breath, so far from breaking the apparent immobility of the sleeper, seemed but to stress the slumbering suspension of all movement. The small swaddled bundle of his body, the membrane delicacy of his skin, the somber fringes of his sleep-puffed lids—all spoke to Miriam of infinite peace. And yet Miriam felt anxious and fearful.

She was alone with the child in the long empty room of her house. Joseph and Hannah had left early, before the onset of the rain, for the Sepphoris market. They had taken the ass, loaded with yokes from Joseph's workshop and fresh vegetables from their garden.

No doubt the rains had delayed them, for night was falling and they were still abroad. Miriam lighted a lamp and, despite the wind, hung it up between the doorposts to beacon the latecomers' way. The lamp threw out a haggard half-light and Miriam watched the restless shadows, trying to focus her thoughts. The great miracle of her life—the angel in her room—wanted to be constantly recalled, for time was out to wrest the memory from her mind, to steep it in the blurred namelessness of the past. Miriam thought of the night in Bethlehem, almost a year ago, when winter, for a fleeting moment, put on the face of spring and the night was ablaze with stars and flaming seraphs. In procession through her mind passed every event since the angel had pronounced her pregnancy. It had all come to pass according to the angel's word. And here was the man-child of the prophecy, the child born unto Israel, the "rod come forth out of the stem of Jesse, who should judge with righteousness the poor." Would the other prophecies be fulfilled also in a literal enactment of every foretold agony? This child that was her flesh—was it he of whom the Prophet had spoken that he would be the sacrifice which Abraham had offered but not consummated? In Abraham was man put to the proof, in her the ordeal was to be completed. And Miriam's body cringed as she forefelt a sudden gashing of her flesh.

She did not feel the pang in any part of her own body; she felt it in the sleeping body of her child, felt it by the power of her compassion. She thought she could have better borne the sting of the spear in her own side than see the laceration of her child's flesh. And Miriam, in a despair of shame and dejection, lowered her head to the ground and let the tears run without check.

"Thou Who gavest him to me, Who didst entrust to me the salvation of the world, that I nurse him and raise him up to the fulfillment for which Thou hast appointed him—give me also the understanding to know the mysteries that Thou plantest in

132

him; give me the knowledge to behold the secret of his being. With him let me drink the cup of joy and bitterness; let me be with him in his falling and his rising, however deep his shame, however high his exaltation. Cut me not off, Father in heaven, from my own flesh and blood. . . ."

Miriam rose wearily from the ground—and caught her breath. Unheard, someone had entered the house, and through the gloom Miriam recognized the massive build of her neighbor Adamia. The earthen dish was in her hands and from it rose smoke curlicues of burning incense.

"Oh, it is you, Adamia, you frightened me. . . . What do you want?"

"I came to return your vessel," saying which Adamia placed the dish of burning incense on a table near Miriam and the child.

"Adamia, what are you doing?" Miriam cried in dismay. "We are not idolators who burn incense before human beings!" And she hastily moved the smoking dish away from the cradle.

"Miriam," said Adamia, and her dark skin flushed with the humbling of her spirit, "I know not who you are, nor your child. But today I have no god left to receive my prayers or my offered incense. My god is dead today."

"How . . . dead?"

The woman looked down and said in a voice compressed with shame: "We serve Astarte, the mother of the gods, who bestows fruitfulness on man and beast and even upon the earth. We had her effigy of molded clay in our house. We kept her well concealed from your people. To her we burned incense and prayed that she might deign to multiply the fruit of my womb. But since the coming of your child, we found no goddess in our house—only the broken shards of her image lying in a heap of incense. Now we are deprived of god; Astarte has died. I brought this censer to smoke before you and your child."

"Why before me and my child? Are we idols, then?"

"I know not what you are, Miriam, but I have heard that the Jews wait for a Messiah who will bring peace and salvation to all men. And once, when I watched you from my house as you sat in your doorway and nursed your child, I thought I saw . . ."

"What did you see?"

133

"I thought I saw the saviour of the Jews in his mother's lap. . . . You are the earth-mother, and this is why I brought you my spurned incense."

"This is heathen talk, Adamia," Miriam said gently. "You heard it from idolatrous priests and magicians. If this day you have lost faith in your idols, sweep your heart clean of every taint left therein by Astarte. And if you wait for the salvation which Israel's God will surely send to all mankind, then do as all of us; turn your heart to the Lord and bring your prayer before the only God, for He alone has ears for your supplication and means for your succor. And He is called the God of Israel." With that Miriam took up the earthen censer and replaced it in Adamia's hands, saying:

"Take it back, Adamia. His priests in Jerusalem kindle incense enough for the God of Israel. From you God requires only a contrite spirit and hands disengaged from sin."

The Edomite woman fingered awkwardly at the dish in her hands and said humbly: "I shall do as you say, seeing that God is with you. But yet, when I see you with the babe in your arms, I feel a glow of piety between my breasts and my knees itch to bend. Forgive me, Miriam; do not judge me harshly, since my legs melt from under me for fear of God."

Adamia then went to the door and emptied the censer on the wet earth. She handed the dish back to Miriam and said as she walked out of the house:

"Your vessel has cleansed me before the Lord."

Miriam thoughtfully resumed her seat at the child's cradle. The room was sultry with the fumes left by the burning incense, and mingling with its scent was a smell of old earth, a smell like that exuded by the mother of the nations in her nightmare vision many months ago.

The rain outside had stopped and Miriam heard the tread of her husband followed by Hannah and the ass.

The widow was first in the room. "Who has been here?" she asked, wrinkling her nose and forehead. "I smell the smoke of incense."

"It was Adamia, our neighbor," Miriam replied. "She came to return a dish she had borrowed."

"Then the dish is unclean! Adamia used it to kindle incense to false gods."

"The dish is clean," said Miriam.

CHAPTER II

Two years were regarded as the proper period for the suckling of a child in Israel. But Miriam found it hard—almost painful—to separate herself from the infant. She looked with fear and sorrow to the time when her son would no longer depend for his nourishment on her own body. And so she continued to delay the weaning beyond the customary limit, despite the raillery of her kinsfolk in Nazareth who asked if she would not drag her breast after her son when he was on his way to school.

Ultimately, however, the child was weaned, and Joseph's family, to honor the occasion, called a feast day in the widow's house, to which all relatives and friends were cordially invited.

First of the visitors was the elder Miriam, Mariama, wife of Cleophas. Mariama was barren; five years she had lived with her husband and had borne him no heir, a circumstance which had done much to aggravate Cleophas's naturally sour disposition. He did not fail to show his bitterness at every opportunity, yet, at the same time, his sense of deprivation gave him a closer bond to Hanan's household which had been so nobly blessed. His thwarted paternity found an outlet in the care he could take of the family which had accepted him as son-in-law. And since he was the elder of the sons-in-law, he chose to look upon himself as the official guardian of the entire family, without whose consent no step should be taken. Deep in his heart he may also have nursed a resentment against the child whose weaning was now being celebrated; for he could not forget that the circumstances of its birth had brought shame to the family.

Nevertheless, the occasion was a joyful one in Hanan's house, for Hanan had died without male progeny and Miriam's weanling was the first man-child born to his household. Cleophas might feel a sting of envy that this first-born was not his, but he sought compensation in the fact of his seniority and accordingly comported himself throughout the festivity as though he were the man to whom all compliments were owing.

His wife, Mariama, felt no resentment; wholeheartedly she rejoiced in the good fortune of her younger sister, for whom, since, early childhood, she had borne a firm devotion. Grown to womanhood, Mariama continued to look up to her sister. It seemed natural to her that, if God had blessing enough only for one of them, it should fall to Miriam's portion. And thus, without jealousy or regrets, she loved Miriam and loved Miriam's child and, for some reason which she herself could not have explained, called him after his mother's name—thus, Miriam's child, or Miriam's son, and never Joseph's, which would have been the normal appellation.

Miriam's son she could not have loved better had he been her own. Not a day passed but she found in him new virtues and signs of precocious wisdom, before they were manifest even to Miriam's watchful eye. She played with him and every day invented new diminutives to call him by, many of which were later taken up by the whole family. She predicted firmly that he would grow up to be no less than a rabbi in Israel; one could tell, she would say, by his high brow and the bright light of God's grace which shone from his eyes. And on this night, while Miriam sat on a decorated couch that had been especially set up for the feast—it was covered with snow-white linen and heaped with olive branches and blossoming twigs—while Miriam, sitting on the couch, held her first-born in her arms for all to see, Mariama sat at Miriam's feet, and her face beamed for joy over the child.

"Yeshua," said she, "you will grow up to be a great man and help your people Israel, will you not, Yeshua?"

Her husband, the thick-set Cleophas, could not restrain his vexation, for his wife was, he felt, too happy with her nephew to grieve as she should have grieved over her own barrenness. And he said:

"Is that all you have in store for him? Why not call him the Messiah and have done?"

"And why not, indeed?" said Mariama, turning impulsively. "May not any Jewish mother of David's house bear the Messiah? And is there not a light of salvation in Yeshua's eyes? Look at him, Cleophas!"

Old Reb Elimelech interjected: "It is our custom in Israel to praise the child before the parents to make the mother beloved of the husband."

"But I have nothing against praising the child," Cleophas remonstrated. "I only object to my wife's rattling tongue."

"He only objects to his ass pulling another man's plow," chuckled a guest in his neighbor's ear.

Mariama remained unperturbed. Bent on displaying the child's wisdom to the company, she said coaxingly:

"Now, Yeshua, let us hear you say the *Sh'ma* that mother taught you."

The child looked up and searched his mother's face.

"Do as your aunt says, *tinoki*," Miriam said, nodding her head.

Whereupon the child slid down from his mother's lap and, standing up in his new white linen tunic, recited in a clear voice:

"Hear, O Israel, the Lord our God, the Lord is One."

The women in the room were dumbfounded.

"Did you hear that? He said it just like a grown-up!"

"And how do little children ask the heavenly Father for rain?" Mariama continued, swelling with pride.

"Father, Father, send us rain; do it for little children's sake."

This caused even more of a stir among the women and they began to vie in vociferous praise.

"Is it true what they say, Miriam, that you taught your child to pronounce a blessing over the milk of your breast?"

"It is true," Miriam replied. "Since he was a year old he has been making the blessing."

At this point the menfolk who sat around the single table in the room began to evince interest in the child. Forsaking the dates, eggs, olives, and wine which Joseph was serving them, they approached Miriam's couch to inspect the prodigy more closely. Old Elimelech curved his height over the child and said:

"Tell me your verse, child."

137

Yeshua placed a finger in his mouth but, looking fixedly at the old man, said nothing.

"Has he learned a Bible verse yet?" Elimelech asked of the mother.

For answer Miriam turned to her son: *"Tinoki,* speak your verse for grandfather."

"The Lord," said Yeshua, "is nigh unto them that are of a broken heart, and saveth such as be of a contrite spirit."

The old man kept silent, thinking of the Psalmist's verse which the child had spoken with the inflection of full comprehension. The furrows of his ancient face deepened, then relaxed as he broke into a smile.

"Well, children are full of surprises," he said, trying to shake the concern from him. "The way of the world is to begin the teaching of children with the first verse of Leviticus. Who taught you your verse, child?"

"Emi,"—and Yeshua's hand groped for his mother's knee and held it tight.

"Your mother, was it? It is a strange verse in the mouth of a child. May God grant that he grow up a faithful son of Abraham, and may there be many like him in Israel." With these words the old man lifted Miriam's son to his face and kissed his head.

"Out of the mouth of babes and sucklings hast Thou ordained strength," quoted the tanner Taddi, who had come with his children to the feast. He was wearing his clean Sabbath dress; his hair was cleansed of dust and grime, his beard combed free of its habitual agglutination, rendering him almost unrecognizable. He, too, raised the boy in his arms to press a kiss on the crown of his head. Then, turning back to the men, he launched into a learned dissertation on the child's verse, as was his wont.

"Why?" he asked rhetorically, "do we begin by teaching children the first verse of Leviticus that deals with sacrifices? Why this third Book of Moses rather than the first? My friends, the rabbis tell us why; it is because children are without taint, even as sacrifices must be without blemish. Therefore, they say, let the pure abide with the pure. But it is not only the aspect of a child which is pure and pleasant in the sight of God. The very voices of children are as a breath of holiness. When the Lord of the world hears their voices raised in the study of the Law, the sounds that ascend from the schoolroom are to Him sweeter than the fumes of frankincense; the quality of mercy is awakened in Him for the creatures of His hands; no accuser can then come before Him to impeach His chosen people; and every evil decree, though it be already sealed, is made null and void. For with the voices of children even the angels cannot compare their chant. And this is why the minstrel of Israel has said—'Out of the mouth of babes and sucklings hast Thou ordained strength.' And with this strength of children's voices shall the Messiah triumph over Satan. For the Psalmist has sung: 'Touch not my Anointed,' which is to say, the little children in the halls of study."

Following the tanner's discourse, which pleased the men by its eloquence and delighted the mothers by the dignity it conferred on the fruit of their womb, sweetmeats were distributed among the children present. The tanner had arrived early, with his children, and it was they whom the women were now regaling with nuts and honey-wafers baked by the widow Hannah.

Joseph had considered inviting the children of his neighbor, the incense-planter. But from this he refrained to avoid giving offense to Reb Elimelech, who would certainly not have crossed his threshold had the Gentile's children been within the house. It is true, then, that he did not invite them; but he did take a large wicker basket and filled it with fresh figs, cucumbers, pumpkins, peaches, and almonds, all lapped in olive leaves, and deposited it outside his door, thus honoring the old Jewish custom which required that visitors' gifts brought to a feast be placed outdoors with the tacit invitation to all passers-by to approach and eat their fill. Joseph knew that the hungry children of the Edomite would make abundant use of the occasion.

But Joseph asserted his disregard of convention by inviting, with his wife and children, the notorious outcast, nicknamed Nafchi, "the blacksmith," a powerful man with a fierce, black-bearded face, an eye afflicted with trachoma and a hare-lip that gave a whistling sound to his words whenever he spoke in a passion. His pariah status in Nazareth was self-chosen, chosen with conviction in deliberate defiance of the scholars and municipal authorities. It was assuredly not the price of ignorance, for Nafchi had a respectable share of learning. It was said of him that he had spent his youth at the feet of the rabbis, but had subsequently fallen into lawlessness. True or not, the fact was that Nafchi had been driven almost to distraction by hard toil. He had once owned a few acres where he grew vegetables and flax to sell to the merchants, and several olive trees had stood on his land; but their fruits he could never enjoy since he brought them to market, where he also sold the fleece of his sheep while he himself covered his nakedness with frayed tatters of burlap. Nafchi moiled all week like a beast of burden, yet when the Sabbath called he had not the wherewithal to welcome it. His family looked like a pack of paupers. All day they toiled and at night could not sleep for hunger. During the week their fare consisted of a mess of barley gulped down with leek or onion. On Sabbath they fed on the garbage and the little fishes which Nazarene fishmongers, returned from K'far Nahum and Bethsaida, let drop on the market square to rot and stink in the sun. Even Nafchi's starveling family could eat such offal only when fried and kneaded in dough.

In the end Nafchi lost his land. He was forced, like many others, to abdicate his father's inheritance to the usurer Talami bar Kazin, who was threatening to sell him into slavery for debts outstanding. Indeed, Talami would not have scrupled to carry out his threat, had Jewish slaves been better bargains on the slave markets. As things stood, Israelite bondsmen were not much sought after; the Law accorded them certain privileges over Canaanite slaves—and who was there that would buy himself a "master," as Jewish thralls were called with bitter irony by the rich. It paid Talami better to leave his debtors where they were and have them work the fields as laborers, for which he paid them with a part of the crop, retaining the rest.

At that time, when Talami the moneylender claimed his field, the desperate Nafchi joined one of the robber bands that infested the hills—as many embittered farmers, plundered of their holdings, had done before him. It was the robbers who conferred on him his name Nafchi, the blacksmith, because he had a nimble hand in forging the scythes and sickles of newly-enlisted farmers into swords and daggers which one could conveniently hide in

140

one's cloak while standing in a crowd and sink unnoticed into a victim's back. The name Nafchi stuck to him even now, long after his withdrawal from the robbers, when he had long been a day-laborer in Talami's employ, working as before on his own soil.

His family lived but a short way from Joseph's house, for the powerful Talami had not managed to dispossess the mother and her children after the father's flight to join the outlaws in the hills. Nafchi's wife was a large woman, bony with strength. With her two young children she had literally dug herself into her husband's land and, like an olive tree that could not be uprooted, refused to be moved. For several years she lived in a ditch at the back of her field, dressed in a few shreds of sacking which rotted slowly on her body. But in regard to food they were now better off than formerly. For they could now claim the pauper's right to a sixth part of every harvest; the gleanings and the corners of each field belonged to them by virtue of the Law, though they had done neither the plowing nor the sowing. They further had the enjoyment of derelict property, that is to say, they were within the Law if they made off with a sheaf of wheat dropped acciden-tally by the reaper on his way to his silo or barn. For the Law accorded to the poor man the "forgotten" portion of every crop.

It cannot be gainsaid, however, that the family lived little better than wild beasts. Nafchi himself occasionally paid a clandestine visit, as after a successful raid upon a merchant caravan, on which occasions he would bring the family his share of the loot. It was during one of these visits that he and Joseph met for the first time. Joseph upbraided him for the neglect of his family, and, pointing to their miserable state and how the children were growing up like animals, prevailed on him to return home, albeit as a serf to Talami. Remembering the words with which Joseph had clinched his argument—"For every thief there is a gallows"—he submitted to the harsh conditions set by the moneylender's agents. Once more, he and his wife farmed the familiar soil, this time as hired hands. And Nafchi eked out his wretched income by helping Joseph fasten wooden beams and handles to iron plowshares which he himself forged out of scrap metal on an improvised anvil.

But, as the proverb goes, the wolf hankers for the forest. Before long Nafchi was itching to rejoin his brigands. This time he was drawn by the halo of patriotic valor which invested the outlaw organizations in the hills.

At long last the tyrant Herod had sighed his last gasp in his Jericho palace. Jerusalem was flaming with revolt against his successor Archelaus, appointed by his father to be king of Judaea. The mutiny was suppressed at the cost of three thousand lives, at the cost, too, of Archelaus's last vestige of influence with the Jews, who hated him thenceforth with such intensity that only the sword of Rome could preserve him in power. Augustus himself had dispatched a Roman legion under the ruthless Sabinus to keep order in Judaea. But the patriots succeeded in driving him into the royal palace in Jerusalem, whither he had transferred his headquarters to be near the hub of the revolt, and there laid siege to him.

Word of the insurrection quickly reached freedom-loving Galilee, where it found a resounding echo. One man, relentless, unforgiving, lusting for vengeance and steeped from childhood in the bitter waters of revolt, rose up to lead his country in rebellion. Son of the fabled Hezekiah who had been executed for leading an abortive uprising some years before, the young Judas raised again the flag dropped by his father. With his slogan—"Government by God alone"—he rallied the patriots who were in hiding in the hills and lined every Galilean highway. His agitators were even now in Nazareth, drumming up recruits for his armies. Judas the Galilean, therefore, was a likely subject for the men gathered at the weaning feast in Joseph's house.

"Not by might, nor by power, but by My spirit, saith the Lord of Hosts," Joseph was saying. "We shall accomplish nothing with the sword, for they are stronger than we."

"But where is the Lord's spirit? Answer me that!" cried Nafchi, sawing the air furiously with his hands. His open eye glowered at the company while a drop of wax-like fluid oozed from the inflamed lids of the other. And as he spoke his hare-lip discharged a jet of saliva and his fingers raked rudely at his beard: "Are we worse than the sin-besotted generations whom the Prophets castigated? Why will no Prophet of the Lord arise in our time?"

"The prophets of our time are our scholars," said Reb Elimelech in his soothing, meditative voice. "We walk in their paths, being guided by their wisdom. They are the eyes of our souls, and the speech of their mouths is our law, for their light is our beacon in the pathways of the Torah." The old man's eyes shone with pleasure as he recounted the virtues and the grandeur of Israel's sages.

But Nafchi broke into his speech with a tart laugh: "There's little we can hope for from our sages. All they know is how to turn the Law of Moses into so many bonds and thongs to tie the hands of the poor and the illiterate. Show them some starving beggar and they will load him high with rules and regulations until the wretch breaks down and doesn't know which way to turn. And then they bear down on him with their holy indignation, anathematize him, and throw him to the wolves. Oh, no, they're not the flour that will make God's bread! A new Prophet is wanted in Israel, a Prophet who can sweep evil from the earth like a whirlwind, crush the heads of the proud and the mighty, and strengthen the backs of the poor. An Isaiah is what we need, a man to reassure us that God wants no sacrifices other than a pure heart and a pair of guiltless hands; someone to remind us not to rob the widow and afflict the fatherless child. That is what the Lord requires—not that we wash our vessels three times a day. I say we need a Prophet and a comforter to rid us of this law the rabbis have turned into a yoke. And let him declare with the authority of God that all Israel is holy, that all of us together make up the chosen people."

"That was a good speech, Nafchi," said the tanner. "But if this is your craving, how will you accomplish it by armed rebellion against the government?"

Nafchi continued, his breath whistling through the cleft in his lip: "First things first," he said. "To begin with we must purge our land of this insolent tyranny. With it we shall be rid of the abominations which now thrive under Edom's sword—I mean the bloodsuckers of Herod's House and their toadies; then we shall deal with those priestlings who turn the Temple into a lion's mouth, as if the God of Israel could not survive without the blood of sacrifices; and then the Mammon worshippers and those who lighten the burden of the rich to the cost of the poor; and those who connive with usurers to rob poor wretches of their family plots. This time land will be confiscated from the rich. We will proclaim a jubilee year and the land will belong to none but God. 'For Mine is the earth and the plenty thereof,' says the Scripture, and he who tills God's earth is in God's service, not in Talami's. And the government, too, will belong to God and not to the sages and rabbis."

"But what power will accomplish these things for you?" the tanner asked again.

Nafchi whipped out a small poniard: "The power of this," he replied.

The men said nothing for a while, but Joseph, standing aside, shook his head and said at last: "I repeat, not by might, nor by power, but by the spirit of God. Where God has not designed the house, the masons labor in vain."

Nafchi spun round to face him: "And why should not God design the house? How do you know we are not building with His spirit? For whom is this revolt? Is it for our own families only? Are we not championing God's cause? Or do you think the Lord wants to see Edom's heel upon the Holy Land?"

"It is not the death of sinners that God wants, but the end of sin," Joseph replied. "You rebels are not eradicating sin; you merely kill a handful of evil-doers, and so long as evil itself survives on earth there will always be new sinners taking the place of the old."

"Then what would you have us do?"

"Prepare for the day when the whole earth shall be covered with justice, the day spoken of by the Prophet, when all the nations shall come to Zion—in other words, when mankind recognizes the only living God. Till the coming of that day Israel will have no peace. Israel cannot live alone in an island of righteousness while mankind wallows in the mire of sin and pollution. We shall never escape defilement in our little isle of perfection. If it were not Edom it would be some other power equally heathenish. There can be no salvation for Israel alone; salvation is for all or for none."

"You speak of the Son of David, who will come to save the

world according to the word of the Prophets?" asked Reb Elimelech.

"Yes," Joseph replied. "I see no hope for Israel without the King-Messiah."

"Then I agree with you," said Elimelech softly.

"And it is my view also," said the tanner, nodding his head emphatically, and would have launched into another learned disquisition had not Nafchi stopped him with an angry rap on the table.

"And where is he, the Son of David! What is he waiting for? Generation after generation lies smothered in blood—all of them men who waited for his coming and perished miserably having waited in vain. And our own generation, ground small between the millstones of Herod and Rome—we have lost stomach for this waiting game; why does he tarry so long? Why does he delay while men die with his name on their lips?"

"That is not for us to answer," Joseph said soothingly. "We know only what our sages tell us—'Even though he tarry, come he will.' And we are told that he will come of a sudden. Who knows but that he may be even now at our door; perhaps he has already found our generation. Perhaps he sits among us now and this day, or tomorrow, we shall hear Elijah's footfall in the hills and hear the voice calling, 'Prepare ye the way of the Lord.' Tomorrow we may rise to the voice of the Messiah's bugle. But we must wait for it—every day, every hour, with every breath of our life."

The company kept silent; the tanner offered no further discourse; old Reb Elimelech shut his eyes, musing over Joseph's words. Nafchi's stocky body closed about itself; his elbows rested on his knees; his head, showing a bald pate, lay heavy in his hands as though it were seeking the ground.

Miriam, seated in the women's corner, picked up her child from the floor where he was playing with the other children. She placed him on her knees and searched his face with a look of anxiety. The child's hand went for her cheek and its tender touch cooled his mother's skin. It made Miriam's face radiant with young beauty. A smile parted her lips and her eyes dimmed with tears of happiness. She pressed the child to her breast and murmured

145

in his ear, so softly that none caught her words: "It is you for whom they wait, *tinoki.*"

CHAPTER III

SINCE Yeshua had been weaned, a separation, as it were, had fallen between Miriam and the child. Yeshua grew of himself and Miriam suddenly felt banished from the spirituality of her nursing period and sent back to the commonplaces of everyday life. The soul in which she had been united with her child had flown. The child had become a creature separate; the bond of flesh was irretrievably broken, leaving only the intangible fact of her motherhood. But this sufficed to establish for her a new communion with her son, a communion born of daily contact and shared experiences. And the child began to repay her with the milk of the spirit, and Miriam began to see the world in a new illumination—in the light of her child.

One would have thought that the child was drawing wisdom from hidden springs. He looked upon all things with eyes of his own, as though his first vision was always that of nature's secret, not of its manifested form.

He was standing one day near his mother in the vegetable garden as she weeded a row of peas. The child detached a pod from the vine and, upon opening it, exclaimed delightedly:

"Look, *emi,* look!"

"What have you found, *tinoki?*" Miriam asked, turning to see Yeshua's black eyes wide with excitement.

"Look, *emi,* each pea has its own cradle to sleep in! Who made this?"

"Why, God did; our Father in heaven who made them all."

"God must have many hands, *emi,* to put each pea in its own bed when no one is about."

"Yes, my son, God has many hands, and they are called His angels."

146

In another while the child came running up with a plucked poppy in his hand.

"*Emi,* see how many coats this flower wears. Who wove them, *emi?*"

"God has His angels weave them, child."

"God must have many angels to dress so many flowers in so many coats. As one falls off, another takes its place. God keeps changing their coats. Here's a plain workaday coat and here's a coat of many colors for the Sabbath, like the one Jacob made for Joseph."

"Who told you of Joseph's coat of many colors?" Miriam asked in wonder.

"You told me, *emi*. Don't you remember, when you put my Sabbath tunic on me?"

Miriam could not recall speaking to her son of Jacob and Joseph. Nevertheless, she nodded in affirmation and, taking the boy in her arms, pressed him close and sighed faintly.

"My darling child, *tinoki.*"

Miriam had many fond names for her son. Before strangers she would call him by the Hebrew *"yeled,"* or the Aramaic *"riba,"* both meaning child. Alone with him she addressed him with the more intimate *"tinoki"*—little child—or *"chavivi"*—my beloved. Yeshua called her by the Hebrew word for mother—*"emi"*—, which he often pronounced *"ema"* in the Aramaic idiom, to go with *"abba"*—father—, the name by which he called Joseph.

Not a day passed but the child discovered some new fact about plants or birds which roused his wonder and enthusiasm. Observing how the mother swallow fed her nestlings under the palm roof of the stable, he insisted upon showing Miriam his find. An incessant whir of bird wings and voices filled the stable from early dawn to night. The mother swallow would dart into the stable and, threading a sure way past several dozen foreign nests, pick out her own unerringly, where she unloaded a worm or insect on her callow young—to take off again at once on a new expedition. The performance made the child clap his hands gaily.

"Who taught her this, *emi?*" he asked.

"Taught her what, my child?"

"How to feed her little ones?"

Miriam pointed to the cloudless sky. "Our Father in heaven," she replied.

"Our Father in heaven nourishes all," said Yeshua softly, as though speaking to himself.

"Where did you hear this verse, *tinoki?*" Miriam asked.

"Nowhere; I don't know; but is it not so, *emi?*"

"Yes, *tinoki,* it is so. Our Father in heaven nourishes all. He remembers the littlest worm in the crack of a stone, be it never so well hidden, and sends it nourishment in time."

"I want to see it," said the child.

"See what, *tinoki?*"

"How our Father in heaven sends food to the little worm in the crack of a stone."

"Come and see," said Miriam.

She took Yeshua by the hand and they began to search the ground of the vegetable garden for small worms. Before long they noticed a muster of ants crawling out from under a stone and making straight for the stalks of the morning glories whose blue eyes adorned the fence which served as the sheepfold. Bees swarmed about the flowers, drinking of their sweetness and sending an assiduous buzz into the air. The ants climbed in procession up the stalks of the flower, vanished in the thick of the vine, and reappeared in flawless formation on one plank of the fence, loaded with fibers of leaves and grains of pollen and sand, finally stringing their way back to their native stone.

"Do you see, *tinoki,* how our Father in heaven provides for His littlest creatures though they hide under a pebble?"

The child stared long without speaking, then said pensively: "How manifold are Thy works, Father in heaven."

It made Miriam's heart stand still to hear the child utter this verse. Almost three years ago, standing in this same garden, she had quoted the identical words—and then the angel had come to tell her of this child.

"Who taught you this verse?" she asked haltingly.

"No one. I thought of it just now. Is it not true, *emi?*"

"Yes, *tinoki,* God's works are wondrous and manifold, as you say."

Yeshua did not notice his mother's alarm. He continued clap-

148

ping his hands, and his face shone with pleasure as he repeated to himself the correct wording of the Psalm:

"How manifold are Thy works, O Lord."

Already little Yeshua had friends among the sheep of the household. There was one in particular, a tiny white lamb born this last winter, who dogged his every step. Yeshua called it "Moon" for its silvery white color, and more than returned its affection. He fed and watered it and insisted on having it always near, so that the animal had to be taken in at night to sleep on a bundle of straw beside the child's cradle. Wherever Yeshua appeared the lamb was sure to follow at his heels. By itself, this fact would not have been remarkable, since many youngsters of his age had their pet lambs or kids. Yeshua's pet, however, stood out from the rest by virtue of its unblemished snow-white fleece. Every known ram or ewe in the region was to some extent speckled and spotted, and if it had been born white, after a few months of exposure to windswept sand and dirt, its wool took on the sallow shade of dust, which darkened with the growth of the fleece until the shearing season. Moon alone, though as richly shagged as any lambkin in the neighborhood, remained a pure white, looking always newly-scrubbed, as though the coat were not a hairy fleece, but feathers washed in the brightness of the sky. When little Yeshua was abroad with Moon at his side, no one could pass without first stopping to stare.

For like the lamb the child, too, was never seen but in clothes of the purest white which Miriam was constantly washing. Her many household duties notwithstanding, she found time to weave his garments of the lightest gossamer which her spindle could twist; and she sowed the finest flax in her garden to keep her spinning wheel supplied. The child's dress was a little shirt that reached past his knees, woven from a finer thread than was usually seen in these parts, and people told each other in confidence that the mother was lavishing the family fortune on a toddler's shifts. They spoke of Miriam's prodigality as though it were one of the seven wonders, and some would have it that those snow-white fabrics, like the sacred vestments of the High Priest, were made of pure byssus, that the entire garment, rolled into a ball, would be lodged at large in a nutshell.

149

Over his shirt Yeshua wore a sleeveless tunic of cotton or wool, in accord with the season. It half covered his body, and four tassels of hyacinth blue, the ritual fringes, dangled from its corners. For Sabbath and feast days Yeshua had tunics of silk or Judaean muslin patterned with colored stripes—his "coats of many colors."

In the summer the boy went barefoot, like his mother, and his soles soon grew accustomed to walking on sun-scalded sand and stones.

His hair had not been cut since birth. Lustrous black locks danced about his head and Miriam was careful not to clip them until he should be going to school at five or six years of age. Then, in conformity with ancient custom, the parents would declare a feast day—the so-called "shearing of the son." Meanwhile, Yeshua's curls enjoyed a buoyant freedom, being always the first to respond to his impulses and multiplying the childish rapture of his joys.

The child's forehead and eyes were remarkably like his mother's; the brow was high and fully domed, and his large black eyes had a shimmer like the glaze of tears. Earlocks hung over the concave hollows of his temples where the skin was of such fragility that it made the heart ache to look upon it. His coloring was like his mother's—dark, and made one think that the eyebrows and the long jet lashes had somehow cast their shade over the whole face.

Often, in the early mornings, Miriam took her little boy to the well. The other women, when they saw Yeshua approach in his white dress, followed by Moon, would say to one another:

"Here comes the well-beloved!"

For they never had enough of his laughter and boyish enthusiasm. Expectant mothers hugged and kissed him and muttered to themselves, "God grant that the fruit of my womb be a man-child like unto this child." And even the other women would surround the boy and praise him to his mother:

"Assuredly, the Lord's grace is upon him."

It was not long before the child began to discover both the sweetness and the bitterness of life. Awake to everything that passed within his orbit, he reacted to every impression with an intense, almost morbid, sensibility. He saw with childish distress that the life of the women around him was one of unremitting toil, his own mother being no exception. From early morning until late at night he saw her engrossed in household duties. The ancient widow Hannah had grown too feeble to do her share of the work, leaving a double load upon Miriam's shoulders. To begin with, there was the problem of supplying the house with water. The water was of two kinds—the "live" and the "dead," that is, the water which Miriam drew fresh from the well and bore home in two massive pitchers, and the rain water which lay stagnant in the cistern and which was used for personal ablutions and watering the stock.

But the cistern water would speedily cloud over with dust and reek with a scum of insects and worms. Thenceforth the animals would refuse to drink from it and the water could be used only for irrigation purposes. Then Miriam's well water had to suffice not only for the family's drinking and cooking but for the sheep as well. Joseph would help her fasten two large leather bottles to the saddle of the ass. Miriam herself carried the pitcher with which she drew the water. The well was but a short distance from their house, yet it took Miriam a good hour to return, since in the early morning hours it was crowded with long lines of waiting women. Some of them, to save themselves time, came with their sheep to water them on the spot in the trough nearby. This, however, created an often impassable crush of women and animals which in turn meant greater delays for everyone. Miriam preferred to make the greater exertion at the well and bring the water home.

While Miriam was away at the well, Joseph prepared the boy for his matin prayers, for it was a father's sacred obligation to accustom his sons from earliest childhood to their duties before God, to study Scripture with them and teach them the recitation of the "Hear, O Israel." Joseph helped Yeshua to dress and purify his body for the sacred hour before saying the prayer in unison with him.

Later, when little Yeshua had grown somewhat older, Joseph would include verses from the Prophets or the Psalms in these morning sessions; or he would run through the Ten Commandments, inscribed separately on one of the parchment scrolls which were widely disseminated among Jews for the education of children. It was the reader of the synagogue who made these scrolls available to parents, and sometimes pious men engaged a scribe to write the Decalogue on pieces of parchment for free distribution among the children of the poor.

Joseph spread the scroll on Yeshua's knees and made the boy repeat his lesson until he could say it by rote.

Then he sallied out with Yeshua at his side to fill the sheep's manger with fodder in readiness for Miriam's return. He wished the child to learn that man must feed his animals before sitting down to his own morning meal. When Miriam came home, Joseph helped her unload the replenished skins of water, filled the trough from which the animals drank, and poured the remainder into the large earthen pitcher that stood in the doorway of the house for the family's use.

After the washing of their hands Joseph and Yeshua sat down to their first meal of the day. Miriam served hard-baked wheaten loaves, garnished with fresh vegetables—such as onions, radishes, and cucumbers when these were in season—and a small charger of olives and dates. Joseph liked to drink down his meal with fresh water or a cup of home-made beer brewed from pearl barley. For Yeshua there was always a bowl of honey milk and a slice of fig cake, dried on the open roof under the sun. Next Miriam would take a bowl of whey and the rest of the loaves, which she spread on a low stool by her mother's bed where, finally, she seated herself on a bamboo mat to eat her breakfast with old Hannah. The widow dipped her bread in vinegar and would not eat it until it was well soaked—then chewed it with her toothless gums. The vinegar quickened her enfeebled system and allowed her an illusive pang of vitality. She felt the acid stealing through her throat and body, and her dim, wrinkled eyes, framed by protruding bone, recovered for a moment a semblance of life. She sucked the bread sop in her gammer's mouth, nursed it long without swallowing, and strained her ears to hear her grandson say grace after Joseph: "When thou hast eaten and art full, then shalt thou bless the Lord thy God." Her withered lips would move at such times, almost inaudibly, and Miriam, inclining her head close to old Hannah's mouth, would hear:

"I thank Thee, Father in heaven, for preserving me to hear Thy praise in the mouth of my grandchild before I close my eyes."

And then Miriam would whisper in her mother's ear: "You shall yet see your grandchild a teacher and a rabbi in Israel."

"Yes, Miriam," old Hannah would say. "The Lord's grace has surely found him. May he never draw the evil eye of the envious."

After breakfast Miriam changed her mother's couch, made up the other beds, put the dishes away, and swept and dusted the room. And only then did her working day begin in earnest.

Meanwhile Joseph repaired to his workshop outside the house. He worked hard at his trade, though the proceeds were niggardly. His main difficulty was to procure the lumber which he required for raw material. Israel as a whole was not rich in timber, and the wood of the Galilean hills was too soft to serve a joiner's uses. It derived almost entirely from cypresses, carobs, and olive trees, or derelict vines. At the same time, the difficulty of transporting logs from Lebanon made the cost of such timber prohibitive, and Joseph's penurious customers could never have paid their steep prices. Thus the only wood Joseph could profitably use came from the stumps of felled sycamores. It was this wood which he fashioned into plows and tried to render sturdy by expert workmanship to offset the scarcity of iron, metal being an imported and expensive item, to be had only from the foundries of Phoenicia. None but the wealthy farmers could afford iron-studded plows. For this reason there was a high value placed upon sycamores, so that when a man sold his field which happened to contain any such trees, they were explicitly excluded from the bill of sale. But even sycamores grew only in warm regions and Joseph was forced to look for them in the Jezreel valley and as far as the Jordan plain. He had to dig out the roots himself, strap the stump on his poor donkey's back, and return on foot. Some of the tools and vessels that came from his workshop he sold to his neighbors, the small farmers and the outcasts who were as poor as he. Many of them could not pay cash at the hour of purchase. Some paid in grain or other crops. Joseph's income, therefore, barely stretched to defray the many taxes imposed by Herod's government and its Roman overlords—the head tax, the road and bridge tolls, the purchase taxes levied in the markets and bazaars.

Furthermore, it was essential to pilgrim to Jerusalem with votive offerings and sacrifices and gifts for the Temple, to say nothing of the obligatory Temple-tax. Then there was the perpetual expense of small luxuries that could not be produced at home or done without—like salt and saffron and incense plants and various spices such as ginger and cinnamon, all of them the products of climates warmer than the Galilean. And since a family lives not by bread alone, money was needed also to pay a scribe for a new scroll of Holy Writ, particularly when a learning child, a son, was of the family. And as for Miriam, it was notorious that she used part of Joseph's earnings to buy costly Sidonian linen and even skeins of Persian silk from which she wove the garments of her son. It was a reckless item in the budget, but Joseph did not hinder her.

The main body of the family's food supply was provided by old Hanan's wheat field, the vegetable garden and orchard, and the small herd of animals. The field itself, close to the house, lay against one of the hillocks that looked down on Nazareth. As Reb Hanan's legacy, it was the property of the entire family, so that the two Miriams, and now their husbands, were joint owners. The Law precluded any sundering of the family estate and even if it were sold entire it would revert to its original owners at the jubilee year, that is, at the half century.

Like every other family in Israel, that of Reb Hanan was a close-knit clan. Each member's possessions were owned in common by all. Cousins thought of one another as brothers and sisters, despite their having different parents. The Jews, one may say, cultivated an overwrought sense of family and lineage. Where one man had a windfall, it became at once a joyful family occasion; if misfortune fell upon one, the calamity was family-wide. Where one man had been offered an offense or injury, the whole family smarted under the blow. Similarly, if, God forbid, a member of the clan had failed in his conduct, the family conscience was pricked as though it were an organic whole.

As husbands to the sisters who had inherited the late Hanan's estate, Joseph and Cleophas were the heads of the family. With the coming of spring, after the latter rains, they prepared the field to receive the summer crop. The men brought out their respective asses, harnessed them both to the plow, and proceeded to open the field for the second annual sowing. But there was more to be done than merely plowing and sowing; since the field lay on the slope of a hill, there was the constant problem of holding the topsoil down. Joseph and Cleophas spent many wearisome days erecting ramparts on the down side of the field and fringing it with terraced rows of stones, but the fury of the spring and autumn rains was often such that layer after layer of fertile red soil was washed into the valley. Each spring the men fattened the field with animal manure from Joseph's mixen, scrupulously gathered through the winter; and each spring, they prayed that the rains come plentiful but without tempest, so that the dung be stamped into the earth and not carried away.

Yet the field was good for a moderate harvest. To evade the complicated rules that governed the mixing of seeds, Joseph and Cleophas sowed only the one crop which they deemed most essential—wheat for the bread that formed their staple food. And the field served both their houses; in a good year the harvest took care of the family's bread needs and no additional grain had to be bought.

The weeding was done by the two sisters. In times of exceptional drought, when, as frequently happened during the spring months, the simoom blighted the countryside, the brothers-in-law dug irrigation ditches down the length of the field and Joseph's ass trudged patiently to and from the well, laden with two skins of water to keep the ditches filled. As the harvest approached the men slept on the plot to guard it both from feathered thieves and from those riflers who were wont to come at night to cut other men's grain. Oh, there was sweat enough poured over that small field before the bearded spikelets weighed the stalks to the ground! But then, at last, when the day of mowing came—and come it did shortly after the Passover to give the farmer time enough to bring his first-fruit to the Temple before Pentecost— on that day the men sallied forth with their women and children, and with songs on their lips reaped what they had sown in tears.

But though the reaping was done amid singing and laughter, it was not done in forgetfulness of the Law. Remembering the poor on this day of rejoicing, the sixth part of the harvest was left uncut, and the sheaves that were forgotten were not afterward brought home, and there was no gleaning after the first gathering in—for the corners, the gleanings, and the forgotten sheaves belonged rightfully to the widow and the orphan and the stranger who dwelled within the gate.

The time of reaping, threshing, and winnowing was a festive season for the family. Cleophas and his wife moved into Joseph's house and all lived and worked together until the shucked kernels had been divided between the two households. Almost the entire time was spent by them in the open field. The men threshed with the thresh-boards which the asses dragged across the harvested grain. In accordance with Jewish Law, and contrary to Gentile usage, the asses' mouths were left unmuzzled, so that they were free to eat the grain which their toil beat from the husks. Meanwhile the women followed after, lifting the threshed kernels with shovels so that the chaff might blow away, piling the grain on one side, and on the other stacking sheaves of straw to dry before the sun.

At midday, when the sun blazed fiercest in the cloudless sky, the reapers sought shelter in the shade of a large olive tree where they kindled a small fire for a light repast of roasted wheat. Joseph knew that he was here taking a liberty with the word of the rabbis, who stipulated that none of the cut grain should be enjoyed before the Levites' tithe had been deducted. But he silenced his brother-in-law's misgivings with an adroit *a fortiori* argument:

"If," he expostulated, "we are taught by the Law of Moses that the ass working in the field shall have his mouth free to eat as he will, then assuredly it follows that man all the more may eat the fruit of his toil while he labors." And as proof incontrovertible he cited the case of Boaz and his young men who ate parched corn from off their field during the harvest. But eating in the field to break their labor was as far as Joseph would go; there could be no question of taking home any part of the crop before the priest had called to separate one tenth for the Levites and priests, and another, the second tithe, for the family's own use to be eaten in Jerusalem on their pilgrimage to the Temple. When these deductions had been made, and not before, the brothers-in-law divided the rest of their crop into two piles and each took home his share and stored it in the grain-box which was the family's chief treasure, the granary from which they drew their sustenance throughout the year.

They were eating the midday meal of roasted corn, drinking it down with parsley beer from cool jars. Miriam had brought a slice of fig cake and a dish of clabber for her son, who spent all day in the shorn field, playing with Moon among the stubbles. Then they stretched out in the shade, the men falling asleep while the women dallied with little Yeshua, who entertained them with his prattle. And when the sun began to down, they rose again to complete the work of the day, leaving Yeshua alone once more to gambol with his lamb.

Though Miriam worked as hard as any of her companions she never let the child out of her sight for long. And suddenly her hands dropped and she stopped petrified, helpless with terror, unable even to cry out. What she saw was a large snake, half its length upreared before the child, its head rigid with contained momentum. Miriam could see its dotted eyes and the green quivering flame of its tongue.

She felt her limbs freeze with horror and neither called for help nor moved toward the child. And then she saw him, Yeshua, in his spotless tunic, rising up from the ground and stretching out his hand as if to stroke the serpent's head. Stop, *tinoki,* don't!—but the scream stuck in her throat and issued as a silent groan from her paralyzed tongue. And the child took a step toward the snake, followed by its faithful lamb. Miriam's poor heart pounded at her throat, and still she could produce no sound of warning, even when she saw the hand of her son actually lighting on the serpent's head. Father in heaven!—she heard a voice deep in her heart; but in another moment saw the snake collapse like a pricked bladder.

Miriam then felt the sudden release of her body and, without staying to call for assistance, dashed over to her child. She found the snake's head resting between Yeshua's feet, being still touched by the child's hand. Isaiah's verse came to her mind: "The suckling child shall play on the hole of the asp, and the weaned child shall put his hand on the cockatrice's den."

157

She sealed the matter in her heart and spoke of it to no man or woman.

CHAPTER IV

I T WAS not long after the weaning of her first-born that Miriam conceived another child. And when Yeshua was three years old she bore her husband a son who was called Jacob, after Joseph's father. This time she was spared nothing, as though God wanted her to know every pain and pang of motherhood.

Since Miriam was bearing sons, her standing rose in the community of Nazareth, for was not this an unmistakable sign of the Lord's grace? Joseph's good name, too, was restored. People came to think more charitably of his little indiscretion at the time of the marriage. And, naturally, every man regarded Yeshua as Joseph's son, seeing no difference between him and his little brother.

Not so the children's parents; remembering well the circumstances of Yeshua's birth, they made a clear distinction in their minds between the elder and the younger. For Miriam, the natural birth of her second son served by contrast to emphasize the mystic and unfathomable character of Yeshua's genesis, in which she had been used as the instrument of higher powers.

Her first-born was the child of her virgin dreams, the child of her Sabbath and holiday, the child of her prayer. In sudden awe of his incomprehensible ordainment and the mystic nature of his birth, she would sink to her knees by his cot and raise her hands to him like a devout pilgrim who meets a divine revelation on the road. Often, when she saw him playing in a corner, or memorizing the Biblical verses which tripped so lightly from his childish lips, or when she watched him asleep in the wooden cot that Joseph had carved for him, she would speak softly to her anxious heart: "Who are you—who came to me so wonderfully? Who sent you to me in my distress? What worlds did you leave behind to come to me? And what is your destiny, you who are the fruit of my womb?"

But such transports occurred only at exceptional moments when she recalled her own election. At other times she treated Yeshua as she treated Jacob, and she taxed her strength to the utmost to provide for their needs.

In Joseph, too, the birth of his own son had reinforced his sense of responsibility for the sacred trust placed in his charge. He was perpetually apprehensive lest he fail in some duty toward the child who bore within himself the hope of Israel, as had been told him in his vision. He knew himself to be outside the sacred mystery, and without hope of access, a mere mortal into whose hands a sacred charge had been delivered, for him to guard with life and soul. He watched over Yeshua's safety, teaching him the ways of the world and taking the place of his father before people until his time should come.

In good years, when the rains came in season and fell plentifully without turning into floods, it was possible for him to provide nourishment enough from the family field. But every accident of weather—drought, tempest, or simoom—might blight the harvest and condemn the family to bitter want. This year, after the birth of his own child, a violent hailstorm, coming in early spring, smote the wheat so that for days and weeks the stalks lay prostrate, clinging to the miry earth. When the sun emerged once more and the stalks, infused with new warmth, reared themselves up again, Joseph realized that the coming harvest would bring no wheat kernels, but empty ears only and straw.

His fears were well founded. Winter was not half gone before the bottom showed in the small box which held their grain reserve, and Miriam's heart sank each time she took from it another handful of corn to grind into flour.

When the field failed them the vegetable garden had to make up the lack in the family larder. This meant more work for Miriam, and she began to cultivate the beds earlier in the year, when the ground was still sodden with moisture. Rising with the sun she plodded barefoot in the mud, planting carrots, broad beans, beets, and onions. Hour after hour she bent over her plants,

159

unstrangling them of weeds, opening up new seedbeds, digging holes to drain away the excess water.

There was no time now to weave new tunics for her eldest. These "coats of many colors" which Yeshua had outgrown were now worn by his young brother on Sabbath and feast days. But there were some which Miriam kept apart, because in weaving them in the small hours of the night, she had seen supernal visions. These she kept hidden like precious mementos in her own reliquary to lie there with his first swaddling clothes, a memorial of her brief sojourn in Bethlehem. For by now her son Yeshua, like all the children of the neighborhood, was garbed in the common dress of the poor—a habit of sackcloth tied with rope at the loins. On festive occasions only he still donned a shirt and tasselled tunic of delicate cotton which Miriam had woven.

Childhood was a short season in the homes of the poor. Little Yeshua was soon called away from his play to contribute his labor to the support of the household. He was entrusted with the small flock of sheep which it was his business to graze and drive home in time for the milking. From the vegetable garden Miriam could watch her son turned shepherd on the hill opposite their house. And when she heard him call each sheep by its name and saw the animals gather around him as for protection, she thought to herself how easily the calling of his ancestors came to her child, how like Abraham, Isaac, and Jacob he was become a shepherd, and surely, like Moses and David, the Lord would make him a shepherd to his people.

But not the animals alone were assigned to his care; from early childhood he was expected to watch over his young brother. And little Jacob did not stir from his side when they went out hand in hand to pasture the flock.

One morning, the children being out with the herd, an inoffensive, bluish cloudlet appeared on the horizon. It hovered there for a while, apparently motionless, but was suddenly overhead and, bursting open like an unclenched fist, discharged masses of black clouds. Before the sky was yet overcast, a sheet of rain dropped from above and waters spouted from the earth as though the abyss gaped and gushed in answer. It had all happened in the twinkling of an eye—with the suddenness characteristic of the spring rains in Galilee. But Miriam's children were out with the flock, cut off from home by impassable rapids that sped through the hollow between the hills. Yeshua was sinking ankle and knee-deep into the fast-softening earth as he ran hither and thither trying to gather in the herd. One lamb escaped with the stream and he plunged after it. Joseph meanwhile had scurried out of his workshop, followed closely by Miriam. But Yeshua, instead of rushing into his mother's outstretched arms, instead of obeying Joseph's cry to hasten home, continued waist-deep in pursuit of the lamb which was hurtling downstream with the torrent.

Little Jacob, barely two years old, did as his brother did, equally bent upon saving the lamb. But he slipped in the water and, losing his footing, began to roll with the stream. His shift, inflating like a bladder, kept him afloat as he was rushed headlong away. Yeshua saw him pass and caught him with one hand and thus held him tight, but still without abandoning the chase after the lamb for which he kept on reaching with his free hand, hoping still to seize it before it was mauled against some rocky obstruction or ditched irretrievably in the trough of the valley.

Miriam stopped, helpless; the flood was swelling in volume and ferocity as it approached the ditch, and she saw all three, her children and the lamb, carried toward it in one indistinguishable floating bundle. "The Lord will help," she murmured, choked with terror, her hands clapped over her mouth. And the next moment she saw the three abruptly halted; Yeshua was standing firm in the water, only his head and shoulders showing, and with one hand he upheld Jacob, with the other the truant lamb, and the torrent broke against his face. Each vaulting wave buried him from sight, so that he seemed each moment gone forever, but Yeshua held his ground, like an olive sapling well rooted. His stand lasted only a few seconds, but this short reprieve enabled Joseph, who had been following with water-clogged tread, to reach the children on the verge of the ditch and drag them to safety.

Drenched to the bone, with jets of water squirting from his soggy locks and out of his ears, Yeshua was laughing aloud, rejoicing as at the most delectable treat of his life.

And Miriam asked, as she changed his clothing: "Were you not afraid when the stream carried you away?"

"Why should I have been afraid?" Yeshua queried in turn. "Did I not know that the Father in heaven would prevent any ill coming to me?"

"How did you know this?" Miriam asked, urgently.

"I was doing His work, was I not? Did our Father in heaven not want the lambkin saved; did He want it to drown?"

Miriam marveled at the boy's words, and even more at the manner in which his will and conscious wisdom had checked in him the natural reflex of fear.

"Who told you this, *tinoki?*" she asked.

"No one, *emi;* I thought of it when I saw the lambkin seized by the tide."

Joseph, who was sitting by, remarked: "Your son, Miriam, speaks with the mouth of the sages, for the sages have taught— 'They shall suffer no injury who do My work.' "

And yet the episode was not without consequences. During the night, little Jacob, restless in his cot, called weakly for his mother. Miriam, approaching, found him burning with fever—and from that moment did not leave his bedside.

For three days and nights Miriam watched as her child fought with death.

Joseph's son was no less dear to her, no less her child than the child of her election. The infant claimed and subdued her total love not by that unearthly joy which her first-born could render in return for every contact, but through its pitiable, mortal helplessness, and the infliction of maternal sorrow. For he was born in woe and travail. So hard and so protracted were the throes that Miriam, with limbs rent asunder, despaired of her life. Like Rachel, it was thought she would never rise from the childbed.

And then the babe itself was feeble and sickly, a prey to violent convulsions as though it were engaged with malignant spirits. Not infrequently they found him covered with an ashy pallor, his little lips bright with foam. And more than once was Miriam's sister ready with a black veil to cover the aspect of death stamped on the infant's face.

"But Miriam, you can see that his struggle is over," Mariama would say.

Time and again Miriam held her back. She did not cease to rub the infant's belly with heated olive oil, nursing the vestige of her hope. If the angel of death could be seen to loom over the cradle, Miriam kept him off with prayers so fervid they would have pierced the averted ear of any power above or below. Several times she had brought little Jacob through bad fevers, and whenever she saw his eyes open and heard his recovered voice issue in a piteous whine, her heart overflowed with grief and compassion for this most wretched of God's creatures to whom she had imparted life and for whom she would gladly have yielded up her own. And she would fall upon her knees before the cradle and call with weeping on the Lord's name till the child was restored.

Thus had Miriam nursed Joseph's son through illness and near death. It was her pride and pleasure to see him, at two years old, a healthy, normal child—until that fateful day when the cloudburst overwhelmed her two sons in the open field.

Yeshua had shrugged it off playfully as a trivial adventure; for his young brother it became immediately a mortal threat. Joseph himself despaired of his life. He stood bent over the mother, begging for her surrender.

"Rest yourself, Miriam. God is taking him from us and His will is unalterable, even as His design is past our understanding. He gave him to us and has taken him away. May His name be blessed."

"Joseph, what are you saying! The child is breathing still; it still has life. Shall we abandon our trust in the Lord with Whom nothing is impossible? And is it not written—'He recalleth them that dwell in dust'? I will not give up this child."

And she continued at the sickbed. It was the third day she had taken neither food nor rest. Her face looked worn and gray with misery; her eyes, streaked and crimsoned by sleeplessness, stared down at the still body of her child and she bent over every little while to mop the sweat of agony from his face. She could see the throb of his heart through the thin coverlet, saw the rise and fall of his chest, the glassy rigidity of his wide-open eyes, as of a young bird during slaughter. His little head was thrown back, motionless, in a gesture of utmost resignation, and Miriam's heart shrank under the violence of her grief. With clenched mouth and fingers, with her eyes tightly closed against every stimulus of the living universe, she tried to make herself undergo the throes of her child, to shoulder by sheer empathy his struggle with death. And then her valiant hope gave way and she cried out aloud:

"Father in heaven, Thou art a merciful God. Canst Thou look down on the agony of my child? If it is me whom Thou seekest to punish, punish me and spare this child who knows no evil. Take my life away, take it for his. Have mercy, Father in heaven!"

And where all had been dark before, her grief-racked mind suddenly lit to a gleam of comprehension. It was not the child who was meant here; it was she, the mother. Her motherhood was to be preserved entire for the rearing of God's chosen Messiah; it was not to be lightly dissipated, for it was consecrated to the divine mission of her first-born son, as the angel had said in her chamber. She could be only once a mother. A jealous God had chosen her of all man's daughters to mother the world's hope of salvation.

Miriam recoiled in terror from her thought: this, her last perception, had sealed the verdict on her child—her own sanctification was his doom. And her maternal passion for this child of flesh welled up in her, transcended and outreached her love for the child that had come to her by grace alone. He, Yeshua, stood secure in the shadow of God; angels were guarding his every step and no harm could come his way. Divine providence had carved a highway for his mission and until this was fulfilled no force for good or ill could shake his progress. But this little child that lay before her at the point of extinction—a friendless bundle of mortality, vulnerable to every pernicious fiend and demon; his was no merit, earned or ordained, and only a mother stood between him and the world. Little Jacob was not God's elect, no exception even among children of his age. He was a child of man, everyman's child. In sacrificing him to her own sanctity, she would be offering up all human children. And this her sanctity, such as it was, conferred without merit or desert—could she, to preserve it intact, consign a human soul to death?

"Father of all worlds," she whispered, clasping her hands in anguish, "Holy God of Israel, take from me my election. Give it to another who shall be worthier than I, for behold, I cannot bear

164

the burden. I, too, am of flesh and blood, like this child whose mother Thou madest me in Thy bounty. Behold, I love Joseph's son as I love Yeshua whom Thou hast put into my charge for the saving of the world. But if I have sinned in Thy sight, then is the sin mine and this child is blameless. Punish me and take my life in expiation for my child's."

It was late in the night when Miriam, keeping her lone vigil by the dying infant's cradle, poured her heart out before God. Exhausted in body and mind she rested her head against the cot and fell into a heavy sleep.

When she awoke some hours later, Jacob's little face, freed of the cold sweat of death, bore the soft roseate glow of infant slumber, and Miriam, turning her tearful face to heaven, thanked God.

CHAPTER V

AFTER her prayers had wrung the child Jacob from the arms of death, Miriam conceived again. The child was named Joses, in honor of its father, and it was in this year that old Hannah died.

Miriam's standing among her kindred, and even with her brother-in-law Cleophas, increased steadily, and in the town they said of her that she was blessed by God to build houses in Israel, than which no higher praise could be bestowed.

Since his dream of the angel who had told him of Miriam's divine mission, Joseph had looked upon his wife as a thing holy and untouchable. Not for a moment did he doubt that she had been elected to bring forth the Messiah. But then the child was born, and though she remained sainted in his eyes, his attitude, now that the sanctity was separated from her body, underwent a change. For to the Jew the sacred thing was motherhood, not sterile purity. Rachel had been rightly jealous of her fruitful sister, deeming her own barrenness to be the curse of God, a withholding of the heavenly grace bestowed upon Leah. Thus also

Hannah, Samuel's mother, and, before her, Sarah, first of the holy Matriarchs, who partnered Abraham's covenant with the Lord, so that the chosen seed of Abraham could fructify in her womb only. "Be ye fruitful and multiply" was God's commandment which raised the act of generation to a sacred office, rendering man and wife participants in the omnipotent work of creation. And when he, Joseph, looked upon his sons, he saw them as the tokens of God's grace. He read in them the proof that he had well acquitted himself as the guardian of God's pledge, for which the Lord of Justice had rewarded him with fatherhood.

More children meant more work for the parents, and Miriam and Joseph were at endless pains to satisfy the daily needs of the growing family.

Yeshua was used to seeing want—in his own home as well as without. All around him toiled wearily for their morsel of bread, their shabby garments, and the hovel in which they weathered the nights. He saw poverty, too, in the form of wandering beggars who knocked at Joseph's door on their way to Nazareth—of whom not one was sent away hungry or thirsty.

With the dawn of his consciousness, therefore, Yeshua developed an aching sensitivity to want and toil. It tormented him to see his parents overworked from Sabbath to Sabbath. Even in his cradle Miriam had noticed his eyes pursuing her every gesture, watching her anxiously as she dragged up the pitchers from the well, and stretching forth his tiny hands, as if to help.

Or he would watch her as she ground wheat kernels into meal. It was a task that called for great physical exertion, and for no less dexterity. The handmill consisted of two circular flat stones, both of considerable weight, the rider, or uppermost stone, being furnished with a handle. When old Hannah was living, the two women would do the turning together. Now, since her mother's death, Miriam had to do it alone.

She was squatting on the threshold of her house, with both hands turning the rider. After many revolutions the sweat broke out on her face and trickled down her neck and body. Little Yeshua was standing by, pouting, and said at last:

"*Emi,* why did not God so order it that the earth produce meal

166

ready for baking, or even the finished loaf? Why must man work so hard for bread?"

"They did not, *tinoki,* before man sinned. Then the earth did yield the finished loaf and man never knew the taste of work. Adam and Eve lived in the Garden of Eden where every food grew ripe and ready. But man fell, God drove him out of the Garden, and he cursed him to eat bread in the sweat of his face."

Yeshua frowned and said: "What is sin, *emi?*"

"We sin when we fall away from our Creator and transgress His will and keep not His commandments."

The child pondered this gravely and asked again: "And why, *emi,* do people sin? Is it not good to do the will of God?"

"Because 'Man's heart is evil from his youth,' as it says in Holy Writ."

"Why did not God make man to be good from his youth?"

"God did make him good, *tinoki,* but since man fell, the imagination of his heart has turned to evil and now he must labor to be good and subdue his wickedness in bitter struggle."

Another pause—then Yeshua:

"Will God never forgive men for Adam's sin and let them become good again without struggle?"

"Yes, Yeshua, when He takes pity on us and sends His Redeemer, then He will purge man of Adam's sin and man will walk in righteousness as he did at the beginning of time."

"When shall that be, *emi?*"

"When the Redeemer comes."

"Who is he, the Redeemer?"

"The King-Messiah whom God will send to Israel to redeem His promise to our fathers."

"I want him to come soon!"

"He will come, *tinoki;* he will come when the hour is ripe."

"*Emi,*" said the boy, "let me help you." And he laid his little hand on hers that had not left the handle of the mill.

It might have been Miriam's fancy, but the child had no sooner touched her hand than the heavy rider began to spin more swiftly.

Just as the boy could rejoice over every token of goodness or beauty, so he could grieve at every injustice—no matter whether it be perpetrated by man or animal, or inhered in the very order of the universe. His sensibilities might have been said to lie open, like the strings of a lute which the gentlest jolt could make to vibrate. His large black eyes that sparkled so vividly in moments of delight, could, at other times, express an innocent mournfulness that no one could contemplate without an aching heart.

One morning, shortly after sunrise, Miriam went into the stable with an armful of hay for her flock. She was at once heard to cry out in alarm, and Joseph, hastening to her side, found her crouched over the mangled body of a lamb, but two weeks old, that had apparently been attacked by a jackal during the night. Its dam must have attempted to shelter the lamb under her own belly, from whence the beast had dragged it out, for the ewe's fleece was daggled with encrusted blood.

Joseph had been offering the morning prayer and he had arrived, breathless, still in his prayer shawl, with the philacteries wound about brow and arm. Young Yeshua, wearing his tunic with the ritual fringes, came running after him. At this, Miriam leapt up to turn him away from the sight of blood, but the boy saw too swiftly what had passed and let out a disconsolate wail. His impulse was to hurl himself over the mutilated carcass which the jackal, finding the gap under the stable walls too low, had been forced to abandon.

"*Tinoki!*" cried Miriam, seizing the boy and pinning him between her knees. But the child went on wailing, while Miriam stroked his head and tried in vain to stay his sobs.

"Why, *emi,* why, why did he do it?"

"It is the beast's nature, Yeshua. God has ordained that it must kill to eat," Joseph said, taking the boy from his mother. "Come, Yeshua. We shall finish our prayer. And you still have your verse to repeat."

The boy cast up his reddened eyes and asked incredulously: "God makes it kill for food?"

"Go, *tinoki,* with father; he will explain it to you," Miriam said, and pushed him gently toward Joseph.

Back in the house, when the frenzy of his grief had passed, Yeshua asked again:

"*Abba,* why did God order it so?"

"What, *tinoki?*"

"That animals should live upon each other's flesh?"

"Because of Adam's sin," Joseph explained. "You see, Yeshua, before Adam fell, all the creatures of God, all animals and birds and fishes dwelled with Adam in the Garden of Eden, and none hurt any other. They ate of the greens of the fields and the fruits of the trees which God had made to sprout for them, as God commanded in the beginning of creation: 'And to every beast of the earth, and to every fowl of the air, and to every thing that creepeth upon the earth, wherein there is life, I have given every green herb for meat; and it was so.' But when Adam sinned and was expelled from the Garden, all animals were driven out with him. And to them the Lord said: 'Go forth and feed upon each other.' "

"And, *abba,* will it always be so?"

"No, *tinoki,* when the Messiah of righteousness appears, all animals, both wild and tame, shall graze together, and they will do no injury one to the other—for so we were told by the Prophet Isaiah. And this, Yeshua, is the verse you shall learn today. Here is the scroll; sit, Yeshua, and we will read the Prophet's vision and you will know what shall be at the end of days."

Joseph drew the boy on his knees and, unrolling the parchment of the Book of Isaiah, read out verse by verse:

"The wolf also shall dwell with the lamb,
And the leopard shall lie down with the kid;
And the calf and the young lion and the fatling together;
And a little child shall lead them."

"A child?" asked Yeshua; "like me?"

"Yes, *tinoki,* like you."

"Like me, like me!" Yeshua exclaimed, clapping his hands, and his eyes found again their native luster.

"Come, *tinoki,* come with me," Joseph said, rising. "Much is to be done in the workshop and I can begin while you learn your verse."

"Soon, *abba,* soon, but I must first tell *emi,*"—and shouting brightly for his mother he called as he ran to the stable:

"*Emi,* listen! A wolf and a lamb shall feed together, and a little child shall lead them!"

169

Yeshua's mind returned often to the violence of nature; the death of the lamb would not let him rest. Once, after Joseph had read with him the story of Cain and Abel, he came to his mother with a question.

"Why," he asked suddenly, "why did God accept Abel's sacrifice and reject Cain's?"

"God reads the inward thoughts of men," said Miriam, "and knows His servitors who are pure and contrite of heart and bring their offerings in love and goodwill. And He knows such as sacrifice in greed and hope of preferment. For there are men who have the grace of God and others who walk in darkness, destitute of grace."

The boy weighed the words and asked at last: "And what shall they do who have not God's grace? Are they not to be pitied?"

"Have you not learned," Miriam asked in reply, "what the Lord said to Cain?—'If thou doest well, shalt thou not be accepted? and if thou doest not well, sin lieth at the door and unto it shall be your desire, but thou shalt rule over it.' God said this not to Cain alone, *tinoki,* but to all his descendants who envy their brothers and, like Cain, wear a wroth and fallen countenance. God says to them—why art thou wroth and why is thy countenance fallen? You can conquer the sin at your door, for the choice is yours. You can choose the good or the evil. Punish then the evil that lies in your heart and seek to do well."

Yeshua pondered this in silence and, sighing with finality, said: "*Emi,* do you know what I think? I think God should appoint a helper for those who have not the Lord's grace, to take their part before God. These men more than the righteous need a helper, for the righteous have father and mother to take care of them."

Then Miriam's eyes grew moist, and she said: "*Tinoki, tinoki,* when you grow up you shall be their helper."

"No, *emi,* not I but you!"

"Why I, *tinoki?*"

"Because you have pity for whosoever stands on your threshold, and there is no one can prevail against your tears. When your tears fall God will have compassion for them."

"Please, *tinoki,* I can bear it no more." She turned her head away so that he would not see her tears.

Despite his six years, despite the oracular pronouncements which he delivered in inspired moments, Yeshua was in some ways the most childlike of her sons, with an intenser need of her solicitude. Miriam struggled always to make no distinction between her children, that no gulf should come between Yeshua and his brothers. Yet, inevitably, the child of promise, with his provocative questions, his tenderness, and her sense of his destiny, absorbed more of her time and attention. Every night, before he would lie down to rest, the child demanded his concession of brief intimacy with Miriam.

The hushed hours Miriam spent with her eldest before putting him to sleep were noted by his brothers. Jacob slept untroubled, cradled, as it were, in the security of prayer uttered without stint or question. Not so the younger Joses, who lay waking in his cot and scoured the half-darkness with dilating eyes, while his mother, whom he wanted close, stroked Yeshua's curls and was so much absorbed in Yeshua's talk as not to feel the hunger of his gaze. Young as he was—and he was barely two years old—he sensed obscurely that his eldest brother Yeshua was favored. And he craved for his mother with a child's avid yearning for the evidence of love. Sometimes, without apparent provocation, the child started and cried out as though he had been stung, and could not calm himself but had to be rocked into security within his mother's arms. There he pressed close, as though, against his mother's body, he could become one with her until the terror had passed over.

One night, as always before bedtime, she sat with Yeshua in a corner, feeling herself transported again by his speech. Then, suddenly, like the cold piercing impact of bared iron, she felt the eyes of young Joses upon her. She turned and dimly saw her little son awake beside the slumbering form of his brother Jacob. Miriam rose at once and, leaning over his cot, asked why he did not sleep.

"Mother, I am afraid."

It made Miriam's heart shrink to hear him speak so surely of his fears.

171

"What is there to be afraid of, *tinoki?*" she said, picking him up.

"I saw shadows moving."

"Shadows?"

"Yes, with large wings."

Yeshua was now forgotten. Miriam became only this child's mother; in one instant her earthly motherhood asserted itself as the sovereign passion, and displaced as by violence the raptures of the previous moments.

"Don't be frightened, *tinoki,*" she said. "I am with you now," —and she fell to pacing the room with the child in her arms, and little Joses dug his head into his mother's breasts while his hands clawed painfully at her arms. His hot breath grazed her throat and chin and his child's voice, husky with sleep, repeated over and over:

"I want to be with *ema,* I want to be with *ema.*"

"But you are with *ema,* you are."

"More with *ema,* more, more!" cried the child, sobbing hysterically.

A chilling shudder ran down Miriam's spine, and she clutched the trembling child more tightly. In Joses' childish woe she heard all mankind's longing for maternal love. The child in her arms was not her little Joses only, it was the son of man, questing for a mother-intercessor and lying at her breast that had nourished the salvation of the world. In this child raged the thirst of man, even as the slaking thereof welled in Yeshua. And she, Miriam, who was mother to salvation, was mother also to the need of it— mother both of thirst and deliverance.

From earliest infancy Jacob and Joses observed that their eldest brother enjoyed a special standing. They knew also that more was involved than the privilege of the first-born. Things forbidden them were allowed Yeshua. Clearly, the parents left Yeshua to discover his own way, and acquiesced joyfully in whatever he did. They saw well enough that Yeshua's status was unique in the household, and the perpetual awareness of this rankled in their young hearts and caused that restless anxiety which is not far removed from open envy.

Mariama also had seen the distinction the parents made between Yeshua and his brothers. Even though she could not fathom the reason, she sensed that Miriam's eldest son was marked for a special destiny. And her loving heart recognized the difficulties. Always a great help to Miriam in her daily duties, she more and more took over the responsibility of the younger boys. As they grew older, she took them home with her, and the two households formed so close a unity that it did not matter under which roof the children passed their days. Cleophas, one may say, was a father born; he liked to give orders, instruction, guidance. He more than welcomed the opportunity to display his patriarchal leanings and enjoyed entering the synagogue with Joseph's sons in his train.

For their own part, the children became so attached to Mariama that they called her not aunt, but mother—a title that clung to her in the references of the townspeople. When she appeared in the street of the sandal sewers with Jacob at her side and little Joses in her arms, the neighbors nudged one another, saying:

"There goes the mother of Jacob and Joses."

CHAPTER VI

CAME the day when Yeshua, now six years old, must be presented to the preceptor of the synagogue who had the supervision of all children's schooling.

A little while before, that is to say, on the thirty-third day of Omer, Yeshua was, for the first time, shorn of his curls, a ceremony which gave rise to another family festivity. And as usual, the neighbor children were invited and feasted with nuts, honeycakes, and fruit.

Miriam saw Yeshua's ringlets fall one by one from the shears. Later, she gathered them in stealth and secreted them in her shrine that held the family treasures. Two curls only were left in their place—the earlocks which women of later times have called "lovelocks." Framing the child's face, they emphasized its delicate length, while the forehead, liberated of rioting curls, asserted for the first time the height and fullness of its dome.

To present the child in the synagogue was traditionally the mother's privilege. Early on the morning of the Sabbath Miriam bathed her child and dressed him in a new linen tunic which had cost her many night hours at the loom. And while Joseph was anointing his own head and beard with olive oil, Miriam, in excess of custom, poured some of the precious fluid on the child's head.

The parents, too, dressed in their finest; Joseph donned his black Sabbath cloak, Miriam a black cape, a veil of star-studded gauze, and the silver-buckled girdle which had been Joseph's wedding gift. Then they took the boy by the hand and walked him to the local temple, the "little synagogue."

They passed through the street of the joiners, through the crooked alley of the sandal sewers, and into the street of the potters. The grave serenity of the Sabbath lay over the town. The streets, that had rung all week with the sound and bustle of trades overflowing from houses and shops, were now voided of life, except here and there for a wandering sheep or a week-wearied jackass making the most of his hebdomadal rest between the doorposts of his stable. And the houses and huts released at intervals small groups of citizens, accompanied by children in their Sabbath finery, converging all upon the house of congregation.

The synagogue, a small structure of massive stone blocks with an Ionic colonnade (too squat by Grecian standards of perfection) upholding a flat lintel roof, stood foursquare in the market place, dwarfing the merchant booths and shops of the town. Seven tiers of steps led up to the façade whose modest portal was shaded by a cornice carved with Jewish symbols—the grape cluster, the urn, and the Menorah.

Joseph allowed his wife and Yeshua to precede him up the steps. Indoors they were received by a tall man with a black corkscrew beard suggesting the Syrian fashion. He was draped in an ankle-length black gown—the outward mark of his learning—and a prayer shawl flung stolewise across his shoulders. He bowed courteously and asked their errand.

"Master," said Miriam, "I have brought my first-born son into the House of God that he may learn the Torah."

174

"You have performed a mother's duty," said the preceptor. "What name in Israel does the child bear?"

"Yeshua."

"Yeshua, the son of . . .?" and the preceptor inclined his ear to hear the name completed.

Miriam faced him open-mouthed, as though she did not grasp his question.

"Yeshua ben . . . ?" the man asked again.

Joseph, standing back in the rear, called out firmly:

"Yeshua ben Joseph!"

"I see," said the preceptor, looking down benevolently at the boy. "Now, Yeshua ben Joseph, can you say the *Sh'ma?*"

"Yes, *emi* taught me."

"Then *emi* did well," said the man, smiling at Miriam. "And now, child, tell me your Bible verse."

Unhesitatingly the child quoted his favorite lines:

"The wolf shall dwell with the lamb, and the leopard shall lie down with the kid, and the calf and the cub and the fatling together; and a little child shall lead them."

"But this is Isaiah's verse. A child should first be taught the opening of Leviticus, as we were taught by the rabbis."

"The child takes pleasure in Isaiah," said Joseph, as if to beg pardon. "He will bring me the book and insist on being taught the words of the Prophet."

"One should not teach a child for its pleasure but for its instruction, as ordained by the rabbis," the preceptor replied with a reproving shake of his head, and he took Yeshua by the hand, saying, "Come with me."

Yeshua allowed him his hand, but he turned about and his glance searched Miriam's face; and Miriam motioned him to go as he was bid. . . .

She saw him again later from the women's gallery. Peering through its wooden balustrade, she saw her son in a line of children whom the preceptor had placed together on a low platform in the center of the synagogue, close behind the pulpit at which the preceptor was declaiming the prayers. They were facing the apse where, below the ark of Torah, there was a built-in stone chair, called the seat of Moses. It was reserved for the town rabbi, the man appointed by the Pharisees of Jerusalem to guide the sacred congregation of Nazareth in matters spiritual. The rabbi was flanked by the seven elders of the town, the learned men in their black gowns.

The common folk sat behind the pulpit upon low benches, scarcely higher than the ground, their knees drawn up to their shoulders. They huddled together in groups, according to their trades. Joseph sat with the carpenters at the rear, the foremost pews being given over to those who practiced more honored crafts, such as silversmithing, sandal-sewing, and perfumery. Not but that there were lowlier trades still—weavers, tanners, shearers, and vendors of salves and perfumes, whose low repute must be ascribed to their constantly associating, in the way of their profession, with women of ill fame; and on a lower rung still, the wretches who, beyond alms-begging, could point to no trade whatsoever—the ass-drivers and unassorted poor who lived on gleanings and forgotten sheaves and who stood no closer than the entrance of the hall; and behind them, small farmers whose orthodoxy had fallen under suspicion, a handful of Gentiles, native Edomites and Moabites. These last attended an occasional service because, after the readings of the Hebrew Writ, the same, or parts thereof, were done into Aramaic, the *lingua franca* of the Syrian East.

Of women there was but a small number. The synagogue was a man's place. The small gallery above, a triangular balcony over one corner of the hall, was allowed only for those women who were drawn by some special occasion—as was Miriam's case on this particular Sabbath.

Miriam continued to look down through the balusters at her child. She saw him standing erect in the midst of the children, his face raised up to a mosaic on the synagogue wall, an awkward representation of the Sacrifice of Isaac. The boy gazed at it in a kind of fascination, with unblinking eyes.

The children's role was to act as choir under the preceptor's direction. At a sign of his hand they chanted the "amen" to consummate his prayer. And they recited the "Hear, O Israel" and, toward the end of the *Hallel,* or Hymn of Praise, repeated the last lines word by word after the preceptor.

176

The orisons were over. The rabbi and one of the elders of the town rose from their seats and, being joined by the reader, all three ascended the steps to the sacred Ark, immured in the east wall. The congregation rose as one man. The reader opened the doors of the Ark and with caressing fingers withdrew the scroll of the Torah. Unrolling it a short space, he then raised it high above his head and turned to face the congregation. The latter, with faces joyfully upraised, sang in chorus: "And it came to pass when the Ark set forward, that Moses said, 'Rise up, Lord, and let Thine enemies be scattered.'"

And when Miriam saw the white-robed reader standing between the black forms of the rabbi and the elder, holding the opened scroll high over the heads of the praying multitude, and they looking up with their workaday faces transfigured by their faith, it seemed to her—no, she saw with waking clarity the image of her son grown into manhood. It was a fleeting vision that would not have survived the twinkling of an eye; but it was long enough for her to recognize his face, the face of her child bearded and earlocked, surmounting a gown paler than white heat. There was a cloak about him as of woven air, and in his hands was an open scroll of the Law.

The vision faded. Miriam looked about her; below, in the hall of the synagogue, the boy Yeshua stood with the other children. His large eyes were wide open and fixed upon the Torah scroll which the reader was still holding aloft.

On the following morning the boy was wakened at sunrise with his elders, and Miriam prepared him for his scholarly inauguration. A style and waxen tablet and a handful of scrolls inscribed in a clear hand with verses from the Prophets, the Psalms, and the third Book of Moses, had been prepared for Yeshua some time before against the day he should be going to school. Now she washed him and dressed his hair, then helped him into a white, freshly-laundered shirt and a fringed tunic, and finally hung about his shoulders a pair of sandals to be used only when a field of thistles was to be traversed, or perhaps a muddy stream whose unseen bottom might offer heaven knows what treasonable snares. Then she pressed a slice of fig-cake into his hands, along with raisins and almonds and other titbits choice and plentiful.

In moody silence, little Jacob watched the preparations. With his own four-fringed tunic hanging limply from his shoulders, he stood in a corner of the room, ostensibly memorizing the alphabet from an open scroll. But his abecedarian zeal was belied by a surly narrowing of his large eyes and a heavy pout on his lips. He looked, in fact, as though he would any moment burst into tears.

Miriam quickly caught his expression. She walked over to him and took his head between her hands, saying consolingly:

"You, too, my child, shall shortly go with your brother to learn God's Torah." And she handed him a slice of the fig-cake as partial consolation. And Joseph took him into his workshop to hear his Bible verses, as he had used to do with Yeshua.

A few minutes later, Bar Evion (Pauper-Boy), the tanner's eldest son, arrived at the house. His real name was Tayma, but he went by his nickname, conferred on him by other children in consideration of his father's poverty. Tayma bar Evion, according to previous arrangement, was to take Yeshua every day to school.

A hefty, sturdy-boned lad, reared by want and privation, he led young Yeshua through gardens and fields, leapt with him over wattled fences, trespassed on private property, and still brought him in time to the synagogue.

The hours began early at school and lasted almost till noon, for it was held essential to attach young children to the Torah in their formative years. Childhood study was likened to an inscription in fresh ink upon newly-pressed papyrus—it remained indelible forever. Thus it was the rabbis' effort to heap the minds of children with Scriptural lore, and thus to render each of the sacred verses unforgettable.

In a cool chamber of the synagogue the children sat in line on a mat spread on the floor, looking up at the rabbi, their preceptor, who sat over them on a high stool. He was making them repeat endlessly one verse from Leviticus, dealing with sacrifices. A few scrolls lay open before the children but were rarely consulted. The teaching by and large was oral and the verses to be learned by heart. They were recited aloud in a staggering attempt at unison, and the higher a pupil raised his voice, the more praise he earned.

The preceptor's assistant stood nearby with a birch rod ready lest any of the children flag in their zeal. And the preceptor repeated once more the first verse of the Third Book, where God told Moses to speak to the children of Israel and say unto them, "If any man of you bring an offering unto the Lord, ye shall bring your offering of the cattle, even of the herd and the flock." And the preceptor went on to expound: "Come and see," said he, using the traditional formula; "come and see how God enjoins the children of Israel to offer only their oxen and their sheep, and not, as the Gentiles do, sacrifice human beings to Moloch, their idol." And he further gave them to understand that a man's offerings were purposed to expiate his sins.

Yeshua kept his eyes fixed on the preceptor, drinking up his words. But he puzzled at every syllable. Why did God want sacrifices brought to Him? Why must an innocent lamb pay for a man's transgression? How did the Gentiles come to offer human sacrifices to their gods? Yeshua would not ask the preceptor, but he would go home and put his questions to his parents, who could surely explain. In the meantime he repeated the verses, together with the other children of his age.

At length each boy was summoned to recite the verse by himself. His ability to do this was held to be of the highest importance. Often, when adult men needed advice to steer them safe through a dilemma, they would ask the first child in their path to quote a verse at random. This verse they would act upon, the child's recitation being regarded as a minor oracle. And it followed that the child with the best memory for Holy Writ was the most deserving of adult praise and regard.

When the children in the classroom had their verse well by heart, the preceptor and his assistant pointed it out in the written text. Then, when everyone knew how to read it, the tablets were brought out and each boy learned to inscribe the verse letter by letter with his own style, his hand being guided by the preceptor or the assistant. First came the simpler characters—the "yud," a little floating comma, the plain down-stroke of the "vov," and thence on to the more complex symbols till the child could write the full twenty-three letters of the alphabet. And thus, finally, if all had gone well, after the thick end of the style had been often applied to the wax to smooth out errors, each boy could copy out the verse without assistance.

Little Yeshua knew the alphabet already; Miriam had taught him, drawing with a wooden stick on the bare earth. And he remembered many verses from the Prophets and Psalms and many more from the Law of Moses, so that he was an exceptional scholar among those of his age. It was not long, therefore, before he attracted the rabbi's special attention. How, the rabbi was curious to know, did young Yeshua come to know so many verses? Sometimes Yeshua was able to satisfy him; this one quotation mother had taught him, this other he had heard his father use. But about many others the boy could give no information, as though he had snatched them out of thin air, or, as Miriam liked to think, as though the angels of the Lord were teaching him by night. Whatever the true explanation, the rabbi set up little Yeshua as a model to his mates. Before the day was over his reputation had reached the higher classes and older boys came to hear little Yeshua recite Scripture. The rabbi called him his "shining scholar," injecting the rest of the class with a compound of envy and awe.

The schedule ended with the singing of the *Hallel,* followed by the day's second recitation of the *Sh'ma.* And with that the children were released to eat what they had brought from home, to play in the court of the synagogue, or to return to their houses if they so desired.

Yeshua soon found himself mobbed by children of his own grade as well as older boys eager to meet the "shining scholar" in a trial of strength—to see who could run off the most verses. But little Yeshua, who, at the rabbi's prompting, had volunteered so many Bible sentences, showed no inclination to enter a quotation race with his fellow pupils. And to the many questioners that asked who it was had taught him what he knew, he replied with monotonous insistence, "Mother," an answer which made everybody laugh, for whoever heard of learning from a woman, when it was the father's job to teach? And little Matthew Saucebox, a merchant's son who was the noisiest blusterer in his grade, promptly dubbed Yeshua the "Mother's Boy."

Yeshua's fellow pupils were drawn from all sections of the

population. There were among them the children of rich houses; even the sons of Reb Tudrus and Reb Sheshet bar Kaspi, the town's richest man, took their religious training in the local synagogue school. They came each morning with their private tutors—Greek slaves who waited outside the building to take them home again. Several others, too, came accompanied by Greek slaves, among them the sons of Talami bar Kazin, the moneylender. The majority, however, hailed from the poorer quarters, day laborers' and artisans' children, and here Yeshua found his old comrade Pezachi, the son of his father's neighbor, Nafchi. Though Nafchi himself had been abandoned as a hopeless case, the leaders of the town, with the rabbi at their head, had undertaken to educate his children, for it was considered noble work to teach the Torah to an outcast's son.

Yeshua sat down with his friend and gave him of his cake and nuts, which Pezachi devoured like the starveling he was. The others, meanwhile, tried to involve Yeshua in one of their games. Simeon bar Talami, chief wag of the second grade, who acted as master of ceremonies, came running up with this urgent appeal:

"Yeshua bar Joseph, which game will you join? Nuptials or funeral? We're playing both!"

"I don't know how to play either," Yeshua said honestly.

The others gasped with profound astonishment.

"You don't?"

"No."

"Well, look here, when you play nuptials, this is what you do: you find two birds and pair them in one cage and then you celebrate as at a real wedding, with tumblers and singers and all the ceremonies that go with it. And when you play funeral you take a dead worm and give him honest burial with mutes and wailing women and funeral orations and what not."

"Oh, have done, Simeon, Yeshua bar Joseph has no relish for your weddings and funerals," said little Matthew Saucebox with a knowing air. "I know what he will play—merchant and customer. Here are the scales all ready," he added, showing a contraption of nutshells and sticks. "Come now, I have a large store of spices and seeds from Persia and Parthia."

"Why not just play ball?" suggested Yehuda bar Talbi, the

ropemaker's son, reaching into his shirt to withdraw a clue of hempen yarn, pilfered from his father's shop and held together by a clumsily tied thread. "I have a ball here and we can play it against the north wall of the synagogue where there are no windows."

Little Yeshua was embarrassed by the richness of the choice presented. His mind was busily eliminating first the funeral game, then the merchant-and-customer game, which seemed to offer even less diversion. He would have liked to play the wedding, with the singing and dancing, and felt drawn irresistibly to the ball game which he had never before tried. But he remembered suddenly how he had promised his mother to return at once after the school session. And to make doubly sure the promise would be kept, Miriam had taken Bar Evion's word to bring Yeshua home without useless delay.

"Tomorrow," he blurted out at the boys who stood about awaiting his decision. "I will ask my mother to let me play. Today I cannot; I promised to come home at once."

"Mother's boy, mother's boy," teased Matthew Saucebox, and the others took up his cry.

"Mother's boy! . . ."

Little Yeshua did not seem to resent his nickname; he liked it.

Thus, with his neighbors Bar Evion and Pezachi on either side, he began to make his way home.

He had told them in the court of the synagogue that he must without delay return to his mother. Yeshua now found that the matter was not so pressing as he had thought. This was his first independent sally into the town and he stopped every stone's throw to stare at novelties. Nothing failed to interest him; every new sight goaded him to ask questions of his comrades. The streets through which they passed rang with the sounds of labor, for the houses and huts that lined them on both sides were little more than sleeping quarters, and the work of the day, no less than the buying and selling, was performed out-of-doors.

Under wattled canopies that spanned the roofs of adjacent houses in the street of the weavers the men sat at their looms turning out linens for the Sepphoris market. In the next street the potters sat with straddling legs over their wheels or praised their finished vessels to casual passers, trying to outshout the spice dealers, their neighbors. And the noise of chaffering voices, raised in anger, outrage, or entreaty, issued without cease from clumps of customers gathered here and there about some artisan or hawker.

Again and again little Yeshua stopped, raised himself on tiptoe, peered around corners and obstructing bodies to see what was going forward. He elbowed his way through packs of laden asses and carriers, buyers and idlers, making always for the thickest crowds, until he reached the street of the sandal makers. Here he found Uncle Cleophas in his open shop tapping at his last, his hairy chest that showed under a frayed tunic, glistening with sweat. Cleophas nodded carelessly in recognition and, without turning his head, called into the house:

"Mariama, come out and see who's here. It's the sun and the moon, your elect, the apple of your eye, your one and only."

Mariama came running out at the summons and welcomed Yeshua as though it had been her own child who had come home from his first day at school. And as usual she began to stuff him with sweetmeats and honeycake, saying:

"Here, eat, *tinoki,* and may the Torah be as sweet as honey to you and may your mother live to see you a rabbi in Israel, surrounded by disciples."

"I should have thought you'd ask for a son of your own to be a rabbi in Israel," said Cleophas, with more than necessary verve in the beat of his maul.

"If Miriam's son grows up to be a rabbi, I shall be just as proud as if he were my own. Are we not one flesh and blood? And is he not as good as a son to us?"

Cleophas laid his hammer down and thought it over.

"Yes and no," he said. "All the same, I should have liked to see a son of my own come home from school with a scroll under his arm. Your sister, God be praised, has three already. Now what harm would there be if—but, no matter—there is nothing more to say. And as for this lad, you had better send him home to Miriam; she will be spent with waiting by this time." And he resumed his tapping.

Mariama turned Yeshua homeward by his shoulders.

183

"Run along, *tinoki,* we will come to you later," she said and handed the rest of her dainties to Yeshua's friends.

They stopped again to watch a group of day-laborers waiting and ready for hire, some with porter's ropes about their waists, others with hoisted shovels. And when this palled, they sauntered on to where "Blind Samson" sat, a day-laborer too, who earned his keep turning other people's mills. Here they fell talking with the ragamuffin who daily steered Blind Samson to the scene of his employment and back to his beat. They gave him of their titbits and moved on, and, after tickling a braying jackass and scaring a covey of birds from a sown field, followed Bar Evion's lead on a short cut home, a route which offered the attraction of leaps over puddles and trespasses through private fields and groves.

Miriam was standing in her doorway, looking out for them. This was the first time she had been separated from Yeshua for so many hours. It was also Yeshua's first jaunt on his own, Joseph having insisted that the boy go without his parents lest he become the laughing stock of his mates.

And so Miriam stood waiting in her vegetable garden with a spade idle in her hands, for her heart was beating in high agitation and anxiety.

At last she saw him hurrying up the hill, the fringes of his tunic straining after him in the wind. He was holding a scroll in one hand, the wax tablet in the other, and he was running straight into his mother's outspread arms.

It was the father's privilege to feed his children when they came from school. Joseph therefore laid his work aside and washed his hands. Then, drawing Yeshua on his lap, he gave him to eat from the bowl he had carved for him; hot barley soup with morsels of bread. And Miriam, to celebrate her son's inauguration as a scholar of the Torah, added the reckless luxury of a boiled egg and a dash of honey in Yeshua's milk. Then she sat down at a short distance to watch him eat and listen to his account.

Little Jacob was as eager as she to hear Yeshua's story. Dressed in one of Yeshua's tunics, which allowed for two more years of growth at least, he circled about his older brother, somewhat shy and somewhat envious, and asked at last what was engraved on the wax tablet. Needing but little encouragement, Yeshua proudly read out the verse of the day. Little Jacob was instantly filled with delight.

"And you wrote it yourself?" he asked happily.

"Yes, the rabbi showed me how, and I wrote it on the wax. It is not hard at all. *Emi* already taught me in the sand."

"*Emi* will teach you too," said Joseph, leaning over to draw Jacob on his untenanted knee. "And now let's hear from Yeshua what he learned today." And, using the traditional formula, he added:

"Tell me your verse, child."

Once more Yeshua recited God's will concerning sacrifices, that they be brought Him from the herd and the flock and not from among men after the usage of idolators.

"*Abba*, is it true that the Gentiles kill human beings for their gods?"

"Some of them do, *tinoki*," Joseph replied, "our neighbors for instance, the sons of Tyre and Sidon who dwell by the sea. They sacrifice children to Moloch, their god."

"Why, do they do it, *abba?*"

"Because they think to please their god."

"But God does not want it, does He, *emi?*"—and Yeshua, from ingrained habit, turned to Miriam for his answer. Miriam said God did not want it.

"And He does not want cattle and sheep killed for Him either?"

"Did I not show you what Isaiah said?" Joseph asked.

"Yes, I remember: 'To what purpose is the multitude of your sacrifices unto me? saith the Lord.' Why then did Moses order these offerings?"

"Because men are sinful."

"But what is sin?" It was the question to which young Yeshua returned again and again, as though the answers that had satisfied before had ceased to be valid after further reflection.

"It is when people are wicked," Joseph explained. "When they rebel against the will of God, Moses told us, they are to expiate their transgressions by means of sacrifices which serve as symbols of repentance."

"But what fault is there in the lamb that we should offer it up

185

for our sins? And then, could not a rich man commit many sins because he has enough oxen and sheep to sacrifice, while a poor man, having no flock of his own, cannot pay for his sin?"

There was a smile on Miriam's face; Joseph too was richly delighted, and he sent Miriam a glance beaming with satisfaction.

"You have mastered me, *tinoki*," he said, almost playfully. "It is as you say; the rich man can sin plentifully because he has sheep and oxen enough for all manner of sacrifices—like our Reb Tudrus, for example, or the usurer Bar Kazin, of whom they say that when he kisses a man's face let the man look to his teeth—and count them afterward."

"Joseph!" Miriam broke in with mild reproach but without serious effort to repress a smile.

"Why not, Miriam? The children should know."

"There will be time enough to tell them when they are older," said Miriam. And turning again to her eldest, she asked: "You remember, *tinoki*, what *abba* and I told you about Adam's sin when the beast tore our lambkin?"

"Oh, yes, I remember," said Yeshua eagerly—"and the wolf and the lamb together."

"Well," Miriam continued, "till that day comes—the day of the holy Messiah who will remit the sin of Adam—until that day man must offer sacrifices from his stock to God." Then, taking Yeshua from her husband, she added: "Now, come with me, *tinoki*, and we shall look after the wheat. *Abba* must return to his work."

Not every day did Yeshua come home with questions of such weight on his mind. For these opening verses of Leviticus were taught only by way of a general introduction to the Torah. Once the law of sacrifices had been presented and elucidated to the children's satisfaction, which, on the whole, was not hard to come by, the curriculum proceeded to a systematic study of the Law of Moses in its proper sequence. Thus it was only a few days later that Yeshua came home deeply familiar with the facts attending the creation of the world. This had been new to him, unlike the story of the fall of man which had so often been discussed at home. One day the sky glowered over the man-killing deluge, and soon after everything was bright again, irradiated by the patriarchal grandeur of Father Abraham. Then again came stories

186

he had heard—the fettering of Isaac and the pre-eminence of Joseph among the sons of Jacob—and verses without number with which he had for long been well acquainted, though no one knew whence their knowledge had come to the young child.

CHAPTER VII

WHEN Jacob was old enough to accompany Yeshua to school, the family of Joseph had increased. Miriam had borne him two more sons, Simon and Jude; and little Shoshannah was a suckling babe. Mariama's pride in her sister's growing brood rose to new heights, and her energies expanded to take a full share of Miriam's increased duties.

As the two brothers grew older, it became clear how fundamental was the difference between Yeshua and Jacob. Where the elder was lively, volatile, insatiably curious, Jacob was staid and sober with the ways almost of an adult. Yeshua knew every neighbor for miles around and was known to them in turn. He felt at ease in every house and showed interest in every activity and occupation. More, he could name every domestic animal in the environs of his house, though as often as not the names were of his own invention. He was forever crawling under hedges and running across foreign fields to visit his good friends—who might be animal or human. For hours together he would sit up in a tree to find out what was going forward in a bird's nest he had lately discovered. Many times, following a prolongéd search, Miriam spied him in the upper branches where, with contained breath, Yeshua was watching a bird grooming or feeding her nestlings.

Jacob, on the other hand, rarely took a step that caution might not have dictated. He knew only one trail through the town and this led without dilly-dally to the synagogue. He stopped at no merchant's stall in the market, stroked no animal on his way, engaged no one in conversation. He plodded home from school with his eyes intent on where he was going and his lips endlessly repeating his verse for the day.

But the most telling difference between the brothers lay in this: that, while the elder could never ask questions enough, the younger could think of nothing to question. He accepted whatever he learnt at school as the incontestable Law of Moses which left no room for doubt. The word of the rabbi was infallible, and his own task was to learn the Torah by rote, to store it in his memory as you would fill a well, when your only care is to avoid leakage.

These differences in temperament could not fail to affect the attitude of all who knew the two boys. Thus Jacob soon became the favorite of his preceptors. The rabbi saw in him the ideal scholar who was never backward with his "amens" and who devoured hungrily whatever was spread on the Torah's table—not like his brother, who questioned and caviled and plumbed always beyond his depth. As for Cleophas, he never could say enough about Jacob's surpassing merits. It was little Jacob, his favorite nephew, who won from him an unreserved affection for Joseph's family. Cleophas came to love him like a child of his own and repeatedly set him up to Yeshua as an object lesson in meritorious deportment:

"Do you see now," he would say, "how your little brother does his prayers in the synagogue? His eyes are down and his attention so keen that he responds with every 'amen' in its proper place—not like you, who goggle about as if you did not know the earth from the sky."

"You say well, cousin Cleophas," put in Miriam. "Indeed, my son does not know heaven from earth when he prays."

"What do you mean, Miriam? Do you condone it? God put us down on earth and wants us to know our station as His creatures. Is it not written, 'the heavens are the Lord's, but the earth hath He given to the children of men'?"

"It depends on the worshipper," said Joseph from his corner.

Cleophas turned on him with pained surprise:

"And I thought a father's rod was to redress the mother's indulgence."

"Does not the Scripture speak of a father who pitieth his children?"

Young Jacob, however, was no stay-at-home. Often he accompanied Yeshua on long strolls through the fields, visiting sometimes the tanner—who instructed them in the secrets of his art, interspersed with snatches of Scriptural lore—and sometimes the Edomite incense planter. They never crossed the latter's threshold, it is true, but ambled about among his plants and herbs, learning which were poison and which could heal the sick.

Sometimes the boys strayed into the vineyards of the rich Talami bar Kazin, where they listened to the plaints of the men who were working off debts to the usurer, hearing time and again of the injury these men had suffered at Talami's hand. For some time the boys had known of the infamous system in which the poor pledged their lands to wealthy creditors. Joseph had been at pains to enlighten them on this point. If the children spoke with enthusiasm of the abundant harvest gathered in the vineyards of the rich Talami by hosts of laborers aching under the load of plenty, Joseph was sure to comment wryly:

"Yes, they work the tilth, and it is theirs, like the sweat that waters it; but the fruit is eaten by others."

Joseph's hatred of the rich was thus passed on to the children, and it fell in Jacob on particularly fruitful soil. Never again was he to free himself of his childhood impressions of human squalor, or forget for a day Joseph's teaching.

Nazareth was a hardworking town. The inhabitants, small artisans for the most part, took their finished goods over the northwestern hills to sell in the bazaars of Sepphoris. But before they had enough merchandise assembled to make the journey worth their while, they were usually forced to appeal to moneylenders for the cash with which to purchase raw materials, maintain their families, or pay the royal tribute. And not infrequently they pawned their finished goods for immediate sustenance, only to find themselves unable to redeem them later. And meanwhile, heaps of finished sandals, earthenware of all kinds, and piled-up bolts of cloth accumulated in the strongrooms of the moneylenders. The earthen pots chipped and broke, the wooden tools grew

189

wormy. The town wanted the goods, its men and women went hungry, went barefoot in winter, and the work of their hands, fashioned for human use, lay rotting in the usurer's hoard.

Sepphoris, capital of Galilee, was but a half day's journey as the donkey walks from Nazareth. The Nazarene craftsmen brought their goods to the metropolitan fairs which Sepphoris conducted almost every other day. Joseph, too, brought his wooden yokes, his plows, and household dishes, to the market town, since it attracted custom from the entire region—from the great sea to Genesaret.

While Miriam's mother lived the family had sold their surplus crops in the markets. But now that, God be praised, the household had almost doubled in number, no food could be spared for sale and Joseph's ass bore only the products of his shop.

Now, it was customary for a father in Israel to keep his son at his side during his peregrinations, so that he could instruct the child in the ways of its ancestors under all possible vicissitudes. Thus Joseph soon began to take Yeshua with him to Sepphoris, arguing over the protests of his wife—who preferred to have the boy at school—that life was the better schoolmaster.

It was in those marketplaces, where he stood with Joseph by their pile of wooden gear, that Yeshua became familiar with men of different extractions. Here, where Joseph led his donkey through the toll-gate, at the entrance of the town, Yeshua had his first encounter with grasping toll clerks. Here he became acquainted with the ways of the various overseers, bailiffs, guards, and watchdogs who patrolled the open markets and bazaars, nosing for untaxed merchandise or keeping the peace between buyer and dealer. He saw how tithes were extracted and paid; what farmers had their goods certified free and clear, what others saw their wares condemned or thrown under suspicion. He perceived further how the various sects in Israel kept aloof from one another, how some were ostracized to shield the rest from uncleanness.

For Sepphoris was a metropolis. Here, more vividly than before, Yeshua saw the immeasurable gulf that divided the rich from the poor. He gazed at gaudy overdecorated palaces, from whose protective shade the city mendicants were being driven by giant Ethiopian slaves. He marveled at the impenetrable walls of cypress trees, planted like palisades around vast private gardens, at the opulent dress of wealthy swaggerers, whose gold chains clinked about their necks while their lickspittles followed them behind.

At home the boy knew but one Gentile—the incense planter in whose garden he spent many hours. In Sepphoris he learned that their Nazarene neighbor was not the only Gentile upon the face of the earth. Here he saw the legionaries of Rome; with bodies of burnished metal and helmeted heads they cut through the market square, marching with disciplined precision. The panicky crowd sundered to clear their lane and the soldiers spanned the square with thumping tread, with clenched fists swinging, with glances more inflexible than speeding arrows, overturning whatever lay in their path of potter's ware or fruit—and not a murmur from the press of men that hugged the verges of the square.

Yeshua watched in silence with the rest. He knew these men to be of Caesar's cohorts who kept Israel under Edom's heel. He had already seen several Roman platoons march through Nazareth and he knew that they sowed panic wherever they went.

"*Abba,* look!"

"What, *tinoki?*"

"Look at those people, who are they?"

Joseph glanced in the direction of the boy's pointing finger and saw a file of chained Canaanite slaves, driven by men with scourges in their hands. Before them walked a stately group of Sidonian merchants, wrapped in expensive purple, their plaited beards rich with the gloss of oil. The slaves, like pack animals, bore immense bales of raw wool on their naked spines. And from time to time their guards let fly at them with the leaden-tipped scourges—not in punishment, but as a routine measure to maintain the pace.

"Yes . . . ," said Joseph, his tongue lingering on the hiss of the word. "These, my boy, are Sidonian slaves. Since the Sidonians are shrewd and thrifty men, they employ slaves to carry the raw wool, which they buy in this market, home to their native city. They will not use asses and mules as our kind do, because human slaves come cheaper and are known to thrive on less fodder than common beasts of burden."

The boy watched pityingly as the sordid caravan drew past. The like of this he had not seen in Nazareth. The men who labored in the fields of his home town were hired hands or else defaulting debtors who had to work off obligations to their creditors. And where some rich citizen did keep a slave, it was as a tutor for his sons, an extra servant for his household, a manager for his affairs, a flute player to make table music, or a Jack-of-all-trades for whatever business might come to hand. Of Jewish slaves there were certainly none in Nazareth, chiefly because their possession burdened the owner with no end of legal obligations. It was in Sepphoris, then, that Yeshua had his first glimpse of man's inhumanity as slaveholder and slave.

"Who are these people?" he asked Joseph after a lengthy pause.

"You mean those slaves? I told you; the Sidonians buy them in their slave marts to use as beasts of burden."

"But how do they find these people to make into slaves?"

Joseph told him how they were supplied by the victorious armies of Rome which kept so many nations in subjection. If a people, country, or city revolted, he explained, Rome sent its legions to quell the mutiny in blood, killing the feeble and selling the strong for profit. Finally, the Sidonians followed the Roman camps to buy the slaves fresh from the harvest. The account gave Yeshua to think for several minutes before he spoke again.

"*Abba,*" he asked, "they do this because the human heart is evil and they know no better?"

Joseph nodded and let the boy proceed.

"*Abba,* will God ever change the hearts of men?"

"Surely he will, my son. Did He not say through His Prophet —'A new spirit will I kindle in their hearts'?"

"But when shall this be?"

"When the King-Messiah appears in our midst. For that is the day of our hope, even as the Prophet said: 'And the Gentiles shall follow Thy light.'"

With the dawn of his consciousness, the boy Yeshua had begun to feel the nearness of God. No doubt, his mother was in part responsible; she had so often told him that God would hear his prayers, that he stood in some special relation to the heavenly Father which was shared by no other child. Joseph, now and again, passed similar hints. Not that he was ever told outright of his miraculous conception, for he continued to look on Joseph as his natural father; was he not everywhere called Yeshua ben Joseph? And yet he had an obscure conviction that Joseph was not his father as he was the father of Jacob and the others. Something had betrayed itself in Joseph's attitude, which was never entirely without restraint. Then again Yeshua had caught some rumor of his premature conception, although it was not clear whether he had actually heard it stated or had merely read intuitively in the looks of his elders. And he had noted, furthermore, that Aunt Mariama always called him Miriam's son, as though to the exclusion of his father. No such title was ever given his small brothers.

And then he often heard his mother speak of a man-child, one Jochanan, who was born at the same time as he, though in a distant place, and that this other child's birth had some obscure relation to his own. His mother showed a vast concern for this other child's fate, as did his father, too.

It had lately come to Joseph's knowledge that the priest Zachariah and his wife Elisheva both had died in their old age. At once Miriam and Joseph resolved to journey to the Wilderness of Judah whence they would fetch the orphaned child to raise with their own. But before they could make ready there appeared a strolling beggar, who stopped at Miriam's door and called for the boy Yeshua. He led him into the open field and there spoke to Yeshua, saying:

"Go tell your mother that she is not to trouble herself about the orphan. Zachariah's son has been taken by them who were appointed for his guardians; with them he abides in the desert, preparing for the task which has been laid on him."

And when Yeshua repeated these words to his mother, Miriam exclaimed:

"It cannot be but Elijah the Prophet has brought you these tidings."

And a short while later they received confirmation that the

193

orphan boy had been taken in by the Essenes. Then Miriam knew that God's design was working itself out.

The boy Yeshua was not surprised at the beggar's sudden appearance. He had been brought up to believe that God's spirit resided among lowly strangers, and that to make such men guests in the house was to play host to God Himself. He therefore courted their company and listened avidly to their discourse. He heard them speak of distant lands through which they had wandered, of foreign peoples and outlandish customs. Some of these wanderers, gaunt and ragged though they were, had once sat at the feet of the rabbis and were conversant with the Law. And from them Yeshua learned interpretations of Scripture and many verses culled from Prophets and Psalms. And like his mother he catered to their needs with joyfulness of heart as though he were engaged in sacred service.

It was an exceptional summer. Each year, when the Khamseen ushered in the dry season, there was a marked shortage of water, though it was rarely such as to imperil the lives of beasts and plants. For the latter rains, which came at intervals beween midwinter and early spring, were usually sufficient to fill the cisterns and soak the ground with an enduring moisture that could outlast the harvest. But this year the showers had been scant. The damp was felt in the topsoil only; it did not seep to the roots of the vines and the fruit-trees; it barely slaked the surface furrows of the fields and left the reservoirs half empty. To make matters worse, the hot dust of the Khamseen had come sooner than was commonly expected. To be sure, the clouds had appeared as usual in early spring, but instead of discharging the fresh water of the latter rains, they brought a shower of hot parching desert sand. Its minute grains clogged the pores, lined the eyelids, settled on tongue and throat. Men and beasts breathed with heavy effort and the young shoots of spring lay wilting over sapped, suffocating roots. Worse still, the dew which commonly maintained plant life throughout the summer—this year it failed. The short nights proved as barren as the day. And over all hung the impenetrable sky, its unflecked blue boastful of heat and sterility.

From the first days of spring Miriam required her husband's

194

help in drawing water from the well. Her little flock refused the murky liquid in the cistern. And even this, dust- and insect-laden though it was, soon gave out, so that it was insufficient even for the vegetable garden which was the household's sustenance. Miriam now needed well water not for her family and stock alone, but also for her blighted plants.

Soon, however, the press of water-drawers at the well became so dense that it was all one could do, after hours of patient waiting under the blinding sun, to fetch enough for the animals at home; little indeed could be spared for the torrid ground. And far and wide the animals of the poor lay languishing where they had fallen, their tongues cracking for want of water.

Well before their season the grapevines were ready for harvest. Again Cleophas and Mariama moved into Joseph's house to take their share of the labor. Cleophas was out of sorts; the grapes he cut down were obviously scorched by sand and sun, and looked as though they had been harvested and dried a month before. Their pips were full and large, but their skins stringy as a miser's heart and their juice niggardly.

And yet wine was a crying necessity. It was drunk with every meal, drunk to save precious water. It supplied essential vinegar, and the dried grapes, when baked with dough, made a staple food throughout the year.

Cleophas, his massive head let down to show a bald red pate, keeping a surly silence for hours on end, helped Joseph rid the cistern of the sediment left there by the exhausted water. Into the clean reservoir the men placed their harvested bunches of grapes and, having washed their feet, entered the hollow to stamp out the juice.

The sisters watched from a distance. They were squatting, with the children, in the doorway of the house, speaking of the one topic which obsessed all minds, and all flesh and all grass, throughout the countryside: the drought. Miriam's few sheep and solitary ass lay near the stalls, as dead and still as the leaves of the fig-trees nearby—too weary even to rise or roll into the shade.

"Our figs, this year, will be as dry and lean as our grapes," said Mariama, looking at the trees. "It will hardly pay to take them down."

Miriam nodded and said: "And look at the animals; they do not even bleat for water any more. Today I gave them all the water I could fetch from the well. They would not drink it, it was so thick and slimy with mud."

"Last night our donkey sent up such a cry he roused all the neighbors."

"That is his way of praying," Miriam said, smiling bitterly. "Do you know if anything is being done by the elders?"

Mariama shrugged briefly.

"They have proclaimed a universal fast."

"But it has done no good. And what more?"

"They sent a special messenger to a rabbin in Sepphoris, imploring him also to ask for rain. The rabbin, they say, is a great miracle worker, being a righteous man. Well, he did pray, but to what purpose? Now the rabbin says that there can be no rain without a miracle, seeing that we are well in the dry season and, says he, this generation is not worthy of a miracle."

"Dear God," said Miriam, "and it is so long before the early rains. I am sure the rabbin is right and we are not worthy in this generation, but if the great ones have sinned, why should the animals and the little children suffer so?"

Yeshua had been listening intently. He, too, was aware of the dry anguish about him, had seen the torment wrought by thirst in men and animals, and in the very earth at his feet. He had seen his mother—after sunset and again at dawn—spreading her hands and calling on God to bring rain to His creatures. He had seen the sick rage of thirst in her eyes, as he had seen it in every lamb of the flock. And still the sky was sealed, and the Lord turned a deaf ear to human prayers and the cries of the beasts, to the wail of the earth and the tears of his mother. All this because men were sinful. And little Yeshua suddenly burst into tears.

Miriam later found him alone in the field. He was on his knees, sobbing, his hands covering his face.

"Why do you cry, *tinoki?*" she exclaimed in alarm.

"Because God will not forgive man's sin and withholds rain from His creatures."

"Why don't you pray to Him?"

"How, *emi?*"

196

"Come, I will show you, *tinoki*." Miriam took her child by the hand and brought him to the hilltop. "Tell your Father in heaven what is in your heart, what your eyes have seen, what your ears have heard. To your prayers God will listen."

As Yeshua knelt down and raised his hands to heaven, Miriam turned quickly away. But as she descended the hill, she heard the beginning of his prayer.

Miriam had not reached her door when she heard a low roll of thunder in the distance. Little knots of cloudlets suddenly dappled the sky. They loosened, stretched themselves like men waking, and oozed out dark masses of cloud until, in a little while, they hung overhead like bloated skins of opaque water. And then, as though some unseen hand had slashed the skins, water—water began streaming from the sky.

"Heaven be praised! Rain in the midst of Tamuz! The autumn rains in mid-summer! The rains! The rains!" cried Joseph and Cleophas, scampering out of the winepress to arrive thoroughly doused under their roof.

Indoors, the women greeted them with radiant faces, and Mari-ama exclaimed:

"Surely the Lord has inclined his ear to the rabbin of Sepphoris and his petition!"

Yeshua, breathless, rushed in the door and to his mother's arms. "*Emi, emi,*" he cried. "God has sent the rain!"

Cleophas plumped down in the corner and, biting his lips, said he feared the wine would become watery.

"As to that," Joseph replied, "you may rest your fears. The rain will only wash the grapes. The juice has not yet issued."

CHAPTER VIII

THERE came a day when Yeshua was face to face with sin. Now a sturdy lad of eleven, he had become a scholar in the higher grades, learning to interpret the Law according to the various rabbinical traditions, which is to say, the oral law, the innumerable unwritten addenda to the Mosaic code, transmitted through the generations by word of mouth alone.

He was on his way to the synagogue soon after dawn, Jacob, his younger brother, walking at his side. Ahead of him there was a sudden tumult, and then a horde of legionaries burst into the street, their broadswords flashing in the sun, their cries of battle mingling with the grueling wail of a mob horror-driven. Pots and pitchers were overtoppled and crushed underfoot, wines and oils poured down the streets, doors of houses caved in under iron-soled boots, and men and women stampeded through the town in a wild panic, leaving here and there a corpse blocking the road.

Yeshua and his brother crouched against a wall, but were spied by a desert Arab in a Roman harness. His sword followed his drugged eyes. He towered over the two children with the blade upraised, when, out of the universal uproar, a woman's piercing howl suddenly struck at his ear and he let go to run off madly in pursuit of the crowd. A few moments later Yeshua and Jacob found themselves breathless and bewildered in the court of their aunt Mariama's house. And at once Cleophas and Mariama took hold of the children and, grabbing up hastily some bundles of food and belongings, set out by back ways for the outskirts of the town where, with Joseph and Miriam, they thought to come unnoticed through the terror.

Here, outside the town, the pillaging bands had not passed, though there could be no surety that the Roman legionaries who were streaming in from all directions, would not find them out. The sisters, therefore, took the children and hurried them into the open fields whose many gullies and ditches offered a fair measure of security. Joseph and Cleophas remained on the lookout in front of their house.

Towards evening the cries of Nazareth were dying down. Nafchi's eldest boy returned from a daredevil reconnaissance with the news that the Romans had moved on in a northwesterly direction, bound for Sepphoris.

The sisters and the children slipped back into the house, and the entire family sat down to an uncertain wait in the darkness, fearing still to light the lamps. And then, looking out into the night, they saw the vermilion glow of fire staining the sky over Sepphoris. Far to the north the clouds flared red like flocks of sheep caught in a forest fire.

"Sepphoris is burning," someone said.

"And every village in the neighborhood."

"A city and a mother in Israel is perishing in flames," Joseph said.

Miriam called her children and huddled them together in the curtained chamber to spare them the sight of the holocaust. Yeshua alone refused to have his eyes shut; he remained sitting silently in the doorway of the house, his head lying flat on his drawn-up knees, his eyes watching the glare of the fire.

The death of Herod the Wicked had plunged all Israel into turmoil and anarchy. No longer would the nation endure the monstrous government of the Herodian dynasty, whether it were headed by Archelaus, the dead king's son and nominee, or by his brother Antipas, the young pretender whom Shulamith, Herod's sister, tried to foist upon the vacant throne. Both men, at this moment, abode in Rome, each with his company of flunkeys and rhetoricians, waiting to present his royal claim before Augustus Caesar.

Archelaus had not carried out his father's order for the execution of all prominent rabbis and teachers on the day of his death. He had openly crossed his aunt Shulamith who had had these men arrested. Yet he failed to win the people's confidence when he refused to answer their clamor for the punishment of Herod's henchmen and advisers. The people's bitterness over the wilful slaughter of the men who had helped to rip the Roman eagle from the Temple gates—and not least over the burning of the two celebrated rabbis, Judah ben Sarifai and Mattathias ben Mar-

199

galot, the intrepid leaders of that great revolt—this bitterness became so unendurable that before long Jerusalem broke out in a new mutiny against the heir of the old king and his protectors, the hated Roman garrison in the Antonia.

While Archelaus and his champion, the grammarian Nicolaus, on the one hand, and his brother Antipas with his supporters on the other, were in Rome soliciting the support of influential men to line their enterprise, Judaea was rocked by a succession of insurrectionary outbursts. Transjordania seethed with revolt. In the north, Judas the Galilean called for open war against Rome. Jerusalem itself was occupied by rebel forces, and Caesar's procurator, Sabinus, who had entered the Judaean capital at the head of his troops to quell the insurrection, was trapped, with his legion, in the Antonia fortress. In Jericho a liberated slave of Herod's household, one Simeon by name, wrapped himself in the royal mantle and, amid the plaudits of the people, proclaimed himself king. His first sovereign act was to plunder Herod's palace and put it to the torch.

There were few Jewish towns or cities where the flag of revolt was not unfurled. Highways became unsafe for peaceful travel and the rich trembled for their lands and chattels.

Galilee went with the rest of Israel. Some Galileans, who lived only from one disturbance to the next, packed themselves off to Jerusalem to help the men of Judaea lay siege to Caesar's procurator in the Roman citadel. In Galilee proper the dreaded Judas had long surrounded himself with men of unquiet spirit, victims of oppression and rapacity who waited, sword in hand, for the day of their vengeance. For years Judas had lain low in the hills, arming his camps and drilling them for action. In the end, deeming himself at full strength, he came down on Sepphoris, overpowered its garrison, occupied its palace, raided its arsenal and exchequer, and declared himself master of the city.

Nor was his seizure of Sepphoris an isolated act, for what he did in Galilee was emulated by every rebel chieftain in the provinces. Soon every regal residence was topped by columns of ascending smoke, proclaiming far and wide the wrath of the incendiaries.

In the end Quintilius Varus, the ruthless Governor of Syria, called out the two legions stationed at Antioch, mobilized every military force obtainable in the surrounding lands, and marched south to raise the siege of the Antonia garrison. With him rode a company of German horse, provided by the city of Beyruth, and a loose horde of Arab ruffians under Roman command, placed at his disposal by Aretus Silius, King of Arabia Petra. Varus chose the port of Acco for his point of assembly as being the Roman stronghold nearest Galilee. From there his cohorts marched on Sepphoris.

Silius of Arabia and the deceased Herod had long been rivals for the Caesar's favor, each hoping to enlarge his domains at the expense of the other by leaning on Roman support. The Arab king bore a bitter hatred for his Idumaean competitor and, by an unreasoning transference, for Herod's empire and people. His military forces, if such they could be called, consisted of mere desert riff-raff, without the discipline and training that distinguished the legions of Rome. Their native brutality had never known a curb, having met with no better example than the corrupting influence of resident Roman officials. It was this savage rabble which Roman power now unleashed against the towns and hamlets of revolted Galilee; and, with them, auxiliary units of German cavalry, specially trained for punitive expeditions, that is to say, for slaughter multiplied, for carnage and rapine and the cremation of every city in their course.

And so it came to pass that, in their man-murdering zeal, a small band of Arab footsoldiers and Teutonic horsemen lost the main highway between Acco and Sepphoris and, for the space of a few hours, raged tempest-like through quiet Nazareth on that memorable day when the boy Yeshua met with them on his way to school.

Now, after nightfall, the Nazarenes crept back to their town; the dead were gathered and silently interred, without accompaniment of pipers and wailing women, without even due elegies, for the danger was not past and every moment might bring a new invasion to do with Nazareth as had been done with other towns in the environs of the capital. Through the following day the townsfolk sat brooding in their homes or congregated in the synagogue, where the rabbi and other elders of the town were exhorting the people to prayer and repentance and deeds of right-eousness. The artisans put away their tools, the merchants their commerce. Children stayed away from school and the women shunned the market. And when the sun had downed again, the Nazarenes climbed on their roofs, each man the sentry of his house. The northern sky had retained its hue of hellfire; it was to show lingering red for eight long nights together.

By degrees the Nazarenes recovered their senses. Scouts were dispatched in the direction of Sepphoris to ascertain the fate of their stricken brethren in Israel. The scouts returned with Job's tidings; the road to Sepphoris was lined with shambled villages; Nazareth alone and a handful of hamlets had been spared an-nihilation. The populations that had escaped the carnage, the scouts reported, were hiding in hole and corner, in arid mountain gorges and ravines, some dying and some already dead of hunger and thirst. And their bodies were carrion for birds of prey. Verily, the ire of God had poured over Sepphoris, for she was no more among the cities of Galilee. A vast smoking funeral pyre stood for its stately palaces and mansions, its houses of learning and houses of prayer. The homes of its inhabitants were plundered naked. Such goods as had not been removed lay charred and flindered in a laystall of ashes. The people of Sepphoris had received judgment, who should die by the sword and who by hanging, who should be sold for a slave and who should go free. And carcasses of young and old littered the scorched lanes of the city and there was none to gather them up. And coveys of vultures converged on Sepphoris from far and wide. And outside the town —forests of crosses, hung with human bodies transfixed and still, some that had undergone the crurifragium, or breaking of the legs, and some whose hearts had mercifully burst before the final torment. And the rest of the people, the whole and the sound, the comeliest of the women and the children that were without blem-ish of body, were herded together with gyved hands to be con-veyed to the slave marts of Tyre and Sidon.

Such was the report of the scouts, and every soul in Nazareth sent up a keen of woe. For there was none in Nazareth but had some kinsman in the capital. And all the people made ready to bring food and succor to the stricken remnant of Sepphoris.

Every ass was laden with sacks of grain and kids of wine and jars of oil and honey. And some brought out bundles of clothing and medicinal herbs and salves for the relief of the wounded.

Joseph and Cleophas, too, loaded their ass with anything that came to hand, ready to join their brother citizens in the saving of the Sepphorite exiles. Only the women were to stay behind to look after the household and children, for the journey was known to be perilous. The dignitaries of the town were even now negotiating with the government to admit relief measures for the sufferers. Nevertheless there was the danger that rescue caravans would fall into the hands of pillaging soldiers.

Yeshua demanded to go with his father. He was old enough, he argued, to share the risk of the men. And Joseph, who was never slow to champion the boy's independence, consented to take him along, in defiance of danger. He maintained that Yeshua was now adult enough to witness the sorrows of Israel and the infamy of mankind. But at that Miriam declared that she would not let the boy go without her. "Wherever my child is in danger, there shall I be in danger," she said. And thus she, too, went with the caravan.

They passed no major settlements on their way, only small villages whose rubbled heaps marked a trail of destruction. Most of them were laid in ashes and black vultures wheeled tirelessly overhead. Nazarene Jews who had gone ahead of the main body were already busying themselves with the dead—to whose location they were surely guided by the birds—and giving them a hasty burial.

Gradually, as they approached their former capital, the air grew acrid with smoke and a breath of wind-borne ashes crept into their throats. They trekked on farther and passed a column of bound prisoners, guarded by Roman soldiers who were marching them to the sea for shipment to the slave-trading ports of the Gentiles. Joseph's family and their companions halted by the roadside and, with fruit and breadbaskets on their arms, fed provisions to the lamentable train. These captives were all healthy, robust men and girls and women with small children. The men were of mature years, their strong backs arched more or less acutely, depending on the length of the chains that joined their necks and ankles. Some had had most of their clothing ripped away so that Yeshua's eyes involuntarily followed the trickle of sweat down their bared bodies. Others wore costly ill-assorted garments snatched in a moment of panic. Some wore sandals; others were barefoot. None was old, ailing, or wounded; all had been picked with a slaver's discernment. They marched with hands manacled over arched backs, each man tied to his fellow so that they had to be fed out of their helpers' hands. To this the centurion in command made no objection; it was, after all, highly desirable that the slaves be delivered in good form and without telltale signs of undernourishment.

The women were allowed more liberty. Their hands were left free to hold and soothe the squalling infants in their arms. Only their ankles were bound. They, too, were the pick of Sepphorite womanhood, healthy and young and with that firmness of flesh that commanded high prices in Tyre and Sidon. A brood of children, some in arms, others on foot, surrounded almost every one of them. Here and there a pregnant woman might be seen. And all of them had loosened their dark hair to cover what they could of their nakedness.

Youths and girls brought up the rear—among them children old enough to fend for themselves, children of seven or eight who had come unscathed and unblemished through the fire. They were not fettered, and the legionaries who drove them kept them walking in close formation.

Miriam stood with her son by the roadside, watching in silence with the other Nazarenes as the prisoners went by. The little food and drink they had brought had long run out. Joseph and Cleophas had run ahead of the procession where prisoners from an earlier batch had staggered to a fall and been abandoned. Some of these still had life, and the two brothers-in-law moved them swiftly into the fields lest they be crushed by the oncoming train.

Mother and son were holding to one another, silently watching, and Miriam thought of Rachel to whose tomb she had pilgrimed on her way to Bethlehem. Even so had Nebuzaradan driven the Jews into their Babylonian exile. And even as she herself wept, so had Rachel wept over her children—"and would not be comforted." And as she watched, Miriam felt the constriction of every mother's heart that dragged her child along, sometimes by force, fearing to leave it behind lest it become carrion fodder for those famished birds whose croak followed the cortege. She felt the pain of every mother wincing when the soldier's whip lighted on the head of her child. And then Miriam became suddenly aware of the grief of her own child which she could feel like scalding lava pouring from Yeshua's heart. Yeshua did not weep; he was asking no questions; he only stood and watched. His eyes were streaked and bloodshot, looking red and hot like gaping wounds. He said nothing, but his eyes drank deep of the misery before his sight.

The procession passed. Cleophas and Joseph returned, weary and sore, their faces dark with pain and helpless anger, and they, like the others, held their tongues. Joseph finally made to go home, to follow the rest of the Nazarenes. There was nothing more to be done, he muttered almost inaudibly, their small store of provender and rubbing oil being long spent. But Miriam would not have it. They must, she said, at least attempt to reach the city; someone might be about who needed help. Gruffly, Joseph consented and, grabbing the ass by the halter, led his party toward the smoking ruins of Sepphoris.

Soon they drew near to the outer gate, where there was a bend in the road. And when they had turned it they were greeted by a vision of stark horror: two rows of crosses astride the road, each made of intersecting timbers that had the nakedness of recent cutting. And each rood bore the impaled body of a dying man, his belly writhing, his veins swelling and cracking in the heat of thirst, his wounds festering under the steady sun. Joseph and Miriam accelerated their pace to put the crosses behind them, but these stretched in endless succession deep into the heart of what had been the city. And Yeshua would not be hurried. He halted to stare briefly at every crucified Jew. Joseph's repeated calls availed nothing, and in the end the boy stopped before one of the crosses and refused to move altogether, for it seemed to him that it bore a familiar figure. Its powerful bald-pated head had fallen across the hairy chest. And the massive bulk of its body so weighted the beams of the cross that it seemed any moment likely to collapse.

"Emi, emi, it is our Nafchi!" the boy shrieked suddenly.

Miriam threw a fleeting glance at the convulsing body and at once seized her son's head to press it against her breast and shut out further agonies.

"Let him see, Miriam," said Joseph softly. "He must see all and know."

"'No, no, there is time yet! He is too young to see!"—and Miriam shuddered and cowered closer over the head of her child.

There was no talk any more of entering the town. All ingress was barred by a thickening forest of crosses, by knolls of mounting rubble, smouldering like huge braziers of live coal, their crests strewn with the charred corpses of animals and men. And amid the desolation Roman and Arab loiterers were sifting the ashes for precious stones and baubles of gold.

Miriam turned her back on the town, still holding Yeshua's head against her body. Joseph and Cleophas followed without speaking.

CHAPTER IX

No one had disciplined Yeshua to the love of God; it sprang unprompted from his innermost being. God could be responsible for no injustice. He was the end of fulfillment and the end of perfection. And whenever Yeshua saw evil practiced, he felt the sting of it in his own soul. For he saw it not only as a crime against fellow men, but as an affront to his heavenly Father. It seemed to him that whatever sorrow man sustained at the hand of sin, God suffered infinitely more; and so he grieved at sin as a son grieves over an indignity offered to his father. And if at such times he felt that something stood between him and his Father in heaven, he wept through the night, like a child forsaken by its parent.

Since his return from Sepphoris, Yeshua had turned inward, as though he lived only in the recesses of his own mind. He developed a brooding taciturnity in marked contrast to his former self. In vain his parents tried to console him. To their pleas and efforts at distraction he opposed an unremitting silence. Many weeks were to pass before Joseph succeeded in lifting the gloom which had fallen over the boy's spirit.

Yeshua and he were walking together in the fields and, when they had climbed one of the hills that overlooked their town, Joseph began:

"Come and see, Yeshua, how great is God's world. That dark mass to the east is Mount Tabor, beyond which lie the cities of the Gentiles. And beyond these to the south spread other lands where the dark sons of Ham have their habitations. And to the north lies the great chain of the snow mountains of Hermon, and beyond them the lands of the peoples of Syria. And toward sunset our own hills descend to the great sea at whose shore, beyond Mount Carmel, sit other Gentiles, those of Tyre and Sidon. And on the far side of the great sea lies Rome and her Empire. Thus are the nations spread over all God's earth and we among them are as an islet set in a Gentile sea.

"Wherever you may turn, there will you find Gentiles who worship the work of their hands, for they make images of silver and leaden idols and fetishes whittled in wood or chiseled of stone, and some burn their small children to the demon Moloch and commit such beastly misuse on their bodies as may not be spoken of without shame. And they foul themselves with all manner of unclean things and have not God in their hearts to teach and to tell them what is good and what is evil, and they have not the Torah to instruct them what may and what may not be done; nor have they, as we do, the example of the Patriarchs with whom God closed an everlasting covenant; and they have no Messiah to await, no Redeemer to change the order of this world and bring peace to all men.

"And since they do not know that there is retribution in the world to come, why then should they not kill and burn, and murder the old and sell the young for slaves? Were they taught to do otherwise? Were they given a Torah as Israel was? Their gods bid them do evil; their misdeeds are perpetrated as by command. And, Yeshua, they are better than their gods, for their gods require them to burn their children on the altar, and to pollute their womenfolk, and yet there are many who do no such thing."

"And why does not God show them mercy?" Yeshua asked. "Are they not also His creatures?"

"Yes, my son, you ask well. Surely they are God's creatures. Does not God say the earth and all the life therein is His? And did not God spread the sky over all men's heads? And, seeing that God has mercy for the least of His creatures, shall He have less for men, the choice of His creation? But God desires that man return unto Him, and He waits for all the world to come to Mount Zion to follow His ways, even as the sweet singer of Israel has sung: 'God looked down from heaven upon the children of men, to see if there were any that did understand, that did seek God.' Mark well, Yeshua, God looked down from heaven upon the children of men, not on those of Israel alone.

"Israel is but His first-born son to whom He has entrusted the Torah. He has chosen Israel to be His sacred congregation, to nurse within itself the will of God, because the fathers of Israel were the first to know their maker and submit to His purpose.

"Israel was chosen from amongst all the nations to keep aglow the light of God unto the day of fulfillment. And whenever His chosen people, His congregation of saints which was to have been a light to the nations, falls away from its Creator and follows the corrupt ways of the Gentiles, then sends the Lord a scourge to smite them. And He chastens them at the hands of the Gentiles to put them in mind of Abraham's covenant. For the Lord fears lest His vineyard, which He planted in the desert of this world, be wasted by the sands of iniquity, to go down with the Gentiles together."

"Are the Jews alone guilty of sin, then?" Yeshua asked. "Are not the Gentiles more sinful by far?"

"The Jews took upon themselves the yoke of the heavenly kingdom; more is expected of them because they have the Torah and Abraham's covenant. The Gentiles have shouldered no such obligations. And greater might resides with them; they have the swords in larger number. And they who resort to power are judged according to their power, for the Lord has said, 'Not by might nor by power, but by My spirit alone.' We shall not subdue

208

the Gentiles by force. Nor are we to hope for the death of their evil-doers, as the Sepphorites mistook to do, but rather for their enlightenment, so that the people that walk in darkness may see the light of the Lord. Our hope should be that God send His Messiah in our time, when all the world shall congregate about the hill of Zion—as you have learned in the book of the Prophet."

Yeshua nodded and began softly to repeat Isaiah's words— "They shall not hurt nor destroy in all my holy mountains; for the earth shall be full of the knowledge of the Lord. And in that day there shall be a root of Jesse, which shall stand for an ensign of the people; to it shall the Gentiles seek . . ."

"Yes, Yeshua," Joseph resumed, "only then will Israel be secure. Not when the Gentiles are destroyed, but when they are ready to receive the light which Israel has kept burning for them through the long night. For by the iniquity of the world all nations suffer, Israel with the rest. And remember, Yeshua, the scourger is as much to be pitied as his victim. Do you think the Gentile is happy and content in his office as the scourge of Israel? No, he, too, in his inward heart longs for deliverance."

Yeshua looked into Joseph's face and, for the first time in many days, he smiled.

"*Abba,*" he said, "you have comforted me."

The boy Yeshua, both at school and at home, was invariably found to dominate his immediate company. What the other boys found irresistible in him was an unquestionable, absolute sincerity. And Yeshua asserted his domination with a light hand, like a born prince—not by any display of superior scholarship, but by a natural authority of character which radiated from his least action or remark.

His fellow students naturally attached themselves to him, and when Yeshua strolled home across the market square with his followers behind, the shopkeepers and artisans looked up after him and said, not unkindly, "Behold the rabbi with his trooping disciples!"

Yeshua was a good student. But, though this might have endeared him to his preceptors, it could never have won him the regard of his playmates. And for that matter, the school could

209

point to several scholars—all of his own age—who were generally reckoned to be both more learned and more astute than he. Thus one might name the young Sakkai bar Zadok, a dyer's son, whose agile brain was everybody's admiration, and who emerged the victor of every mock trial staged by the students.

For the old children's games of nuptials and funerals had been long outgrown. The boys of the higher grades, all learners of the oral Law, found their diversion in mock trials to which they brought all the penetrating sagacity of scholastic *pilpul,* as taught during school hours. They would choose one of their number to act as judge, and he, after hearing the case—usually an involved contrivance of improbabilities—handed down a sentence framed in the spirit of the scribes and Pharisees. Not infrequently the sentence passed was of such astuteness that it was reported to the rabbi, who, on occasions, had been known to pass it on to Jerusalem. The elders, therefore, encouraged the game, seeing it as a welcome means for whetting a child's intellect and fortifying him in the knowledge of the Law.

Young Yeshua showed no ambition to excel in the game. The truth was that he had little relish for the oral Law with its labyrinthine technicalities. And when his friends challenged him to take part in the mock trials, he answered with finality, "I don't like to pass judgment on people."

And there was another game—conundrums. A rhyme was propounded, blindly or ambiguously worded, and had to be unriddled. Skill at this game was a touchstone of knowledge, just as the trials were a test of wits. Whoever distinguished himself at the trials was dubbed "sharp"; the riddling champions became "the erudite."

Yeshua proved to be neither the one nor the other. His skill was rather in spinning yarns and parables. If there was anything he wanted to explain, he at once improvised some pointed story, for which his fellows named him "the parable boy."

The other children enjoyed his inventions, which enabled Yeshua to hold his own with "sharp" wits like little Sakkai bar Zadok, who was credited with having tricked a confession from a criminal by a ruse so artful that the rabbi, hearing of the case, predicted for the boy a glorious future as a prosecutor. In fact, the children preferred Yeshua's parables to others' brilliance at solving riddles or finding counterparts for every numerical value in the alphabet, as: *aleph* is one, which stands for the Lord of Creation; *beth*—two, stands for the tablets of the Law; *gimel*—for the three Patriarchs; *daleth*—for the four Matriarchs; *he*—for the Pentateuch; and so forth.

Yeshua lived in the world of the Prophets. He did not shine in the other studies, some of which called for great keenness and subtlety, involving as they did complex calculations concerning measures and crops. Nor was he much taken with interpretations of the Law, no matter how ingenious they might appear to others. His affinity was with the Prophets, whom he interpreted according to his own judgment.

In Yeshua's grade they were studying the Book of Jeremiah. They had come to the passage where the Prophet comforts his people and, in the face of the direst peril, foretells a future of radiance and joy. No man could more cruelly damn and execrate his people—and no one knew better how to console. The majestic mourner of Israel was also the sweetest minstrel of Israel's hope. Even now he had brought his fiery scourge down on their cowering backs, adding the Prophet's lash to the enemy's sword, as though he gloried in his nation's wounds and had sworn to unscab their sores that they might never heal—but all at once he changes pitch and sings again of forgiveness to make the heart burst with hope. No man expressed more intimately his nearness to God than this Prophet of wrath and lamentation. Never once did he utter a plaint for his own torments, which were the wages of his exhortations. Not a drop of his personal bitterness stained the cup of comfort which he held out to his people. The spittle in his face was forgotten, his bruised body covered over, his prisoner's ditch consigned to oblivion. From the mouth of Rachel he let pour an undying lament for his people, a mother's lament for her sons. And the voice of God itself he invoked to restrain Rachel's tears with assurance of love and forgiveness. And, finally, he stirred the deepest longing of his people till the end of time, when, like a messenger of love, he delivered the mystery of Israel's marriage with the Lord: "Behold, the days come, saith the Lord, that I will make a new covenant with the house of Israel and with the house of Judah. Not according to the covenant with their fathers in the day that I took them by the hand to bring them out of the land of Egypt; which My covenant they brake, although I was an husband unto them, saith the Lord. But this shall be the covenant that I will make with the house of Israel. After these days, saith the Lord, I will put My Law in their inward parts, and write it in their hearts; and will be their God, and they shall be My people. And they shall teach no more every man his neighbor, and every man his brother, saying, Know the Lord; for they shall all know Me, from the least of them unto the greatest of them, saith the Lord; for I will forgive their iniquity, and I will remember their sin no more."

By these words Yeshua was so deeply stirred that he could not hold back his tears while he recited them in class. There was laughter among some of the boys; others wept with him. All felt moved by the Prophet's compassion, and even those who pretended to laugh did so with forced bravado as if to show their manly self-possession.

After class Yeshua sat down in the court of the synagogue and, with his friends about him, interpreted the words of the Prophet:

"Come and see," he began, using the formal exordium of the preachers, "to what may this thing be likened? It may be likened to the rosebush in my mother's garden. This rosebush has been long with us, for it is very old. My grandfather brought it from the Plain of Sharon and planted it in our garden. Now, my mother loves this rosebush dearly, for she remembers when it blossomed with fair flowers in the days when she was yet a child, and on the day of her betrothal, when she wore a garland of its roses on her head. For many years my mother tended it, and showed it to her friends, saying, 'This is my rosebush from Sharon's plain.'

"And now this same rosebush is run to scrub. The main stem is almost withered away, its branches carry many thorns but bear few flowers. And every time my mother mulches its roots, or waters it, or trims its branches of dead growth, the thorns prick her fingers. Her friends and kinsmen, when they see her so engaged, urge her to give it up: the rosebush, they say, has grown too wild and there is no more hope for it. It will never bloom again and only grow more thorns, to cut her hands.

"But my mother says to them: 'How shall I abandon it now? Was it not always at my door for every feast? And did I not use it to pollinate the other rosebushes in my garden? Its thorns are dearer to me than the flowers of every other bush.'

"Thus my mother continues tending her rosebush. She hides the wounds which it tears in her skin and says over and over, 'To-morrow it may bloom; how can I throw it away?'

"It is even so with the people of Israel. For Israel is God's rose-bush, planted by the Lord to pollinate its wilder cousins. Now that Israel is run to scrub, God sends His Prophets to prune it of its wildness even though they come away with bruised hands and think that there is no more hope for it. But God thinks in His heart: 'This rosebush is the most precious of My plants, for through it I mean to pollinate all the roses in My garden. And though now it be wild, I do yet remember the days of its youth when it was glorious with clusters of flowers that made a garland for My head!' . . ."

When the children told the rabbi Yeshua's parable, he was well pleased, and he said:

"Surely, surely, he will grow to be a great teller of parables in Israel."

Late that night little Jacob repeated it to his parents, and having finished, asked:

"*Abba,* where did Yeshua learn to tell such parables?"

"We do not know, my son," Joseph replied. "It is God's gift to him—and God's secret."

Jacob thought for a long while and at last said:

"Do you know, *abba,* I would forget all I have learned for one of Yeshua's parables? Sometimes I think he has all the Torah in his stories."

Miriam heard the words and, coming over to her son, she softly kissed his head.

As Jacob grew, he submitted increasingly to the influence of his older brother. Yeshua to him was everything a boy could be. He had only to open his mouth to explain a thorny passage in the Scriptures to his friends—dealing with it in his usual fashion by means of some telling allegory—and young Jacob was immediately at his feet and trembling lest he miss a word. Jacob, even more than the others, had fallen under the spell of Yeshua's mysterious authority. With all his scrupulous adherence to the Law, his taste for self-mortification, his fastidiousness in keeping clean, and his incessant alternation between study and prayer, he felt nonetheless that he could never be his brother's peer; that Yeshua had access to sources of wisdom and strength from which he was debarred forever. He felt that Yeshua served God not in the hour of prayer, nor during sacred studies, nor yet in the performance of good deeds, but by every casual word that fell from him, as when he pointed to a flowering shrub, or a bird on the wing, or when he brought proof for an argument by recalling a day-laborer he had observed at work. It seemed to Jacob that his brother's least significant act or remark was invested with a divine grace.

Uncle Cleophas did not share his sentiments. He persisted in preferring the piety of the younger Jacob to Yeshua's flightiness. And, no doubt, it was to assuage his thwarted longing for a son that he almost adopted Jacob for his own. Sometimes he kept Jacob at his house for days and weeks on end, walked with him in the streets and to the synagogue, bragged of him to the townspeople and held him up to Miriam as her best little son.

"This is the son of my choice," he would say, "Jacob, from whose mouth the words of Holy Writ spurt out like living water from a mountain spring. And note this, Miriam, much as he knows already, he is still learning to know all—not like your eldest boy, who has one ear at school while the other is out on the street."

On hearing such disparagement of Yeshua, young Jacob would rise at once to his brother's defense:

"My brother," he once said, "has no need to study as I do. For he knows each verse by heart before the rabbi ever utters it. You would think he had his learning from a guardian angel."

Or:

"My brother need not pray as often as I do, since everything he says or does is in the manner of a prayer."

Such statements were painful to his uncle.

"What do you mean, child?" he would ask with a puzzled frown.

"My brother has God's grace upon him in everything he does."

"If this is how you feel about your brother," Cleophas asked, "do you not feel envious too?"

"Envious of Yeshua? How could that be? Where he is, there is room for no one else. For he stands under the Lord's grace, and I stand under the Law."

CHAPTER X

IN Nazareth was an abandoned child, somewhat of Yeshua's age, whom the town called "the bastard." He was known to be of Jewish parentage, but he was a love-child, his mother, a married woman, having had him out of wedlock. The woman had made off—doubtless to avoid being taken to Jerusalem to drink the bitter waters prescribed by the Law. Her subsequent history was not known—only that she had disappeared without taking the child. The elders of Nazareth could have wished for his disappearance, too, so that this blot upon their town might be wiped out. But the child lived. At one time he was taken in by a poor peasant family who let him tumble about with their own children and animals. Then he caught the merciful eye of an ass-driver, who had the infant waif ride with him by day and let him spend the nights in the stalls.

But the child had hardly learned to do more than crawl on all fours when he made shift to provide for himself. Thus he frequently crept up to a milch cow and, taking hold of her teats, got himself an udderful of kindly milk; or he snatched a bun from a baker's shelf and bolted; or slipped unnoticed into an orchard to emerge unseen with a bunch of grapes, a pomegranate, or a drum of figs. He made full use, too, of his legal rights to derelict property and, like all the poor, reaped in the corners of the fields at harvest time.

He had grown up a tall, powerful boy, with want and invention his foster-parents. His dress was one ragged piece of burlap, parts of which managed to reach his knees, where his skin was earth-colored. His face was scarred and pitted. His hair had never known washing. He came each Sabbath to stop before the synagogue, though he never braved the steps that led up to its entrance, knowing that he would on no account be admitted. But he came, just the same, apparently to watch the other children on their way in. And every time he appeared in the market square on the synagogue side, someone was sure to shoo him away—a worshipper, a street loiterer, or even one of the Gentiles who came to hear the Prophets read in Aramaic:

"Begone, away! You have no business in the congregation!"

Thus, too, when he turned up in midweek at the school entrance; as often as he was turned away, he came back. There he stood, sentry-like, at the door, waiting for the children to make their boisterous exit, though he knew, from experience, that he would most likely be met with a hail of stones.

"Why, it's the bastard again; be off with you! You know you may not come in!"

Yeshua had been noticing him for some time. Such treatment angered him, and though he had heard something of the boy's origin, he could not see how his bastardy rendered him personally guilty. Several times Yeshua had tried to approach him, but was restrained by the warning cries of his friends. On one occasion the boy himself made off like a frightened hare when Yeshua drew near.

Yeshua was troubled. He asked his parents to justify the boy's ostracism but elicited no better answer than, "His mother sinned, and we are taught by Moses that the child of sin should be cast out from Israel."

"It cannot be," he objected, "that God commanded the punishment of a child for the sins of his parents. The Lord is a righteous God."

Miriam said uneasily:

216

"Never repeat in public what you said now, *tinoki*. I beg you, let no one hear it again."

"Why not?"

"Because one must not speak against God."

"I was not speaking against God; I spoke for Him,"—and Miriam did not know what more to say.

Thenceforth Yeshua undertook with obstinate determination to make friends with the neglected orphan. Once, as he and Jacob were going to school, he saw the boy a little way off. Yeshua at once offered to approach him while Jacob stopped in the middle of the road, speechless with terror as if he were seeing his brother walk blindly to the edge of a precipice.

"Yeshua, what are you doing? It's the outcast," he cried in dismay.

"And what if it is?—he has done no harm," Yeshua called back over his shoulder, still moving on.

"Yeshua! You are breaking the Law; you are offending God!"

"You don't offend God by taking pity on His creatures."

The ragamuffin understood none of this; he saw only that someone was coming at him and so, from long habit, picked up a stone and hurled it at Yeshua's head. He missed, though Yeshua made no move to dodge it. Yeshua smiled and took his bundle of food which he had from his mother, and threw it to the boy. The latter, thinking Yeshua was giving blow for blow, beat a quick retreat.

"It is food!" Yeshua called after him. "Pick it up, it's honey rolls and fruit and . . ."

The boy stopped. He turned and his eyes narrowed suspiciously in his dark, mud-stained face as he slunk slowly back. He kept looking at Yeshua, fascinated by his lingering smile and still mistrusting it.

"Go on, pick it up," Yeshua said again when the boy had reached his bundle. "It's food—honey rolls and nuts."

The boy's hand went for the bundle, groping for it on the ground, for he did not trust Yeshua enough to take his eyes off him. Finally, he snatched it up and, finding it to be food after all, ran off to the nearest dark nook to ram its contents down his gullet.

217

From that day on the orphan never let a morning pass without waiting for Yeshua on his way to school. It seemed that he had enough good sense not to intercept him near the doors of the synagogue, where his presence would surely be embarrassing. He waited for his benefactor in a narrow side lane, which Yeshua soon learned to know as his ambush. And Yeshua passed through it each morning with an extra bundle of provisions, given him by Miriam for the wild street Arab of whom he had told her.

Now, when Yeshua came on, the boy held his ground. It was only when Yeshua drew too near that he sprang away, forcing Yeshua to address him from a distance of several paces.

"What is your name?" he asked.

"Bastard," the orphan replied in a curious snorting voice.

"That is no name. I mean, what is your name in Israel?"

"I have no name in Israel; I have no father."

"Everybody has a father. Your father is God, and I shall call you Adam."

"Why Adam?"

"Because Adam is every man's father. You shall be Adam ben Adam."

The boy gaped at Yeshua; the white of his eyes flashed with brilliance and—for the first time—his dark, grime-encrusted face cracked into a smile.

"Well then, shall I call you Adam ben Adam?"

The other nodded vehemently as though he feared to lose the offer by retarding his response.

"Then I shall call you so. Can you say the *Sh'ma,* Adam ben Adam?"

"No."

"Shall I teach you to say it?"

"I must not say it," said the bastard.

"Why not?"

"God does not want it."

"You are wrong. God wants to hear your *Sh'ma.* He made you and He loves everything He made. And all His creatures sing His praise, and so He wants to hear your prayer too."

"I am not allowed in the synagogue with Israel."

"Who says so?"

"Everybody."

"Will you come home with me to my father and mother?"

"Your mother will kick me from her doorstep because I must not come into a Jewish house."

"My mother will not kick you out," Yeshua said.

"The others always do."

"But not my mother, I tell you, nor my father either. You will see. Will you come to see me in my mother's house?"

"But I must not be in a Jewish house."

"You may be in my mother's. Wait for me here. When I come back from school, we shall go home together and you will be my friend. Will that suit you?"

After school Yeshua evaded his friends, even his brother Jacob, with whom he usually strolled through the town before making for home. He ran straight to the narrow lane, where he found the orphan waiting for him.

"Come," Yeshua said and offered to take Adam by the hand. But at this final moment the boy suddenly lost heart and took to his heels. Yeshua cried after him:

"Adam, don't run away. You'll see, no one will hurt you!"

It took many more days of patient persuasion before the outcast dared to accept Yeshua's invitation. Even then he would not walk at Yeshua's side; he let his benefactor walk ahead, following at a pariah's distance.

He had not been in Yeshua's house more than a few minutes and his forebodings seemed to be coming true. Miriam gave him one look and at once fell to stripping him of his black rotten sack. That done, she immersed him in the tub in which she was wont to bathe her children and, unmindful of his yells, began to scrape him free of his agglutinated filth. And Adam was not reassured until at last she brought him a shirt of Yeshua's, together with a tunic and a pair of breeches and a bowl of bread dipped in honey-milk. Adam dressed in silence and looked steadily at Miriam. He saw her motioning him to eat but took no notice, and suddenly, throwing his hands up to his face, he gave a prolonged groan and burst into a fit of weeping.

"Why are you crying, now?" Miriam asked, reaching out to touch his head.

219

"I don't know."

Miriam continued stroking his hair and waited for the fit to pass. Joseph was watching the scene from his corner, and he now turned to Yeshua and asked:

"What is his name?"

"I call him Ben Adam."

"Ben Adam, eh? The son of man . . . It is a great name, Yeshua, an honorable name. It is what the Lord calls His Prophet. But there is no man that has not a right to it. You named him well, Yeshua."

Could Yeshua stand against the will of God? Jacob was frightened at the thought. He had too long been used to see his brother in the image of moral perfection. The respect which in every Jewish family was due to the first-born, the father's deputy—in Jacob it was multiplied by love and veneration. He saw clearly that Yeshua was licensed in the doing of certain forbidden things by the holy spirit which rested on his head. And yet, when Yeshua struck up a friendship with the orphaned bastard, Jacob was deeply troubled. And when he saw his mother following Yeshua's example—and his father acquiescing in the importation of that uncleanness which the Law ordered kept at arm's length—he felt the ground slip from under him.

He was sure that his parents could never be at fault. They were, and always had been, his ideal of rectitude, and he loved and honored them without reserve. His mother's kindness of heart had been among the first of his childhood impressions. He had seen her give unstinting welcome to the most ragged callers at her door, washing and aneling their sores, giving them food and drink though it be her last morsel. And he had daily evidence of her pious, law-abiding ways; was it thinkable that she, heaven forbid, should do wrong in the eyes of God and His Law?

Jacob would not ask his parents; the very thought of suspecting them was a violation of the fourth commandment. His part was to accept for right and just whatever they did.

He resolved to question Taddi, for like his older brother he had early recognized the tanner's merit. The two boys had often put to him those questions which they would not, or dared not ask of their parents. And Taddi was never lost for an answer, which he delivered by way of fable and parable.

Jacob found him at work, stamping with his bare feet on the dripping hides he had been soaking. The boy bowed and said with ceremony:

"Teach me, master, may one commit a sin the better to perform a righteous deed?"

The tanner stopped treading the hides and looked sharply at his questioner:

"A difficult problem, my son," he said, "and not to be answered with a yes or no. It depends on how the intention is directed, and for whom the sin is committed. Because ofttimes, you see, a sin may be turned into a noble deed, provided it is committed not against another but for the glory of the Lord. And sometimes what you call a sin will serve God better than an act of piety. The intention is the thing. For when the heart is with the Lord, it cannot be a sin—as our sages said: 'God wants no more than the heart of man.'"

"But, master, if this be so, where is the limit? Cannot every man break the Law and say, 'Look you, I intended it for God'? And would not this be the end of the Torah? I thought we were judged by our deeds, not our intentions."

"Ah, but it depends upon the doer," Taddi said. "Now, you and I cannot break the Law. We are little people who must travel in harness. But there are others, you know—people who not only love the Law, as you or I, but who love God. And for their love's sake they are ready even to commit a sin against God's teaching, if but to do His will. Remember the words of the Psalmist: 'I delight to do Thy will, O my God.' Such people strive not for good deeds, but to execute God's will."

"But who shall say he knows the will of God?"

"Not you or I, heaven forbid! But take your brother—he knows."

And as Taddi resumed his treading, he added, having easily divined the boy's perplexity:

"What he does is proper in God's eyes."

Jacob watched silently for a while and said at last:

"Sometimes it seems to me that whatever Yeshua does is done

in God's way. I thank you, master, for you have comforted me greatly."

The affair, however, did not pass unnoticed: this was indeed a novel turn, that a scholar of the synagogue school should go hobnobbing with a bastard, link elbows with him in the public street, bring him home to his mother, take up the cudgels for him at the least provocation, and sit up with him of an evening to teach him holy liturgy. If Yeshua ben Joseph were not warned in time, would anything prevent him from defiling the synagogue itself with the bastard's presence?

In the end the preceptor of the school decided that his intervention could no longer be delayed. One morning, as his young pupils sat about him on the matted floor, instead of broaching the day's business he continued for a long time without speaking, merely looking from one boy to the next and smoothing the black strains of his beard. Then he began:

"Our sages tell us that he who teaches the Torah is like a father to his pupils. And just as it behooves a father to chide his sons as occasion requires, and chastise them if it be necessary, so also the teacher cannot escape his parental task. For teacher and pupil are as one entity together, and the teacher bears responsibility for the conduct of his wards. Accordingly, when a pupil fails in his conduct, the rabbi is no less blameworthy than he. Now, certain rumors have come to my ears which trouble my spirit and make me feel like one of those sinners who danced about the golden calf. For it is bruited that there is one among my disciples whose late behavior cannot be condoned. I will therefore ask my students if they can point to one who has been lately failing in his public conduct. Let them rise—those who know—and point him out."

The first to arise was Matthew Saucebox, the second Sakkai bar Zadok, two boys who bore Yeshua a grudge for reasons of their own; the former because Yeshua still disdained to play with him at buying and selling, the other, "the erudite," because Yeshua's exalted standing among the boys robbed him of the glory due his erudition. Both boys now pointed their fingers at Yeshua and said:

"Here is the disciple who has failed in his conduct."

"Of what do you accuse him?" asked the rabbi.

"We have seen him walk abroad with the bastard who lives in this town, befriending him and teaching him to say the *Sh'ma.*"

"Has each of you seen it severally? Have you, Matthew ben Hanah, witnessed it with your own eyes?"

"I have seen it with my own eyes."

"And have you, Sakkai ben Zadok, seen the student Yeshua ben Joseph walk with the town bastard?"

"I have seen Yeshua ben Joseph walk with the bastard and consort with him in violation of the command of our teacher Moses—'A bastard shall not enter into the congregation of the Lord; even to their tenth generation shall they not enter into the congregation of the Lord'"; and having quoted the full text, Sakkai, "the erudite," dropped his eyes piously.

"You were not asked to state what law he violated. You cannot be witness and judge in one. Leave judgment to your rabbi. I called on you to state what you had seen with your own eyes."

"I have seen Yeshua ben Joseph with the bastard who lives in this town, befriending him, and teaching him to say the *Sh'ma,*" Sakkai said, taking care to repeat the phrasing used by the first witness to make the testimony tally.

"Yeshua bar Joseph, you have heard the charge of your fellow pupils. Do you plead guilty to having consorted with the bastard?"

Yeshua rose to reply:

"I admit that I befriended him, as I befriend him now. But I can see no ill in what I do."

"Are you unaware that Moses enjoined us in the Torah to keep the bastard out of the congregation of the Lord, even to the tenth generation—as was cited by your fellow pupil?"

"But when the parents sin, why is the son to blame? Did we not learn a few days back what the Prophet Jeremiah said—'Every one shall die for his own iniquity'?"

Yeshua's words faded into a hushed silence. No one, it seemed, had expected him to defend his conduct. At last the rabbi, somewhat taken aback, said in a conciliatory tone:

"The Prophet's words do not apply to the commandments given us by Moses. The Torah states expressly: 'A bastard shall not en-

223

ter into the congregation of the Lord.' God forbid that you should speak against the holy Scripture."

"Amen," said Yeshua. "But did not Moses himself say in the Fifth Book: 'The father shall not be put to death for the children, neither shall the children be put to death for the father; every man shall be put to death for his own sin'?"

The rabbi nodded with satisfaction and replied:

"You quote well, Yeshua ben Joseph; Moses did say so, but this verse—'The children shall not be put to death for the fathers'— applies to verdicts of death as handed down by courts of law. The sense is clear; 'they shall not be put to death.' But here, in the case of the bastard, a death sentence is not under consideration. Moses did not say a bastard should be put to death for the sins of his parents; he said he should not come into the congregation of the Lord."

The rabbi's words were beginning to assume the precise emphatic diction of restrained exasperation, for as he spoke Yeshua had begun to shake his head impulsively.

"Is it less cruel to banish him from the Lord's congregation than to take his life?" he cried. "And for what? Because his parents sinned? He is one of God's creatures, like all of us. And did not God say through the mouth of the Prophet Ezekiel, 'Behold, all souls are mine; as the soul of the father, so also the soul of the son is mine'? And then, if he is God's creature, we are enjoined to show him mercy, even as God has mercy for all."

The rabbi frowned and his mouth twitched under his heavy beard. He was evidently losing patience and making every effort to hold his temper down. When he spoke again there was a tang of sharpness in his voice:

"Where did you hear this verse? The Prophet Ezekiel has not yet been studied in this class."

"I heard it from my parents."

"Indeed? You heard it from your parents? And I trust you heard the interpretation also, in which case you are hardly in need of what this school can offer, for it is well-known that two instructors are as bad as none, seeing that their interpretations differ. Your parents, evidently, interpret the verse, 'Behold, all souls are mine,' as meaning that we should take pity on a bastard,

224

or an Amonite, or perhaps a son of Amalek, for behold, they are all creatures of God; and yet God said of the Amalekites, 'not a soul of them shall live'—and this despite Ezekiel's words, 'all souls are mine.' And remember, Yeshua bar Joseph, the Prophet Ezekiel also has a word to say about death sentences: 'the soul that sinneth, it shall die,' says he, even as Moses said. But there is, as you say, no death sentence for bastards, only a banishment from the congregation of the Lord; and this shall be enforced."

"I have heard the words of the Prophet," Yeshua replied with heat. " 'The son shall not bear the iniquity of the father'—and by this precept will I live. I will not break my friendship with the bastard, for I will not believe that God repudiates a guiltless soul for a crime in which he had no share. 'God,' says the Scripture, 'is just in all His ways.' "

The rabbi, listening, colored with rage and knew not what to say; of such insolence no record existed. A word hovered on his lips, but was suppressed, and he said in a firm, quiet voice:

"Yeshua bar Joseph, you have raised your voice against your rabbi, and rejected his Torah which our Teacher Moses on Mount Sinai handed over to our tradition. You have embraced another Torah which our sages have not taught. Now therefore you shall be expelled from this school with dishonor. Henceforth you are no pupil of mine, and I forbid my students to have further dealings with you, until such time as you repent of your speech here and return to us filled with remorse and ask for readmission in obedience and humility."

Thus ended Yeshua's years at school.

CHAPTER XI

"MY SON," said Joseph, "think of King David's words, 'From all my teachers I gained wisdom.' The teachers, Yeshua, are many, and life is the greatest of them. Now, you are almost twelve years old, and it is time you learned your father's trade. 'Whoever teaches not his son a trade,' the sages say, 'may as well teach him to be a robber.' "

And Joseph led Yeshua into his shop, where he handed him a bar of wood and showed him how to arch and curve it for a yoke to make it fit snug to the animal's back; how edges were beveled to prevent their chafing the animal's skin. He taught him how to splice pieces of timber, how to join two boards for a table-top, and how to carve out a trough. And other things he showed him concerning the joiner's craft, as, what leftovers, shavings, and filings reverted to the customer who had supplied the lumber for the work in hand, and what others belonged of right to the artisan.

Nor was the Torah neglected. Each evening after work, when Joseph and Yeshua had washed their hands for the evening meal, Miriam produced the scrolls from her family chest—a psalter and the books of Isaiah and Daniel and others of the Minor Prophets. In addition, Joseph possessed several inscribed fragments of that apocalyptic literature which had not found its place in the Bible canon—the Secrets of Enoch, the Book of Jubilees, and the Assumption of Moses, all of which, along with other spurious writings, enjoyed wide currency among those pious who awaited the Messiah's coming. And Joseph acquainted the boy with the circumstances of Enoch's translation, his journey through the seven heavens and his vision of hell.

The Psalms Yeshua read with his mother, who remembered a great many from the time she was a young girl in Jerusalem, living in the house of her priestly cousin among the holy women who were gathered about Elisheva.

And it was Taddi the tanner who first told him of Reb Hillel, the fabulous rabbi who taught in Jerusalem. Yeshua often went down to the damp hollow below the wellstead where Taddi kept his tannery. Kneading the hides with his bare feet and bespattered top to toe with the bluish-black juice in which they had been pickling, Taddi taught Yeshua the wise sayings of the sages, their aphorisms, their "fences" and additions to the Law by which a man must live if he is to inherit the world to come. The tanner's learning seemed inexhaustible. He had forgotten nothing from his younger years when he had sojourned in the capital at the feet of the greatest rabbis in Israel. But Taddi had repudiated the rabbinate for the slighted calling of the tanner because, in the tradition of many Jewish scholars, he did not wish to make his living by the Torah.

Taddi told him the oft-repeated tale of the insolent Gentile who came to Reb Hillel and declared himself ready to be converted on condition that Reb Hillel teach him the entire Torah in the short space that he could bear to stand upon one leg; and the great rabbi, so far from driving the scoffer from his sight, accepted the bargain, saying, "Do not inflict on others what you would not undergo yourself; this is the whole Torah—all else is commentary." And Taddi went on to quote the old rabbi's famous maxims: "If I am not for myself, who will be? And if I am for myself only, what am I? And if not now, pray, when?" Or: "Be not sure of yourself till the day of your death, nor judge your neighbor till you have been in his place."

Taddi never tired to speak of his beloved rabbi. He told Yeshua how Hillel, in his earlier years, had supported himself as a woodcutter. It was Reb Hillel who taught that no trade was contemptible if it served human needs. And the tanner went on to tell how the young Hillel had divided his woodcutter's earnings into two equal portions—a moiety for his upkeep, the rest for admission money to the school. And once, said Taddi, when Hillel had no money left wherewith to pay the price of admission, he climbed up on the roof and eavesdropped on the scholars' lesson through the chimney flue. It was winter, and a heavy snowfall buried the young student as he lay there, oblivious to all but the words of the rabbis. Fortunately, he was discovered in time, though almost frozen to death.

But Taddi had more to offer than a knowledge of the Law and a fund of stories about its great expounders. Circulating among the academies of Jerusalem he had heard no end of myths and fables from the old storytellers who teemed about the Holy City —legends hallowed by ageless tradition, added to and amended in each generation, legends that wove further the storied lives of Israel's Patriarchs. For just as Jacob had set his variegated rods of poplar, hazel, and chestnut in the watering troughs of his flocks —that they should conceive before the rods and bring forth speckled cattle only—so tradition painted the lives of the Patriarchs that they be always before the eyes of Israel, an example to be imitated and a spur to righteous doing.

The tanner imparted to the boy the ancient traditions of the people, those concerning the Mystery of the Celestial Chariot, the Mystery of the Creation, the primordial serpent, Satan who was born with Eve, Adam's first sin, and the resultant degradation of mankind since a residue of that sin lingered in each one of us; he told him how the Patriarchs had endeavored to redeem man of his sin, how their efforts had raised them to heights never attained by humankind before. He told him of the fettering of Isaac as amplified by legend—how Satan strove craftily to bar Abraham's passage to the land of Moriah where the Lord had commanded him to offer his son for a burnt offering; how Satan sought to weaken Abraham in his design, the manifold temptation he laid in his path to shake Abraham's purpose which was to do the Lord's bidding with full abandon to the divine will. Nor was Abraham alone harried by the Tempter: the boy Isaac, guessing at his father's errand—he too came safely through the snares laid in his track, joyfully to offer himself up.

"You see, my son," the tanner said, "Isaac knew what his father was about as soon as Abraham laid the wood of the burnt offering upon his shoulders, for this is like burdening a convicted man with a cross to bear to his own crucifixion. And when Isaac saw that his father had no lamb for a burnt offering, but only wood and fire and a knife, he asked his father where the lamb was for the sacrifice. And his father said, 'The Lord has chosen you, my son, for a sacrifice.' And Isaac replied, 'So be it then, since He has chosen me, for my life is His; but yet my heart aches for my mother.' And they went on, both of them, together. And when the time came for the offering, Isaac said: '*Abba,* bind me by my hands and feet, for behold, the flesh is insolent, and perchance, when you come to plunge your knife, I may resist so that the weapon graze me only and I will no longer be a fit, unblemished sacrifice for God. Now hurry, *abba,* and when you have done, take up my ashes and bring them to my mother, but take care not to bring her the report when she stands near a ditch, or on her roof, for it may be that the blow make her fall. And you must console my mother and tell her that it was the will of God.'"

That evening, after he had heard the legend told by the tanner, the boy Yeshua lay on the roof of his house with his face upturned, watching the stars kindling in the sky. Beyond those glimmering lights heaven was filled with its own life. The Patriarchs were there, and David the King with his crown and lyre, and Yeshua closed his eyes to see them better, them and the celestial chariot which upheld the throne of glory, and the Seraphim; he heard the chant of the earth surging through the ether to expire faintly in the far reaches of the sky, and, mingling with the chant, men's tears and supplications arriving at the gates of heaven. And Yeshua's thoughts returned to the fettering of Isaac. He thought what he would do in Isaac's place. He tried to visualize himself laden with the wood that was to burn him as an offering. Would he be willing, as Isaac had been, to go meekly to his slaughter? Would he need to be bound hand and foot lest he resist the sacrificial knife? . . . But one thing troubled him—one ordeal he could not be sure of overcoming. Could he knowingly inflict grief on his mother? What if his pity for her tempted him from his willingness to die for God?

"*Ema,*" he called softly.

He rose and looked about and saw the kneeling form of his mother at the farther end of the roof. He held his breath not to disturb her prayer. He did not know how long he had waited before he heard his mother rise; and then he called again.

"What is it, *tinoki?*" Miriam asked.

"*Emi,* tell me, must every man who is condemned to hang carry his own cross to the place of execution?"

Miriam gasped and felt a cold clutch on her heart.

"Why are you asking this, *tinoki?* What, in the name of God, gave you such thoughts?"

"I was with Taddi today and heard him tell of the fettering of Isaac. He said that when Abraham laid the wood on Isaac's back it was as though a cross were laid on a condemned man to bear to his own crucifixion."

"Taddi spoke to you about the offering of Isaac?"

"Yes, among other things. And he said that when Abraham

229

was about to make the sacrifice, Isaac asked to be bound for fear that he would balk at the last. I was thinking, I would be as willing as was Isaac to be sacrificed. And you, *emi?* Would you let me go, like our mother Sarah, if God desired my father to offer me up?"

"*Tinoki,* I beg you, do not ask me. How should I compare with Sarah? Be still, *tinoki,* be still and think of other things. Look at the stars and how they shed God's mercy upon all."

Miriam took the boy's head and laid it on her lap, and they gazed up together at the sky.

But Nazareth remembered and made its own reckoning. Even though, to avoid further scandal, Joseph had taken Adam ben Adam, Yeshua's illegitimate friend, to Cana, where he could stay incognito with Miriam's kinsfolk in the house of Bar Levi, the barley miller, helping to turn the millwheel and earning his own keep, the incident in Nazareth was not forgotten. The children brought the story home, the parents spread it in the market, and before long every man and woman in the town knew how Joseph's eldest son had been impertinent with his rabbi, had quarreled publicly with the Law of Moses, and had been ousted with dishonor from the school.

The town's population was divided between various families, many of which were in constant strife with each other. The feud was bitterest between the sons of Pinhas and the sons of Issachar. The former descended from a family of common priests, the local priest being their chief. Most of them—such as had married widows or divorcees—had long been pronounced unfit for sacerdotal functions, for the rabbis kept a strict eye on the lineage of all priestly families in Israel. Nevertheless, they preened themselves with their exalted pedigree and saw to it that it was not forgotten.

The sons of Issachar, albeit they were not so rich as their rivals, claimed connection with the House of David, and to their camp belonged Reb Hanan, the deceased father of the two Miriams.

The feud was stubborn and long-drawn, and it had become more bitter because of Miriam's marriage. The widow of Hanan, instead of accepting one of the sons of Hanina ben Safra, leading

230

spirit of the children of Pinhas, had given her daughter to Joseph, a stranger and an outsider. In retribution, the sons of Pinhas debarred those of Issachar from using their property or setting foot in their courts or coming near their dwellings. And the sons of Issachar countered with similar measures.

Joseph, who was still somewhat of a stranger among the Nazarenes, despite his long stay in their midst, took little interest in public affairs, and less in inter-clannish feuds. He had his hands full, as he said, looking to his own plot and family. To the synagogue he went every Sabbath and on the day of the New Moon, and since he was known to befriend men who were unlettered, and possibly unclean, the town in turn took little notice of him. Cleophas, the elder son-in-law of Hanan's house and a native of Nazareth, made up what Joseph lacked in public spirit. He was a prominent spokesman for the sons of Issachar and, since he looked upon himself as the head of Hanan's house, anything that touched upon the family was brought to him as to the responsible party.

Now that the scandal of Yeshua's familiarity with the bastard and the boy's reprobation were matter of public discussion, the sons of Pinhas thought they had a golden opportunity to quit scores with the sons of Issachar.

In the synagogue on Sabbath eve Cleophas observed their meaningful glances, their way of shaking their heads over him, of evading his eyes and whispering with one another. But it was not until the next day that he had a full account of the story.

He was sitting in his workshop that opened on the street of the sandal makers. Opposite stood Hanah ben Tekufi, the father of young Matthew Saucebox, who had his merchant's stall in the same street.

"What better fruit can you expect from such a tree?" mumbled the shopkeeper with a listless shrug, as if he did not care who heard it.

Cleophas, matching his indifference to his neighbor's, put a sandal on the last and asked lightly:

"What canker is eating your innards now?"

"It's your brother's son I'm thinking of, and his fine behavior at the school. My boy Matthew has told me all."

"Your boy Saucebox, indeed; may there be no more of his ilk

in Israel! Why, the poison fairly drools from his mouth. And what new slander has he brought home now?"

"Merely that your precious nephew has defied his rabbi and made light of the Law."

"Well, well, the apple never falls far from the tree. Your brat Matthew is as impudent as you are boorish."

Hanah himself was one of the sons of Pinhas. Yet in their feud with Issachar he hoped to maintain the merchant's wise neutrality which is loth to antagonize potential customers. But, being by nature incapable of keeping out of other people's business, he made himself the universal poker, stoking every quarrel that had some promise in it of a conflagration, and always setting families against each other. His shop occupied a nice strategic position for his game, for the Pinhas men, some of whom, like Cleophas, were sandal makers, while others were shopkeepers like himself, all lived in close proximity to Cleophas.

"So you will not believe me, eh?" he said. "Why not ask Zadok bar Levi, the father of 'sharp' Sakkai who was present. Sakkai came home with the same story,"—and Hanah pointed to his neighbor shop where Bar Levi dealt in wines and honey.

"A fine witness, Zadok of the sons of Pinhas! The proverb says, 'Liars bring witnesses from far away,'" Cleophas replied, protecting himself in advance against whatever testimony might be forthcoming.

"And there's another proverb warns us that 'birds of a feather flock together,'" put in a voice from the side.

Cleophas, growing hot, turned toward the unseen speaker:

"What I don't understand cannot hurt me—and so much for your proverbs."

More men now joined in the altercation, and one called out angrily:

"A curse on all who bring infamy on a house in Israel. Cleophas can have you up before the Court for what you said!"

A shock of ginger hair emerged from an opening:

"What did I say? Nothing at all! I only mentioned a harmless saw about birds of a feather!"

"And he took naturally to the bastard because he too is slightly suspect."

"What do you mean?" cried Cleophas with no effort to conceal his mounting fury.

"Well, we have a notion that his father ate sour grapes . . ."

"Adders and vipers stop your mouth for such vile slander on a daughter in Israel! I'm warning you again, he can haul you to court!"

"But what did I say? Only that his father ate sour grapes . . . Everybody knows that, and knows it for sure. Our children remember it; we saw to that, for they were dealt nuts to help their memory when they grew up."

At this Cleophas could hold back no longer; he leapt away from his bench, still clutching his mallet.

"I'll split any man's skull that dares malign my family. Every man knows that my brother-in-law married within the Law of Moses and Israel! His marriage contract was endorsed by the rabbi and his son was born in holy purity! I'll have you all before the judge for your vile slander!"—and Cleophas kicked open the door of his stall and sprang out with raised hammer ready to strike down his jeerers.

There was no telling how far the matter might have gone had not the local agoranome, Ben Clinumus, intervened at this moment. Anticipating a possible brawl he had stood by for some moments, watching the proceedings. Now, with his two assistants, he restrained the rabid sandal maker and called out in a stentor's voice:

"Who has started this fray in Israel?"

"These men have been slandering my kin. I'll haul them up before the court for this!" Cleophas cried.

"That's your good right, Cleophas," said the agoranome, still barring his way. "But you cannot be all things in one—plaintiff, witness, judge, and executioner. Now, who are these men that you indict for slander? Give me their names and I will have them summoned."

"No one has slandered his kin, no one at all! We spoke of no one in particular," cried the sons of Pinhas. "Did we name anybody? Did we point in any one direction? Let them speak up who heard us, there are witnesses enough, God knows!"

"No, that's true," came a jumble of voices from the crowd.

"No names were mentioned . . . We heard no names . . . No grounds for a slander charge . . ."

"Well, then, leave quarreling," said the agoranome. "Our sages say that he who starts a quarrel is like one who destroys the world."

And from the gathering crowd a learned Jew called over to the sons of Pinhas:

"You priests should take your cue from your ancestor. Our wise men tell us to be, like Aaron, hunters of peace; but you, for shame, sow discord in Israel!"

"God forbid we should sow discord! What more did we say but that his brother's son had been expelled from his school with dishonor and would not be readmitted till he come with remorse before his rabbi. This is the news we had from our children and this is what we said and not a word more."

And thus the public quarrel rested.

That evening Cleophas sat in Joseph's house, repeating to him and his wife the talk of the town. He demanded, in the name of the family honor, that Joseph send the boy Yeshua to propitiate his offended rabbi—barefoot, dressed in black, his head sprinkled with ashes, as required by the Law. Cleophas contended that Yeshua had imperiled the honor of their house, and he gave Joseph to understand that the story of his own marriage to Miriam was coming in for another round of sordid publicity as a result of Yeshua's defection.

Joseph did not immediately reply, waiting for Miriam to state her position; and Miriam said:

"Whatever shame my son may bring upon me—I shall wear it like a crown. He shall not say an untruth for my sake."

Cleophas smiled, half earnest and half in mockery:

"Women have light opinions, and should be taken lightly. We know how blindly mothers dote on their sons, to spoil them by too much indulgence. Not so the father; while he caresses with his right hand, he chastises with his left. He loves as King Solomon said of God, 'Whom the Lord loveth He chastiseth.' I wait to hear you, Joseph."

"My son has reported the incident to me," Joseph said. "I could find no blame in his conduct. Yeshua brought proof for his argument from the Law of Moses and the Prophets, and since we are free sons of the Torah, each of us is free to interpret the Law in his own way, provided only the Torah is on his side."

"But not a pupil before his rabbi," Cleophas objected. "Even if the rabbi were wrong, it is not for the pupil to correct him in public, slurring his dignity which stands no less high than a father's. And your son defied his rabbi in the hearing of the other students and scorned to accept his judgment. This matter touches all our reputation, the dignity of our house, because, as I have told you, Joseph, the townspeople already have renewed their scurrilous talk about you."

"Never fear, brother," Joseph replied. "My honor, and that of my family, is firm as a rock. And if their rattling tongues cause us to suffer—why, then, my wife has answered you, we shall bear willingly whatever infamy they have in store; but the child shall not be moved against his sense of justice. Let me call him now, and I shall ask him in front of you whether he has indeed slighted his rabbi. If the boy is ready to make an apology of his free will, I shall not stay him, but I will prevent him from doing anything contrary to his belief."

When Yeshua, whom Joseph had called in from the workshop, had heard his father's question, he replied:

"I did not mean to slight my rabbi, God forbid. What I did and said accorded with the words of the Torah and the Prophets. But if my rabbi feels that I have given him offense, I shall not fail to come to him in humble submission to do whatever penance he may ask. I would not have him bear me a grudge, for it were better to leave a thorn in one's flesh overnight than a grudge in one's heart."

The boy's words made a profound impression. Cleophas himself was so moved that he leapt from his seat to plant a kiss on Yeshua's head.

"Yeshua, my child, you are a true son of Abraham; may your kind increase in Israel."

But Miriam, in one impulsive gesture, threw her kerchief over the boy's head, as though to protect him.

"No, my son," she said, "penance is not required from you, for you have neither injured nor offended any man." Then, turning

235

to the men, she added: "What he did was done for heaven's sake. He stood up for the honor of God. Shall my son slur the honor of God to mollify creatures of flesh and blood—his rabbi or his parents?"

Joseph bowed faintly to his wife.

"Well spoken, Miriam," he said. "It needed a woman to open our eyes, for it was God's glory we were wanting to shed for the honor of a man. Hear me, brother Cleophas—we are ready to bear the worst they can deal us. This is our answer to you and the townspeople."

Cleophas rose wearily to go.

"It was with good reason our sages said, 'Better to follow a lion than a woman,' "—and left without farewell.

The upshot of Joseph's and of Miriam's attitude was not long in coming. Once, as Yeshua passed through the street of the sandal makers where Cleophas's shop was housed, he caught the sound of bellicose voices:

"There goes the issue of the man who eats the grapes before they ripen."

"As it is written—'The fathers have eaten a sour grape, and the children's teeth are set on edge.' "

"A whippersnapper who insults his rabbi!"

Yeshua still did not understand the meaning of these repeated allusions to unripe fruit, or what they had to do with him. But that they must throw some light on his origin had become clear to him long ago when the student Matthew Saucebox had made a similar remark. A child of unripe grapes, Matthew had called him, and even then Yeshua had thought of asking his parents. But Matthew had been immediately hushed by the others, who said he was shaming his neighbor, which the rabbis held equal to shedding a man's blood. And so the matter was for the time dropped.

But now Yeshua could not pass through the vintners' street where the Pinhas men had their booths without running a gauntlet of odious insinuations cracked down on him by young and old. And so he finally brought the matter to his parents.

Joseph heard him out and threw a weighted look at Miriam.

236

Clearly he wanted her to initiate the boy into the mystery of his conception; Yeshua was old enough to know and none but Miriam could tell him.

Miriam went to the family chest where the sacred scrolls lay wrapped in cloths. She took the parchment of Isaiah and said softly:

"*Tinoki,* come with me."

She preceded Yeshua to the roof.

"My child, let us pray together, that God reveal to you the things that concern you."

Yeshua bowed his head and remained long in the attitude of silent prayer. And suddenly he raised his eyes to his mother and whispered:

"Holy, holy, holy . . ."

"*Tinoki,* what are you saying?"

"*Ema,*" Yeshua said, "I know what I know."

The boy unrolled the parchment and read out in a quivering voice:

"'Behold, a virgin shall conceive and bear a son, and shall call his name Emmanuel . . .'"

That night no more words passed between mother and son. But Yeshua came over to Joseph who was meditating alone in the dark of the house. He bowed deeply and said:

"You are my father upon earth. All the days of my life I shall obey your word."

CHAPTER XII

THE second tithe, separated from the harvest after the first tithe had been rendered to Levites and priests, had to be brought to Jerusalem, to be consumed there by the pilgrim farmer and his family. It could not be conveyed to the capital by proxy; and only that part of it might be sold which was clearly perishable, and then the proceeds of the sale must be spent, like

237

the second tithe itself, in the Holy City. It was exacted annually but for two years in every seven; twice in the sabbatical cycle its place was taken by the poor man's tithe, when the tenth part of the crop was ceded to the pauper and the stranger within the gate.

These provisions of the Law enabled farmers from the remotest districts to make frequent pilgrimages. Even the poorest of the population undertook the long journey, regardless of the cost and the loss in working hours. And yet it was obligatory for every family, whatever its condition, to make the festal pilgrimage at least once in two years. And this also was Joseph's custom.

He could not hope to take his entire family, his younger sons being too small. Nor could the household be abandoned altogether; someone must stay to tend the animals, the garden and the field, and to keep watch against marauding Gentiles, for many times the homes of pilgrimaging Jews had been rifled in their absence by their Gentile neighbors. For this reason Cleophas and Mariama took possession of his house whenever Joseph went up to Jerusalem.

It was high time that Yeshua, as the first-born, see the Temple with his own eyes. He was a full twelve years old; soon he would be subject to the Law and answerable for himself, releasing his father from responsibility for his actions.

This was a great event in a boy's life—the first ascension to the Holy City. Months in advance preparations were made for the journey. Miriam wove a new cloak for Yeshua to be worn over shirt and breeches, a cloak of dignity fit for a scholar, only that its color was not the sable dye affected by the men of learning. For Miriam could not bring herself to dress her child in black. She used instead the whitest wool, though she knew how this would draw attention and make the boy seem like one of the young priests.

A girdle too she wove for him as for an adult. It was a broad sash, white, with a thread of azure tracing on it the forms of grape and pomegranate, five fingers deep and long enough to be wound many times about the waist. For the girdle had a special significance in the masculine dress. It was his outward token of maturity. Without it he felt somehow divested, for he could not then sit down to table or recite the Sh'ma.

238

It had practical uses too. A girdle could be employed at night for a partial covering against the cold and damp. Flinging it over a projecting branch a man could swing himself across a patch of swamp or ditch. Some used it as a breastband to carry weights on their backs, or as a fallrope for the lowering of heavy objects from a roof. Others had their girdles furnished with fobs for the hiding of trinkets and coin, and all men wore their purses suspended from it. Such a girdle often served its owner his life long and many a man bequeathed his, like a family ring, to his first-born son as a token of transferred seniority. And since this girdle was to last her son throughout his life, Miriam took special pains in its making, that it might form the pride of his garment when Joseph should for the first time wind it about his waist, an emblem of his attained manhood.

With Taddi the tanner she bartered a measure of meal and honey for a length of leather from which cousin Cleophas fashioned two pairs of sandals with long sturdy thongs—one pair for Yeshua, and one for Jacob, the heartbroken Jacob who had to stay behind with the other children.

In a special corner of the house stood the pitchers, inscribed "The City" or "Jerusalem," containing the flour, the oil, and the wine destined for enjoyment in the Temple precincts as part of the second tithe. Dried figs and raisins lay stored in newly-sewn bags, and the cash realized from the sale of perishable goods was set aside not to be touched before arrival in Jerusalem. And there was, in addition, a store of provisions for the road—parched corn, bags of nuts and almonds, which made useful substitutes for bread, baskets filled with fruit and vegetables, gourds of fresh water, cruses of honey, and a horn or two of fragrant rubbing oil in case of accident or illness. This in addition to quilts and blankets of felt and wool to keep the dew out if it proved necessary to weather the nights under the open sky.

Joseph's old ass, who had served the family so many years, was loaded high, and even then some of the burden fell to the man and boy at his side.

No lamb or kid from the domestic herd was taken for the paschal offering; for even if it came alive through the journey, it might well sustain some injury on the road which would disqualify it as a sacrifice. The alternative was simple and inexpensive. A whole family, and sometimes a company of citizens could pool their resources and purchase from the Temple administration in Jerusalem a warrant which entitled them to one lamb from the Temple stock. For it was enough to eat but a morsel of its meat no larger than an olive to have fulfilled the ritual minimum, provided only that the man in question belonged to the family or the company who had together brought the sacrifice.

When the month of Adar came, and the last ewe had brought forth, the authorities of Jerusalem dispatched bands of laborers to mend the pilgrims' highways, fill in ditches and gullies, drain wayside marshes, and repair the foot bridges which the storms of the spring rains had damaged or destroyed. And on a lesser scale the same was done by the town mayors of Galilee.

In the middle of the month, a few weeks before Passover, the hopeful pilgrims of Nazareth assembled in the market place, leading their mules and donkeys by the halter, with packs and bundles weighting their own shoulders, with staffs in their hands, with wife and child and fellow-traveler at their sides. The whole town, headed by its seven elders, turned out for the joyful rite of valediction and, when the procession began to move, gave it an honorable escort several leagues beyond the limits of the town, and over the flowering fields of spring drifted the pilgrims' chant, "I rejoiced when they said unto me, into the House of the Lord let us go. . . ."

Two possible routes led to the capital. The longer hugged the course of the Jordan as far as Jericho and thence to Jerusalem athwart the Judaean hills. The advantage of this route was that it lay wholly within Jewish borders, for which good reason it was preferred by those who traveled solitary. The other road ran through the Valley of Jezreel and, without detour, by way of Sichem and the hills of Ephraim straight to Jerusalem. But this, despite its greater comfort, was a dangerous road for all but larger caravans, since the Samaritans who populated it to right and left were wont to rob and slay those travelers who moved with insufficient escort.

The company of Nazarenes chose the shorter route. Descending from their native hills, they entered the wide champaign of

240

Jezreel, which now in the first flush of spring, looked like the garden of the Lord, with flowering almonds and olives in full bloom. On the left hand lay the fair town of Na'in, lapped in green, whose market place offered asylum for the night.

Na'in was the first station. Here the party from Nazareth met with pilgrim caravans from the Sea of Genesaret, from Bethsaida, K'far-Nahum, and Magdala, who had greatly multiplied the hardship of their journey to by-pass the Gentiles of Beth-Shean and had reached Na'in by way of Mount Tabor to join trails with their Galilean brothers. And it was here in Na'in that the assembled travelers chose a captain from their midst to lead the pilgrims' host the rest of the way.

It was here also that Joseph met his kinsman Zebedee, who lived at the sea shore. A fisherman by occupation, Zebedee was a man in his best years, with a face leathered by sun and wind. His part of the shore, near Bethsaida, was famed for its fisheries. From here the catch was ferried to K'far-Nahum, where it was smoked and salted and packed for shipment to the great fishgate at Jerusalem.

With him were his two sons, boys of about Yeshua's age, named Jacob and Jochanan. Shoshannah, their mother, was a large, overfleshed woman, kind of heart and ready always to laugh or lend a hand where help was needed. Her bags were cramful of sweetmeats, nuts, and pastries, which she dealt out to all young comers with a lavish hand. For she loved children to the point of absurdity, strangers no less than her own, and praised them all to the same excess, predicting for every straying toddler a future bright and wonderful.

"So this is your eldest," said she, smacking a kiss on Miriam's cheek. "He looks like a prince, surely!"—and with that, fell to fondling Yeshua's head.

"Look," she said, reaching mechanically for the dainties in her bags, "these are your brothers Jacob and Jochanan. May the Lord bless me to see the three of you great men in Israel, seated at the King's table."

Her sons were well-grown boys. Jochanan, the elder of the two, looked more than his years. Ready-witted and given to blunt speech, he had also a curious way of throwing up his arms when he spoke, as though he were constantly warding off blows. For

241

some years he had been helping his father at the family trade, as witnessed by his raw red hands and his dark, roughened face. And like his father, he reeked of fish and rope and open water.

His younger brother Jacob was a more delicate boy, with heavy corkscrew earlocks framing a small face and an absent expression in his eyes. He tended to his own meditations and, when addressed, looked up with a startled, timid smile.

Jacob was Miriam's favorite, whom she loved like her own. When, in the past, Cousin Shoshannah had visited Nazareth—as once on her return from the Sepphoris market where she had used to sell her husband's catch of fish—, she had come with the infant Jacob in her arms, and Miriam, warmed by the love he showed for her, had given the child her breast. Now again, many years after, the boy's unworldliness and fragile charm won her immediate affection.

She embraced both boys and praised them to their mother, then introduced her son and said, putting her arms around all three: "Like David and Jonathan you shall be to one another."

And indeed the boys were soon staunch friends, for the spell of Yeshua's conversation caught Zebedee's children as it had caught Yeshua's playmates at the school. And when, on the day following, the pilgrims moved on from Na'in toward Mount Gilboa, the boys made an inseparable threesome with Yeshua the undisputed leader.

They told Yeshua of Bethsaida, of the two fishing boats they had afloat on the Sea of Genesaret. Yeshua had never seen a lake, nor even a river, and he was curious to learn about this sea of Galilee and how they went about their fishing. And his new friends, particularly Jochanan, were proud to instruct him, telling him of the many towns by which the Sea was encompassed, of K'far-Nahum, largest of them all, where they were sometimes taken by their cousin Simeon and where you could watch the fish salted and packed in barrels for shipment to distant places.

Meanwhile Cousin Shoshannah was questioning Miriam about her eldest son.

"Your first-born's fame has reached even to our Sea," she was saying. "Your artisans who come to K'far-Nahum speak highly of his wisdom and his gift of parable. They say expectant mothers

242

pray for fruit like him. And I can see why; God's grace shines on him and no mistake. And look how my boys cling to him—they might be his disciples and he a famous rabbin."

"My other children, too, praise God, have turned out well," said Miriam. "Jacob, the Younger, is a sponge for learning. They say he should grow up to be a rabbi in Israel . . ."

The troop that descended from Na'in into the Jezreel plain was not one contingent but a great host of pilgrims drawn from all the ends of Galilee—among them old and young and rich and poor. Some trudged along in miserable rotting shreds of sack, with but a loincloth to conceal their shame, without so much as a small bundle to their backs. Day-laborers they were, and some near-slaves who had absconded from their masters to spend the festival in the courts of the Sanctuary. For the Passover was the poor man's yearly joy, when Jerusalem was his estate and the Temple his treasure.

Others in the pilgrim's host were dressed in fine linens, hung with multi-colored cords, with embroidered sandals on their feet, rings on their fingers, fragrant oils rubbed on their heads. Slaves and servants bore them up the hills in stylish litters, followed by asses loaded with provisions and bales of soft bedding and dyed woolen counterpanes.

But in this procession the difference between the rich and poor was ignored, or at least minimized. The pilgrims, one and all, felt like the children of the exodus from Egypt, bound for the land of promise. The God of Israel whose glory beckoned from the Temple united all as in one clan, one congregation, and no one asked, "Who may you be?" or "Is your place with mine?" When the band halted for a resting, every man stretched out where he happened to be and partook of whatever refreshments were at hand. Thus too when they laid themselves down for the night; they used the open fields where stranger lay with stranger under the same cover. Children who by day had joined with other families, or other groups, stayed with them for the night, mothered by strange women as they would have been by their own.

They pitched the second night at the well of Gilead, since it was

243

necessary to proceed by easy stages to spare the many children in the train. The lands here were the private estate of a great Jewish land-owner, who, whether he welcomed them or not, had to admit the pilgrims to his fields and supply them with fresh water and roasted kernels of wheat.

At night, when the three boys lay together under the open sky, tucked into Miriam's blankets, they talked of the legendary places they had passed. Their names, heavy with historic memories, had long been familiar. Mount Gilboa which soared overhead recalled the disaster that claimed the lives of Saul and Jonathan when they warred with the Philistine. David's impassioned curse still brooded over its bare crest. And the boys' talk turned to the well of Gilead, at whose water Gideon had put his host to proof; how with his last little band of thrice a hundred stalwart men—those who had not lapped the water with their tongues as a dog laps, but had cupped their hands to drink—he had defeated the arch-enemy of Israel, Midian and Amalek, though they lay in the valley like grasshoppers for multitude.

The boys grew still and looked with waking eyes at the night sky. And at last Yeshua said softly:

"I can hear every thing grow . . ."

Stillness had settled on the land. The voice of the Creation sang a muted lullaby, blending in one music the subdued hum of insects, the rustling of grasses, the hushed whisper of the leaves, the distant wail of wild, nocturnal beasts which echo made to sound again, the wandering motion of the stars. Yeshua heard the glimmering music of their trail in the sky. They were so large, so many, and so close together that Yeshua thought he saw spark showers clash-begotten in mid-heaven.

"I hear the thunder, too," he said, "and see the lightning. And I see all Creation as it lightens."

"The rabbis say there is an angel behind every leaf of grass, urging it to grow, in obedience to the Lord's Law," said Jacob at his side.

"Not to His Law, but to His grace," said Yeshua. "It is God's grace that makes all things grow, without distinction. His love is a raiment for all. . . ."

244

In every town and village the pilgrims' horde was joined by newcomers from the surrounding countryside. And when they entered the land of the Samaritans, which is Sichem, they came down innumerable as a swarm of locusts. They shunned the royal road which ran south from Beth-Shean to merge with the Caesarea highway down to the king's palace of Sebaste. This was the hated road Herod had ordered built to link his palace with the Roman centers. It was a sop to Roman power and to native leeches, for it facilitated both the rapid movement of troops and the erection of new toll-gates and bridges for the bleeding of pedestrian and mounted travelers. The pilgrims chose footpaths and the lesser by-ways and endeavored only to find Jewish estates where they might rest themselves by day or sleep overnight. For this was alien territory, thickly settled by Samaritans, Tyreans, and Greeks. Here also Roman legionaries were quartered to be near Herod's palatial city, built for the Caesar's glory.

Ten years after Herod's death, Caesar Augustus had at last banished Archelaus, his successor, from Jerusalem and allowed the Jews their wish to be governed from Caesarea by a Roman procurator. But the Emperor had carved up the land of Israel among the rest of Herod's heirs, who sustained their father's policy, throwing up luxury palaces and pagan temples to deify the Caesar and lavishing godless entertainment on patrician Romans in the numerous Herodean palaces which defaced the Holy Land.

Herod's palace boasted a major arena for chariot races, second only to its Alexandrian prototype. Its approaches were lined by marbled colonnades; not far away was a circus for athletic displays and gladiatorial combat. And all these places of diversion were now entering upon their busy season.

For the week of Passover signaled the holiday season throughout Palestine, not among the Jews only, but equally among the foreign overlords. In the springtime of the year the Tetrarchs of the divided provinces of Israel, Antipas of Galilee, Philip, and the rest of the Herodean princelings, staged spectacular entertainments for the Roman dignitaries at their courts—chariot races and gladiatorial slaughter to show the Caesar that they, the heirs of the

245

great Herod in their Asiatic outposts, cherished the civilization of Rome no less than their royal father.

The pilgrims' host rested on the hills that overlooked Sebaste, and Yeshua saw for the first time how the Gentiles and the mighty ones of this world whiled away their leisure hours. He saw the merciless lash of the charioteers crack against the foaming fell of horses at full gallop. Below him he caught a glimpse of a platoon of sword-bearing gladiators, naked but for small leathern aprons and elaborate helmets, parading in closed ranks on the way to the arena.

From their high coign of vantage the Jewish pilgrims watched these Roman pastimes and pointed with anger at Rome's paganry —a foreign nettle planted by the Herods on ancestral soil.

"There go the gladiators," said one man bitterly; "look how they strut to their worthless death."

"We are in Sichem now," said his neighbor. "This is the land of Jeroboam ben Nebat, the idolator, of Ahab and the hellhag Jezebel, Baal's minions, for this is Baal's province, and Astarte's. What wonder if you cannot turn about for defilement? But in Jerusalem—to put a circus there and stage gladiatorial contests— in the sight of the Temple!"

"They have a circus in Jerusalem?" someone asked from the crowd.

"You will see for yourself; under the Sextus bridge, directly opposite the seat of the Sanhedrin at the place of the polished stones."

Yeshua, who had been listening closely, was anxious to learn more about those naked men who went singing into mortal battle, and he asked his mother:

"*Ema,* those men we saw with swords in their hands; were they the Caesar's soldiers going to war?"

"No, *tinoki,* they were going to fight one another. It is their business to fight till they fall dead."

"Why?"

"To amuse and divert others who watch their fighting skill."

"*Ema,* why do they do it?"

"Because Adam's sin weighs us down like a heavy load. Our lives are ruled by sin. And that is why men rejoice at the sight

246

of evil more than at the sight of good. And that is why the earth cries out to God that He may speedily send a Saviour to wipe the sin from its face."

Later that night, before falling asleep, the boys spoke of the brutal ways of Sichem. Sichem and Jerusalem were in eternal strife—the pure against the dross, Jeroboam's polluted altars with their golden calves against the hill of Zion and its Sanctuary; Elijah the Prophet facing Jezebel, Ahab's unholy wife, mother of harlots, the beldam of evil, the votaress of Baal and Moloch, female embodiment of filthiness. She fought the prophets of the Lord and spilled their blood. Elijah and the bloodied queen were locked in everlasting battle. The battle never ceased, not even when the priests of Baal were put to death on Mount Carmel. Elijah of Tishbi was still fleeing the false queen, to be fed by ravens by the brook Cherith. Jezebel was still the regnant power, priestess and prophetess of Baal. Suckling babes she hurled into the searing embrace of the insatiable Moloch. The poor she plundered of their birthright and immolated the Lord's chosen at the feet of Baal. Like a harpy she winged monster-like over mankind, sowing iniquity in human hearts and gloating at the swollen tide of tears and blood that stifled the groans of the earth. And thus she warred still on Elijah, until the Prophet's tread should resound in the hills and the blast of his horn herald the hour of victory, Messiah's coming. And the Messiah would wash the earth clean of iniquity, even as Noah's flood. Then all the Gentiles would go down in the deluge, and Noah-Israel alone would be saved in the Ark.

"Not so," said Yeshua, correcting his companions, "for God told us through His prophet: 'As I live, saith the Lord God, I have no pleasure in the death of the wicked; but that the wicked turn from his way and live', and so, I tell you, the Messiah will not stamp out the Gentile nations, but rather the evil that lives in all men."

"How do you know all this?" asked Yeshua's friends.

"I know it," Yeshua replied.

Jacob and Jochanan continued whispering to each other for a little while.

"He speaks as though he had received a revelation," said Jacob to his brother.

"It could be that he has," said Jochanan. "I have thought it before, since everything he does or says seems justified in him."

"I know," his brother said. . . .

There was a blare of trumpets in the hills and in a few moments the camp was astir. The boys shook off their hour of slumber and saw the morning star over the heights of Ephraim.

"Let us arise and go unto the holy mountain," came the chant of the pilgrims. They were in haste to leave this Gentile ground, straining toward the hills of Ephraim, the beckoning realm of Israel.

CHAPTER XIII

"Look, *emi,* look, Jerusalem is like a stag leaping the hills!" They were gazing down on Jerusalem from Mount Scopus, they and the pilgrims' host. Before them King David's city rose and fell. On one side towers and palaces climbed to a hilly crest and were absorbed in groves of olive trees. On the other, a slope of chalk-white roofs dipped into a vale, blended by light into a cascade of iridescent silver. Here and there the city crouched in the flats, only to rise again to greater majesty where it crowned itself on Mount Moriah with the Temple, or with Herod's turreted palaces on Zion Hill.

They entered the purlieus of the city by the second wall, and passed through the new quarter of Bezetha into the valley, where representatives of the Temple had prepared for their official welcome and where the pilgrims' host finally dissolved and scattered. From there on every family looked after its own, finding kinsmen or friends with whom to stay for the duration of the festal season. There were too many of them for all to be housed in private homes. And since the Jerusalemites were forbidden by law to take money for the quartering of pilgrims, it was with difficulty that those who were friendless in the city found any lodging at all. They accommodated themselves under the open sky or on the hills and dales that surged about Jerusalem. Here each company of townsmen had its prior rights based on previous pilgrimages; here they pitched their tents or spread their burlap mats by the brook of Kedron, in the Ge-Hinnom valley or—with better fortune—somewhere within the lower city or at the city walls. Others camped with their bundles under the portico of some wealthy mansion, preferring to keep close to the Temple through the length of their stay. For Jerusalem, during Passover week, belonged no more to its inhabitants alone; it became truly the queen city of all Israel, the nation which had come in force to pay it homage. Whether a man had come from far or near, his entrance in the Holy City was his homecoming. To be a member of Israel was to have a portion in Jerusalem, and for one festive week the pilgrims made the town their own. All private rights to landed property were for the time suspended; the pilgrims spread themselves where they found room.

Not that room was easy to find, for Jerusalem was fairly inundated by the visiting hosts. Crowds filled every house and mansion like grape clusters bursting on the autumn vine. They streamed through every lane and thoroughfare, debouching at each market place into a greater conflux of humanity.

Joseph's family struggled to get through to the King David wall in the lower city, not far from the pool of Siloam. They chose the least frequented by-ways, but even there the city was heaving and churning and one needed sharp elbows to beat a lane through the press. Yeshua had never seen so many people in one place, nor so many varied types: Jews from every province of Syria, whose habit and manner of dressing their hair betrayed their multifarious origin. And there were many from beyond the confines of Syria—Babylonians with trailing black robes clasped at the throat; Jews from the Phoenician coast, in many-colored, pictured cloaks and breeches, with beards variously braided and gathered; families from Asia Minor, from Antiochia, Philippi, Ephesus, all in their native dress, from the pauper's habit of goat's hair to the scintillating colored Persian silks of the rich; and, not least, Jews from the provinces of Italy, vaunting the latest styles of the Tiber,

249

proud of the toga which proclaimed their citizenship in the first city of the Empire; and—winding in and out of the throng—half-naked anchorites, desert dwellers draped in sacks or untanned animal hides.

The families of Joseph and Zebedee, accompanied by some of their townsmen, threaded a way through the dense crowds, past open shops and merchant booths, over piles of pots and pitchers which lay in their track. They traversed the valley at the foot of the Temple mount, crossed over the high arches which supported one end of the bridge that linked the upper city with the Temple mount, and came at last into the valley of the cheesemongers, or —as it was called in Greek—the Tyropoeon.

They found the valley garrisoned by sizeable patrols of Roman legionaries, fully armed and harnessed, as well as auxiliary German horse, standing watch over the great gymnasium under the bridge. During these holy days of feasting, the Roman gymnasium, an unsightly sore in the eyes of the pilgrims, required a powerful guard to forestall rioting.

Having crossed the valley, they arrived next at the market in the lower city.

It was a good while before they had forced a way through the crush of buyers and chandlers which peopled the market. This was the hub on which every mercantile street in the lower city converged. And though its merchants and artisans catered primarily to the pilgrims and the poorer sections of the population—there being another market in the upper city for the rich—the booths and stalls in this lower part of the town were sought out by all as the traditional center of the oilmen and incense-mixers of Jerusalem.

No city in the world could vie with Jerusalem in the use of unguent oils and perfumes. A popular jest, it is true, claimed that the ladies of Jerusalem required no perfumes since their entire city was adequately scented by the fragrant fumes borne down from the Temple altars. But the ladies preferred to make sure. They followed faithfully those of their grandmothers who had fallen foul of Isaiah, walking "with stretched forth necks and wanton eyes." They kept perfumes in atomizers hid inside their sandals. When they met a comely youth in their way, it needed but the pressure of a toe to send out a heady scent which inflamed his desire and benumbed his sense. And among all the daughters of Israel only those in Jerusalem were allowed the privilege to spend the tenth part of their dowry upon oils and balms.

The market overflowed with would-be buyers, male and female, indigenous and newly-arrived, eager to provide themselves with perfumes for the high festival. They had their choice here of the most exotic spices, oils, and aromatic gums, and they bought to the limit of their means, since there were few things more highly cherished in a household than its store of fragrance.

Wending their way through bargaining crowds, Joseph's family at last reached David's wall near the pool of Siloam.

As the pilgrims had taken possession of the bazaars, courts, and columned porches of the city, so they had occupied its spacious walls. The ancient walls of Jerusalem, with their grottos, alcoves, niches, immured casemates, and embrasures, where thousands could lodge overnight, teemed with populace—strangers as well as local poor who, with the rest of Jewry, were owners of the city walls. Here every family could find some built-in opening or breach to provide shelter.

Miriam had an old acquaintance living in the city wall near the Ge-Hinnom valley. His name was Hillel—Hillel the water carrier, his occupation being to draw water in the pool of Siloam and bear it over the steep, narrow stairs to the upper city where he peddled it from house to house. He was a small man with a meek, apologetic smile, a member of the Essene brotherhood. Miriam's father in his youth had been his companion in the sect and, after the custom of the Essenes, the two men had shared all their belongings. Even now, so many years after Reb Hanan's death, Miriam's family had, as it were, its own home in Jerusalem in Hillel's lodging.

The water carrier was expecting them. His first act of welcome for the two families was to bring out a pitcher of cool water with which he washed their hands and feet. Then he kissed their cheeks with ceremony and led them into his house—a recess in the city wall—where straw cushions had been readied on the ground and bread and salt on the table. The two families sat down to eat and Hillel served them with his own hands; for as an orthodox Essene he lived alone and celibate.

In one corner of his chamber was a ladder leading to a roofless cell which had formerly served as a watch tower. The water carrier had turned it into a retreat for his devotions. Now Miriam claimed it for the children, spreading on its floor the pallets for Yeshua and his two friends who were soon fast asleep.

Then she undid her bundles and set about fitting the water carrier's home for her family's stay in Jerusalem.

When the time came to bring Yeshua to the Temple, Joseph was busy preparing the sacrifice. With Zebedee and his boys he had gone to purchase the warrant which would entitle them to one lamb for their paschal offering. It left Miriam alone with Yeshua to deliver her gifts into the Temple treasure—as it was written: "Thou shalt not come with empty hands before the Lord."

She dressed her son in his new white cloak and girdle and, taking him by the hand, set out for Mount Moriah. They climbed the steep rock-hewn steps to the upper city, shaded by the massive bulk of Herod's triple towers, Yeshua dragging her along at a great pace, for he was impatient to see at last the glories of the Temple. They passed the upper market with its splendid bazaars and profuse palaces and the old castle of the Hasmoneans opposite Mount Moriah. They crossed over the wide Sextus Bridge which spanned the Tyropoeon, linking the upper city with the Temple mount, and came finally to the outermost gate of the Sanctuary where it was sentried by Roman soldiers. They ascended the wide stairs that led into the enclosed outer court, the vast "court of the Gentiles," the hub of the great city. It was flanked on either side by columned arcades which housed, below and in the galleries above, innumerable chambers, shops, and merchant booths, mobbed by a multitude of pilgrims.

Many of them had come like Miriam to deliver presents or to procure a warrant for a sheep, a pair of turtledoves, some twigs of incense, cedar wood, or other items suitable for sacrifice. In a medley of native and foreign costumes they stood lined up before the cashiers' wickets, officials of the Temple—each with a plaque on his chest to show his rank in the Temple bureaucracy—who sat in small closed booths and gathered in the Temple tribute.

There were many forms of tribute and as many offices for its collection; at one booth they were taking the obligatory "half-shekel of the Sanctuary," at another the free gifts and donations of money, at a third the money held in trust for orphans, for which the officials handed out bills of receipt. Several more stands dispensed warrants for sacrifices. There were also two closed booths behind whose wickets sat no officers; into their openings people threw money and sundry articles of value. The first of these was called the "silent charity booth," marked for the reception of anonymous bequests and oblations. The money here realized was used by the Temple to support deserving persons who had fallen on bad days. The other "blind" booth was a kind of dumping ground for those of the pilgrims' gifts which were rejected as unfit for Temple use.

Miriam's gifts for the Temple were a cruse of refined oil, which she had pressed from flowers and herbs in her own garden, and a length of fine-spun linen. Of this the Temple used enormous quantities, since the vestments of the priests must never be washed but, at the first sign of soiling, were put away to be burned in a great bonfire at the Feast of Water-Drawing—a prodigal custom which made linen an ever welcome gift.

Miriam passed by the booth where the half-shekel was taken, since she had paid the tax in Nazareth to roaming emissaries of the Temple on the first day of Adar. She and Yeshua went straightway to the booth of gifts and took their place in the line. There were many before them, some of them wealthy men in colored robes with large rings on their hands, bearing costly presents for the Temple—some with purses of gold or golden vessels, others with bolts of Persian silk and Sidonian linen embroidered with thread of gold and purple. Others still bore figured vases filled with the rarest oils. The officers spent much time with these wealthy donors, welcoming them with proper courtesy and calling out the chief treasurer himself to greet them and inquire after their well-being. The poorer donors were briefly dispatched, with every now and then some wretch of a woman turned back altogether because her gift was not fit for the Temple. She was then told to drop her contribution in the wicket of the "blind" or "silent" booth whence it was later sold for the Temple with the rest of the rejected offerings.

Miriam was one such case. When she offered to hand the official her cruse of oil, he eyed it sceptically and, without reaching, asked what was in it. Miriam explained how she had brought a little oil from Nazareth which she had pressed herself for the great Temple candelabra.

"But I trust you have no galbanum in your garden," said the official, and a faint smile stirred the oily ringlets of his beard. "And then you are not likely to have brought us nard or myrrh. Nor does this cruse look to me like the one from which Samuel anointed David. This is no more than ordinary oil; no, my good woman, we have no use for it. Go back and throw it in the silent booth. The clear oil for the Temple candelabra is made in our own distillery by men who are past masters of their craft and who have their trade secrets handed down from time immemorial. . . . And what else have you there?"

"A piece of linen—that I wove."

"That's better," said the cashier reassuringly. "That we can use for the priests' vestments,"—saying which he took the cloth from Miriam's hand and tossed it on a high pile of linen at his back. "Now go, my good woman, and the Lord will reward you."

Miriam found her son's hand and led him away. She walked past the blind wicket but instead of throwing in her cruse of oil, hid it under her cloak. Then she and Yeshua proceeded to the fifteen steps that led, through the Gate of Nicanor, into the Court of the Women. But before they had reached it, Yeshua stopped suddenly short and exclaimed:

"Look, *emi,* the rabbis with their disciples!"

He was staring greedily at assemblies of students seated on low benches in the open forum. In the midst of each group, on tall cathedras, sat the presiding rabbis. Yeshua could not tear himself away from the sight. He gazed at the rabbis, the old and the young, at the students who represented all ages of man, the younger in the foremost rows, the others at the rear. And they were rising by turns to voice their carefully deliberated queries, to which the rabbis made answer.

254

Yeshua too had many heavy questions on his mind, some that had gnawed at him for years past, and some that had arisen during his brief stay in the Temple precincts. For he felt God's house to be his own, as it was every Jew's, and each lapse committed near its walls affected him like a personal affront. His first impressions of the Temple had not answered his expectations and had added fresh disappointment to his doubts so that he was impatient to clear his mind before the rabbis of whom such wonders had been told him by the tanner, by Joseph and his teachers in Nazareth.

"Are these the rabbins, *emi,* who interpret the word of God?"

"Yes, *tinoki,* these are Israel's sages. And with God's help, when you grow up, you shall sit among them. And who knows but that . . ." Her last sentence was not completed. "Come, *tinoki,*" she said.

"No, *emi,* wait," said the boy; "I want to sit with the disciples and hear what the sages say."

"Not now, my child. Your first footsteps in God's house should be to God, not to the rabbis. Come, we will go into the court and pray."

As they entered the Court of the Women the scene changed abruptly. The space here was filled with women, many of them kneeling, their eyes turned to the wide opening of the Nicanor Gate that towered above its fifteen tiers of steps. It was here that the Temple proper began. Here the Levites stood ranged on the steps, dressed in white robes, plucking the strings of their harps as they chanted the Psalms. Behind them the wide wings of the Gate shone with the blinding glitter of gold under sunlight. And beyond, in the Court of the Israelites, Yeshua caught glimpses of worshippers who prayed with their brows pressed to the ground. In the distance more steps could be seen, climbing higher and higher toward the innermost sanctum—white steps as far as Yeshua's eyes could reach, and over every marbled façade curtains and veils sparkling in a thousand colors. And deep within, in the Court of the Priests, the hard glare of burnished copper came from the great sacrificial altar. Files of priests in tall white miters moved ceaselessly over the steps that led to its base, of whom some bore golden chargers, others smoking incense boats or resinous woods. In unending procession oxen and sheep were being led

255

into the slaughterhouse. Puffs of smoke, mingling with the fumes of incense and the hot reek of blood and scorching fat, issued through its curtained portals, filling Yeshua with misgivings and clouding his joy in the worship. He knew that the smell of blood and burning flesh came from the animals whom the priests were sacrificing within. Did God then take pleasure in the smell of blood? Had not the Prophet said that the Lord was weary of the blood of bullocks and lambs; that He asked no more than a purified heart and hands that had ceased from evil?

He felt saddened and perplexed. The scene before his eyes, he knew, accorded in every rite with God's commandments to Moses, and yet a rebellious impulse in his heart moved him to reject it. Oh, for a prophet to sweep the Lord's house clean of burning flesh, tear down its curtains, and release the pent-up steam of blood, and bring back to God the heart of man—not by the ashes of burnt offerings, but by uprightness and prayer.

Yeshua wondered that he had no consciousness of wrong-doing in pursuing these thoughts. He felt instead that he was living in the breath of the Prophets who knew God's will better than these priests of the Temple. The Prophets had revealed God's will to men. Why was their word not heeded?

Yeshua thought he would ask the rabbis in the seats of Moses whose calling it was to resolve doubts. They, surely, knew how much longer the priests would bring their sacrifices of animal flesh and when the genuine offerings would begin, as spoken of by Isaiah.

While Yeshua was thus absorbed in his own thoughts, Miriam was kneeling at his side, her eyes closed, her lips moving faintly to the words of her unuttered prayer:

"Father in heaven, I have brought him safe into Thy house who is Thy pledge to the world. Behold, he is grown to manhood, but in his seeing and hearing he is not like to other men. For his young heart is bruised by our sinful lives and his spirit troubled by the injustice he has met so soon in his way. Even now, standing at my side, he burns with the sacred indignation that raged in Thy Prophets. With contempt he views the flesh and fat they kindle on Thy altar, and like Isaiah he demands that the heart alone be offered before Thee.

"I know not to what pass he shall be led, nor what road Thou hast paved for him. But I do see him, like a launched arrow, speeding toward the target Thou didst set, and my heart trembles between joy and fear. Father, I fear for him, for I see walls of fire in his path. He is too young, Father in heaven; the thread of his life is too frail. For a little while yet, let him see the flowers, not the thorns. Leave him to me for a little while longer. And teach me what to do, Father in heaven, for I am in awe of the power of his spirit and feel too weak to be his mother."

In the intensity of her prayer Miriam forgot herself. Her eyes were still tightly closed and she saw herself in a land of green hills where a youthful shepherd was grazing his flock. An old man with a white flowing beard stood on a hilltop over the dale. A cruse of oil was in his hand and with the other he was beckoning to the young shepherd. Miriam knew the hill and the valley; it was a site near Bethlehem, and Samuel the Prophet was calling the young David to anoint him king of the House of Israel.

Miriam then knew what to do. With one hand she beckoned to her son, even as Samuel had called David, and when Yeshua had come quite close, she seized the cruse of oil from under her shawl and poured it out over his head.

"*Emi!* It was the oil you brought for the Temple!" said Yeshua.

"It is the cruse from which Samuel anointed your father David."

CHAPTER XIV

YESHUA saw little of his parents now, and not much more of his friends. Alone he rambled about the courts of the Temple, watching every detail of its ritual and administration. He saw many things that displeased him, as for instance the multitude of overseers, watchmen, guards, and officials who walked constantly about the courts, some with bludgeons in their hands to maintain order. For what did God need so many guards, or so many priests of all ranks, pacing back and forth in groups, like soldiers on parade? And to what purpose were those innumerable

257

rams and bullocks which they drove without end into the sanctuary as though it were a charnel house and not a house of God?

And all the while he thought of the Prophets, of Isaiah, Ezekiel, and Jeremiah who had inveighed against the Temple and its blood sacrifices of which the Lord had long sickened.

"Father in heaven," Yeshua cried in his heart, "can they not see that Thou art wearied of their doings?"

The only men before whom he could voice his perplexities were the rabbis who taught in the shade of the Temple. They were the recognized champions of the Law, who understood God's will better than the priests. Yeshua would go to them for his answer.

He began by looking among them for the grand old Rabbi Hillel of whom Taddi had so often spoken. But he could not find him in the Temple and at last learned from Hillel's namesake, the water carrier, that the old rabbi had passed away some years before. The teacher who now took his place was his youngest disciple, a man universally respected and revered beyond his years. His pupils in the Temple court crowded about his feet as though he were an ancient venerable sage.

He was indeed very young and had but recently assumed the rabbinate. His gentle eyes and slender body could belong only to a man in his early thirties. His lean face tapered down from a broad forehead whose height was cut short by the black cap of his calling. His soft dark beard barely hid the hollows of his cheeks and merged over the chest with a black gown. And when he spoke he had a way of molding the air with long beautiful hands and rolling his eyes upward, as to the prime source of knowledge.

The young rabbi was expounding to his hearers—who included men with hoary beards and fellow rabbis—the rules of the Passover sacrifice, speaking humbly in the name of his great teacher, old Reb Hillel. For the youthful Jochanan ben Zakkai was known as a zealous defender of his master's teachings, which in Hillel's lifetime had acquired the full authority of Israel's oral tradition. And what is more, he not only conveyed his master's legal code, but lived faithfully by his moral precepts. Like his rabbi he was a passionate lover of peace and a difficult man to put out of humor. It was said of him that no one had ever anticipated his greeting, be it man or child, Gentile or Jew.

Yeshua stopped near the rabbi's circle. Some of his listeners he found to be draped in sackcloth, with ropes girdling their loins. He saw one with a sledge-hammer at his side, whose dusty dress showed him to be a stonecutter fresh from his labors. His neighbor's naked shoulders were hung with a carrier's ropes; others held spades or saws between their knees. And Yeshua observed that these common artisans, if they were the rabbi's learners, received no less respect than the black-gowned scholars in the audience and the men whose wealth was meretriciously displayed in rings and precious girdles.

In the midst of his exegesis Jochanan ben Zakkai's glance lighted on the boy who stood nearby in his white cloak. Something of the boy's total absorption must have arrested his notice for he stopped in mid-sentence and smiled. Then he beckoned to Yeshua to come close.

The students looked round to see whom the rabbi was calling. They knew that the great Reb Jochanan would not break his discourse but with good reason, and so they waited eagerly to hear what he would ask of the boy.

"Tell me your verse, child," said the rabbi, addressing Yeshua with the customary formula of introduction. And Yeshua, without hesitation, responded with a verse from the Psalms:

"O Lord, open Thou my lips, and my mouth shall show forth Thy praise. For Thou desirest not sacrifice, else would I give it; Thou delightest not in burnt offering. The sacrifices of God are a broken spirit, a broken and a contrite heart."

The rabbi's face brightened with pleasure and his hand went out to stroke Yeshua's locks:

"You say well, my child—you are a true son of Abraham." Then, turning to his listeners, he said: "Learn from the mouths of children. This boy with his verse has revealed for us wherein lies the secret of sacrifice. For the sacrifice is nought but the heart, the contrite spirit. A good heart is every human virtue, and when a man offers his heart to God he can offer no more, for he returns to God the best of what he has received—which is called mercy. For the name of God is the All-Merciful, even as our sages taught —'The All-Merciful demands no more than the heart.'"

"Is God called the All-Merciful?" Yeshua asked eagerly.

"Yes, my son, God is a king of mercy and demands only that we offer Him the heart, which is the seat of mercy."

"Why then do they sacrifice lambs and bullocks? Does God require their blood? Teach me, rabbi, why do they not heed the word of the Psalmist? Why do they continue the slaughter of innocent beasts?"

There was a surprised movement among the students, for they were not accustomed to such candor in a questioner; they expected now to hear the rabbi dismiss the boy with the curt answer he had so often given to men who challenged the rites of purification—"See how you live," the rabbi would tell all comers; "it is not the unclean thing which defiles, nor the water which cleanses, for the Lord says—'So have I ordered it and it is not for you to question My orders.'" But now, instead of evading the question by invoking the infallibility of the divine law, Jochanan ben Zakkai looked intently at Yeshua and took the boy's hands in his own and said:

"This is a mighty matter you have opened, child." He sighed deeply and turned to the audience to resume his discourse, using the boy's question as a point of departure: "No, heaven forbid, God needs no sacrifices, for it is written—'I spake not unto your fathers, in the day that I brought them out of the land of Egypt, concerning burnt offerings or sacrifices.' And to Moses God said: 'If ye offer a sacrifice unto the Lord, ye shall offer it at your own will.' At your own will, mark you—not at the Lord's. For the soul of man thirsts after God, even as David said—'My soul pants after Thee.'

"Observe now; man's soul—his heart, which is a spark of God —longs after God, craving for nearness. His sacrifice is his approach to God; the smoke of the burnt offering—it is the ladder by which the creature climbs to its Creator.

"But, you may ask, how can mere man attach himself to God, being a hulk of flesh and blood, a clot of corruption which seems alive today and tomorrow sickens and dies? It was for this God gave us sacrifices. For by means of sacrifice we do attach ourselves to God. What indeed is a sacrifice? Is it the lamb? No, for it is the soul of man. When the soul sins it is removed from its Creator. When it seeks to return through penitence, man brings a sin offering. And what is this sin offering? A fine to indemnify the

260

Lord? No, heaven forbid! The sin offering, it is the lamb sacrificed by the sinner, upon which he brands his confession of a contrite heart. And then the sinner's soul enters the sacrifice, and the silent lamb that cannot open its mouth, that never sinned since it was born, that is immaculate and free from all iniquity—this lamb then undertakes the sinner's guilt, becoming indeed like the souls of the righteous who suffer for the sins of many and do atonement for mankind."

Yeshua was listening with whole attention. The rabbi's words had moved him deeply and his eyes filled with tears.

"Then the innocent lamb is transformed into the soul of the man who offers it as sacrifice?"

The rabbi nodded.

"And through this lamb the man attaches himself to his Maker?"

"It is as you say, my son."

"Then it is as the Prophet said of him who would bear the sins of us all—'He is brought as a lamb to the slaughter'?"

"What the words of the Prophet may signify is past our certain knowledge, my son. It will be clear only to those who shall have grace to witness it with their own eyes. In the meanwhile, my son, abide by the words of the wise Ben Sirach: 'What is hidden from you, seek it not to uncover.'"

Yeshua bowed deeply and gave the customary answer to a rabbi: "I hang on your words; from your mouth I gain new life."

"May you be a rabbi in Israel to spread the word of God," said Jochanan ben Zakkai.

Yeshua hesitated.

"May I come again to hear you?"

The rabbi spread his long, pale hands: "There are no doors to my school," he said. "Come when you can and let us hear your verses."

Throughout the length of their stay in Jerusalem, Joseph and Miriam had never a moment to spare. Each company of pilgrims, composed of townsmen usually, made common cause of their sacrifice. Thus most of the Nazarenes had pitched their tents together in the Ge-Hinnom valley close to the King David wall where

Joseph and Zebedee lived with the water carrier. And it was here that the Nazarenes prepared to meet the Passover feast.

The women brought out the bags of flour they had separated for the second tithe, and together baked them into wafers of unleavened dough. And they set out wine and vegetables for their communal paschal supper. The men dug a ditch in a court near the wall and filled it with brushwood for a fire to roast the sacrificial lamb.

And then came the great moment for the sacrifice itself. The company of Nazarenes, including Zebedee's family, Joseph, and Yeshua, repaired to the Court of the Israelites where only a few steps and a curtain separated them from the priestly sanctum. The court was choking full of pilgrims who had come on a like errand.

The walls here were lined with gutters to conduct the blood of the sacrificed lambs to the slaughter house, situated in the innermost Court of the Priests. Across Joseph's shoulders lay the yoke which upheld the white, unblemished lamb, its head dangling limp over the gutter. Zebedee stood by, knife in hand, waiting his turn, for there were many ahead in the line, with lambs similarly slung over their shoulders.

Two rows of priests, barefoot, in holy vestments crowned with miters, formed a lane that stretched from within the sanctuary and through its curtained port down to the slaughterers. They passed a golden chalice from hand to hand, and when it reached the priest who stood abreast with Joseph's lamb, Zebedee swiftly slashed the animal's throat. The priest caught a spurt of its blood in the cup and handed it to his brother priest. The chalice traveled on from hand to hand until, brim-filled with bubbling blood, it passed into the sanctuary where the officiating priest sprinkled it on the great altar.

Yeshua was standing at Joseph's side, staring intently at the lamb "that opened not its mouth" while it died for the sake of others. He was pondering Jochanan ben Zakkai's words, and so absorbed was he in his meditations that he seemed deaf to the chant of the Levites on the steps above, with their blare of trumpets, their lyre-strumming, and their chiming bells. He forgot almost where he was, aware of nothing but the sacrifice. He tried to follow the course of the lamb as it shed its own substance to assume the burden of a human soul, the soul of them all, and this soul it brought as a sin offering to God, even with its blood, as it was written: "It is the blood that maketh an atonement for the soul." And through this animal that perished mute and unprotesting, the souls of Israel were fused with God. They met together on His altar. In the commingling blood of many sacrifices, poured from one golden cup, the souls of Jewry were mixed indissolubly and conjoined with Israel's God.

Yeshua started as at a sudden blaze of light, and he knew then what the Prophet meant when he spoke of the man of sorrows who would bear our griefs and be wounded for our transgressions and be brought as a lamb to the slaughter. The rabbi had warned him against seeking to uncover the Prophet's mystery, but the mystery had bared itself to him in one instant of revelation, like the open page of a book written in a clear hand.

He knew now that the Messiah was the Lamb of God. His bruised body bore the souls of all, and by his life, which he would offer with his blood upon God's altar, he would take away the sin of Israel and bind its common soul to his Father in heaven. . . .

The slaughtered sheep was carried back to the King David wall. The fire was kindled in the ditch, the lamb trussed upon a spit and roasted on the flames. The Nazarenes seated themselves in a circle and ate of its flesh a fraction no less than the size of an olive. And Yeshua, swallowing his morsel, thought to himself how his soul was now bound to his Father in heaven by virtue of the lamb that had died for his sake.

No more than a few days had passed since his arrival, and already Yeshua was the fondling of the rabbis in the Temple Court. All knew the boy in the white cloak and girdle, with his black locks that tumbled down the nape of his neck. The sight of him, standing before a famous rabbin and quoting a verse from the Prophets, had quickly become familiar. For his verses were sufficiently apposite and pregnant for mountains of interpretations to be piled upon them by rabbis and disciples, and his questions were generally so incisive that they enabled the expounders of the Law to launch the longest exegesis, and the storytellers to unwind the darkest threads of legend. He was called from one rabbin to the next, each time to cite his verse, as though his choice had something in it of prophetic inspiration.

Yeshua liked it well among the rabbis. They heard his questions patiently and answered from the wealth of their knowledge so that many torturing problems in his mind were happily resolved.

One such problem that had long been a source of disquiet concerned the laws of purity which cut such sharp divisions not only between Jew and Greek, but between one Jew and his fellow, between the learned and the ignorant. Yeshua did not scruple to lay his doubts before the rabbis.

"Did not God say—'In Thee shall all families of the earth be blessed'?" he demanded.

Then the rabbis explained to him that Gentiles too were free to sacrifice to the Lord in His Temple, and that the righteous ones among the nations had their portion in the world to come. But none of this could satisfy the boy, until a full explanation for the Law's insistence on purity and segregation came to him from one of Jochanan ben Zakkai's disciples.

Once, after he had asked his question, Yeshua was approached by a handsome young man with startlingly bright eyes. He greeted Yeshua with a cordial smile and said:

"I heard you ask a question today about the Gentiles, if they were not also sons of Abraham; and I liked the text you brought to support your contention—'In Thee shall all families of the earth be blessed.' That was aptly quoted, my boy. It means that all the nations of the world may, if they wish, draw on the blessing which God laid on Abraham, and that, by faith, they may all become sons of the covenant, which is to say, children of Israel."

"If this is so," said Yeshua, "why then do we keep Gentiles at arm's length; why do we make them agents of pollution—like lepers?"

"But don't you see, my boy, that Israel must keep apart? Look about you: we are hemmed in by uncleanness. No one wished to accept the Torah but Israel alone. On this account we are hated and spurned by the nations. And if we did not harness ourselves with the bonds of the Law, how long should our zeal for the Lord's cause endure? Our teacher Moses sought to render us a holy peo-

264

ple—not for ourselves alone, but to serve as a beacon to the nations, an example of purity and righteousness, that they might learn from us and thus draw nearer to their Maker. But suppose Israel were to leap the barriers and abrogate the laws of purity—why, then the Gentiles would not come to us; we would come down to them. Our women would still sacrifice—but to Moloch and Astarte and not to the living God. So, you see, Israel must continue with the yoke of heaven on its back, and must bear it for all the world to prepare it for the advent of the kingdom of heaven."

This led them to talk of the Messiah, and the young man and boy soon found themselves drawn to each other. For the young man, like many more in Israel, was waiting with passionate longing; the time, he said, was ripe. And as he spoke his eyes grew brighter still with love and longing for the Saviour, and he looked like one speaking out of a dream.

A fast friendship sprang up between him and Yeshua.

Children among Jews were not looked down upon as minors. They were, on the contrary, treated with a certain reverence since their freedom from sin was held to keep them in proximity to God. Their pronouncements were respectfully heard and interpreted for hidden intimations of a possibly oracular nature. It was not unusual to find an older man cultivating the friendship of a child and valuing it without a thought of patronizing condescension. Such a relation now sprang up between Yeshua and Nicodemon, the young disciple of Jochanan ben Zakkai. Nicodemon was entranced by the boy's intelligence and once, when they had remained together past the fall of night, he took him home to his own house.

Nicodemon was unmarried, living not far from the Temple in the low section of the Tyropoeon, where he had an olive press and plied the trade of an oiler.

His shack was littered with bundles of dry incense, but he kept a chest in one corner filled with precious scrolls. Yeshua found here the apocalyptic writings which told of the Messianic future. Yeshua drank deeply of their message and, as the night wore on, forgot to go home. And so he continued to spend the daylight hours with the rabbis and scholars in the Temple, and the nights with his friend Nicodemon, who found for him among his books the passages relating to the Messiah. Several days thus passed and Yeshua, wholly absorbed in his new-found riches, did not remember to return to the King David wall.

Meanwhile Joseph and Miriam and the band of Galilean pilgrims prepared for the return journey. Those who had households and stock to look after could not afford the luxury of spending the full holiday season in Jerusalem. Once they had brought their offering and kept the first days of the feast, they were impatient to be on their way.

Miriam knew nothing of her son's whereabouts. For several days she had taken it for granted that Yeshua was out with Zebedee's boys, making explorations of the city. It was common for children to leave their parents for several days at a time, so long as they remained near their townspeople. Grown boys particularly banded together and sallied out on their own where no parental authority could dim their excitement. And there was no cause for alarm if they failed to return for the night; presumably they had dropped to sleep wherever the night had overtaken them—in the homes of kinsmen or friends, against the columns of some city mansion, or in the spacious "King Solomon Stables" which served so many pilgrims for a night or two. Miriam therefore was convinced that Yeshua was somewhere in the Galilean band, and it was not until Jerusalem was a day's journey behind that she, preparing Yeshua's pallet for the night, became concerned about his absence.

"Where is Yeshua?" she asked.

The few women around her had not seen him.

"Where did you leave him; was he not with you?"

"No, he has not been about for a few days—we thought he was with the B'nai Jacob."

Miriam ran to the B'nai Jacob, and from them to the B'nai Hanina.

"Is my son with you?"

"No, we never saw him."

All that night Miriam and Joseph went from family to family, asking the same question. And in each tent the people thought that they had seen him in another.

"He is not lost, Miriam," said Joseph, trying vainly to console his wife. "He is a grown boy and has probably joined another Galilean group."

They waited anxiously for the dawn. Then Joseph bridled his ass and led Miriam back to Jerusalem.

No, Hillel the water carrier had not seen him for some days; Yeshua had not come home.

They searched the length of the King David wall, ready to seek him with every family, known or unknown, that had stayed in Jerusalem. The boy had not been seen.

They did not neglect to search for him in the Temple, where they combed the courts and peered in every booth. Turning back again they scanned the incense market and even delved into the valley of Siloam to look for him among the water carriers where Yeshua had spent some of his hours.

It was on the third day only that Miriam—footsore, weary, and consumed by anxiety—remembered. She recalled that first visit to the Temple when Yeshua had stopped at the rabbis' forum and how she had with difficulty pulled him away. She rallied Joseph and hastened with him to the Temple—through the Court of the Women as far as the Great Gate that gave on the Court of the Israelites. From here the forum of the rabbis could be seen.

Yeshua caught their eye at once, a slight white figure among the black robes of the scholars. He was standing in their midst, his forehead wrinkled with concentration, adducing verse upon verse to line his argument, while men with nobly flowing beards sat thoughtfully listening, and young men with clipped beards showed wonder on their faces. And next to Yeshua stood a handsome young man, listening to him with bright blue eyes that radiated joy and pride.

"And hear what the Prophet of Israel says: 'Tell me, O man, what God requireth of thee but that thou walk in justice?'"

"Yeshua!"

Joseph made his way to the boy and brought him to his mother, whose face twitched between sobbing and laughter.

"*Tinoki,* why did you do this to us? Your father and I have searched for you in sorrow and fear."

Yeshua looked up in astonishment:

"Why did you search for me? Did you not know I would be in my Father's house?"

Miriam paled at his answer and made no reply. Joseph took the boy by one hand and Miriam by the other, and they walked with him out of the Temple.

CHAPTER XV

RAPT and spellbound, Yeshua's brothers heard his tales of Jerusalem. And when they learned how the rabbins and scholars in the Temple had listened to his parables and verses, their admiration soared, and Jacob told his father he thought there must be angels in heaven who taught Yeshua the Torah without need of a rabbin.

"Who knows, my son?" Joseph said to him. "God guides your brother over strange and unknown paths."

Cousin Cleophas was of different opinion. On hearing of the boy's exploits in Jerusalem, he said:

"And yet I do prefer the donkey tread of Jacob to the skipping short cuts of your eldest. Because, you see, a donkey goes where his master takes him; but if you try to cut the journey, you are liable to lose the way."

When the town learned how Yeshua had acquitted himself in the Temple, how the rabbis had relished his words and foretold that he would shine as a great light in Israel, it was generally assumed that the young rebel would return to the local school to resume his interrupted education. There was a mild shock when it appeared that Yeshua had no such intention, preferring rather to ply the joiner's trade in his father's shop.

A few months after his return from the pilgrimage the boy proved himself so proficient at his craft that he could take a root of vine and fashion it into a yoke without assistance. Joseph took the boy's work and proudly showed it to his mother, praising his skill. Later he brought it to the town market to sell with other products of his workshop.

He had them piled on the ground before him, waiting for a buyer. An old man crossed the square and stopped near his merchandise. Joseph had seen him before; he was notoriously one of those crazed wretches who ferreted among the children of the country for a sign of the awaited saviour. He appeared, as always, in a rope-girt sack, dust-blown like one who had come from a distance. For a while he looked with interest at Joseph's modest array of tools, then pointed to the piece Yeshua had carved.

"Master whittler," said he, "was it you who fashioned this yoke?"

"No, stranger, my boy made it; it is his very first."

"Tell him he made it well, master. If he can carve in such wise for an animal's back, he is fit to lay the yoke of heaven on mankind."

Joseph, whose eyes had proudly rested on the boy's handiwork, now looked narrowly at the stranger. He saw an antique, weatherworn face, with hair and flowing beard disheveled, the whole marked with the stamp of hermit solitude.

"What do you mean?" he asked haltingly.

"Can you not see, master, what God-like compassion went into the carving and the smoothing of this hollow, that the wood neither press upon nor chafe the animal's back? I say that he who lines the concave of a yoke with so much love, though it be destined for a beast, is fit to lay the yoke of the kingdom of heaven upon men. Go tell your boy the world awaits his yoke."

With that the stranger paid the price and, bearing the yoke on his shoulder, went his way.

Maturity came to Yeshua in his fourteenth year, in strength of character no less than in outward appearance. His work as small farmer and carpenter had steeled his body. He was tall of stature, light as a hart on his feet, and with a face bronzed by the Galilean sun. He could take ditches and brooks in long bounds and scuttle surefooted down the Nazarene hills when business called him in the valley. His hands were strong and sinuous and, clamped on the plow, cut a straight furrow.

269

His coal-black hair fell in waves about his face and neck and, when the wind blew it apart, revealed a high, bold forehead. His large eyes of vivid brown—their corners seemed always ready to crack into smiling wrinkles—suggested both cheerfulness and an alert curiosity. And his full youthful mouth, which recalled the slighter lips of his mother, was animated by welcoming smiles which made every man meet him with goodwill. But, more significant, there was in him an intangible quality of spiritual enthusiasm which quickened and illuminated every gesture of his face and body.

There was less noticeable change in his mother. Despite the hard toil of her daily life and the care of six children, Miriam had retained, in habit and appearance, much of her innate girlishness. It was as though, by-passed by time, she had escaped nature's law of decay. The change from maiden to motherhood had been wrought in her almost without external symbol. Maternity seemed not to have lessened but intensified the serene strength of her body, adding only a sense of fulfillment and of ripened confidence. She was still a slender woman, though she seemed somewhat taller now, fortified, as it were, by the habit of maternal endurance. And though her delicate features had remained unaltered with the passing of time, their message now was of acquired fortitude, not, as in her maiden years, of yielding, shy fragility.

Joseph's appearance told a very different tale.

Like those plants whose underground roots diffuse vigor to others, his lean frame had grown more haggard with the years. The flesh lay dry and stringy on his bones; he was light as a plume. His limbs seemed no longer human in their bony length, and when he moved, his body, like a solitary reed, seemed swayed by the wind.

His face too had grown gaunt. His drawn cheeks were shaggy with whiskers, prematurely grizzled like his beard and the thin hair which now failed utterly to hide the pointed dome of his skull. What vitality he had was gathered in his eyes—two burning coals that looked as though their fire was sustained at the expense of an extinguished body.

And yet there was no air of tragedy in his looks, though his old eyes were walled in by the hollow bone. The familiar smile of kindness and contentment still played about his lips, and when he saw the mother with her son together, their bodies charged with enduring health while their faces expressed a common spiritual elevation, he nodded happily and thanked God for having suffered him to fulfill his assigned task.

Joseph one day bought a pair of sycamore stumps in a denuded grove which its owner was turning to wheat. The next morning early he took Yeshua and the ass and set out for the Jezreel valley. Yeshua was to help him dig up the stumps, which would keep them in timber for several weeks. The ass would haul them back to Nazareth.

It was a good time for their errand. The first showers of the winter rains had softened the ground and there was that nipping keenness in the air which turns exertion into pleasurable exercise. And they had not far to walk; the field lay on the northern verge of the plain, at the foot of the Nazarene hills, close by the village of Xaloth. Nor was there likelihood that rain would overtake them, for those first showers of winter were usually followed by a run of dry, cold days, when the sky was wind-swept clean. Nevertheless, in case the rain should come, Miriam had packed a pair of burlap coats with their tools and provisions.

Yeshua had never before accompanied his father on one of these journeys. But Joseph now felt that Yeshua was sufficiently a man to learn every phase of his profession.

Their way led steadily downhill over damp pliable soil, which gave Joseph to hope that the day's digging would present no undue hardship. They reached the site of the sycamores, found their two stumps, and fell to work. They dug all morning under a dry sturdy sun and by noontime had lopped one of the stumps clear of its roots so that it was ready to topple.

Their midday meal was taken hurriedly, since they were anxious to complete the work before the short day waned. They ate bread and onions, drank them down with beer and fresh water, and resumed their labor before the perspiration on their foreheads had yet dried. Father and son worked with vigor, and Joseph marveled to see the boy do a man's day without seeming to flag. Yeshua's spade plunged deep into the earth and his axe cut boldly

271

through the hard tenacious roots. Sweat trickled ceaselessly over his face and neck, saturated his black curls, and made his tunic cling in clammy patches. Yet he never fell behind Joseph. It was still a good hour before sunset when they had freed both stumps. They bound them in heavy netting, trussed them to the ass's sides so that the load was poised astride its belly, shouldered their tools, and turned homeward with their precious hoard in tow.

"Today we have fulfilled the commandment of eating bread in the sweat of our faces," Yeshua said, smiling.

"The commandment?" asked Joseph, who had never known the word applied to the divine curse.

"Yes, *abba;* whatever God ordained for man is a commandment for good and to be taken as a blessing."

Joseph pondered a moment and replied with a sigh of relief: "You have prevailed, my son. I see it now. Each of God's words to man is a benediction, never a curse. There is great joy in the sweat of one's brow."

So they moved on uphill, hoping to reach their threshold before night darkened the road. But when they had begun to climb the trail that led to Nazareth over the open hillsides, they noticed suddenly, in the clear sky, a small, ash-colored, compact thunderhead. They knew well what this meant: a cloudburst and a violent flooding of the land at one stroke; the ungraduated change of weather which was the peril of their climate. The cloud opened and puffed forth billowing masses, which stretched a murky blanket between sky and earth. Then the rain came—not drops but sheets of rivering water obliquely slanted to the ground and churning it into a viscid pulp. In the sudden deluge of darkness and water the earth vanished under their feet. They waded in a running slough as though another flood spurted from unsealed subterranean wells, as though the sod, like a thin film of solid, had been crushed in the vise of water.

Yeshua, clutching the ass's halter, labored on to reach at least a tree that would give partial protection. But the darkness had grown so impenetrable that he lost every sense of direction. He stopped, realizing suddenly that Joseph was no longer at his side.

"*Abba,* where are you?" he called.

He called three times and at last heard a stifled groan. He let go of the ass and plunged back through the mire, following the sound. Joseph's legs were caught in a narrow gully; he stood waist-deep in the torrent, ready to collapse.

"*Abba, abba*," cried the boy and stretched out his hands to his father.

"Go on, Yeshua, let me be. I cannot walk any more."

"No, *abba*, no!"

"Leave me, *tinoki*," Joseph whispered, and Yeshua felt his body sink under water. Then he remembered, and, throwing his face up into the beating rain, roared out:

"Father, Father, whence shall my help come!"

And then he saw, darkly as through a screen, an olive grove no more than a few paces away.

"*Abba*, brace yourself, I will take you to the grove; the trees stand thickly and will give us shelter."

"What grove, *tinoki*?" Joseph asked, speaking as from a trance.

"This grove of olives here—it is right before our eyes."

"You are mistaken, *tinoki*, there never was a grove on this hill."

"But, *abba*, it is here, can you not see it? I will take you there."

The boy lifted Joseph out of the gully and supported him as they staggered together toward the shelter of the trees, Joseph mumbling to himself—"I never saw a grove on this hill before."

They entered the grove and wondered that the ground here should be so dry; no rain at all had seeped through the foliage, and the earth between the trees was softly padded with dry moss. Joseph at once sank down to rest himself, for his legs melted like wax under his body.

Meanwhile Yeshua ran out again into the rain to return presently with the ass. He found his father drowsing under an olive tree, a faint smile deepening the furrows at his mouth.

Yeshua stood over him, holding on to the drenched animal. It was dark in the grove, and still, but for the sound of raindrops lashing against leaves.

And Joseph felt well at ease. He saw a narrow path winding through the grove and coming to a stop before a little house. Its front was laved by radiant brightness as on a sunbright morning. His young wife Miriam sat near the doorway among flowering blue and white mallows. The infant Yeshua was in her arms,

273

palming her throat and face, and his little lips chattered away as though he had something to tell. And the mother listened with attention to the gush of infant sounds, listened as to a tale of enchantment—as Joseph had often seen her do, watching from a corner of his workshop in years long past.

"*Abba, abba,*" said Yeshua, "it is all over; it is time to go home."

"Go where, my child?"

"Home to *emi*. Look, the rain has stopped."

Joseph's eyes opened wearily.

"Yes, *tinoki,* take me home to *emi*."

Yeshua tried to help his father to his feet, but Joseph's legs no longer obeyed him. Then Yeshua resolutely untied the stumps from the donkey, hid them in a ditch nearby, and lifted Joseph to the animal's back. He covered him with Miriam's burlap coats and tied a rope as best he could to prevent his falling. Then he took up their spades and axe and led the ass back to the Nazareth trail. The rain had indeed stopped, and under a mild twilight sky grasses and leaves were shaking off the wetness.

Night had fallen on Nazareth when Yeshua reached his mother's house. Miriam was standing in the doorway with a lamp in her hand. She did not speak as she helped Yeshua untie the failing body of her husband. They carried him into the house and laid him on his pallet, where Miriam stripped him of his rain-soaked clothing and began rubbing him with camphor oil.

But Joseph had never left the grove of olives in the valley. Holding up his head, Miriam saw his lips lightly stirred. She bent her ear to him.

Joseph was gasping his last breath: "Take back, Father in heaven, into Thy hands the pledge Thou gavest me to keep. My work is done."

"Joseph, Joseph," Miriam whispered in his ear. "You were a faithful guardian to us and the best of fathers to him as to your own."

Then Miriam kissed his forehead and with her veil covered his face.

And Yeshua was fourteen years of age at the death of his earthly father. And he took upon himself the burden of the eldest to sustain his orphaned house.

PART THREE

PART THREE

CHAPTER I

FIFTEEN years had passed since Joseph's death. For fifteen years Yeshua, as eldest son, had borne the burden of supporting the family. He had succeeded to Joseph's workshop and calling and in his leisure hours had helped raise his brothers, as the saying is, to learning, marriage, and good deeds.

Miriam's younger children now lived with their wives and husbands, the plot of the widowed mother being too small to feed so many mouths. Miriam and her eldest son alone remained in the small house on the hill beyond the town.

Jacob, or the Younger, as he was called, had won a high reputation in Nazareth as a God-fearing young man. The learned respected his piety and scrupulous orthodoxy, while the simple folk took him for a holy man with perhaps the power to work miracles.

Jacob's fear of heaven proclaimed itself in his very appearance. He was tall and thin, with no loose jollity of flesh about him. During prayer his body swayed back and forth like a sugar cane. He married early with a poor man's daughter—married her unsighted and only to fulfill the law of generation. Very soon he forsook his young wife to take himself to the gray, weedless waste of the Dead Sea, where he joined a colony of Essenes in a life of holy poverty and abnegation. When he returned several years later, he brought a body haggard and wasted. His eyes loomed larger than before with a black sunken gaze resting in cavernous sockets. His beard and hair had grown wild. He went about barefoot, covered only with a sack and rope in the manner of the poor.

He had developed an obsessive concern for cleanliness, washed his hands constantly, and never passed a brook without immers-

275

ing his emaciated body, so that it was never surprising to see water trickling out of his long earlocks and curled beard.

He had gained a knowledge of the healing art, having learned the virtues of each herb and bark and how to decoct a sick man's potion from their oozings. From his father Joseph he had inherited a profound, settled scorn for the rich; and the rich to him were all those who tilled with hands other than their own. Not that his disdain ever took form in act or even speech; he merely shunned their company and made a wide arc to avoid the most casual contact with moneylenders and contractors and that brood of leeches who hired workmen for their vineyards. His associates were paupers, vagrants, and day-laborers, and it was with these that he stood at the door of the synagogue. They thought, in Nazareth, that he had picked this place out of humility, and said no more about it.

Jacob had not lost his conviction that his older brother was endowed with a peculiar grace. He thought Yeshua a favorite in heaven, and no doubt this special standing gave him a certain license. Nevertheless, he could by no means reconcile Yeshua's laxity with rabbinic teaching which, to him, represented the divine will. And so he prayed each day that God open his eyes to see his brother's ways in their true light.

That his brother did have a way of his own was beyond question. And Jacob honored him for it, but at the same time kept himself aloof lest he place his own soul in jeopardy.

Of a very different cast were Jacob's younger brothers. Joses and Simon were a robustious pair, with enormous hands and solid necks, their faces darkly framed by curly beards, their noses jutting forward in bold grasping arches. They married early, and Miriam lived to see them blessed with sons. Under the guidance of their uncle they had both become sandal makers, working with Cleophas in his shop near the public market. And they were the terror of the sons of Pinhas whose old-time feud with Hanan's house was not forgotten nor forgiven.

Like their uncle Cleophas who had raised them to their craft, Joses and Simon were honest toilers and reliable artisans. Like him, again, they were no paragons of scholarship but made up the deficiency by accepting the rabbis as the light of their eyes. Being themselves observant of the Law in all its multiple ramifications, they too were somewhat vexed by Yeshua's slackness and his perversity in spurning the company of scholars for that of illiterates and other questionable types. They were most sorely irked by Yeshua's flouting of the holy places. For Yeshua rarely went up to Jerusalem and once, when pressed for an explanation, replied in these words:

"What is Jerusalem? Jerusalem is the city of the Great King. It is also a city built of stone. Does God need stones to dwell in? Were we not told that all the earth was filled with His glory? And did He not say—'Wherever thou shalt call on My name, I shall come for to bless thee'? God wants no more than a pure heart and hands that work no evil. And I say to you: If Sodom and Gomorrah were to do penance and practise righteousness, they would be better fit to be the house of God than a sinful Jerusalem."

It was fortunate, at any rate, that the remark was made within the family circle. The brothers, whatever their own sentiment, could be trusted not to spread it abroad.

Youngest of the sons of Joseph was Jude. He was his uncle's pride, combining as he did the virtues of learning and orthodoxy with practical good sense. Jude had spent longer than his eldest brother in Jerusalem and he returned a full-fledged scholar. He was, moreover, careful of his habits, being both punctilious in his religious observances and uniformly courteous in his social intercourse. There was no question of his popularity in Nazareth and it may be said that he did much to reinstate Yeshua's mother in the good graces of her neighbors.

Jude's education had been Pharisaic, and he had had no contact whatsoever with the Essene sect. In fact, their separatism and egregious concern with cleanliness offended him, as contrary to the teaching of the rabbis. His dress was always spotless, his hair impeccably oiled; he carried himself throughout as befitted a scholar. People could not but comment on the very striking differences between him and his brother Jacob. Jacob's penchant for solitude was matched by Jude's love of good company; where Jacob guarded his tongue—speech, he said, was the one faculty man had over animals and should be reserved for prayer and benediction—Jude gave it free rein, whether in public or at home. And he spoke well, with a nice sense for adroit phrasing and elegant metaphor, which he delivered with an even fluency acquired after years of sharp debating in Jerusalem.

With the characteristic confidence of the good talker, Jude did not scruple to voice his opinions at every pass, and he made full use of his ability to deflate opponents with a well-aimed sting. Whereas the older Jacob was, as the sages put it, "difficult to anger and easy to conciliate," young Jude carried a grudge as a sponge carries water. He had the scholar's relish for the taste of revenge, as when he stabbed his enemy with an insult that turned neatly in the wound, or hurled at him some epithet—such as "cloud without water," "grapeless vine," or "ocean billow voiding its own scum."

All these qualities, his handsome looks, his learning, and his silver tongue which men preferred to have on their side, made Jude a welcome addition to the scholarly circle in Nazareth. Before very long he became one of the spokesmen of the local Pharisees and scholars.

With four such nephews Uncle Cleophas could well afford to hold his head up high. The only one among the sons of the late Joseph who dimmed his good name in the town was Yeshua, the eldest.

"See, woman," Cleophas said one day to his mother, "what has become of Yeshua, the head stone of the corner of your house? If I am not mistaken, you all said he was destined to be a rabbi in Israel. And where are his disciples? Where is his good name and fame which you predicted with such fervor? You keep dressing him up like a bridegroom in white, but in the bride's place, what is there but the dark grind of a joiner's life, and in the place of his disciples, who is there but a handful of riff-raff? He is the laughing-stock of Nazareth. No, my good Miriam, God's way is paved with law and piety, with fear of heaven and good deeds, even as the rabbis show us. As you see, your other sons who chose this path have heaped honor on themselves and on their mother."

"There are many ways to God, Cleophas. I do cherish the blessing my younger children have brought to me, for the praise of the children is what best adorns the mother. But for my eldest

278

God has designed another way. Where he walks no one else can go."

"Miriam, Miriam, forget your dream," said Cleophas with a sudden change of voice. "Look, there shall be hair on the palm of my hand before your dream shall be fulfilled."

"What dream, brother Cleophas?"

"The dream you had when you were pregnant with him; everyone knows of it. But if you think that you alone among Jewish mothers had such a dream, you are wrong, Miriam."

Miriam's face grew pale.

"What dreams do Jewish mothers have?"

"You know as well as I. Every mother in Israel dreams of giving birth to the Messiah."

Miriam said nothing and Cleophas continued:

"It was this dream of yours, Miriam, that led your son astray. . . . Now it is time for him to marry, to build a house in Israel and become what his brothers are already—an honor to their mother and to their father's house."

Was it only a dream then, a girlish fancy conjured up by her passionate wish to become the Messiah's mother?—and this a wish which she shared with every other daughter in Israel? But no— what she had seen was not a dream! She had stood face to face with the angel; and Yeshua was born in virginity according to the angel's word. He was no common mortal, though he was of woman born. Heaven had appointed him—not to fulfill the commandments of men, but to do the will of the one God. And she was the vessel that had borne God's pledge to the Patriarchs, and Yeshua, the child of salvation, had been placed in her trust. And though the time was long and there had come no reassuring sign from heaven, she knew nonetheless that Israel's shepherd would not deny her.

Meanwhile there was nothing in Yeshua's demeanor which could have seriously roused the elders of the town against him. He minded his own affairs, worked long days in his shop, observed the rabbinic laws as they related to sowing and harvesting and to his own trade. In accord with Pharisaic precepts he kept the Sabbath and the holy days, dispensed charity in excess of his means, earned his livelihood by his own labor, spoke modestly of himself, and met every man with goodwill on his lips.

The learned, it is true, had their suspicions and frowned on him, as they had frowned on Joseph, for consorting with unclean pariahs. But the common people, the fellow artisans and field laborers who were his daily contact, held him in great respect. For Yeshua taught them the Torah in his own way, not by legalistic *pilpul* but by showing them how one must live to feel close to one's Maker; and invariably he made his point with some new tale or parable and drove it home with a verse from the Psalms.

And there was one trait Yeshua had which won approval even from the local sages—his love of children. Often and often he could be seen surrounded by a host of them, amusing them with his tales and speaking to them as to his elders. Even during services in the synagogue he seemed to feel happiest in their midst and, like a child himself, he joined in their "amens."

If called on to defend his conduct, Yeshua would say that God loved the voices of children raised in the *Sh'ma,* and that it was easier for your own prayer to reach the throne of glory if it mingled with that of the children. Some of the Nazarene scholars found much pleasure in his explanation. This, they said, was Yeshua's way and there could be no harm in it. Others, taking a more serious view, insinuated that this Yeshua ben Joseph had never quite grown up. For it was common knowledge that he did not behave like an adult, witness the fact that he was still unwived.

The rabbis' counsel was to marry at eighteen. And since procreation was a divine command they disapproved the single state. Nevertheless, there had of late been a marked increase in celibacy among Jews. Men who sacrificed all private interests to devote their entire lives to the study of the Torah could now be found even within the rabbinate. Nor was this true only of men; voluntary spinsterhood had become something of a cult among the most pious of women. Their error was fed by the "Psalms of Solomon," a spurious tract which had gained regrettable currency among the people and which lauded "the virgin who knoweth not defilement nor lies upon the couch of sin." More and more women in Israel vowed by their maidenhood to give their lives over to charity and good deeds. Among Hellenized Jews they were known as "the eternal virgins." But even so, the custom was not as yet widespread, except in certain sects like the Essenes. The mass of Israel abided by the injunction of the rabbis: "the marriage canopy at eighteen years." To be fruitful and multiply was God's design for all creation, and whosoever strayed from this law destroyed the order of the world.

Yeshua's single status was therefore viewed with mild surprise and disfavor by his townsmen; it was not sufficient cause for bitterness or serious dissatisfaction, except perhaps among his nearest relatives, notably Cleophas, who was continually urging Miriam to make her son marry and found a family as his brothers had done. The old Reb Elimelech, who might have cared as much, was no longer living.

Thus Yeshua continued to live alone with his mother. At dusk, sometimes, when he returned from working in the field or shop, Miriam came over to him and with her kerchief wiped the sweat from his face, or washed his hands in scented water. Often she prevailed on him to let her wash his feet. In vain did Yeshua protest; Miriam regarded such small offices as a form of sacred service.

She had not ceased in all these years to think wistfully of his childhood when he had been in constant need of her assistance. Now, in his maturity, she sought as far as possible to anticipate his needs by attending to his dress and preparing his meals. And when he came home from labor she insisted on anointing his hair with oil.

Yeshua had long succumbed to his mother's will; the fact that Miriam found so much joy in attending his wants had disarmed his objections. It was more even than joy. The littlest service that Miriam could render him was performed with a measureless devotion as though there was for her no holier task. She kept his clothes as spotless as the vestments of the High Priest in the Tabernacle, and Yeshua, despite the drudgery of his day, never appeared in public but in fine-spun, immaculate linen. Indeed, some Nazarenes who had nothing better to do wondered how Miriam's son, the carpenter, came by such delicate fabrics, which were more costly, surely, than those worn by the son of Talami the moneylender, who was never seen but with a bravery of sparkling rings and chains. The splendid white tunics and cloaks of Yeshua's wardrobe even stirred up a certain envy among the less generous who charged the joiner with wanton ostentation. They pointed out that Yeshua's dress not only belied his humble calling and the poverty of his house, but that it made him seem like the son of a king. Had he ever been seen, they asked, in the penitential sack-cloth of his brother Jacob? or even in a workaday smock such as was worn by Joses and Simon?

Miriam was no less painstaking with her son's food than with his garments, thinking of his every meal as of a sacrament. The earthen dishes in which she served their modest fare shone with repeated scouring. The low table was spread with a clean linen cloth, white as new snow, come Sabbath or weekday. And when Yeshua approached it, his mother never failed to rise for him, like a priestess dressed in her best attire, ready to serve. And before he had yet time to bow to her in customary greeting, Miriam would quickly come close to plant a kiss of submission on her son's shoulder.

"*Ema,* what are you doing?" Yeshua once said with light re-proach. "Why will you prevent me from honoring my mother as the Law bids all men do?"

"Are you like all men, Yeshua?" Miriam replied.

The matter was not discussed again and Yeshua thenceforward suffered his mother to serve him.

Miriam's behavior was to Yeshua a constant reminder of his mission. Every time he saw his mother pay him obeisance as to a prince he felt a surer confidence in his divine election and ex-perienced a thrill of renewed vigor. He could not have been more irresistibly moved if a heavenly voice had called him to go forth and claim his Messianic kingdom. And as year upon year went by without sign or omen that the time had come, Miriam, by her conduct, kept his faith burning like the eternal flame in the Temple.

Thus they lived on together, sharing their common secret. Nor did they cease to wait for a sign to tell them that the mystery was ripe for revelation.

Often Miriam was conscious of a spiritual struggle in her son.

At such times she had no speech to comfort him. She could only leave him to wrestle alone with demons and angels. As Jacob had fought a lone fight with the angel, so her son must rely on his own powers. But she could in spirit share his fevers and torments. She saw him seek arms and protection in the books of the Prophets. He would pore a full day over the scroll of Isaiah, the Psalms, or the Book of Enoch which Joseph had bequeathed to him.

Sometimes his spirit rested serenely like the blue sky after a passing storm. To Miriam it was clear that he had drawn strength from the words of David or Isaiah. At other times his agitation was intensified by the perusal of the Prophets. His face clouded over, and he would gaze at Miriam sadly and searchingly.

Then Miriam's lips would move impotently and she could bring forth no words. She wanted to ask him what it was that so troubled his spirit, but in the end her courage always failed and she could only look with pleading eyes and quivering lips while her cup ran over with fullness of love and compassion.

And sometimes, without previous warning, her son would disappear for several days together, more often than not with Taddi the tanner. She knew that it was not for her to pry beyond the secret borders of his being. Her part was to accept his every act as one more step along the road God had carved out for him. And yet, despite this better knowledge, her fear of the miraculous event which might come with every hour, almost cleft her heart. If Yeshua was absent without explanation, she, Miriam, spent many hours kneeling in a corner of her chamber, relieving her anxiety in prayer:

"I have no right, O God, to follow his ways. I know that what he does is done according to Thy word and for the cause for which Thou hast appointed him. Heaven forbid that I should seek to lift the veil which Thou hast made to fall between him and all Thy creatures. From my womb hast Thou drawn forth this child and hast veiled him from my understanding; and yet Thou didst plant in my breast more love for him than I can bear. Leave me then to go with him to the end of his earthly days and take not from me my fear and grief for him, for, behold, my soul is bound to his."

CHAPTER II

BESIDES his mother, his aunt Mariama was the only member of the family who had early recognized Yeshua's high vocation, and throughout the years she had remained true to her belief. She did not have Miriam's imperiousness of conviction; but she felt intuitively that she saw more in her oldest nephew than did other men and women, though they might have more learning and intelligence than she.

And once she saw her sister's son revealed in the fullness of his grace, and she knew thenceforward that Yeshua could not be measured with the yardstick of human frailty and achievement.

There was nothing spectacular in the incident; a common everyday occurrence served to open Mariama's eyes.

It was seedtime in late spring and Yeshua was sowing their sloping plot to barley. Mariama was busying herself with spade and shovel, digging a trench round the verge of the seedbed where the field descended steeply into a rocky hollow that had once been a watercourse. She raised her head and saw her nephew striding down between the open furrows. A cloth over his head protected him from the beat of the sun; the flaps of his white coat were tucked into his girdle and from an apron gathered in one hand he scattered the seedcorn. It was a familiar sight, no different from any other sower, and yet Mariama was suddenly struck by the dazzling brightness of his dress and the light that shone again from his face.

Her heavy dark-skinned neck stiffened momentarily. Then she felt her body growing numb and her legs gave way so that she sank upon the ground. Her heart was pounding high and the sweat of panic broke out on her forehead.

She thought the sun was shining upon him alone while all the world was blurred in a universal mist of wandering atoms. She saw his white garment shining like a silver armor and he seemed like an archangel bestriding a small earth and disseminating grain with open hand. The motion of his arm was as the sweep of a tempest, for some of the dispersing grains fell like raindrops deep into the drills, while others, caught up by the wind, were borne past Mariama's head to fall dead among the sterile stones of the wadi. And Mariama saw other seeds broadcast by Yeshua's hand that might have been caught on invisible wings, for they were carried into distant fields far beyond her vision. She wondered that there should be so much grain in one of Yeshua's handfuls; it was as though the spray of grain flung from his hand was inexhaustible. Yeshua came on with a powerful tread and Mariama, crouching on the ground, hid her face from his sight as though she felt the dread of an angel's approach. When she looked up again Yeshua had gone past without seeing.

Mariama picked herself up quickly and ran home, neither looking back nor stopping on the way. A great awe had fallen on her and she was frightened to remain with Yeshua alone, lest she perish, having seen what was not meant for her eyes.

She arrived at her door flushed and out of breath, her eyes wide with terror.

"What is it, Mariama?" asked her husband, not without agitation, "why are you shaking?"

"I was out in Miriam's field . . ." said Mariama and stopped short.

"And what happened?" asked Cleophas, while his younger nephews drew close.

"I . . . I saw Miriam's son sowing . . ."

"Well, and was it he that frightened you?"

"Yes, because what I saw was not meant for my eyes."

The men stared at her without comprehension.

"Well, woman, tell us what you saw," Cleophas said.

"He was walking down the field seeding the barley crop. But suddenly, he changed and looked like an archangel in a silver coat of mail come down from heaven. And he was sowing, but I could not tell what seed it was that scattered out of his hand; it seemed to be not grain but something else. Because some of the seeds dropped in the soil but others were driven off to fall among stones and thorns, and still others were carried far afield, farther than I could see. I saw the seeds leaving his hand but I did not know them, for it was not a human sower who was strewing them abroad."

285

She spoke as none had ever heard her speak before. Her eyes were glassy and her dark face flushed, so that she seemed more like a sibyl speaking in a moment of entranced prophecy.

"You are beginning to see visions like your sister Miriam and you talk without sense," said Cleophas. "You say you saw Yeshua seeding the barley crop and yet you don't know what he was sowing. Well, I will tell you: he was sowing last year's seedcrop which we retained for this year's planting."

"No, Cleophas, it was no earth crop he was sowing. These were seeds that grow only in heaven. And those that fell on the tilled furrows will yield the bread of salvation. But others fell among stones."

Cleophas did not know what more to say. It was not Mariama's way to speak so confidently of things that were clearly beyond her understanding. For the first time since he was married he felt a touch of respect for his wife.

The vision Aunt Mariama had had in the field became at once a heated subject for discussion among the men of the family. Jacob heard the report and said briefly:

"I always knew Yeshua was selected for great things. Who knows what our brother has sown?"

"Let us wait for the fruit of his sowing," said the younger Jude. "Then we shall know whether our brother's grain was earth-grown or heavenly." And with a graceful bow to indicate that he had finished, he added: "You shall know the seed by the bread."

His doting uncle winked at him and grinned.

"At last, the word of a sage," said he; "nothing fantastical or womanish, but plain good sense."

Another one in Nazareth had maintained a staunch faith in Yeshua throughout these years: Taddi the tanner.

At one time, when Yeshua was a young boy, Taddi had taught him law and legend. Now the tanner was an old man who listened avidly to the speech of his one-time disciple.

Taddi had remained his old contented self, though he was now a widower and as poor as he had ever been. He had moreover inherited his wife's rheumatic ailment—the years of soaking his bare feet in tannin having caused his ankles to swell up like pumpkins. And yet the tanner had lost little of his youthful agility. With his feet pathetically bandaged in old rags, he hobbled about from one village to the next, seeking out the poor to tell them that a new light had risen in Israel. For he had heard the words of comfort with which Yeshua consoled the poor, and had seen how his personality sustained their spirits. Yeshua was to him a messenger of God sent to illumine their darkness by the light of his word.

Taddi's children were now grown-up men. Some had become day-laborers in a rich man's olive press or vineyard, digging his wells or drawing his water. Others had left Nazareth to seek better fortune elsewhere. For the first time in his life Taddi found himself with time on his hands. There was no longer a family to be fed, and he himself was a poor trencherman by lifelong habit, who could last a full day on a cane of sugar picked up in a field, a few unripe dates, and a tiff of fresh water from a spring.

Dressed in a coarse burlap cloak, he would limp into the vineyard of some rich employer and tell the laborers of the new comforter who had risen in Israel; or he would come as a wandering stranger into the synagogue of some small town, take his place among the laborers and artisans and inform them in words of ardent rhetoric—"Behold, there shall be a reward for your pains when the lowly are exalted, for the Lord has sent a comforter to comfort the poor!"

Taddi was one of them, a toiler like the rest, familiar with the mood of the dejected. He knew the outcasts, the unlettered pariahs who had no portion in Israel, who had no share in this world or the world to come, since their poverty debarred them from the enjoyment of this life while their ignorance of the Law banished them from Eden. These were the men to whom Taddi brought his harangue, the men who thought themselves humbler than the dust at their feet. And sometimes he brought Yeshua himself, or made them come with him to Yeshua's house.

Southward from Nazareth, where the Galilean hills declined into the Jezreel plain, lay the great vineyard of Reb Sheshet bar Caspi. It ran for many miles along the sunny southern slope of the hill chain. Throughout the country it was celebrated for the sweetness of its grapes. Its wine, owing to the cooling dew which fell so plentifully in the nights, possessed richness and body so that it was much in demand even in Jerusalem. And lastly, the fattish red soil of these hills made for an early crop so that Bar Caspi could successfully compete with the vintage of the Jordan valley.

Time was when the vineyard consisted of numerous little holdings owned by small growers. Little by little Sheshet bar Caspi had appropriated their mortgaged land and annexed them to his property. By now the entire south side of the Nazarene hill chain was his private estate, worked by innumerable hired hands. True, all these original splinter holdings must revert to their former owners in the jubilee year at the half century; but that was a long time away and much could be done in the interim to circumvent the Law. For the time being Sheshet bar Caspi remained the local Midas. His wealth, which was to some extent the object of exaggeration, was great enough to render him a boon companion to the nobles of Jerusalem. And what is more, he was universally respected as a man of charity, for that he let his former debtors work on his estate was allowed by all to be an act of pure philanthropy.

Yeshua, who knew every hole and corner of the country for miles around, was well acquainted with the vineyard. For many years he had watched Bar Caspi spread his usurer's net over the small plots of the poor. He had watched the former owners during harvest time when, instead of singing and rejoicing, they worked in morose silence, some with curses on their lips, others in sullen gloom and despair. He had watched the bare backs of the men glistening with sweat as they bent over their shovels or lugged heavy vats of water from the cistern to irrigate the vine. There was to him something horribly abject in the dull curve of their backs. With the forfeiture of their lands these men had lost both independence and self-discipline. They had lost, too, the lighted highway of the Torah, to fall into the pit of ignorance and sin.

Yeshua had often gone to see the men in Bar Caspi's vineyard. He had not spoken to them, since the hours of their working day were bought by their employer, and the overseers were a watchful crew who brooked no interruption. And after sunset, when the day was done, the men were so numb with fatigue that they slumped down like animals wherever they happened to be in the vineyard. Thus, throughout the working week, the men slept at the scene of their labor.

Yeshua had not yet begun to spread his teachings, except in Nazareth itself, among the local poor and the visitors whom Taddi sometimes brought into his mother's garden. Now he was asked by the tanner to go speak to the laborers in Bar Caspi's vineyard.

They entered the vineyard shortly before nightfall. The laborers sat in groups on the damp soil which they had lately watered. From the low twisting vine overhead the grape clusters hung down like bloated udders. The laborers were many and of every age—some ancient, with wan, hairy faces, others in the prime of youth; even children were there, working off their father's debts.

Night was settling quickly in the Nazarene hills and the day's heat fled before its cooling breeze. The laborers were kindling bundles of dry vine twigs and squatted about the fires to eat the evening meal by their light.

Yeshua approached one of the groups, his white cloak setting him off from the gathering darkness. Seating himself with the men near the fire, he said:

"*Shalom aleichem*—Peace be with you."

"*Aleichem shalom*," they replied, "and may your coming be blessed."

Yeshua sat for a while without speaking. The laborers too were silent, munching sullenly at their meager fractions of dry bread. Some felt embarrassed by the presence of the learned man; no doubt they took him for one of the hireling preachers whom Sheshet bar Caspi sent up at intervals to sermonize them into orthodoxy. Any moment now the rabbi would open his mouth to bedamn them with fire and brimstone for having failed to wash their hands before eating and carrying their food unwrapped. He would reprove them for companionship with men who had been long pronounced unclean, with whom they dipped their bread promiscuously in one bowl, and shared the gourd of parsley beer as it traveled from mouth to mouth.

But when the young man did open his mouth, it was to say, with a gentle lifting of his palms:

"Blessed is the bread of the toiler, for it is the bread of justice. His table is God's altar, his meal the Lord's most wished-for sacrifice. Would that I might have a part in this offering you make to God."

Every man in the group stopped and held his breath to stare incredulously at the speaker. Then they began to look at one another, uncertain whether or not they had caught the rabbi's meaning.

"The rabbi asks if he may break bread with you," explained the tanner.

"Bread? With us?" came various voices from the group.

"Our hands are soiled; our bread is unclean," said a dark man with short stubby hair.

"Brothers in Israel, I beg to have my portion with you," said Yeshua, extending his arms. And he sat there, with his hands unwashed and accepted a crust of bread from one of the men. He broke it in two so that he could share it with his nearest neighbor, made the blessing, dipped it like the rest in the common dish of vinegar, and ate. It was an act of willful trespass.

By this time laborers in other parts of the vineyard were leaving their fires to gather about Yeshua's circle, for the word had gone forth that a rabbi had come among them.

The dark man who had spoken before waited for the newcomers to settle down and then threw out his challenge:

"Enlighten us, rabbi; have not the sages taught that all bread which is touched by unclean hands becomes itself unclean? How then can you eat our bread, seeing that our hands are soiled?" It was evident from the man's speech that he was a former scholar degraded to pariah level, for he spoke with the burden of restrained bitterness in his voice.

"It is not the hand but the heart alone which makes clean and unclean. If your heart is pure, so shall your hands be, even though you wash them not in water. But if your heart is unclean, then are your hands unclean also, though you observe every ablution. To what may we compare this? Come and see, my brothers.

"There was once a wealthy moneylender who lent upon usury

and made his debtors plight their lands to him for surety. This moneylender was a law-abiding man. He neglected no rite of purification, washed himself many times a day, cleaned and scoured his vessels to be always immaculate, and rinsed his hands whenever he had touched a doubtful thing or person. Now it befell that this same moneylender gave a loan to a pious neighbor whose vineyard abutted on his house. As time went on the pious neighbor could not meet the usurer's rate. He sank deeper into debt until at last the moneylender took his vineyard and set him to work off the increase that had fallen due. The poor debtor was overwhelmed by the long hours of hard toil. No longer was there time to study or to heed the laws fixed by the rabbis, and so it came about that in the end he forgot even to wash his hands before eating and broke bread with soiled fingers.

"Some years went by and both men died, the moneylender and his neighbor. And when they came into the upper world, they were led up to the great hall where Father Abraham sat to take his sons to his bosom. And a voice rang out, saying:

" 'Only they whose hands are clean may enter the great hall! They alone are the true sons of Abraham!'

"Thought the moneylender to himself: 'How fortunate that I never neglected to wash myself before the *Sh'ma;* that I rinsed my hands before every meal and never touched an unclean thing! Who but I am the true son of Abraham?'

"And he approached the keeper of the gate and said:

" 'Open wide that I may come to my father.'

"But the keeper of the gate retorted:

" 'Get thee hence, man, for there is a noisome stench goes up from your soul. Your heart is a sink of worms and obscene vermin and your hands are sullied. This hall of Abraham is not for your like.'

"Then wailed the moneylender and protested. 'Behold,' he said, 'you do me a great wrong. I can bring witnesses galore that I have faithfully observed the washing of the hands throughout my days.'

"And the keeper replied:

"Yes, you did wash your skin with water, but you have let the unclean thing nest in your heart. For rapine and theft and cruelty and evil deeds cannot be washed away by water, but by repentance only and the pursuit of righteousness. Begone now, for your hands reek of your brother's blood.'

"Now when the poor man, who had been the moneylender's serf, saw how his master had fared at the hands of the gatekeeper, he said to himself:

" 'If this be my master's end, how then shall I enter the great hall, I who have sinned in that I have not kept myself clean and have eaten bread with unwashed hands?' And he turned to withdraw from Abraham's hall.

"But the keeper flung the gate open and called after him:

" 'Come, son of Abraham! Behold, your father waits your entrance!'

"Then the poor man replied:

" 'You are mistaken. I have not kept the Law and my hands are unclean.'

" 'But your heart is pure,' said the other; 'it fills our halls with pleasant odors. Shortness of breath and the toil of your labor kept you from washing your hands, for the hour allotted to your meal was brief, even as your fare was niggardly. Yet you washed your hands in your tears, your heart was submissive to the one God, and your spirit meek. And God loves them that are of a contrite heart and such as are of a meek spirit. Therefore, come into the house of your father.' "

The parable was finished. Yeshua halted for a moment while the laborers crowded more closely about him, some of them reaching out to touch his cloak—like children reaching for their mother at the sound of thunder.

"Be of good spirit," Yeshua concluded. "You have gone hungry, but you shall be sated with the bread of life. You have been humbled, but shall be exalted in eternity. Your Father in heaven knows your hearts, and He has seen you purged and cleansed by uprightness, by heavy toil and lifelong suffering. And He will reward you, for in Him only can man find his reward."

Night lay heavy in the vineyard when Yeshua had ceased to speak. He stretched forth his hands and let them hover for a moment over the bowed heads of his hearers. The company became suddenly aware of a deep silence—the ease and harmony of perfect silence which soothes away all bitterness and sorrow like a cooling hand; a silence which penetrated to the heart and purged the soul of evil and the body of all weariness; which freed every back of its burden. In the darkness, which the embers of the fire served but to make visible, the white-robed form of the rabbi was a still image radiating silence and peace. And the voices of men weeping came through the silence.

That night Yeshua slept with the laborers in the vineyard. He returned home in the morning with the faithful tanner at his side, and Taddi, seeing Miriam in the doorway, stopped at a reverent distance and said to the mother:

"I have seen your son as he distributes the bread of the kingdom of heaven."

CHAPTER III

THE Sabbath is the holiest day in the Jewish year, the day of God's kingdom on earth. As you make your Sabbath, so shall your days be in the life to come.

The Sabbath is God's bounty to mankind. But not to humankind alone; it was granted, say the sages, as much to animals and beasts, nay, to the whole creation. Poets have likened it to a queen, a mother, and a bride. And, indeed, the Sabbath is a mother, dispensing holiness as from a plenteous breast; it is a bride, for as a bride brings grace to her well-beloved, so does the Sabbath vouchsafe grace to Israel. And, therefore, it behooves every man to meet the Sabbath in his best attire as he would meet his bride, and welcome it with the most joyous ode of love, the Song of Songs which is Solomon's.

In no Jewish home was the Sabbath more festively observed than in the house of the widow Miriam and her son Yeshua. Friday, when the sun reached its zenith, Yeshua put away his labor in the shop to help his mother prepare for the Sabbath eve. He found her carrying two heavy pitchers, filled with water from the cistern or the town well, to replenish the great earthen tub they used for bathing.

Yeshua hastened to relieve his mother of the heavy load. Then he filled the tub, to which Miriam added heated water and, for fragrance, a few sticks of the wild thyme. And while Yeshua washed himself and donned the fresh white garments readied by his mother, Miriam prepared the Sabbath meal—little fishes from K'far Nahum, dried in the sun and salted, which, baked with dough, formed the Sabbath cheer of the poor; and a pair of braided loaves to recall the shewbread which lay before the Lord in the Temple.

It was considered an honorable privilege for a man to participate in the preparations of the Sabbath. Yeshua accordingly helped where he could, picking the finest greens in the garden, plucking the largest pomegranates, dates, and figs, and, lastly, pouring out the wine for the blessing. Miriam looked to the lamps, which were traditionally the woman's custody. For the eve of the Sabbath she had a cruse of most pellucid oil which she now poured into the earthen bowls to cast a soft light on the table.

To honor the Sabbath she had also tidied and adorned the house. Benches were spread with purple-dyed cloths; the floor was swept clean and covered here and there with mats of bamboo or palm sprigs. The corners were adorned with nosegays of vermilion flowers from the best rosebush in her garden, and the table decked with the refreshing leaves of olive tree and myrtle.

When everything was ready and in order, Yeshua withdrew to his chamber to prepare himself by a re-reading of the Prophets for the reception of the Sabbath bride. Or else he sauntered out into the fields. Alone in this twilight hour he felt a strange elation and yearned at last to see the kingdom of heaven. And when he saw the sun dip to kiss the horizon, swathed in scarlet veils, he heard, coming with the shadows, the still tread of the queen, coming to spread over the earth her mantle of holiness and peace. The kingdom of God would make the crooked straight, undo all bonds and shackles, comfort the dejected, redress every evil, and bring peace and goodwill without end. For such a Sabbath did he wait, a Sabbath never to wane.

A hornblast down in the valley startled him from his revery; it was the ritual *shofar* telling Nazareth that the Sabbath had come. Yeshua turned back to his mother's house.

Miriam was standing at the table lighting the Sabbath lamps. Her dark hair was parted at the crown and combed smoothly back where it was caught in the netting of her kerchief. Her dress was black, black as the night outside, and with a silky shimmer as of starlight. And Yeshua thought he saw the queen that was the Sabbath, radiant of countenance and crowned. She stood tall and erect, like a priestess doing votive service, and, stretching out her loving hands, embraced and blessed the Sabbath lamps.

Yeshua stood aside in a corner while his mother completed the prayer. And in his heart he thanked God for allowing him to see her who had borne him.

Then he approached her gently and, bowing with humility, said:

"May the peace of the Sabbath be with you, my mother."

"And with you, *tinoki*," Miriam replied, and pressed a kiss on his shoulder.

And Yeshua raised the goblet in his hand and from the head of the table, pronounced the consecration of the Sabbath:

"Thus the heavens and the earth were finished and all their host. And on the seventh day God ended His work which He had made. And He rested on the seventh day from all His work which He had made. And God blessed the seventh day, and sanctified it, because that in it he had rested from all His work which God had created."

Thus the Sabbath came and settled itself under Miriam's low roof. And a great silence fell upon the world, like the silence of Genesis, as though the Lord's creation was now coming to its final form, a perfect form to express God's intent without error, blemish, or perversion, as it would be when all crookedness should be made straight on the day of the kingdom of God.

Then Yeshua washed his hands after the bidding of the Law and taking up the loaves blessed the bread and broke it.

Mother and son sat on cushioned benches, each opposite the other at the table. Before them were the Sabbath platters—the bread, the baked fishes, the fruit and vegetables, the gourd bottle of wine and the goblet cut and carved from a horn. And in the silence of this Sabbath eve, in the hour of grace, the mother spoke to her son of her initiation:

"In the Court of the Women, in the holy Temple, I was praying. My heart was filled to overflowing, for a great awe of heaven had seized me and I prayed with a full heart—not for myself, nor for my father's house, no, not even for Israel. I prayed to God to let His glory rest on the whole world. I do not know what made me pray in this manner, but I was lonely for God; I wanted nothing but that His name be revealed to all men, so that every knee might bend before Him and He be pleased to send His Messiah for mankind's redemption.

"And as I prayed I felt my spirit moved as upon waves of water and my love and longing for God rose up in me and I wept and called His name until I thought I could have flown away with new-grown wings.

"I was so filled with hunger and thirst for the Lord that I no longer knew where I was. Then I felt someone taking my hand and saying to me in a voice sweeter than I had ever heard—'Come with me, girl.' And I rose up and followed.

"Surely, I thought, this must be Cousin Elisheva, for the figure that preceded me was tall and draped entirely in black; even the face was veiled. But then I knew from the voice that it was another, and I went after her. And she led me past the press of pilgrims and through an open door.

"I found myself then in a palace hall that was ablaze with many lights. And three long tables stood in the hall. At the first sat three men only, at the second, more, and they had Torah scrolls open before them, many, many scrolls. Some were old, with kingly beards and faces fairer than kings; others were filled with youth and strength. And at the third table sat a king with a harp at his side. He sat on a throne; his head was crowned. At his left, seated on another throne, was his son. But at his right stood a third throne, tallest and noblest of the three, hung with a jewelled crown that sparkled brighter than the others—and this throne was empty.

"My guide led me up to the first table where the three men sat, one hoary with age that had the face of majesty; the second, a young man with curly dark hair and thoughtful features; the third, a man of middle years, heavy-browed and with a skin that seemed coarsened and tanned by all weather. And they looked at me and never said a word. Then my guide placed me before the king, and I bent my knee to him. And he too looked at me and never spoke a word. Lastly she led me to the third table where the venerable company sat poring over open scrolls, and they glanced up and looked at me and some pointed their fingers at the scrolls, but not a word was spoken.

"Then the woman who was my guide led me out of the hall and back to my place in the Court of the Women. But as she offered to let go of my hand, I pressed hers and said with a sudden boldness that made me start at my own voice—'You shall not go without you tell me who you are and where I have been.' Then the woman lifted up her veil and I saw her eyes dimmed with tears, and her face, though it was etched with grief, was the fairest I had ever seen. 'I am the mother Rachel,' she said to me, 'and the hall you were in was the holiest sanctum, the abode of the Patriarchs, the Prophets, and the Kings David and Solomon. And the throne that stood vacant at the right hand of David—it awaits the King-Messiah.' With that the woman laid a finger to my lips and vanished from my sight."

Miriam had reached the end of her narrative and looked down silently. Yeshua rose from his seat and, looking at his mother, said in a firm tone:

"Indeed, woman, there is a higher place than that which you saw; and in that higher place another throne awaits the Son of Man."

On the Sabbath Taddi had begun to bring his fellow artisans to Miriam's garden—spinners and weavers, dyers, potters, cobblers, and carpenters, and such as were too poor even to have acquired a trade. Yeshua spoke to them outside his own house; he still avoided preaching in the local synagogue, desiring no conflict with the elders who must sanction his sermons.

His mother listened, standing in her doorway to hear her son "distribute the bread of the kingdom of heaven," as the tanner had said. The brothers, too, came to hear Yeshua's parables. Jacob and Jude, each in his own way, were curious to know how Yeshua

297

dispensed comfort to the poor, for the old tanner had spoken of it as a marvel in the synagogue of Nazareth.

After hearing him several times, they were compelled to grant that Yeshua's parables were morally uplifting and served to strengthen a man's faith in the God of Israel—even though they differed somewhat from the expositions of the recognized rabbinic teachers. But it was rankling to the brothers to hear Yeshua make light of the Law, to slight such sacred traditions as the washing of the hands and to hear him say this before common gullible folk who surely did not need to have their laxity encouraged. The brothers argued that Yeshua would have done better to voice his differences with the rabbis before the scholars of the town.

There was in every sizeable town a place where scholars could meet for discussion—usually a grove or arbor belonging to a wealthy member of their brotherhood. In Nazareth it was a private orchard where the scholars met, among them some of Yeshua's former schoolmates—Simeon bar Talami, the erudite Sakkai bar Zadok, and even Matthew ben Hanah (the Matthew Saucebox of their youth). The young Jude was here a prominent spokesman, a shining light among the local Pharisees. And it was Jude, at last, who broached the common grievances to his elder brother.

"Yeshua, my elder, enlighten me," he said one evening in his mother's house. "Though I defer to you as my elder brother, and also for the wisdom with which God has endowed you, I cannot conceive why you disdain to bring your words to the wise men of this town. If there are innovations you wish to see promulgated in the field of law or moral parable—which is your special excellence, as we have judged from your wise speech, why, then, it seems to me that your proposals should be made to the rabbis and scribes. But if you differ with the rabbis in the presence of illiterates, you might as well, heaven forbid, break down the fences of God's garden for swine to rootle in."

"Brother Jude," Yeshua replied, "do you imagine that I came to offer dainties to the sated? I have come to bring the bread of eternal life to them who are in want."

The brothers did not, or would not, understand his meaning,

298

and the division between them and Yeshua sharpened from day
to day.

In the shade of the olive tree that stood by Miriam's threshold
sat Yeshua in his white Sabbath mantle, surrounded by a group of
native artisans. Of them some squatted on the ground, others
were standing, and among these last were Yeshua's four brothers,
Jacob, Joses, Simon, and Jude, who came each Saturday in defer-
ence to their mother.

Yeshua was speaking of the eternal, never-ending Sabbath
which the Lord would make descend upon the world:

"He shall bring this Sabbath with him, he for whom you wait.
And this Sabbath shall not be external to you, but shall be within
every man, so that none may take it from you, though he come in
the garb of the Law. For this Sabbath is the new breath of life that
God shall breathe into your nostrils. It shall be a new spirit for
man, and by this spirit shall you judge. It shall be the scale delivered into your hands to weigh good and evil. Then shall you be
sons to another Adam, for the new spirit shall purge you of your
sins and you shall receive the Sabbath everlasting, which is the
peace of God that was destroyed in you by Adam's sin. . . . All
men whatsoever shall have a part in the new spirit, for on that
Sabbath shall every unevenness be leveled. Valleys shall be exalted
and mountains made low. And the spirit of God will hover over
all, as was foretold us by the Prophet: 'I will pour out My spirit
upon all flesh; and also upon the servants and upon the handmaids in those days will I pour out My spirit.'"

This was hard fare for Yeshua's brothers to swallow. Jacob was
deeply shocked and his long reedy hands began to tremble. In
the past he had repeatedly been troubled by certain of Yeshua's
sayings, but these latest words, which broke down every fence
drawn by the rabbis to protect Israel's garden, threw him into an
almost physical panic. But still the respect he bore his older
brother made him keep silent and he curbed his feelings, hoping
for a more propitious hour when he should find himself alone
with Yeshua. As for Joses and Simon, they were too little educated to challenge any of their brothers on a point of law or
creed. Only Jude, the youngest, whose mind had been tempered

in the fires of rabbinic argument, and whose audacity was always at the service of his zeal, was bold enough to fall into his brother's speech.

"May it please my brother and rabbi to enlighten me," he said, "but what is this spirit which shall in future illumine the path of man? Shall it be the Torah, which, we are told, is the light of our eyes?"

"Yes, the Torah," Yeshua calmly replied, "but not the Torah that is taught by men, inscribed on tablets and copied on parchment and folded to fit into a pocket. It shall be a Torah grounded in the human heart, the spirit of God which the Lord will pour upon all men."

"We have but one Torah," said Jude with growing vehemence. "It is the Law which God handed to Moses on Mount Sinai. And Moses handed it down to the Prophets, and they to the elders, and the elders to the rabbis of our own age. The Torah does not abide in heaven; it dwells with us on earth! It lives in every academy and school, and on the lips of the rabbis. It does not come by dreaming, but by earnest effort and ordeal, by sleeping on hard benches, eating dry bread, and imbibing the words of the sages. Remove this our Torah and you remove the knowledge of good and evil, for it alone is our measuring rod. Where the Torah is banished you will not find the spirit of God, as we were told by the great Rabbi Hillel—'An empty-headed man cannot fear sin, nor can an ignoramus be a pious man.'"

"Hear me, brother," said Yeshua. "The Torah of which you speak is valid only until man is engrafted into the spirit of God. For when a man is grafted upon the good root, he needs no more the Torah of another man's mouth. For then he shall have a Torah grounded inward in his heart to teach him better. Come, brother, and I will show you the inmost Torah of the spirit." He rose and, with him, his listeners, and Yeshua led them to his mother's vineyard at the far end of the garden—a large sturdy vine upon which Miriam had grafted several wild shoots. "Do you see these shoots?" Yeshua said. "So long as they grew on their own wild roots they bore nought but wild grapes. They were quickened by dew at night and warmed by the sun by day. The had their law of growth, their Torah, which God vouchsafed to all His creatures, and yet they carried wildness only. For their nature was wild and neither Law nor Torah could help. But now my mother's hand has grafted them on this good vine and behold, they bear fair fruit. They have not now another Torah, nor another Law, for neither of these is the cause of good fruit, but the root only from which the sap is drawn.

"Even so is it with man. Whosoever shall be grafted on the good vine shall bear good fruit, for my Father shall be his vine-grower. And he who shall not bear good fruit shall be cut off."

At this point Jacob could restrain himself no longer.

"Teach me, rabbi," he said, "who shall be grafted on this good vine—the pure alone or, God forbid, the unclean also?"

"There shall be no unclean," retorted Yeshua. "For they shall all be purified in the grafting."

"Even the Gentiles—though they come without Torah and without commandments?"

"They shall all become part of the vine."

This was more than the brothers could bear, and Jude, throwing ceremony to the winds, called out sharply:

"Tell us, brother—tell us without equivocation, whom do you have in mind when you speak of the good vine in whom the unclean shall be made pure without help of Torah and commandments?"

Yeshua did not answer. In the fading sunlight his face looked somber and determined and his lips were tightly closed. Jude pressed on:

"Why will you withhold it from us and keep us in ignorance? Bring us your tidings, Yeshua—who is the good vine?"

"You shall know when his time comes," Yeshua said quietly, with the cadence of finality in his voice. A great silence fell on the company and for a moment every man feared to move. Rooted to their places, the brothers stared fearfully at Yeshua's white-clad figure. Through their minds flashed the sudden thought that their own brother might be Israel's awaited hope, whom in their grossness they had failed to recognize, meeting him with captiousness and carping words. The notion paralyzed their eyes and tongues and they gazed in sheer terror.

301

Jude was the first to recover his senses. Fortified in his faith by the teachings of the rabbis, he said with renewed humility:

"Yeshua, my brother and rabbi: you have spoken to us to make our souls tremble as though we were touched by God's finger. Who are we to judge of things that are the concern of all Israel and whose handling calls for the utmost wisdom? We are indeed the lowliest in our father's house. But now, my brother and rabbi, the feast day of Israel's deliverance is drawing near. Come with us, then. Let us, your brothers, pilgrimage with you to Jerusalem and there you may bring your words before them who were ordained to judge their merit. Bring your tidings to all Israel, not to us, the rejected ones who sit in Nazareth, for no man will court secrecy unless he fear the light."

Jude's words gave courage to his older brothers and they turned boldly on Yeshua.

"Brother, why do you keep us walking in darkness? Reveal yourself to the world!"

Yeshua did not immediately answer. His face clouded over and he looked with sadness and compassion at his brothers.

"This year you shall go up alone to celebrate the Feast of the Tabernacles; my time is not yet."

Then Yeshua beckoned to his old disciple Taddi and they went forth together to the fields.

Throughout this altercation between Yeshua and his brothers, Miriam had sat in her threshold watching her sons from a distance. Their words did not reach her and yet she knew their quarrel. She had long waited with an anxious heart for the wonderful day when her younger sons would recognize her eldest and convert to him. Now that day was passing and the miracle had not been. She watched Yeshua going off alone with Taddi, going without his brothers, who stood rooted in ignorance, arguing hotly and gesticulating among themselves.

Miriam was well aware of the conflict in their hearts. She knew their thoughts because they were as dear and close to her as her own life. She rejoiced in their learning and uprightness and in their good name among the people of Nazareth. But she would have liked to see her sons shine, like many candles on a single stick, in one blended flame—the flame the Lord had lighted in

302

her eldest. She wished to see the others sit at Yeshua's feet, as one sits about a rabbin, and drink at the fount of his wisdom. But it was clear today that her younger sons were not fitted to partake of Yeshua's sanctity. Not learning, nor even piety, could open a man's heart to Yeshua's teaching. A special ray of grace issued from the hearts of those poor artisans who listened to him and fused with him as light fuses with light. Utter strangers who had never looked on him before perceived in Yeshua some mystic quality which was veiled from his own flesh and blood.

Jacob, her second son, was coming slowly toward her on the garden path. He walked with difficulty, like a man newly crippled.

"I know not who my brother is," he said, coming close, "and I cannot judge how far his rights extend. I know only that God will justify him in his doings. But we, we have nothing in our hands but the guide rope of the Law. And he who cuts this rope, whoever he may be, cuts off our path to God."

"My son, my son," said Miriam passionately, "pray God that He plant a new spirit in you, that you may see the new path to the Lord which your brother lays out for the poor and simple. Without God's help you shall never see your brother's light, for what he does is not done according to the laws of men but in accordance with the will of God."

Jacob's sunken eyes opened wide as he stared at his mother. He dropped his head shamefully and stammered out in a choked voice:

"*Ema,* mother, who is Yeshua?"

Miriam laid her hand on his arm.

"It is not for me to reveal the mysteries of God. When the time is ripe it shall be known to you, my son."

CHAPTER IV

A MONG those whom Yeshua had early drawn into his circle were the two sons of Zebedee from the fishing town of Bethsaida. Jacob and Jochanan well remembered their first childhood trip to Jerusalem, and remembered Yeshua's association with the rabbis in the Temple. They knew that their Nazarene cousin had been chosen for some great preferment and, with the rest of their kinsmen, waited for him to become a rabbi in Israel. They did not lose faith when these hopes remained unanswered, convinced nevertheless that God had appointed him for great deeds.

Their own education and environment had been very different from Yeshua's. The town of Bethsaida—or Julias, as it was later named for Caesar's daughter—lay on the shore of the Sea of Genesaret, only a few miles from the commercial town of K'far Nahum. It was ruled by Herod Philip, a brother of Herod Antipas, the Tetrarch of Galilee. The populace of Bethsaida was largely Greek in language and extraction as was the rest of Philip's narrow realm. But Bethsaida was large enough to boast its own tax collectors and small Roman garrison. More even than K'far Nahum, it maintained constant intercourse with the Greek population of Decapolis, the ten Greek cities on the far side of the Sea.

Since his subject population was preponderantly Gentile, Herod Philip—himself only half-Jewish—saw no need to play his brother's irksome game of flattering and fawning on the Pharisees. He was a whole-hearted and brazen Hellenizer. He did not hesitate to have the Caesar's image embossed on his coin, in flagrant violation of Mosaic stricture. He brought Roman institutions to his towns, opened gymnasiums for the diversion of the young, as well as public baths and temples to promote Pagan worship. These Roman institutions, with their attendant ills of luxury and dissolute living, lent Bethsaida the appearance of a Gentile, Hellenistic-Asian city.

Nor was it only the provisions for public games and entertainment that gave the city its Greek character. In a wider cultural sense Bethsaida was a suburb of Decapolis. Its wealthy landowners, sheepmen, and fish merchants kept Greek tutors, purchased at the slave exchange, for the instruction of their children. And the Stoic school was represented by a circle of native philosophers who used an orchard for their public disquisitions—as the Pharisees did in Nazareth—and discoursed on Plato, Epicurus, and Aristotle, while expounding the superior merits of their teacher Zeno. These debates in the garden of philosophers in Bethsaida generated no less heat than those in the Torah grove of Nazareth, since in either case the antagonists were Jews.

If, under these conditions, Zebedee's sons had absorbed a fair amount of Jewish learning—though in Greek translation—they were somewhat exceptional among the younger Jews of the city.

Their father, in his lifetime, had carried on a lively fishing trade and had acquired several small craft to operate on the sea. The smacks were still in the family possession, worked by his sons with the assistance of a hired crew. Meanwhile, in their home hard by the shore, the widowed mother kept an open house for the friends of her sons who foregathered here for an afternoon siesta, a Sabbath, or a holiday. One of these was a young man, Philip by name, who enjoyed wide respect as a follower of Greek philosophies. Another was young Nathaniel from the Galilean town of Cana. And not far from the Zebedee home lived Andrew, whose brother Simon often came from his wife and home in K'far Nahum to join the others in their fishing.

Shoshannah had raised her sons on good food plentifully served, and the two boys had grown up with athletic, brawny bodies. Wind and water had completed their training. Their powerful arms, which could wield trunk-like oars in stormy waters, were used as often to defend their co-religionists from the affronts of local Greeks. In fact, Zebedee's sons had a reputation in the town for teaching Gentiles how to behave toward their Jewish neighbors.

Yet strangely, despite their build and ready strength of muscle, the brothers had the minds of visionaries, dreaming constantly of Israel's salvation and taking interest in little else. They were repelled by the pleasure seeking and the loose living of their Greek contemporaries. They saw a shallow satisfaction in the sport and beauty of contesting athletes, in the howl of a hysteric populace at chariot races. The symmetry and charm of Grecian temple architecture did not seduce their eyes, though Herod Philip had reared several fine structures with marble slabs and slender fluted columns to house a naked god or goddess wrought by human hands.

To the brothers, no beauty that did not have in it a relish of salvation could be more than meretricious tinsel. And thus their great capacity for love, which neither nature, beauty, nor the love of woman could command, was offered to the godhead, to their distressed people, to their ecstatic longing for the coming of the Messiah.

Situated as it was, far from the Jewish centers and steeped in the noxious influence of neighboring Phoenicia, their town of Bethsaida received few visits from transient rabbis or Pharisaic legates from Jerusalem, who alone could have planted or tended the Torah in their midst. New ordinances and rabbinic promulgations rarely came to their attention, and by degrees the small Jewish community became estranged from the rabbinic spirit which moved the mass of Israel. But, as it were for compensation, they found the greater resource in another field of Jewish spiritual life—in the ideal of the Prophets, the hope of Israel, the expectation of redemption.

This yearning for Messiah had found new channels of expression in Hellenistic-Jewish writings. The mystic "pseudepigrapha," which the rabbis had excluded from the holy canon of the Scriptures, became the foremost source of consolation for the estranged, rejected Hellenized Jews. In these writings a man might find the ancient promise of the Prophets pledged again in a new tongue. Here he might find a bridge thrown to the Gentiles among whom he lived, a heroic effort in poetic terms to work a synthesis of the Jewish spirit with the "Logos" of the Greeks. It was these books which set forth the role of the Messiah, how he would spread God's mantle over all the nations of the earth.

The general mood of the Hellenic Jews prevailed also in the small Jewish community of Bethsaida. They drew their spiritual sustenance from the body of Greek-Jewish literature, allowing it

306

to mold their way of living and their attitude to world and man.

Zebedee's sons too had absorbed the message of these writings, and their spell was greatest on the mind of Jochanan, the elder. Unlike his brother Jacob, who was tall and sinewy and with smooth graceful movements, Jochanan had grown broad and stocky. He looked as though his figure had been hewn from a square block of stone. His wide shoulders bore a massive head with a dense profusion of unclipped black curls that multiplied his every motion. And Jochanan, despite his ox-like bulk, was constantly in motion. As though to relieve an excess of vitality, he had retained his childhood habit of swinging his arms outward as he walked—like a pair of wings. And when he spoke he needed little prompting to burst into ecstatic monologues that made one think the vessel of his fervor had been suddenly uncorked. In a voice of pressing urgency he spoke of Israel's approaching redemption—the Saviour was already knocking at the door, his footfall was unmistakable—and Jochanan spoke of him not in the colloquial of his fisherman's tongue, but with the God-framed diction of the Bible. People thought he was possessed by the Lord's spirit, or stood under an angel's lash that drove him to his mission. For when he spoke of the Messiah, Jochanan lost the contours of reality, confused wakefulness and dream, and declaimed in the accents of a new Daniel or Ezekiel, the Prophets closest to his heart. He saw the wheels of heaven with the Prophets' eyes, the fiery wheels of the celestial chariot, and heard the roar of seraphic wings, "like the noise of great waters." Or he would speak with Enoch of the heavenly tablets and of the "Son of Man in whom justice abides."

The power of his oratory had long established Jochanan's influence over his friends. They listened spellbound as he painted for them the resurrection and the end of days and the Messiah's kingdom.

In his younger years, his God-seeking and his yearning for salvation had driven Jochanan from home. He had gone to live with the Essenes in the wilderness and, spending several years in their midst, had learned their mystic lore of the roads of heaven. He fancied that he heard voices, that he knew the potency of the angels in the heavenly host, and by the power of the names of

307

Michael, Gabriel, Uriel, and Mitron, could exorcise evil eyes, drive demons to hell, and deliver parturient women from the claws of Lilith. It was this training, underlined by a naturally mystic temper, which gave Jochanan to see visions and experience ecstasies so that he was perpetually tensed for the advent of the Messiah—a state of mind and body to which the books of Daniel and Enoch gave ready articulation:

"Behold," Jochanan would cry out, "He is the Son of Man; His is the judgment and He dwells in righteousness, and in Him shall ancient mysteries be unsealed, for Him the King of Spirits has elected. And His place is before the King of Spirits in the ultimate justice at the end of time. . . ."

Then came the day when Jochanan, with his own eyes, saw him whose "countenance was like the face of man, yet featured like the holy seraphim." Yeshua came one day to Shoshannah's house in Bethsaida and was told the young men were out on the water, having cast their nets. Yeshua waited until almost dusk, then stepped out-of-doors to await the return of the fishermen on the shore of Genesaret.

The small fleet was rowing shoreward with the day's catch, and Jochanan, from a distance, spied the white form of Yeshua. He turned to Simon, who was helping on this day, and said: "Behold the Son of Man!"

Simon was a simple person, powerfully built, though short of stature. He knew, like every Jew, a little of the Scripture, and could recite the *Sh'ma* and a few of the Psalms. But he was not strong in the Law, and his roster of good deeds, he felt, made a scant showing. Yet his heart was filled with awe of heaven and he held the scholars and rabbis of his people in great reverence. In the synagogue he sat near the door among folk as ignorant as he, praying as best he knew and attending, though often without comprehension, to the reading of the Torah—"Two portions of Holy Writ for one of translation." Like the sons of Zebedee he was full of the hope of Israel and ready in his heart to welcome the Messiah. For he was one of the people and familiar with their plight, and he knew that the Messiah was the only hope and consolation of the poor. Now, since he had joined in partnership with Jochanan and Jacob, and had heard the elder brother's warnings of the imminence of the Messiah, his imagination was inflamed and he thought constantly of the Redeemer's coming, expecting it at every hour of the day.

When he heard Jochanan's words, he started violently and almost capsized the boat. His dark, furrowed face grew suddenly pale and he felt his hair bristling. The net almost slipped from his hands, and he whispered, without raising his eyes:

"Where?"

"On the shore—in the white mantle," said Jochanan. "Yeshua of Nazareth."

Simon had heard Jochanan speak of the Nazarene before. And some of Yeshua's townsmen who purchased fish in Bethsaida had mentioned a young rabbi who had no dealings with the learned and attached himself to the poor. Simon had not heard them report miracles in his name; he had heard only that this rabbi brought comfort and exaltation to sinful and ignorant men, men who were no better than Simon himself.

He had never before stood face to face with a rabbi or a scholar of the Law. Whilst living in Bethsaida there had been almost no opportunities, owing to the rare visits of itinerant rabbis. In K'far Nahum, where he was now living, a few scholars could be met, but Simon had too much humility to dare invade their fellowship. Conscious of his ignorance and possible uncleanness, he kept himself at a respectful distance lest he contaminate a holy place where God's word was being studied and preached.

Now, in the boat, he was afraid to raise his eyes, for the man who awaited their landing was not only a rabbi; it was he whom Jochanan, who was versed enough to know, had called the Son of Man. Simon kept his eyes down to avoid seeing the white flecks of the Nazarene's mantle where it shimmered palely in the faltering sun. With beating heart he steered the boat inshore.

They disembarked close to where the Nazarene was standing and the sons of Zebedee wished him peace. Yeshua gave no appearance of having heard their greeting. He gazed at the cowering Simon, as though to penetrate him with his glance. Simon thought that the rabbi's glance, like a bolt of lightning, pierced his outer shell and illumined his heart, healing and purging it of all blemish. With the rabbi's gaze he felt the infusion of a new spirit, for there was a tremor of holiness at the core of his being. Simon felt himself suddenly rid of sorrows and sins, like a child newly born. He stood with lowered head under the rabbi's gaze and for a moment, though no one had stirred, felt the pressure of a hand laid on his shoulder; and heard the vibration of a voice in his heart—"It is you I want."

It was several minutes before the rabbi lifted his gaze from the fisherman, while the brothers Zebedee stood by helpless and irresolute. Meanwhile Simon's brother Andrew disembarked with Philip from another boat, but seeing the rabbi motionless they too held their breath until at last they heard the Nazarene's clear voice saying:

"Peace be with you, Simon bar Jonah!"

Then for the first time Simon raised his eyes to the rabbi and timidly stretched forth his hand to touch the sleeve of his white mantle.

"And with you, master," he said.

For one fleeting moment their glances met and locked, but Simon's eyes, when he looked into Yeshua's face, offered absolute surrender, a server's unconditional submission to his master— "Yours will I be for all ages."

Yeshua turned from him slowly and hailed the others.

That evening, the night being mild, Shoshannah set up a large trestle table in the yard outside the house overlooking the Sea. On the table, which was covered with a white cloth, she placed lighted lamps and proceeded to serve the food she had prepared during the day with the help of neighborhood fisherwomen. For the rumor was abroad that a wayfaring rabbi had come down to stay at Zebedee's house, who would take supper with the fishermen and offer them his teachings.

Yeshua seated himself at the table with the men of the house, their number being soon augmented by neighbors coming from their houses or fresh from the Sea lest they miss the word of a preacher whose transit here was such a rare occurrence.

Near Yeshua sat the sons of Zebedee and their friends, Philip and Nathanael. But next to him, on his right, sat Simon bar Jonah, the simple fisherman who had neither so much learning as the sons of Zebedee, nor so much philosophy as Philip, or even his

310

own brother Andrew. And to the surprise of all, the rabbi treated him with obvious respect, though Simon had never been esteemed above his brother. It pleased the fishermen to see one of their kind so honored. For they who came into the yard of Zebedee's house were themselves of humble stock, day-laborers for the most part, who did not even own the tackle with which they plied their trade. Many, indeed, had long been in Zebedee's employ, and they respected Yeshua the more for singling out one of their lot to show him special honor.

It was evident, moreover, that the strange Nazarene did not conduct himself like other rabbis who had formerly passed through the town. He was not staying at the house of a reputable Pharisee, nor did he stickle to eat only at their approved tables. No, he had taken up his quarters in the home of simple men and did not shrink from eating in the company of working fisherfolk, without even inquiring into their cleanness. Word of this unusual rabbi spread rapidly along the shore, and men arrived in droves, some thankfully, others from sheer curiosity to hear what he might have to say.

They watched him closely, and when they saw him bless the bread and distribute the blessed morsels among the learned and the ignorant without discrimination, then dip his own bread in the common bowl of vinegar-wine, they felt drawn to him in love and gratitude and waited with a ready ear to hear his teaching.

Yeshua began to speak of loving one's neighbor, enjoining the company to love even their enemies and to pray for them who did them injury. He next turned to the subject of forgiveness, saying: "If you offer a sacrifice at God's altar and there remember that your brother bears you a grudge, leave your sacrifice, I say, and go first to make peace with your brother." Lastly, he spoke of the day of the kingdom of heaven whose approach, he said, was at hand. "All shall be called," he said, "but not all shall be admitted. The gate of the kingdom is a narrow ingress and the warden will probe whosoever knocks thereon. Like a careful herdsman will he choose his flock, and only he who is found worthy shall have right of entry. For great ordeals await him within the gate. He shall be like a lamb in a wolf pack, and the shepherd must have assurance that his flock will hearken to his shawm. In that day no man shall be exempted from his debt, neither on grounds of lineage, nor of learning nor of riches. The haughty shall be humbled and the lowly exalted, the hungry shall be brought to the table and the rich sent empty away. For they who are esteemed of men are not esteemed of God. God examines the hearts of men and knows His servitors. He knows the man who comes before Him in humility and contrition and him who seeks the easy comfort and lull of security. For the Son of Man, who will come shortly, comes not to be a golden nose-ring for the noses of the learned, but to be a comforter and a helper for them who are meek of spirit and pure of heart, and his shall be the kingdom of heaven."

Yeshua paused and from the surrounding darkness the rough voice of a fisherman called out:

"Tell us, master, who you are. You speak like one commissioned by the Lord."

And Jochanan answered loudly:

"Can you not see? He is man in the image of a seraph, as was foretold by Father Enoch. He is the Son of Man who walks with the Ancient of Days."

Jochanan's words faded into a deep stillness. Every man held his breath and, in silent terror, listened to the beating of his heart. There was a movement of affrighted withdrawal among some of the men, for they expected Yeshua's white mantle to emit flames of fire and they would all be consumed in the blast of his sanctity. Others stretched out their hands to him and cried:

"Blessed man of God, let your hands rest on our children and bless them for the sake of your glory!"—and brought their children to him. And while Yeshua blessed them each, he heard the heavy man at his right sobbing like a child.

"What ails you, Simon?" he asked.

"Master, my heart is melted for fear. For my eyes look on the holy one of Israel and I am a man with unclean hands."

"Be of good heart, Simon," Yeshua said. "For I have seen you and know that you have the purity of a child and the wisdom of a mother."

Simon bowed humbly and whispered:

"Rabbi, I am not worthy to hear such words."

"Your humility shall be your elevation, for only they shall be exalted who hold themselves in small regard."

Shoshannah, who was standing aside, watched all that passed before her. And when she saw the brightness radiating from the rabbi's face and lighting the faces of the men with happiness, she thought to herself: "It cannot be but a God-like man has entered my house, and mine is the grace to behold my sons seated beside him."

The company did not disperse until late in the night. For many hours more they listened to the rabbi's speech and sang paeans of praise to the Lord, sang loudly into the bright night so that their voices hung over the silver surface of the waters. The rabbi's peace had penetrated every man's soul, and they went home comforted, each to his own house. . . .

On the morrow of the following day Yeshua left the house of the sons of Zebedee. His hosts wondered at the shortness of his stay; in the past Yeshua had sometimes spent a whole week with their family.

But Yeshua was in haste. His visit to Bethsaida had been for a special purpose which he would divulge to no man. Only Simon bar Jonah knew its nature. When Yeshua bid him farewell, Simon asked, with his head lowered, as was his wont:

"Master, shall I go with you?"

"No, Simon, my time has not yet come. But you shall have a sign."

Then asked Jochanan:

"When will you come, master?"

And Yeshua told him—"It is not for you to know the hour which my Father has appointed for me. Wait for the coming and be always wakeful, for the son shall come of a sudden into his kingdom."

Then he departed alone.

Yeshua walked the rest of the morning and, following the shore of the Genesaret Sea, came at noontime into a town whose name was Magdala. Merchants from Tyre and the surrounding provinces filled its markets, the town being famed for the skill of its dyers, who rendered wool and linen in every color known to man.

313

To cater to the Gentile trade Magdala provided sumptuous accommodation in numerous hostelries and inns. And many women of ill fame, the camp followers of commerce, were drawn into its precincts, like insects to a bowl of honey.

Yeshua of Nazareth was in the market square of the town when he saw a litter carried out of a house. In it lay a woman, indolent and softly cushioned. Pipers as well as dancing girls preceded her train, which was composed of many men in colored garments, with costly rings and chains about their persons. For the woman was much sought after by the rich, being beautiful for all to see, and never stirred outside her house without a retinue of lovers and admirers.

As the litter moved across the market square where Yeshua stood preaching to the people, the woman turned her head and, seeing a young rabbi in a white mantle speaking to common laborers, she motioned to her bearers to stop, curious to hear what such a man might have to say.

But the young rabbi lifted up his eyes and gazed steadily at her who had stopped for a curious whim.

"Woman, woman," he called out to her, "why do you squander the oil in your lamp? Where shall your light be when your bridegroom comes?"

At this, the woman started in her litter and with a fumbling gesture of recollected shame drew the long tresses of her hair over her breasts. For she was naked to her belly but for a veiling of gossamer and a profuse finery of bangles, amulets, and silver coins.

"I do not understand you, rabbi," she said. "Tell me the meaning of your words."

"The Lord has opened a pure fount in you, which is a fount of love. But you have sullied the Lord's gift. And still your bounty is great, woman, for deep is the fount of love which God has given you, and the bottom is yet pure. Why will you not preserve it for the bridegroom who is worthy, but let your bounty run out in polluted gutters?"

The woman dropped her eyes and dared not look at the rabbi. Then, in a sudden impulse, she glided down from her cushions, threw herself at his feet, and cried out in a breaking voice:

"Tell me, holy one, what must I do?"

"Leave sinning," said the rabbi, "and purge yourself for the day of the kingdom of heaven which is at hand."

"Can there be hope still for my kind?"

"To you also the gate shall open. Knock at it in fear and contrition and your Father shall be waiting for you to receive you into the kingdom of heaven as a daughter of Israel. Your time will come, woman; hold yourself ready. For they shall fare well who wait for the day of God."

With that the rabbi turned to go, and the woman snatched the hem of his garment and pressed her lips upon it.

And on that day she abjured the company of her lovers, dismissed her pipers and dancing girls and, selling her house with all its precious furnishings and trinkets which she had had from her admirers, distributed the money among the poor.

All the town mused upon her conversion, for the woman had been greatly renowned for her beauty, and many men of wealth and importance had been among her friends.

And the rabbi left the town behind him and came into a field. It was the hour of early afternoon and he, being weary with walking, seated himself to rest in the shade of a tall olive tree.

Not far from him, a young couple, man and wife, were harvesting in the field, and their child, swaddled in white linen, hung in a hammock from a branch above the ground to protect it from worms and snakes. Now when the sun waxed strong in the midday hour the man and wife came from the field to seek the shade of the tree under which their child slept. The man stretched himself at his full length to rest, and the wife, taking the child out of the hammock, laid it between herself and her husband and lay down at his side to rest herself also.

And the spirit came upon Yeshua and his heart filled with compassion for mankind, and he raised his hands and wept:

"Father, as Thou madest man and wife to be one soul, make Thou one soul of heaven and earth and join them in one kingdom, even Thy kingdom, the kingdom of God."

Then he rose and went to the man and his wife and said:

"As you were made one in the Lord's covenant, may you have grace to see heaven and earth covenanted in the kingdom of God."

And he blessed them and went his way.

CHAPTER V

"**D**ARK are the sun and the moon, and the stars hold back their light."

All Judah, Jerusalem, and Galilee, and all the righteous throughout the vast Dispersion listen in vain for a tread in the mountains and a voice crying out in the wilderness. No omen comes to Israel; the voice of the Prophet is mute; shadows hang over the earth.

The plight of the Holy City, with that of Judah and all the land of Israel, had grown more bitter with the years. In bygone times it was the lion and the leopard who had torn their fellow creatures; now the little foxes were spoiling God's vineyard.

Caesar Augustus was dead—the great Emperor who had burst like Apollo from a clouded sky to snatch Rome from destruction in her hour of need when Mark Antony was snared by Egypt's queen. Augustus had restored to Rome her old-time discipline, renewed the manly vigor of her people, banished the perfumed effeminacy and oriental lust in which Roman virtue had been degraded through Cleopatra's hold on Antony. He had buttressed the people's faith in the gods, restored justice to her place in the courts and chastity to its place in the home. Under his fatherly hand the subject nations of the far-flung Empire were ruled with equity and understanding by governors who catered to the common weal and made the "Pax Romana" well worth the price of independence. Oh, there was cause enough to weep for the great Augustus now that Rome and her conquests smarted under the regime of his adopted son and son-in-law, Tiberius Caesar.

During the first years of his reign Tiberius made blundering attempts to maintain throughout the realm the justice and fair government of his revered predecessor. But where Augustus had embodied every virtue of the Roman character, Tiberius was sly, craven, little-minded, a slave to fugitive pleasures and to personal ambitions for which his ready means were treachery and small intrigue. How was Rome ever to forget his peevish jealousy which

316

led him to assassinate the well-beloved and glorious Germanicus by bribing a handful of his soldiers!

And the Emperor's personal life, evincing a perverted mind in a sickly body, could do little to win the respect of senators and tribunes who had been bred under the moral standard of Augustus. Deprived of power and office, these men withdrew from public affairs and, retiring to their estates, trucked politics for the consolations of philosophy. Those who remained in the Imperial entourage consigned themselves to a career of flattery and traducement; they shared in the Emperor's intrigues, debased the great traditions of Augustus, betrayed their general Germanicus, under whose ensign they had won victory upon victory for Rome, and fawned day and night upon Tiberius by titillating him with solemn titles and proclaiming him a god. The integrity of Augustan government degenerated to a corrupt traffic in administrative posts with which Tiberius rewarded his toadies. He appointed them as procurators over provinces and nations, with orders to do like the proverbial flies who, when they gorge themselves with blood, keep quiet, being too heavy for adventure.

One such favorite he had appointed Procurator of Judaea.

Pontius Pilate had neither the education, nor the strength of character, nor the Roman feeling for order and self-discipline which would have fitted him to rule over a foreign people. Certainly he lacked the subtle wisdom required for the handling of a nation so strange as the Jews. He had no patience with the laws and customs of a foreign faith, even though all religious rituals throughout the Empire were recognized and privileged by statute of the Caesar.

His very first move in Jerusalem caused bloodshed. While it is true that the emblems of the Roman legions—the brazen eagles and the fasces—were not religious but Imperial and military symbols—it had long been the accepted practice of Roman procurators in Judaea to sheathe the standards of the legions when approaching the Judaean capital.

Pilate entered the gates of Jerusalem with the naked Roman emblems reared high above the heads of his men. Then, to top the insult, he had the eagle and the lictor's rods affixed to the

317

battlements of the Antonia, the Roman citadel which dominated the Temple site from the northwest.

This first official act opened an unbridgeable chasm between the Procurator and the people. Their mistrust of his motives became so deeply ingrained that they rightly supposed some crooked scheme to underlie his project to improve sanitary conditions in his province.

Thus, when Pilate made plans for the construction of an aqueduct in Jerusalem, he did not turn for funds to the administration of the Temple, did not even consult them on the project, but captured the entire Temple treasure by main force, though to his perfect knowledge it included numerous private deposits and many legacies for orphans who had not reached majority. News of this sacrilegious plunder spread rapidly throughout Judaea and Galilee. No one would stay to hear for what extenuating purpose the Procurator had laid hands on the hoard. It was enough that sacrilege had been committed, a dastardly assault on the sanctity of the Lord's tabernacle. It now seemed an unbearable affront to have the sacred vestments of the High Priest kept in Pilate's custody in the Antonia tower, for they were hallowed objects and, according to tradition, the Lord Himself had, on Mount Sinai, instructed Moses how they should be made. A thousand times a day the pilgrims looked up to the lamp that burned on the summit of the fortress tower as a sign to the Jews that the holy vestments were being kept inviolate and unprofaned by Gentile hands. It was with bitterness enough that they had stomached this humiliation in the past; now, as the news of Pilate's robbery was noised abroad, the thought of the High Priest's vestments in the hands of Pilate fanned their resentment. From every home in Judah and Galilee men set out for the Temple in a record pilgrimage.

Pilate knew well that disturbances were brewing—and carefully abstained from taking measures to prevent them. With pleasure he foresaw an opportunity to settle scores with the Jews, whom he despised as enemies, and to attain this end, resorted to a scheme which no Roman Procurator before him had dared to employ. He sent out his legionaries, disguised in civilian dress and carrying small weapons under their cloaks. Their orders were to mingle

318

with the pilgrim crowds in the Temple. On a pre-arranged signal the soldiers picked a quarrel with the people, then laid at them with spiked bludgeons, knives, and iron-tipped rods, turning the Temple courts into a reeking human shambles.

Thenceforth Pilate's government became a reign of terror. Not a festival passed in Jerusalem without some bloody clash between the pilgrims and the legionaries who, on Pilate's orders, manned the Antonia in readiness for every holy feast. Most of the disturbances involved the Galileans, more irrepressibly fanatic and more jealous for the Temple's sanctity than their Judaean brethren.

Pilate bore a simmering hatred for these northern zealots who offered such fierce opposition to his petty violations of the Temple. Throughout his tenure there was not one holiday that did not see the blood of Galilean pilgrims spilled with that of their sacrifices before the altar of the Lord.

Ever since Ezra's time the office of the High Priest had been revered by Jews as the supreme authority within the nation, surpassing even that of the crown. To the people the High Priest was not only Aaron's ordained descendant, not only the mediator between God and Israel, but also the symbol of terrestrial power. Under the hegemony of the Maccabees the two offices of kingship and High Priesthood came gradually to be held by members of the same house, that of the Hasmonean dynasty. But they were ousted by the Idumean Herod, and the usurping king saw in the High Priesthood a dangerous rival to his absolutism. Unable to endure the shadow of competing power in his orbit, Herod set out to degrade this supreme religious office and rob it of its sacred luster. He began by removing from it the descendants of the Hasmonean dynasty of heroes, whom he murdered to the last man. He had their place taken by his private favorites and minions, once even by an unknown minor priest as a reward for trading him his daughter. And he was careful to enact a quick succession of High Priests, thereby spoiling their dynastic pretensions which might have vied with his own.

A further degradation of the sacred office set in after Herod's death. To the Roman Procurators who followed his regime, the High Priesthood was a benefice to be trafficked to the highest bidder among the four eligible families. Every few years—some-

319

times annually, depending on the offer—there was a new High Priest appointed to replace the old. This unashamed corruption of the sacred office; the fact that it was held invariably by the members of the aristocratic party of the Sadduccees, who differed with the Pharisees on fundamental issues, such as the belief in angels and the resurrection of the dead; and, not least, the general knowledge that these upstart priestlings were henchmen to the Roman power that had put them in their place—all this led the person of the High Priest, if not the High Priesthood as such, to be regarded as cheap and contemptible.

During Pilate's procuracy the High Priesthood was held by members of the house of Hanan, a family which had succeeded in retaining the office for longer than had by this time become usual. Hanan himself had been High Priest and the office had been held by his sons. Now the position was filled by his son-in-law Caiaphas.

A popular lampoon accused the house of Hanan of high treason, that is to say, of working hand and glove with the Roman Procurator in oppressing the people. In the words of the squib, the family "made treasurers of its sons and tax collectors of its sons-in-law, and they send out their servants to flay us with scourges of lead."

Under such circumstances it was no longer possible to see the High Priesthood as a reflection of Messianic glory, or of Supreme Authority, as it had seemed under Simeon the Just or in the early days after the Maccabean liberation. The nation turned from the sacred office and sought guidance from its sages and rabbins, the scholars of the Pharisaic party.

Meanwhile the economic condition of the people had undergone a sharp deterioration, particularly among the poorer peasants of the Galilean North. Their toil had to support an opulent Oriental court that teemed with useless personnel, Roman officials, assorted military, and a horde of parasites whose tastes ran expensively to elegance and luxurious living.

If the land had barely supported the spendthrift building mania of the great Herod whose sway extended over a large realm, it could by no exertion feed the extravagances of his small-statured son Antipas Herod, whose tetrarchy comprised only the few provinces of Galilee. The great Herod had commanded large reserves on which to draw for his expenditures—a great kingdom, investments abroad, far-flung commercial enterprises, and, above all, a Temple which attracted the contributions of Jews throughout the Diaspora. Herod Antipas the Little had no more than rural Galilee and a few fisheries on the Sea of Genesaret to bleed for taxes. And yet his appetites grew almost as inordinate as his father's had been, particularly after his second marriage. For Herod Antipas sent his Arabian wife home to her royal father and married his Roman-educated cousin Herodias whom he seduced from his own brother, another petty Herod, to cohabit with her in violation of the Jewish law. With this switching of wives Herod Antipas changed his entire mode of living. Bred as a small Oriental potentate in a castle of the Sodom desert beyond the Dead Sea, he now affected the role of a fashionable monarch and set himself to vie with other subject princes of the Roman Empire, including even the queens of wealth-laden Egypt.

Like his father, Herod Antipas was goaded by a mania for building palaces and cities. His first major enterprise as Tetrarch of Galilee was to rebuild the ruins of Sepphoris, sacked by Quintilius Varus and his generals. But he did not choose to take up residence in this ancient capital of Galilee, preferring to rear a new city on the Genesaret Sea not far from the fishing town of K'far Nahum. He named his capital Tiberias, after the Emperor in Rome. The site of it was an old Jewish burial-ground—by which sacrilege he rendered it impossible for Jews to live in the city. Herod accordingly peopled it with Greeks and various local tribes whom he encouraged to settle in his residential city by making them free gifts of lands and properties. The shore of the Sea he turned into a splendid garden, set with palaces and towers, and citadels for his protection and that of his teeming courtiers.

No Jewish blood ran in the veins of Herod Antipas the Little. A foreigner by paternal descent, he was born of a woman who hailed from the Jew-hating tribe of the Samaritans. Nevertheless the diminutive Herod carried within himself the secret ambition to rule over all Israel within the borders of his father's realm, if not beyond. His scheme was by the aid of Rome to assume the royal title or, failing this, to hammer out an alliance of small kingdoms against Rome.

And strange to say, no matter how alien they were to the spirit of the nation over which they ruled, and no matter how they were abhorred by this same nation, the sons of the great Herod persisted in their dream of one day occupying in the Jewish heart the place once held by Solomon, and directing to themselves the hopes and expectations which Jewry had of the Messiah. Yes, these petty princelings had Messianic aspirations, in pursuit of which they strove absurdly to befriend both sides—the Romans without whom they could not stay in power, and the Jews. They played a double game and lived a double life.

At home in their palaces, in their own capitals which few Jews ever saw, they disported themselves like Roman patricians, champions of Roman civilization in Asiatic outposts. They surrounded themselves with Roman soldiery, with Roman ministers and counselors, engaged only Greek or Hellenized philosophers, historians, and grammarians, and maintained close relations with the court of Rome. They decked their palaces with marble statues of Greek gods, equipped the capitals with gymnasiums, theaters, and hippodromes, built temples for Caesar Augustus, and kept large retinues of slaves and freedmen.

But before Jews they put on sanctimonious airs, pretending to a vast concern for correct Pharisaic ritual. Knowing how popular the Pharisees were with the people, they cultivated their goodwill and went by their legal strictures wherever they were under Jewish observation. Herod Antipas even refrained from using the Emperor's, or any human, head on his mintage, resorting rather to accepted Jewish symbols, such as the grape cluster and the grain stalk. Each year without fail, the Herods pilgrimaged to Jerusalem with presents for the Temple rich and conspicuously bulky. With the rest of the people they bore upon their royal shoulders the first-fruits of their lands packed in golden vessels, and were followed by whole flocks of sheep and many bullocks for the sacrificial altar. At times they even interceded for the people, headed deputations to Antioch, or intervened in Rome against the despotism of a local Procurator. By these means they succeeded in winning some of the Pharisees and even in forming a party,

322

called the Herodists, who preached the desirability of the Herodian kingdom.

The soul of all Herod Antipas's ambitions was his new wife Herodias. Both she and her brother Agrippus had been raised at Caesar's court, where Augustus had treated them as princely children and where the girl had been educated together with Agrippina, the daughter of the great Germanicus.

Now, at the court of Herod Antipas, Herodias launched an intense political activity. She formed valuable connections in Rome and secured friends among men of influence by her prodigious liberality in making presents. Under her hands Tiberias blossomed forth into a miniature Rome, a citadel of Latin culture in wild rebellious Galilee. If Roman notables visited Jerusalem on business, they came for pleasure to Tiberias, where the Tetrarch's wife saw personally to their entertainment—chariot races run by the best athletes in the East, banquets executed by hand-picked Syrian cooks, with music by Egyptian harpists and Sidonian dancers.

All of which was paid in sweat by the peasantry of Galilee. Their bread was taken from them for taxes and they toiled only to pay larger tributes. The land was overrun by publicans moving under military escort. The people groaned under the heavy burden of taxation, under excessive toil of which the fruit was never theirs to enjoy. They looked with dull eyes for a saviour, for an omen of salvation, a sign from heaven to reassure them that someone was seeing their distress, counting their tears, and appointing a term to their sorrows.

But was Israel alone in crying for salvation?

Israel was fortunate; it had its rabbis and its laws to protect it from uncleanness, and against wantonness and dissipation. Israel had attained a unique intimacy with its God Who had lifted it out of the morass of pagan beastliness, conferred on it a higher rank within Creation, making it a child of God, with special rights of access by prayer to its heavenly Father. Israel had the Psalms and Torah to light it through the night; it had the pledge made to the Patriarchs and the assurance of the Prophets that there would one day be a Redeemer to redress all wrongs and found on earth the kingdom of heaven. Israel had the Messianic hope to purify and sanctify it and prepare it for the day of God. What consolation, what hope had the Gentiles to compare with Israel's faith?

Woe to the nations whose gods do not keep pace with history! Woe to the gods who lag behind their believers!

The gods of Greece and Rome had been blown like soap bubbles into existence—the playthings of Arcadian shepherds conceived under the pipes of Pan. What spiritual or religious values did their splendid forms embody? What meaning had they for the modern Greek and for the Roman, who not only possessed the physical world but had long outstripped his gods in his quest for moral values? How pitiful did they appear before the spiritual giants of a world that worshipped them with lip service, before men who, like Plato, plumbed the depths of the soul's knowledge and, in Stoic philosophy, ascended to the highest ethical perceptions!

If the Romans still retained their gods, it was no more than national discipline, a matter of propriety and a patriotic duty to uphold the ancestral character of Greco-Roman culture. Their mock divinities were the external ornaments of their society, without a shadow of religious, ethical, or mystic content. The more educated among them sought refuge in various moral philosophies which, however lofty in precept, were backed by no divine authority to compel action. The systems which these best-intentioned men embraced were, no doubt, useful pedagogical expedients for character building; and no one could deny the high educational value of the Stoic school. But it obliged a man to nothing. It lacked the authority to enforce total submission to a moral yoke such as the heavenly kingdom was for the Jews. It remained the intellectual privilege of the learned and the moralists. The rest, the common people, were abandoned to the mockery of a pagan creed that had grown stale with disbelief.

Small wonder that these Gentile peoples looked with anxious fascination to the Jews, though they sneered at their faith and derided their outlandish customs. Wherever stood a synagogue in Roman dominions, Gentiles came of a Sabbath—like mendicants begging for words of hope, for those words of prophecy or consolation that fell so amply from the Writ of the Jews.

Let the satirists with all their wit and malice burlesque the Jewish Sabbath, showing with infinite jest how the Hebrew twiddles away one day in seven; still, an alarming number of respected Romans were infected by this barbaric piece of ritual sloth. Many a Roman who ambled through the Jewish streets on the banks of the Tiber, seeing the Sabbath lamps lighted in the windows, pondered on this seventh day which, regardless of a man's wealth or want, belonged only to him and to his God. And though comedians and mimes in theaters and arenas caricatured their countrymen who adopted Jewish ways, the credo of the Jew nevertheless began to seep into the Roman soul, agitating it with a craving for faith. Many were the Roman officials who donated secret moneys for the building of a synagogue in Palestine or the Dispersion—then came themselves to seek God in the midst of this abominated people, as though the words of Zechariah had suddenly come true: "In those days it shall come to pass that ten men shall take hold of the skirt of him that is a Jew, saying, We will go with you, for we have heard that God is with you."

One would have thought the very earth was sending up the cry of mankind's yearning for salvation. It was as though Man, groping blindly, had found heaven's gate to knock against, and God in His mercy was sending His answer.

For there was a voice sounding from the wilderness.

CHAPTER VI

WHO brought the word of Jochanan ben Zachariah to Nazareth? No man and every man. His voice was wind-borne, echoing at once in Nazareth and K'far Nahum, in Sepphoris and in Jerusalem.

Yeshua heard it returning with his mother from the Sepphoris market. On his way he fell in with a man who bore a bullock's yoke upon his shoulders. And the man said:

"See if this be not the yoke you carved."

"It is," said Yeshua. "I made it with my hands."

"And it was from your father's hands I bought it," said the stranger. "Nor have I failed to bear it since that day, for it stands for the yoke of the kingdom of heaven. And now the time has come. The world awaits your yoke, by which you shall subject all mankind to its Father."

"What tells you that the time has come?" asked Yeshua.

"Have you not heard the voice of him that cries in the wilderness—'Prepare ye the way of the Lord'?"

"A voice in the wilderness?" Miriam said, gasping.

The stranger did not turn from Yeshua and answered sternly:

"Jochanan ben Zachariah has come forth out of the desert calling to baptism and repentance in readiness for the day of God."

"Whither does he call to receive baptism?"

"To Jordan—the place whence Elijah ascended to heaven in a tempest."

"And you, stranger, how came you to know?"

"I have but newly come from him and heard him say—'I indeed baptize you with water; but one mightier than I cometh, the latchet of whose shoes I am not worthy to unloose. He shall baptize you with the Holy Ghost and with fire!'" And the stranger added with sudden emphasis—"He was speaking of you!"

A few days later news of the Baptist reached Nazareth. It was the talk of the town that a wayfaring stranger with a yoke on his back had appeared in the market place, saying that he who had laid the yoke upon his shoulders would lay the yoke of the heavenly kingdom upon all men of the earth; and that whosoever wished to hear more should go forth to Bethany on Jordan and hearken to the voice that called to prepare the way of the Lord.

It was difficult at first to know what the stranger meant. He seemed like one possessed by demon spirits, one of many such wretches who roamed from town to town and spoke always of mysterious portents to which self-possessed men paid but little attention. But the stranger's meaning was not long in making itself clear, for in the synagogue next Sabbath the plain facts were finally reported:

A man had come out of the desert, dressed in a shirt of camel hair and with a leathern girdle on his loins; and he had posted himself on the banks of Jordan, at the supposed scene of Elijah's assumption, and had called to repentance and prayer.

To the Nazarene congregation these were more than bald facts, since the very notion of the desert had a mystic fascination for the Jews. It aroused ancient atavistic memories, dreams hauled from a bottomless past in which Moses led Israel to its first encounter with God. To the Jews' inner ear every voice from the desert was reboant with the clarion thunder of Mount Sinai. It echoed the voice of the Lord enunciating the Decalogue, the million voices of the Jews answering, "We shall do and obey." It was the exultant cry of early love, of Israel's nuptials with the Lord. A voice crying in the desert set up strange vibrations in every Jew's soul.

The desert was the refuge of all who sought detachment from society, who wished to mortify their flesh and purge their souls through prayer and abstinence. They lived in caves, covered their nakedness with the bark of palm trees, and washed themselves in random water or by rolling in fresh dew. For food they used the bodies of locusts dried in the sun and ground into kernels like grain to be sun-baked into flat cakes. Or they went out in the early morning hours to collect wild honey from rocks and cactus plants, or gather the slimy cocoons of caterpillars which came down with the dew and melted sweetly in the mouth like the manna of old.

These desert dwellers were of different kinds. Many belonged to orders and fellowships such as the Essenes and the Hassidim. Some were individual Pharisees who had embraced temporary hermitry to attain a fuller state of self-dedication. Some had followed an obscure saint into the wilderness to learn from him the mysteries of numerology and physic, or to perfect themselves in the secret arts of exorcism and communication with the angels. And, finally, a great many came here to suffer for repented sins, or in fulfillment of personal vows rendered in return for a miracle or act of grace.

But this new voice that sounded from the desert could not be the voice of an Essene or Pharisee. The Essenes were known to baptize only those who were admitted to their brotherhood after severe ordeals; they were a hand-picked company of men who had passed every test of physical endurance. The Pharisees, in their own way, were equally exclusive, admitting only the learned, those who sat "at the Torah's table." The voice of Jochanan ben Zachariah was calling all men whatsoever to their baptism—the scholarly and the unlettered, the men of honor and repute as well as the rejected, the righteous together with the most despised evil-doers in the nation—the publicans and the collectors of the royal tribute. Nor was it calling them to join a sacred brotherhood and separate themselves from the rest of Israel; it was calling them to repentance and baptism to be ready for one who would baptize with the Holy Ghost and with fire.

This was the novelty—that the gate was parted wide to give every man access. And it was this that made a deep impression on the people. A multitude of men and women poured toward Jordan, rich and poor, scholar and dunce, harlot and usurer, and even they who served the Herods and who surely had no claim to Israel's hope. They tramped every lane and highroad, converged from every town and hamlet in Judah and Galilee.

From Nazareth, too, a band of citizens set out for Jordan, of whom the first to go were Yeshua's brother Jacob and his neighbor Taddi.

Miriam and Yeshua had not for many years spoken of Jochanan, Elisheva's son. But both had waited amid hope and fear for a sign of his coming. Both knew obscurely that he was implicated in their fate and through these many years expected every day to hear that he had left the desert. For they remembered hearing long ago that the infant Jochanan had been taken in by the Essenes who were unwittingly raising him up to his mission. Miriam knew that God was watching over the child in the desert and when the moment came which God had appointed for the revealment of her son, Jochanan would come forth from his desert cave and let his voice resound in Israel as foretold by the Prophet.

Now that the event had come to pass according to the prophecy, both mother and son knew that the period of preparation and expectancy was over.

Yeshua was ready. He knew the price that he must pay for his election, and that the road God had prepared for him was paved with fiery thorns. It was often enough he had read the Prophets of salvation, and if he was indeed the Saviour he must be ready with the sacrifice that was his debt.

But was his mother ready?

His mother must go with him every part of the way and, whether or not she was to witness his ordeal, Yeshua knew that every wound on his own body would bleed again in his mother's soul. Would she have the fortitude to see her son a willing sacrifice? He remembered every glad tremor which his childish ways and laughter had called out in her face when he was little. How proudly had she watched him from the women's gallery the day he was presented in the synagogue. And today? How would she suffer his humiliation and the cry which the world must raise against him? *Ema, ema!* Tenfold would I take my trials if you could be spared. He did not say this aloud but, laying his hand on hers, asked haltingly:

"*Ema,* did you know my time is near at hand?"

"I know, *tinoki.*"

"Are you prepared, mother?"

"What matters it, *tinoki?* God will have His will."

"But, *ema,* God's will is my only crutch on this road. It should be your crutch also."

"Yeshua, I am only a weak woman."

"A mother's weakness is her strength. Your weakness, *ema,* will purge Israel like the blood of a sin offering."

When Miriam looked up at her son the tears stood in her eyes. "You are my comfort, Yeshua, my son," she said.

And as he let himself down at her side she clasped his head in her hands and laid it on her knees as she had done in his childhood.

Taddi and Jacob returned together from the baptism, both of them deeply stirred, but with divergent views. The old tanner, his black teeth showing through a rotting beard, was talking hotly of the marvelous wonders he had seen. The son of Zachariah, Taddi said, as he recounted his experience to Yeshua, was standing knee-deep in the waters of Jordan not far from Bethany, his

329

body covered with a shirt of camel's hair, and he was baptizing the multitudes that came each day from every quarter. And, said Taddi, glowing with enthusiasm, Jochanan was not baptizing in the name of any brotherhood or fellowship or party, but in the name of the kingdom of heaven which was soon to descend upon earth. In the name of that day of terror he was calling to repentance because, he said, the great judgment was about to begin. And like a Prophet, Jochanan was scourging the people with the rod of his mouth, calling them a generation of vipers who were seeking lightly to flee from the wrath to come. And he said further that baptism for the body was not enough, unless they baptized their hearts also in the waters of repentance. And he warned them not to make themselves easy because they had Abraham for their father. Pointing to the stones on the banks of the river, Jochanan said: "I say unto you that God is able of these stones to raise up children unto Abraham." These words of the Baptist, said Taddi, were driving a great fear into the hearts of the people so that they were falling at the prophet's feet, begging him to tell them what they should do. And Jochanan was answering: "He that has two coats, let him impart to him that has none." And many people heard him and performed according to his word, for the fear of God had fallen upon all that heard him speak.

Yeshua had listened silently to the tanner's report. But as Taddi stopped for breath he asked what the Baptist had meant in saying that God could raise up children to Abraham from stones.

"He meant," said Taddi, relishing the opportunity to elaborate a favorite point, "that the grace of the Patriarchs would be no help, but that only each man's merit would be considered in the day of judgment."

But these same words, which so inspired the old tanner, saddened and grieved Yeshua's own brother and destroyed his faith in the Baptist.

"What does this mean?" he asked—"'God is able of these stones to raise up children unto Abraham!' How should such words pass the lips of a Jew? Were not all of us who are Jews contained in Abraham's seed when God gave him progeny in Isaac? And as Isaac lay fettered for the sacrifice, do we not all lie fettered on God's altars because we have remained the sons

330

of Abraham, refusing to mingle with the Gentiles and go whoring after their gods? Who bears God's Torah through a world of idolatry, bloodshed, and rape, through filth and prostitution, upholding and cherishing the word of the Lord to purge and sanctify ourselves for our Father in heaven? And if to us was given the pledge of redemption—was it for a better reason than that we were the sons of Abraham? And have we not justified our descent from Abraham, who first recognized his Maker, by our continued faith in God and as well by our works? I say, only he who bears the yoke of the kingdom can enter the kingdom."

"Were there publicans and soldiers at the baptistry?" Yeshua asked, "and did Jochanan admit them also to the covenant?"

"Yes, indeed," Taddi replied; "many publicans from the surrounding towns came for the baptism, and with them their military escorts, soldiers of Herod. I know not whether they were Jew or Greek; they stood away at a distance and listened to Jochanan's thunder.

"And when Jochanan came to speak of the day of God's wrath, of the approaching day of judgment, the publicans were seized by a great fear and they fell shivering and wailing to the ground and stretched out their hands to the prophet and cried:—'We know that we are evil-doers who deserve God's punishment. But tell us, rabbi, is there yet room for us in the kingdom of heaven?' And when Jochanan saw their tears and broken hearts, he said to them: 'There is no man beyond God's mercy.' And they asked, 'What then shall we do?' And Jochanan said, 'Exact no more than that which is appointed you.'

"Now, when the soldiers saw the Baptist speaking with the publicans, they took heart and came near with bowed heads and asked also what they should do. And Jochanan said to them, 'Do violence to no man, and be content with your wages.' And he baptized them all into the covenant."

Jacob broke in, excitedly. "How could it be that publicans and strangers to the Law should be admitted by baptism into the kingdom of God?"

Yeshua answered him. "What is the kingdom of God? Is it the palace of the rich guarded by his strong men? The kingdom of God cometh not from observation. Neither shall they say, Lo

331

here! or, Lo there! for, behold, the kingdom of God is within you. For all the Prophets and the Law prophesied until Jochanan. And if you will receive it, this is Elijah, 'the voice of him that crieth in the wilderness. Prepare ye the way of the Lord; make straight a highway for our God. Every valley shall be exalted, and every mountain and hill shall be made low; and the rough places plain. And the glory of the Lord shall be revealed, and all flesh shall see it together!'"

At the mention of Elijah, Taddi and Jacob started from their seats and remained staring at the speaker with terrified eyes. In Yeshua's voice they were suddenly struck by an unfamiliar ring, as though they had been hailed by an archangel speaking with the voice of power.

CHAPTER VII

THE sign had come at last and every strolling mendicant confirmed its truth; Jochanan, son of the priest Zachariah, had emerged from the desert.

Yet nothing happened. Often, by day or night, Miriam lay on the open roof of her house, praying for a short reprieve. She was not ready to face the tribulations that awaited her son. If it must be bought with the life of her child, she would like to delay the promised redemption, if only for another day, though at the cost of her damnation.

She thought she felt the world grown restless and impatient. Trees and animals and stars seemed to be waiting for the great act of grace, hounding her for the release of her son. In the early mornings, when she sortied from the house to begin her labors, she felt beset by every tree and flower begging her in mute supplication to restore them to the order of Genesis from which they had been banished by the sin of Adam. And on the roof at night she read reproach in the wan light of the stars that seemed to beg of her the return of their primordial brightness. The animals looked at her with importunate pleading and once, Adamia, her Gentile neighbor, surprised her as she bent over the greens in her garden and said in a voice of entreaty:

"Mother, tell me, shall we be permitted to gather the crumbs that fall from the table of your children?"

"What do you mean, Adamia?"

"Jochanan's call to baptism has reached us also," said Adamia. "When will your son begin his kingdom?"

"Who told you of this, Adamia? What has my son to do with Jochanan's call?"

"I have known it since he was an infant in arms. And we too wait for him with all Israel."

Yeshua returned that evening from his work in the shop to find his mother seated in a corner, and the tears were running unchecked over her face.

"*Ema*, why do you weep?" Yeshua asked.

Miriam shook her head and said with difficulty:

"All the world is heavy with sorrow. When will you reveal yourself, *tinoki?*"

And Yeshua said gravely:

"I wait for you, *ema*. Are you willing?"

Miriam did not answer.

"Your tears, *ema*, storm against the gates of mercy, but your love for your child keeps them closed against the world."

Sleep would not come to Miriam that night. She rose from her pallet and went out into the field. The spring night lay warm over the house in which her son was sleeping. Miriam looked into the stars and whispered again and again:

"Lord of the world, render me worthy to be his mother."

But as if to prove her, God had sharpened in her the passions of her earthly motherhood. Miriam knew that she must subdue these passions, that God's will must become her own. Did God then want her earthbound nature to soar to the same heights of dedication as her God-begotten son? Must she, without God's help, find means to confine her mother's love and, by her own volition, like Abraham, sacrifice the child on His altar? But Yeshua had said that there could be no redemption until she also was prepared. Long ago he had told her that even the elect must

333

struggle against the powers of evil. Was the love she bore her child the temptation to evil which God had set on her path?

No, heaven forbid! she cried in her heart. Surely her motherhood, her love for the child, flowed also from God. It was her sacred portion in the child's sanctity, and her divine vocation. It was this love which fortified her being. The simple love she bore her child, this feeble passion of a human mother was her strength, as Yeshua had said. And now this love was exacted from her for the world's redemption, as though it were an inalienable element of the redemption, and her part in God's design.

Then Miriam suddenly understood what was required of her, and she flung herself upon the earth and cried:

"My God, my God, I have no more than what Thou gavest every mother—the love for my child. Take then this love as my offering. I bring it with a willing heart. It is the holiest, the most precious of all Thou gavest me; receive it as a fitting sacrifice."

A mist of dawning gray came over the horizon and spread stealthily across the dark face of the sky. Bright shafts of a still-hidden sun suddenly shot through the darkness, and in the paling sky the stars grew paler. The first rays of sunlight fell on Miriam's tear-stained face. Her eyes were closed. A few tufts of hair, strayed from her kerchief, trembled against her temples with a sparkle of dew. When she opened her eyes, the sky was a white sheet of light, and her garden and sheepfold were draped in a foggy vapor rising from the ground. Miriam smiled.

Indoors she found her son still sleeping on his bench in the main room. She approached him with soft steps and waited. Yeshua was sleeping deeply. His lids lay smooth over his eyes and he breathed with the regular pulse of a child. In his sleep, Miriam thought, his bearded face looked graver than waking, but even now the shadow of a smile on his lips softened his features.

It made her think of him as a child, and it was over the child she remembered that she now bent her face to smile at his closed eyes. Yeshua must have felt the warmth of his mother's glance, for his own smile deepened before he was yet awake. Then he opened his eyes—

"Emi!"

"Yes, *tinoki?*"

He hesitated, and said, watching his mother:

"It is good to pray with such as cannot speak but have only their works to speak for them."

"What do you mean, Yeshua?"

"I mean the trees and the grasses among which you prayed. Their growing is their song of praise. Like them we must all, every one, serve God with that for which we were made."

Miriam said no more; she went into her chamber and took down Yeshua's travel sack that hung there from a wooden nog. In it she placed his *tallith* and *tefillin* and a shirt and provisions for the road. Then she tied the bundle to his staff and, returning into the main room, placed it against his bench.

"You are right, Yeshua. Among the shrubs and trees God sent me the grace to know His will."

That day Yeshua left Nazareth. He took the Jericho road that ran with the Jordan at whose shore Jochanan was giving baptism.

Taddi no sooner heard that Yeshua had set out for Bethany than he determined that he must be present to witness his baptism and revelation. He hastened after his rabbi.

Several days later he returned, feverish with the news that Jochanan the Baptist had recognized in Yeshua bar Joseph the man for whom he, Jochanan, had been waiting.

That same day, following the reading of the Torah in the synagogue, he reported what he had seen and heard to the congregation, among them the sons of Pinhas, the sworn foes of Hanan's house, headed by Matthew ben Hanah and Sakkai bar Zadok, Yeshua's one-time schoolmates. The erudite Sakkai had become the leader of the local Pharisees, having studied deeply in a Jerusalem academy. On his return he had become the son-in-law of the fabulous Sheshet bar Caspi, the lord of the great vineyard south of the town. Matthew occupied a lucrative post in the employ of the rich Reb Tudrus; his task was to collect duties and toll at the local market, for which Reb Tudrus held a government concession.

Also among Taddi's listeners were the aged priest Hanina ben Safra, who had had more than one brush with Joseph, and cousin

335

Cleophas with his four nephews, Jacob, Simon, Joses, and the brilliant young Pharisee, Jude.

In the midst of them stood the old tanner, his dress hanging about him in frayed tatters, his bare skin showing under the rents. Since following Yeshua he had lost much of his burliness; he looked leaner now and his skin was charred a deeper brown. But he had gained in youthful ardor, and as he spoke his wreath of gray hair quivered on his bald head, and his eyes flashed like black coals. He was speaking without halting for breath, garbling the words and substituting wild gesticulation where they failed him. Nevertheless, he did convey the burden of his argument, which was no less than that Yeshua bar Joseph, the widow Miriam's son, who was well-known to all present, was none other than he for whom they all were waiting. He did not pronounce the name, but his upturned eyeballs and raised hands made his point perfectly clear. Nor was this his own view only, for it had been confirmed by Jochanan the Baptist himself at the very moment when Yeshua came to him to receive baptism. Which could be attested by anyone of the multitude who had witnessed the scene.

"Do you see these eyes?" cried Taddi, pointing at himself. "These eyes have seen how our Yeshua was baptized, how he stood up to his chest in the water with his head lowered for prayer. And suddenly a dove came winging down from heaven and remained suspended over his head, and Jochanan said it was the Holy Ghost in the bodily shape of a dove that had descended upon Yeshua. And do you see these ears? These ears heard a voice from heaven which said—'Thou art my beloved son in whom I am well pleased.'"

"You really heard this voice with your own ears?" asked Sakkai bar Zadok, plucking at his small curled beard.

"No—no, I did not hear it myself. But the Baptist heard it and he told it in the face of all the people. For when Yeshua was in the act of being baptized, we all saw this white dove—a very large dove, the size of an eagle—shooting out from heaven like an arrow speeding from the bowstring, and then Jochanan threw up his arms and roared out in a voice of thunder: 'I hear a voice calling from heaven—Thou art my beloved son in whom I am well pleased. As it is written—The Lord hath said unto me, Thou art my son; this day have I begotten thee.' And," added the tanner fiercely, "I believe every word that issues from the holy mouth of the Prophet Jochanan!"

For a brief moment everyone kept silent; then Jude spoke up: "We have reason to believe," he said, "that these words you cited refer to the King-Messiah."

And Sakkai bar Zadok said with slow deliberation:

"King David's words certainly do refer to the King-Messiah, and he who applies them sacrilegiously to a mortal man in our midst, a joiner's son, Yeshua bar Joseph, should have his mouth stopped with adders and vipers."

His words were followed at once by a general uproar.

"Taddi is after his own profit," shouted Matthew ben Hanah. "Own up, tanner! What sinecure did the joiner's son promise you in his heavenly kingdom for spreading his lies?"

"The office of a publican, of course," Cleophas shouted in Matthew's teeth, ready as always to stand for the family honor, though he did not think too highly of Miriam's eldest son and gave no serious consideration to the report of the tanner whom he dismissed as irresponsible.

"*Raika*—villain," someone said.

"Who calls our uncle *raika?*" came the angry voices of Yeshua's brothers, and Simeon and Joses stepped forward together with clenched fists. The situation promised a bad quarrel, but Sakkai and Jude, the two scholars in the company, managed to restrain each his own kinsmen. And some neutral fainthearts said:

"We all know that old Taddi is a fantast who sees things that never were. Shall we quarrel over a man's dreams? If there is any truth in his story we shall all know it soon enough."

And yet, despite their efforts to dismiss Taddi's report as an extravagant invention, the tanner's words were not without effect on the minds of the Nazarenes. It could not be denied that one of their town had become the subject of such rumors that all Israel looked up to him—and even though he was but a joiner and a joiner's son, the fact alone was certainly impressive. Henceforth the attitude of Yeshua's townsmen was colored with a certain awe, even a touch of hidden pride among both friends and enemies. People spoke softly to each other, as though every word were a confidence. Poor folk, who would have grasped at any straw, were ready to believe that there was something in the tanner's tale. The learned for their part felt increasingly disquieted by the persisting rumors from the Jordan, rumors that sent a quiver to the heart of every Jew. All were united in waiting anxiously for Yeshua's return. Sceptics and enthusiasts together grew more impatient with each passing day, and meanwhile, to indulge their hunger for definite news, cultivated the goodwill of Yeshua's near kinsmen. Not only was Yeshua's mother exalted in every man's eyes, but in the absence of Yeshua himself, even his brothers rose to a pale glory in the general estimation. But Yeshua seemed to have vanished without trace; days and weeks went by as all Nazareth, including even his own mother, continued in strained expectation.

Needless to say, the gossip of the town had tongue for little else. Every man, from scholar to laborer, wondered why Yeshua should have suddenly disappeared after his baptism by Jochanan, and every man advanced his own conjectures.

The old tanner buttonholed worshippers in the synagogue to tell them that Yeshua had assuredly been taken up to heaven for forty days, there to receive the new Torah as Moses had received the old on Mount Sinai. His importunities were increasingly resented and Taddi rarely came away without hard words or even a drubbing. He was warned that he could be arraigned for blasphemy, but the old mule refused to be intimidated. There was nothing at which Taddi would stop in his zeal to believe.

Yeshua's mother, despite her concern, was sustained by her belief that God was with her son, but others of her family came each day to ask for tidings. No one could explain to his own satisfaction why Yeshua had disappeared, and his relatives vacillated between hope and terror, expectancy and disappointment.

Cleophas, as head of the family, thought it his duty to calm their anxiety. He explained that Yeshua had most probably attached himself to some famous rabbin—was sitting in the dust at his feet to study the Law; than which no career could be more laudable since Yeshua would return in time to be hailed as a sage in his own right, a great rabbi in Israel surrounded by disciples. Jude, though he could not be sure, thought this a very likely

338

theory. And so the suggestion of the uncle was accepted as an explanation for all questioners.

Alone among the brothers, Jacob continued to be troubled. He prayed much these days and fasted himself without mercy, for his spirit was torn between faith and doubt. Could it be that his elder brother, his own mother's son, whom he had known from infancy, was he for whom Israel had been waiting through the generations? Yet why was there no sign, no miracle, no opening of the gates of heaven? Why were the evil-doers of this world not swallowed by the earth? It made Jacob tremble to pursue these thoughts, and yet, with him, they were thoughts only, and others had already spoken them out loud. What if they were true? Perhaps, in very deed, the time had come and Yeshua was even now in heaven, seated among the Patriarchs, and soon, perhaps this very day, he would reveal himself, surrounded by the Patriarchs and Prophets, borne by the holy Seraphim over the clouds of heaven. God in heaven, could it be true? And Jacob, tortured by his meditations, segregated himself from all, and sat with closed eyes in a corner of the synagogue, mumbling the same words over and over:

"Lord of the world, open Thou our eyes, and illumine our hearts. My soul cleaveth unto the dust: quicken Thou me according to Thy word. Make me to understand the way of Thy precepts. I have chosen the way of Thy truth. O Lord, put me not to shame. I will run the way of Thy commandments, when Thou shalt enlarge my heart. Let Thy mercies come also unto me, O Lord, even Thy salvation, according to Thy word. So shall I have wherewith to answer him that reproacheth me, for I trust in Thy word."

Toward dusk at the end of the fortieth day, as Miriam sat in the threshold of her house waiting for her son's return, she saw him coming from a distance. Miriam rose and ran to meet him and observed at once that he was changed. His face looked strangely worn and haggard and his body taller than Miriam remembered it. Also, his beard and hair had grown wild, which had been always well-kept in the past. But Miriam was struck most by the unfamiliar mood of his face. The youthful serenity and friendliness which had formerly lightened his features had settled into an expression of strength and determination, and his eyes, which seemed to Miriam larger than ever, looked with an ineffable melancholy as though they had gazed too long on pain. Yeshua greeted her with a silent restraint that was new in his manner, and went without a word into the house.

Miriam followed him in silence, though her heart was beating joyfully over his return. She hastened to fill a vessel with fresh well water, then washed his feet, which Yeshua, absently, suffered her to do. And while he washed his hands and face and changed his garments, Miriam lit her earthen lamps and set the table for his homecoming.

They remained undisturbed. No one had seen Yeshua come, for he had reached his mother's house by back ways to avoid the stare and gabble of inquisitive watchers. Clearly, he wished this night to be alone with his mother.

Miriam refrained from asking questions. She proceeded to serve Yeshua in silence, merely watching his movements and drawing solace from his presence. When he had done eating, Yeshua himself began to speak without prompting, and he opened in this wise:

"Whatever the Lord gives, He gives freely; but he who would receive the gift must merit it. Nothing is ever bought from God, save at the price of worthiness. And God puts even His elect to proof to test their desert. And why is it God proves His elect? Because He wishes them to become partners with Him in the continuous act of Creation.

"No creature of God can evade the test, not even the son of man. Thus, when I turned to depart from Jochanan, being filled with the Holy Ghost, I was led by the Spirit into the wilderness. Forty days and forty nights I abode there, neither eating nor drinking. Then the frailty of my flesh cried out to me and I hungered for food. But suddenly a man stood before me. 'If you are the Son of God,' he said, 'command this stone to become bread.' And he drew aside a curtain so that I saw the world from end to end and it was peopled with the generations of man—even from Cain and Abel to the last who shall be. And I saw how man wars upon man even as beasts war on each other; how the strong violate the weak and rob them of their harvest, the toil of their hands. I saw how some work by sword and iron and others by cunning and craft, for it is not to be conceived what perfidy men will employ to cozen one another for a piece of bread. And they spare neither old nor young, fathers selling their children and children their fathers, and all for a morsel of food to line their bellies with. I saw such as sell themselves into bondage, who mutilate their bodies and turn themselves into freaks and buffoons and disfigure the image of their Maker. Mother, it is not to be recounted what man will do to get his daily bread.

"Not only men did he show me, but also beasts in the forests who leap upon their feebler fellow creatures and lock their fangs over the gushing throats of their prey. And in the waters he showed me fishes, the big eating the little. 'Behold,' he said to me, 'man and beast partake of one nature; fill but their stomachs and they shall be your grateful slaves. Throw them their paltry piece of bread and they will hail you for their lord and saviour. Only by bread will you gain their allegiance. Command then these desert stones to be made bread, for it is food alone which underprops the world.'

"But I answered him: It is written that man shall not live by bread alone.

"He led me onward then and drew aside another veil and in a trice I saw all the kingdoms of the world and the power by which they rule over mankind, their armed hosts and the engines of destruction which they employ for the shedding of blood—those that gash and those that stab and those that spout fire like the fiends of Hell. And the man, Satan, said to me: 'All this power will I give you, the government of man and the glory thereof, for mine is the sway over iron and fire. If you worship me, all shall be yours.' But I answered him and said: It is written, Thou shalt worship the Lord thy God, and Him only shalt thou serve.

"Then next he took me up, and in the twinkling of an eye set me on a pinnacle of the Temple in Jerusalem, and with his finger pointed to the charred vale of Gehenna which lies black below the Temple, and said: 'See, if you have eyes!'

"And I saw all the idol-worship and abomination conducted from time immemorial in this dump of abhorrence. A vast concourse of men and women, old and young, came up in procession, with boughs in their hands, misled by their priests. I saw them fall before the idol Baal, while mothers cast their crying infants into the flames of Moloch. And the people raised great shout and jubilation to drown the wail of the children as they perished in fire. Others I saw kindling incense for Astarte and performing obscene rites before her unclean shrine and many deeds of foulness and abomination which shame the eye to behold. In this vale of Gehenna I saw the idols and fetiches of all nations and lands, for the devil has his dominion in this valley wherein Israel profaned itself with idolatrous usage. From the time of Jeremiah, they lie here, with bared fangs, at the very threshold of the Temple, to tempt Israel from the way of salvation. Here Satan deploys his promiscuous host; and I saw idols, infinite and multiform, like beasts misshapen, and like cancerous vermin—Beelzebub, the god of flies, the mice of the Philistines, the cats and crocodiles of Egypt, and such idols which are yet to be, to whom humanity will bow in later ages, sending men to kill each other in their name. And Asmodeus, Samael, and Lilith and a brood of black-winged demons flew about the host, and as I looked upon them Satan turned to me and said: 'Serve me and I shall appoint you king over all idols by whose power you shall rule over men.' But I answered him: It is written, Thou shalt have no other gods before Me.

"Then Satan said: 'If you are the Son of God, cast yourself down from hence and defy them to battle. You have nought to fear, for it is written, He shall give His angels charge over thee, to keep thee; and in their hands they shall bear thee up, lest at any time thou dash thy foot against a stone.'

"And I answered: It is written, Thou shalt not tempt the Lord, thy God. And also: Not by might nor by power but by the spirit of God. God's spirit shall battle with them and blast them from the face of the earth.

"And when the devil had ended all the temptation, he departed from me, and angels came and ministered to me."

And with these words Yeshua closed the account of his ordeal in the wilderness.

Miriam remained still for a while, then said softly:

342

"It is not for me to know what God in Heaven has appointed for you; but tell me this, Yeshua, why was my heart so sorely troubled in the hour of your trial? Did I not know that the Lord's angels had charge over you? Surely the littleness of my faith had troubled my spirit."

"Not the littleness of your faith, but the greatness of your love for your child and your concern for him. I tell you, woman, the guidance of the father and the mother's love—they alone are the strength of the son. And with this strength will I go my way."

"So soon, Yeshua? You returned only today!"

"At dawn tomorrow I must leave you. I came only for your blessing, *ema.*"

"Then let me go with you, *tinoki!* I can still serve you as I did in the past, only let me go your way with you!"

"You shall be always with me, *ema;* nevertheless, this road I take must be traveled alone. It was prepared for the son only. But for you too our Father has prepared a cup which none has drunk before."

Miriam shook her head:

"I do not understand you, Yeshua."

"I say that heavy trials are prepared for you. From this day forward the sorrow of your heart shall be your bread, and your tears shall be your drink. You shall suffer contumely and humiliation on your child's account. People will shake their heads over you for the fruit of your womb. Cruel rumors will be brought to you to pierce your heart like arrows and to shed your blood in shame, and the talebearers will think that they pleasure the Lord. Pray to God, woman, that you be strong enough when the time comes to hold the grief in your heart as you held the child in your womb, for from this day forward your child and your grief shall be one."

Miriam let her head fall on her chest and gave him no answer. Then, after a silence, she said:

"Do you think I shall be able to endure it? My strength is little."

"And I tell you, woman, your fortitude shall cause men to kneel on earth and make the angels tremble in heaven. Your power shall be sung in heaven and on earth until the end of time."

343

"What then will you have me do, my son?" Miriam asked.

"Only the will of God, mother. Wait here for your appointed hour—and pray, for your prayer is my shield."

"How long must I wait?"

"For so long as you receive no sign. But a sign shall be given you at last, and on that day the ways of the mother and the son shall meet once more, never to be parted again."

Morning came, and Miriam's house awoke into a nascent light. Miriam walked with her son as far as the K'far Nahum road and there Yeshua lowered his head to receive the blessing of his mother's hands.

"The God of Abraham, Isaac, and Jacob be with you as He was with our Fathers," Miriam said.

CHAPTER VIII

AND it came to pass, after Yeshua departed from his mother, the marriage of her kinswoman in Cana approached. Peniel and his wife Shifra, who lived in that small Galilean town, were the poorest kinsmen of Hanan's clan. Miriam had long taken it upon herself to look after their needs, just as her mother had done, stretching the small resources of her household. And Peniel had a daughter who had been Miriam's special concern, for the girl, Hannah by name, was of marriageable age and still unwed. In such situations where spinsterhood was seriously threatening, it was usual for pious women to equip and endow a penniless girl in order to enhance her marriage prospects.

When Miriam learned that poor Hannah had at last found a bridegroom in a local artisan, she determined to do her utmost in helping to prepare a memorable wedding.

Week after week she led her little donkey to Cana, burdened with provisions for the nuptial larder. The town lay beyond Sepphoris, a full day's journey from Nazareth and no easy trudge for the ass, which—now that the wedding day had come—bore a particularly heavy load: two bags of flour to make pasties for the children and several skins of wine and oil as well as a small cruse of incense oil for the anointing of the bride; and from the wicker baskets that hung at the donkey's sides protruded the heads of two newborn lambs—Miriam's contribution to the household that was being founded.

A wedding was a costly affair in Israel. Families had been known to ruin themselves in the effort to do justice to this great occasion which called for so much pomp and ceremony. For a wedding was an important religious event, and this not only for the groom and bride who were being joined into one soul, but for all those who participated in the rite. The groom, called "the perfect one," was on this day treated like a king—the bride, "the wreath-bearer," like a queen. The wedding guests were called "the children of the bridechamber, or canopy." The groomsmen, of whom there were as many as the groom had friends, were known as "the companions"; and the entire ceremony symbolized for the participants the marriage of God with Israel—God, the celestial bridegroom, espousing for all time the sacred congregation of the Jews.

A man participating at a wedding was therefore held to be engaged in noble work. And in a small community like Cana it was no surprise to see the entire town involved in the festivities. Farmers forsook their labor in the fields; artisans rested their tools to rejoice with the young couple, to eat and drink and sing what songs they knew, praising the bride's beauty and diverting her with dance and tomfoolery, sometimes for days on end. Neither was any man too rich or too poor to join in the merriment.

The celebration of the marriage in Cana had begun, according to the Jewish custom, on the preceding Sabbath, when the bridegroom was called to the reading of the Torah in the synagogue, after which he had been honorably escorted home by the entire congregation headed by the town's seven elders.

On the day of the wedding the older women who were closest in blood to the bride's family came early to her father's house. They set themselves to heating the rainwater that was stored in a large vat by the door of the house. Then they bathed the bride,

345

anointed her body, and clothed her in the bridal finery—twenty-four stipulated articles of dress and ornament.

For Miriam every detail of the ceremony was of the utmost importance. She wanted this to be a perfect wedding—as though it were her own—for she knew that her son had promised to attend. This knowledge in her eyes lent a profound significance to the event, a feeling she could not have justified had she been pressed for an explanation. She had chosen therefore to come alone, without taking any of her younger sons who might have questioned the necessity of her attendance.

Soon after the bride was ready came the seven elders of the town. They were followed by a crowd of citizens, called to the feast by a specially appointed crier. The bride was seated in a sedan chair, and the young men who were the groom's "companions" bore it on their shoulders to the banqueting house next to the synagogue where the marriage canopy was waiting. And all the crowd followed after in procession.

Heading the parade was a girl with an alabaster pitcher that was filled with fragrant oil. After her came a group of ushers with laurel boughs in their hands to clear a passage for the bride as one would for a queen, and they chanted incessantly: "Make way, make way for the bride!" Upon which, every man must step aside, be he prince or pauper. Next came the musicians with pipes, tabrets, and cymbals, and a handful of respected citizens, tripping along with a dancing step to divert the bride.

Seven maidens with lighted lamps in their hands preceded the litter of the bride, which was surrounded by her kinsfolk and the dignitaries of the town. And they, like a royal retinue, sang loudly, as they walked, the praise of the bride:

> "No paint and no powder,
> No unction, no oil,
> A bride without artifice,
> Fair as a doe."

Lastly, following the sedan, came the multitude—men, women, and, above all, children, who were thrown sweetmeats all the way to the synagogue; and, bringing up the rear, a man carried a cock and hen for luck and fertility.

The conjugal couch, meanwhile, stood ready in the bride-groom's house, freshly made from the wood of a young cedar that had been planted on the day of his birth.

Thus through the narrow winding streets of Cana marched Hannah's wedding train. Miriam too walked in the procession near the bride's litter. Her widow's weeds had given place to a bright blue shawl set with flakes of gold. She was marching like the others to the beat of the tabor and, clapping her hands, joined in the general chant:

> "No paint and no powder,
> No unction, no oil,
> A bride without artifice,
> Fair as a doe."

And so at last the bride was brought into "the house of the canopy," where, on completion of the ritual, all "the children of the canopy" would be urged to the nuptial feast and whence, late in the night, the bride would be borne with the same pomp, to the home of her husband.

Waiting near the canopy inside the hall was the governor of the wedding feast. He was one of the readers of the synagogue, a large man with a smooth wide beard and a heraldic baritone which had gained him the post of master of ceremonies at all public functions. He was robed in white and the badge of his office was prominent on his chest.

The governor conducted Hannah to her prepared throne under the laurel-decked canopy. Then the women of her family loosened her hair and let it fall over her shoulders in sign of her maiden-hood.

At this point the governor took charge of all further ceremonies, his first act being to dispatch the groomsmen to fetch the hero of the hour from his house and bring him to the marriage canopy.

The groom's parade was less ostentatious than the bride's, though he too walked in a suite. And while he was yet on his way, the seven maidens who were the bride's friends sallied out into the streets, holding high their lighted lamps; they were going forth "in quest of the groom,"—as it is written in the canticles of Solomon: "I will rise now and go about the city in the streets, and in

347

the broad ways I will seek him whom my soul loveth." For the groom was not merely the bride's choice; he was the symbol of the lover, the elect, the bridegroom of all maiden lovers. In accord with ancient tradition he was "found" by the maidens not far from the house of his parents which he had but shortly left with his friends and groomsmen. The girls then joined his cortege and lighted its way to "the house of the canopy," where the great banquet would soon be served to all comers.

As soon as the seven white-robed maidens returned to the hall with the bewildered laurel-wreathed groom in their train, Miriam caught sight of her son among the groomsmen. Like the others he was dressed in white and, like them, he held a laurel branch in his hand. It seemed to Miriam that he was not alone; a small group of men stood with him and somehow detached from the rest.

Two of them Miriam recognized, though she had not seen them recently. They were the sons of Zebedee from Bethsaida. How powerful Jochanan had grown since she had seen him last! He stood like a block of granite, with enormous squared shoulders, his massive head capped with a bushy mass of ill-kempt, coal-black hair. Near him was her fondling Jacob, tall and almost delicate in build, with black hair falling in small ringlets from his crown. He, too, had grown into a man, but the startled, vivid look of his eyes betrayed a lingering adolescence.

One other man in Yeshua's company attracted Miriam's special notice. He was a thick-set, heavily compounded man in middle years, and Miriam noted that he never took his eyes off her son. He seemed to have no eyes at all for the bridal couple. His eyes were smiling as he looked at Yeshua, and Miriam knew at once that it meant perfect bliss for this man to be near her son. A shudder of happiness ran through her—but almost immediately she started to the sudden realization that her child had no more need of her.

There was one other, younger, man in Yeshua's circle. Miriam concluded that he must be Nathanael, a kinsman of the groom's and a native of Cana, for he was hailed with joyful familiarity by all present. Yeshua had told her before his departure that he had been asked to the wedding; no doubt, Nathanael had invited him.

Had Nathanael brought them all together? Miriam observed that Nathanael too kept looking at her son, almost as a servant looks at an adored master, trying to anticipate his every command.

Her reflections were interrupted by a shriek, like the cry of a dumb animal. She saw Ben Adam, the once neglected boy of Nazareth, now a tall, large-boned man, fling himself on his knees before Yeshua, as he approached through the hall, followed by his men.

Kissing the hem of Yeshua's robe, the former outcast cried, over and over, "My saviour, my saviour, my saviour!"

The men in Yeshua's company attempted to free him from the embarrassment of this display, but Yeshua motioned them away. With his hands resting on Ben Adam's head, he uttered the words:

"Blessed are the poor in spirit, for theirs is the kingdom of heaven."

He went forward to Miriam, bowed before her and said:

"Peace be with you, *emi*."

"And with you, my child," said she, and kissed his cheek.

"Is this the mother of our Lord?" asked the stocky stranger, and immediately let himself down on his knees, saying:

"Blessed is the womb that bore the hope of Israel."

"*Emi, emi!*" called out the slender Jacob kneeling at her feet. Miriam laid her hand caressingly on his soft curls and said:

"You are my son also, *tinoki*."

And his brother Jochanan, fixing her with his intense dark eyes, said with quiet rhetoric:

"You are the mother of the beginning. Not the beginning, but the source thereof."

"Is there a rabbi with his disciples among us, come unbeknown to brighten our wedding?" the guests began to ask among themselves.

"A rabbin? More than a rabbin!" shouted the impetuous Nathanael, pointing to Yeshua.

"What do you mean?—more than a rabbin!"

"I mean what I say," called back Nathanael, who enjoyed a vast respect among his townsmen, fully conscious of the wonder his words were provoking.

But in mid-sentence Nathanael caught the eye of Yeshua; he

349

paled suddenly, stammered some incomprehensible excuse, and subsided into silence. But his townsmen would not let him be:

"Who is this man who came here with his pupils?"

"Who is he? Do you not know him? Yeshua of Nazareth, the son of Miriam who is a kinswoman to Peniel. They came here to attend their cousin's marriage."

"And who are the men with him?"

"You said it yourself—his pupils."

"Why, then Yeshua is a rabbi and we must show him honor," said Peniel excitedly. "Go some of you and tell the governor to cede him the place of honor at the right hand of the groom. A rabbi with his disciples has come to illumine our feast; let us show him that we in Cana know how to honor the Law!"

"And who is the woman to whom they bow and bend the knee?"

"Why, she is the rabbi's mother, and to the disciples of a rabbi his mother is as sacred as their own."

"In that case we must tell the governor that the rabbi's mother has come to the feast and that she must be allowed the place of honor at the right hand of the bride."

It was not often that a rabbi strayed into Cana, for it was a little town in the high north, far removed from the scholastic centers, and its people were for the most part ignorant herdsmen and peasants. The unexpected arrival of a rabbi in their midst was a signal event, and it was natural therefore that Yeshua and his disciples should be the cynosure of all attention so that for a while the bride and groom were almost forgotten.

The wedding ceremony proceeded smoothly nonetheless, and soon the bridal couple were married in accordance with the Law of Moses. The marriage contract was then read aloud—it committed the husband to the payment of two-hundred dinars in the event of a divorce—and then the governor of the feast seated the guests at the tables, each man according to his station.

The fare, to say truth, was not over-rich. The groom had supplied everything in his power—several flagons of wine, a large pile of vegetables and eggs and even a few fowls. And pastries and honey rolls for the children had been provided by the parents of the bride. The rest was potluck—whatever the guests might choose to bring, preferably wine, of which there could never be too much at a wedding.

For this was one occasion when mirth was a gracious obligation. To gladden the guests and the newlyweds, it was right and proper to drink deep, even at the risk of drunkenness. And from this rule even the learned and the men of dignity were not exempt. Thus the drinking began early, for the guests had no sooner consumed the first course of peppered greens and eggs, but they rapped loudly for the wine. Before long the house sparkled with gaiety. Rings of dancers formed about the bride, with the soberest men joining hands and stamping their heels. The pipers puffed themselves blue and breathless and the drummers hammered out the beat so that the walls rang again and the low roof shook to the rhythm. The men, barefoot or sandaled, with black scintillating beards, went turning and spinning about the hall, and the women, with bangled kerchiefs and bright sparkling tinsel crowding their dress, joined in singing lusty snatches from the Song of Songs, all to praise and to delight the bride.

No Torah was said during the banquet, except that some of the nimbler wits at the groom's table cited a few rabbinic epigrams about the state of connubiality. And one man reported on the difference between the schools of Hillel and Shammai regarding the limits to which a man might go in panegyrics on the bride. It was the view of the stern Shammai, said he, that a man should speak nothing but the truth—so it be complimentary—or hold his tongue. But the good Hillel, his perennial opponent, was of opinion that no eulogy was too extravagant if it served to make the bride beloved of her husband, and he actually enjoined his followers to stretch the truth where necessary, rather than allow themselves to be outdone in lavish praise. To this another guest added that, in the opinion of the rabbis, one should look at the bride's eyes and, if these were beautiful, seek no further evidence, since comely eyes could compensate for every blemish.

But if they did not talk too learnedly about the Torah, the artisans and farmers of Cana surely knew how to eat. The piles of cakes and fruit before them melted away like butter in the sun. The eggs vanished, and the olives, and the legs and breasts of fowl, as if a whirlwind had swept them off the tables.

And they knew how to drink, these sturdy Galileans. The few skins of precious date-wine which Miriam had brought barely slicked their tongues. Then the home-made wine was drained in long draughts and soon the servants were reduced to pouring home-brewed beer from the earthen pitchers which had been held back as the last reserve.

And still the hungry guests were falling to, while the sweat broke from their foreheads and trickled down their whiskers and beards. The men's faces were flushed red and hot with the work of eating, and their eyes were glossy with intoxication.

And they knew how to make merry. Their gaiety burst from their faces and rollicking bodies. One man, an old Jew with a beard like virgin forest, jumped upon a chair, clapped his hands and loudly cried:

"Wine maketh glad the heart of man! Bring in more pipers and drums! We must have music, music!"

And at once the players fell to it with doubled zest, and everyone began to clap in time and the women squealed and laughed from their bellies and held their sides laughing. Men streamed into the open middle of the hall; arms locked around shoulders; twirling hoops of dancers spun across the floor, their sandals stamping out the rhythm. Some so far forgot themselves as to drag even the women into the dance, for there was nothing disallowed at a wedding; while the feast was on, jollity made amends for every infraction of decorum. And all of it had but one goal—to gladden and delight the bridal couple.

At the groom's table spirits rose so high that an elderly man, and a scholar at that, suddenly remembered a trick of his youth which he insisted on displaying. He snatched three platters from the table and began flinging them into the air in the way of a juggler. And the governor did not stop him, but spurred him on to show more of his somewhat rusted skill.

Yeshua sat at the groom's right hand, his disciples near him. He delivered no discourse, nor did any man seem to expect it from him. He, too, as well as his pupils, had caught some of the gaiety. They had drunk and eaten fully with the others and Yeshua's eyes were bright with happiness. They said in the hall that the rabbi was rejoicing in the joy of the simple folk, for there was nothing in his bearing to mark him off from the rest. And yet the natural gravity of his face and the humble respect shown him by his pupils instilled everywhere an obscure sense of awe which tended to control the tongues the wine had loosened.

Yeshua's mother sat at the bride's table in the place of honor. The merriment here was more subdued, in keeping with the modesty expected from the bride and her immediate companions. But, if less ostentatious, they were no less happy as this table, and Miriam, infected with the universal joy, continued to draw pleasure from her son's smiling face. For the first time, and perhaps for the last, she saw him sit at ease in goodly company, among his own people. She almost heard the blessings that fell from his parted lips, and saw the smile of genial fellowship in his eyes. Indeed, he was rejoicing in their joy. And though these people did not know who it was that sat in their midst, perhaps they felt it in their hearts more surely than their minds could ever know. Now they were surrounding him, dancing about him as though he were the groom, clapping their hands and singing to an improvised tune: "A rabbi sits in our midst. Blessed be your stay in our house. May your teaching run as a mighty river and may there be many of your like in Israel!"

Others went even further, dancing for him and singing him the very song they had previously offered the groom. "Like to a king is the groom," they were singing, except that the words had become—"Like to a king is the rabbi." And Miriam, hearing them, thought to herself: "If they but knew that they have Israel's bridegroom in their midst!"

Meanwhile the last gourds had been emptied and the earthen beer mugs were beginning to show bottom. Yawning cups and pitchers were lying upset on the tables, to be lifted now and then by a thirsty guest who thought to coax from it another drop. Eyes looked questioningly to the governor; the governor, his eye on the groom, called out with jovial unconcern:

"Well then, since you have drunk so deep, we will now serve you the inferior wine. The other is all drunk. Bridegroom! Where are the pitchers of vinegar-wine? Your guests are athirst!"

The bridegroom's face went suddenly white. He blinked at the company with an inane apologetic smile, begging their pardons.

353

"All we had . . ." he began to say, but his unfinished mumbled phrase was lost inaudibly.

One could feel the gaiety ebbing away in the hush. The circles of dancers disbanded; the men slunk back to their tables, taking up a gourd or flagon to ogle its dregs with a thirsty eye.

"Ah, if one were to bring me a cup of sparkling date-wine, enough only for one more tiff!" said a guest with a fustian groan.

"Wine maketh glad the heart of man, but what is a poor heart to do without it?"

"Isn't there another thimbleful about?"

"If there is, let's have it here! We're so dry, we're spitting dust!"

And the governor asked loudly:

"Does any man have more wine? Perhaps he has forgotten an odd pitcher on his donkey?"

Silence.

A drowsy languor stole through the hall. Tongues felt weighted and spirits grew heavy. Here and there, sleepy heads could be seen to drop on chests and there was suddenly the sound of a man snoring. Yet it was still broad daylight, many hours before the time when the bridal couple could be decently carried to their wedding chamber. Once more the governor, standing on his dais near the bridegroom's seat, asked if there was not another gourd or pitcher left outside—forgotten or perhaps retained for just such an exigency.

No one replied. In the awkward stillness one brave "child of the canopy" started a solo ditty, hoping to rekindle some of the lost fire. But his tune, like the wick of a dry lamp, flickered feebly and gave out. Too late for other guests to save his effort; their lonely, desultory voices fell and sank into a listless calm.

The governor looked with anger at the bridegroom's dispirited face, but could no longer catch his eye, for the groom was staring hard at a point between his toes under the table.

On Miriam none of this was lost. Pity stirred her heart, not only for the bridegroom, who had done his best, but for these simple people and their thirst. They did not know that the well of salvation was among them, that Yeshua's presence had created in them a more than human thirst. She knew that Yeshua alone

354

could save the luckless bridegroom from humiliation. She must beg him for help, as she had done many years back, when she had made him pray for rain. Now she must make him bring wine to this poor man's feast. Here she hesitated; was it for her to tempt her son to miracles?

In the next moment she was sure that nothing would prevent her. In her heart she felt a sudden onrush of strength; it was that consciousness of power she had felt when she outfaced the angel who had brought her the annunciation.

She alone would judge what was right. Indeed, were it a matter of bread for the hungry, she would not ask it of her son. Bread for the starving was only justice, and over justice she could have no sway. But the wine of salvation, which only Yeshua could bring to these humble people—this was not justice; this was mercy. Justice was a thing imposed; mercy must be cried for from below, must be dragged down from the heights by prayer and by battle. And Miriam made her decision.

Yeshua saw her rise from the table and go into the servants' hall. He saw also the imperious look with which she bade him follow and knew at once that she was calling him, needing him perhaps. He rose from his place and went out to his mother, his disciples following.

Mother and son looked at each other, and it was as though Yeshua could read her demand in her eyes. There was little need for words, but behind the few words spoken raged a timeless struggle, the struggle of justice against mercy, of the possible against what can and must not be, the struggle of the limited against the boundless infinite.

"Yeshua, they have no wine," Miriam said at last, and there was nothing of entreaty in her voice.

"Woman, what have I to do with you? My hour is not yet come."

Miriam held him fast in her glance and said no more. Then she turned away abruptly and in a voice that rang with the authority of conquest addressed herself to the servants:

"Whatsoever he tells you, do it," she said and left the room without again glancing at her son. And Yeshua knew that her last

355

words had been his command as much as the servants'. And he acted on her words.

Turning to the servants he pointed to the half dozen pots of stone that stood in the yard of the banqueting house, intended for the rite of purification. And he said to the servants:

"Fill these pots with water."

The servants hastened to fetch water from the cistern and poured it into the pots till they were filled to the brim.

"Draw out now and fill the pitchers and bear them to the governor of the feast," ordered Yeshua—and the servants did as he said.

All this while the disciples had been standing at Yeshua's side. They had observed the silent struggle between him and his mother and had seen the mother's victory over her son. They felt shocked and bewildered and waited breathless for the outcome of the miracle that was being enacted before their eyes. And then they heard a murmur of subdued excitement in the banqueting hall, a low rumble of joy, but so soft that they fancied they heard the thud of awe as it fell upon the company. For even though none of the guests knew as yet whence the new wine had come, and though the governor wondered why the groom had withheld his very best wine to the end, all the company felt suddenly caught in a spirit of holy reverence. They were no longer drunk, but filled with a serene joy, a joyousness charged with the longing for God. And when the first cups had been drained, one man began softly to sing a Psalm of David, and all the company added their voices:

"When the Lord turned again the captivity of Zion, we were like them that dream. Then was our mouth filled with laughter, and our tongue with singing; then said they among the heathen, the Lord hath done great things for them."

And when they had done singing, a man cried out in a breaking voice: "O God, Thou art my God; early will I seek Thee. My soul thirsteth for Thee, my flesh longeth for Thee in a dry and thirsty land where no water is!"

And a woman of the company lifted up her voice and said to Yeshua: "Blessed is the womb that bore thee, and the breast which thou hast sucked."

356

But he said, "Yea rather, blessed are they that hear the word of God, and keep it."

Miriam recognized the warning. Still she did not regret what she had done.

CHAPTER IX

EWS of the miracle in Cana spread fast through the Galilean countryside and soon reached Nazareth. Scores of men had witnessed how the joiner Yeshua had publicly turned water into wine which, being drunk, had filled them all with a new spirit.

Travelers from Cana told it in the Nazareth market that Yeshua's mother, the widowed Miriam, had wrung the miracle from her son. It was she who had prevailed on him to perform it, as they had been assured by those righteous men who were Yeshua's disciples and who had heard every word that passed between mother and son.

The report, corroborated by so many, made a powerful impression on the Nazarenes. They went about as in a stupor. Great heavens, if this Yeshua, their familiar townsman, could turn water into wine, then could he not work other miracles as well—translate stones into bread and, indeed, change the very order of nature? Who could tell but there might be some truth in the wild rumors that had recently sprung up about this unpredictable man?

For several days the citizens of Nazareth looked on his mother as on a saint, a favorite of God gifted with illimitable powers. Mothers with ailing infants in their arms came to her door and begged her, genuflecting, to induce her son to heal the little children, for they were journeying, they said, to K'far Nahum where, according to report, her son was healing the sick.

And indeed, the tales of Yeshua's wonder-working were now coming thick and fast from K'far Nahum where Yeshua had gone with his disciples after the marriage in Cana. It was said that he had power to command unclean spirits for that at his bidding they came out of the possessed; that he could make the blind to see and the lame to walk and that a multitude of cripples, madmen, and lepers were being brought to him from every city to be cured of their infirmities.

Yeshua's brothers were the most disturbed by the news. They could not dismiss the notion that Yeshua might after all be a new prophet, a new incarnation of Elijah. If this was the truth, then they had a direct stake in his destiny. If one of their own blood had reached the status of a seer, and a miracle worker to boot, then it was right that they, his brothers, should partake of his glory at the scene of his glory.

Jacob was the first of them to go to K'far Nahum. Having always believed in his brother, he longed for nothing but to have his lingering doubts resolved. But almost as anxious to see Yeshua's miracles for themselves were the younger brothers, Joses and Simon. They were simple men whose sluggish minds had come early under the influence of their dogmatic uncle. And, whether consciously or no, they had absorbed much of Cleophas's scepticism in regard to their eldest brother. But now that they heard such wonders reported in his name they began to doubt themselves in earnest. Yeshua, they thought, might yet go far; he might even go up to Jerusalem, and there . . . but it was best to see for oneself and not spend one's thoughts in wild imaginings. Thus, without heeding their uncle's caution, they hastened after Jacob to K'far Nahum.

Only Cleophas and Jude remained behind. They explained that they would wait until such time as Yeshua chose to go up to Jerusalem, and then see how the rabbis ruled on the matter.

Jacob returned from K'far Nahum in the utmost commotion of spirit. He would say nothing of what he had seen, refused both food and company and filled his days with prayer and fasting.

The younger brothers, when they returned to Nazareth, proved almost as ungenerous with information. And it appeared that they came home very much as they had gone out; that is to say, they brought with them no treasure in gold and silver with which, in the opinion of some Nazarenes, the new prophet might well

358

have rewarded his brethren. But, as both Joses and Simon pointed out—to allay the envious cupidity of their neighbors—Yeshua had no earthly treasures to dole out; his treasure was laid up in the world to come, so that there were no immediate returns to be expected.

It was only in the privacy of their mother's house that the brothers, with cousin Cleophas on their side, spoke freely of their late experience in K'far Nahum. They warned Miriam of the great peril Yeshua was bringing on himself by provoking the antagonism of the rabbis and scribes. Still, they said, there was nothing for it but to wait until the Pharisees and the High Priest in Jerusalem should make a probe of the matter.

Nazareth was no more than a day and a half distant from K'far Nahum on the shore of Genesaret. The two towns were in close commercial contact, since K'far Nahum was not only a fishing town where the catch of the Sea was salted and pickled for distribution to the entire province, but also a substantial port whence the surplus crops of Galilee—the grain, wool, and oil and the celebrated fruit of the fertile Genesaret plain—were shipped to the Greek cities of Transjordan.

Wholesale buyers from K'far Nahum were thus a common sight in the Nazareth market, and, similarly, Nazarene farmers and sheep breeders often betook themselves to K'far Nahum to dispose of their salable excess.

Thus, by word of mouth, the Nazarenes were soon advised of the teachings which their townsman was spreading among his followers in K'far Nahum. And, like their counterparts in the large town, the scholars of Nazareth rebelled against the new doctrine, even when it was presented to them in the enthusiastic exhortations of Taddi, the tanner.

The old man was now shuttling back and forth between the two towns, impatient to bring every new word or miracle of his rabbi as soon as possible to his own people. He was like a water carrier, people said, constantly replenishing his pitcher at the well and hawking each new draught about the country.

Taddi could never say enough about his master's miracles; here Yeshua had driven out an unclean spirit, there he had restored a cripple. He even let it be known that his rabbi had raised from death the little daughter of one of the rulers of the synagogue and that the sick were thronging after him whithersoever he went, even they who were not of the sons of Israel. And he told of a Roman centurion, a Gentile living in K'far Nahum, who had turned to Yeshua for the healing of his servant. The Nazarenes, listening to the old tanner, were incredulous. But Taddi, after each miraculous account, closed with these words:

"The miracles which my rabbi performs are not my concern; we have wonder-workers galore in Israel, men who are well able to heal the infirm and know how to rid the possessed of their bad spirits. But who else in Israel has brought such consolation to the simple and the poor, saying—'Ask, and it shall be given you; seek, and ye shall find; knock, and it shall be opened unto you. For everyone that asks receives; and he that seeks finds; and to him that knocks it shall be opened'?"

It was these words, quoted by Taddi in his rabbi's name, which so exasperated the learned:

"What does this mean?" they asked indignantly; " 'knock, and it shall be opened'? It depends at what gate you knock and who it is that knocks, an upright man or a wicked."

Another time the tanner quoted Yeshua as saying:

"You have heard that it has been said, 'An eye for an eye and a tooth for a tooth.' But I say unto you, that you resist not evil; but whosoever shall smite you on the right cheek, turn to him the other also.' "

To Taddi who repeated these words in the synagogue, they seemed no less than God-inspired; to the learned of Nazareth they seemed the very opposite.

"Our sages," they said, "have sufficiently interpreted the word, 'An eye for an eye.' It does not mean that we are to blind a man for having blinded another; it orders the guilty one to compensate his neighbor for the injury inflicted. But what shall we make of this Yeshua's words, 'But I say unto you?' What are these powers he arrogates unto himself?"

"For shame!" cried Sakkai bar Zadok, "this Yeshua ben Joseph will have us believe that he is no shoot of the tree of Israel but its very root itself! Our teacher Moses never said, 'But

360

I say unto you.' He brought the Law from heaven in the name of God. God saith—not I, Yeshua ben Joseph, the joiner's son ..."
And Sakkai halted in mid-speech, closed his eyes, and let his body sway back and forth as he relapsed into thought.

Taddi, as well as Jacob, who sometimes joined the tanner in reporting Yeshua's utterances, assured the congregation that their rabbi had no intention to undermine the Law of Moses. Yeshua, they said, had stated explicitly that he had come not to destroy, but to fulfill. Heaven and earth would pass, Yeshua had said, but not one jot or tittle should pass from the Law till all was fulfilled.

"The thief calls the gallows to witness," threw in Matthew ben Hanah, whose impudence had grown with the years, so that he was now a feared and powerful man in the community, achieving by insolence what he could not grab with his hands. "What reliance is there," he continued, "in the word of Taddi and Jacob? They are interested parties with their fingers deep in the joiner's pie."

Cleophas was perhaps the only man in Nazareth who could be provoked to match his tongue against Matthew's. Whatever private notions he might have about his troublesome nephew, this, he felt, was a situation that called for a bold show of family solidarity. He did not hesitate, therefore, to throw all the heat of his temperament into the fight for the family honor, even at the risk of his own reputation:

"Since when," he cried, "does God choose His messengers among the bigwigs of the nation? If my brother's son pursues the modest trade of his fathers, is he therefore less likely to receive the Prophet's mantle? Did not God call Amos from his oxen in the field to become a Prophet of Israel? And King David himself; did he not say, 'From my sheep didst Thou summon me to rule over Israel'? Since when does God despise the poor? God examines a man's heart, not his profession. And if God's spirit has lighted on my brother's son, no snarling snob shall take it from him!"

At this point, to prevent further acrimony, the town rabbi called a stop to the altercation.

"If," he began soothingly, "Yeshua ben Joseph is a true prophet, sent to us by the Lord, we shall not fail of harking to his voice—

361

even as the Prophet said, 'When the lion roars, who shall not be afeard?' The Lord will let us know in His good time. Meanwhile, let there be peace in Israel. Your angry voices do profane the Sabbath!"

The company dispersed and went meekly to their homes.

But at night, in Miriam's house, Cleophas and his younger nephews pleaded with the mother. Yeshua, Cleophas warned, was bringing misfortune on himself, to say nothing of the shame and indignity he was heaping on the entire family. It might be, God forbid, that they would all be cast out from Israel! No one would deign to marry with the sons of Hanan, for they would all be laughed to scorn; they would become fair game for every wag and scoffer in the nation, a byword and a mockery. Only one way remained to salvage their respectability; the whole family, the brothers, the brother-in-law with his wife Shoshannah, all their children, and Miriam herself at their head, must go up to K'far Nahum and fetch him home before the ruin of the family was complete, because it was a patent certainty that Yeshua's doings and assertions would lead them all to the abyss.

The uncle was hotly supported by his nephews. The brothers complained that they could not show their faces in the market without having fingers pointed at them. Soon they would be driven into downright want, for their neighbors were beginning to avoid all truck with them, and it need hardly be said that they, as artisans, depended on the community's goodwill.

The learned Jude, though on more theoretical grounds, was equally strenuous in his presentments. Yeshua, he said, was assaulting the Law, and he was dragging all of them, including Jude himself, into the pit of heresy.

Even Jacob, who had always been the most loyal to his elder brother, expressed misgivings at Yeshua's last-reported doctrines. It is easy for the common weed to take root in any sort of ground, but the noble shoot, nursed by centuries of careful culture, finds it hard to strike roots in a foreign soil. For all the reverence he bore his brother, Jacob said, he did not know what to make of Yeshua's latest teachings.

362

Jacob felt himself at a crossroads, unable to choose his way. Yet he could not bear to hear his brother's name maligned.

"My brother, who is my rabbi and my guide, preaches the same as did our Prophets. When he says, 'Blessed are the poor in spirit, for theirs is the kingdom of heaven,' he means no more than King David, peace be with him, who also said, 'Blessed are the undefiled in the way, who walk in the Law of the Lord.'"

"If this is all he means," cried Jude, "why brings he not his teachings to Jerusalem, where he can be heard by the sages of the Law who sit in the seat of Moses to separate the true prophet and the false? Why shows he not his miracles to expert judges? Why does he shun the scholars, preening himself only before ignorant numskulls and poltroons?"

Then Miriam rose up and said sternly:

"When his time comes, and not before, my son will go up to Jerusalem, for all he does is done according to the word of God. And whosoever wars upon him, wars upon God, though he be his own brother! . . ."

But not always were the tidings that reached Miriam from K'far Nahum of a disquieting nature. Sometimes she received news that filled her heart with hope and joy. It might come through an old acquaintance, like her neighbor Taddi; then again, it might be brought by an utter stranger, a wanderer or passing vagabond.

One day, emerging from her house, she found an old wretch of a cripple sitting on her doorstep. Never before had Miriam seen a man so dreadfully afflicted. His face was pitted with blains; pustules and sores covered his entire body, which was dressed only in rotting strips and ribbons of sack. His head hung limply on his chest, and, indeed, every part of him—head, shoulders, arms, and loins—sagged and tended to the ground. Yet when he opened his dark-blue eyes, Miriam was shocked to see them radiant with peace and unspeakable contentment.

Miriam gave him her hand, helping him to his feet, and brought him into the house. She rubbed oil on his sores and bandaged them in fresh fillets of cloth. Then, having washed his hands and feet and anointed his hair, she seated him at her table and proceeded to serve him food and drink, for the man was greatly famished.

And when the stranger had strengthened himself, she began to speak with him. Whence did he come, she asked; and the cripple replied that he had walked three days from K'far Nahum. He had heard that a new healer had risen in Israel and so had hastened to K'far Nahum to be unplagued of his sores and infirmities.

"And he did not cure you?" Miriam asked anxiously.

"He cured me better than I deserved," the man replied. "For I had come to him to be healed of my sick body, but he healed my ailing soul. Can the body be sick? No, for it is but a clot of corruption. It comes and goes hence like a passing shadow, and how can that which has no permanence be injured or sick? It can only decay, which is the law of its being. Only that which never decays, being fashioned for eternal proof, can be or sick or sound. And I, fool that I was, thought my body distempered. It was from him, the healer, I learned that my body was sound. It requires no cure, for I am well in my sickness. I rejoice in my disease; it reminds me that this flesh of mine is to become a rotting human fungus. It pleases me to know my head is drooping, for then I cannot hold it high over my fellow men. I am rich when I am of all men the most wanting. I am healthy when I am most sick in the flesh. For the healer has given a new soul into my broken body, a soul of another world which makes me whole and rich above all men."

"I know not what you mean," said Miriam. "Did the healer refuse to heal your body? I have heard that he cured others who brought their infirmities to him."

"Who are these others?" said the cripple; "sick men of little faith, who come mumping and begging, wanting their bad spirits expelled, their blind eyes opened or their sores wiped away. And he, a ruler of spirits, orders them to quit plaguing their victims and thus, from the infinite store of his bounty, he gives the poor wretches the almspenny they seek. And they do not see nor understand that it is not their bodies which he heals, but that the touch of his hand uplifts the fallen soul and gives it a new lease. He raises man up from his wormishness and seats him

364

again at the table of his Father. For what are his miracles? That he delivers a cripple of his bit of misery? No, there are many who do likewise. The healer's miracle is that he alters the unchangeable nature of man; that he adds to the Law the quality of pity and mercy.

"When he opens the eyes of the blind, it is not to show them the beams of the sun, but the concealed light of the seventh heaven which irradiates all things. In this light all the world is glorified, and this is his wonder-working, that he can make us see it. But those men of little faith rejoice in their little body fortune which, they think, is the healer's greatest gift, and in their blindness see not the celestial world which he brings to all men. I did not choose to barter the health of my soul for the little health of my body, and so I said to him: Rabbi, I said, leave me my maladies and let my ravaged body go as it will. But give me the great riches, the great health of the soul which you have to give. And he said to me—'It shall be yours; by the power of your faith you have won it.' And even as he spoke I became rich in health.

"Now," the cripple concluded, "who is my peer among men? I am the richest of all, and the wholest, because I have his blessing in my soul."

He finished and looked proudly at Miriam.

"What is this blessing he gave you?" she asked.

"That he gave me a part in the Father by giving me a part in himself. For he said—'At that day you shall know that I am in my Father, and you in me, and I in you.' Thus I was raised through him to become one with my Father in heaven. And this is the treasure he has given me, which no man shall ever again take away."

"Who are you?" Miriam asked. "Are you one of his disciples?"

"I am a rod of the stem, even as he said,—'I am the vine whereof you are the branches; he who abides in me, and in whom I abide, shall bear much fruit.'"

Then Miriam said to him:

"May the Lord's blessing always follow you, stranger, for you have gladdened the heart of his mother."

The cripple started.

"Mother, you say?"

365

"Yes, stranger, you are in her house who bore him."

For a long moment he gazed at her, then said:

"The house of her who bore him? Is not he the beginning? Is not he the Adam by whose grace we all are born anew?"

And then Miriam heard him murmur these words:

"Our Father who art in heaven, hallowed be Thy name. Thy kingdom come, Thy will be done, on earth as it is in heaven."

"But this is my son's prayer!" she exclaimed.

"It is the prayer he gave me to help me on my way," said the cripple.

Then Miriam knew that Yeshua's words were reaping a rich harvest.

CHAPTER X

SUDDENLY and unexpectedly, Yeshua returned with his disciples from K'far Nahum, coming to spend the Sabbath in Nazareth.

He was weary, exhausted by the long journeys on foot which had taken him through the towns and villages of Galilee. He was fatigued by his continual speaking in their synagogues and markets, by the multitudes who came to him from far and wide to be healed of their sickness.

Miriam noticed how her son had lost flesh since leaving her home, as though his body were consumed by the sacred fire that burned in his inward parts. And she treated him as any mother would have treated a son who came home wearied by his labor; she washed and anointed him and changed his clothing, fed him with his favorite dishes, and spread his pallet on the corner bench that had always served for his couch.

This Friday eve, when the meal had been eaten with the disciples together, Yeshua slept once more under his mother's roof. And when he had laid himself down to rest, Miriam went out into her garden to learn what manner of men her son had chosen for his followers. She had seen them before, at the marriage in Cana; they were the three whom he had apparently elected to be his closest intimates, for they never stirred from his side.

Among them was the stocky fisherman with the leathery face— Simon, whom they were already calling Cephas, signifying "a rock." A curly black beard, which seemed continuous with his hair, framed all his features. His eyes were overhung with heavy brows and made a pattern of crow's feet at their corners, all of which would have expressed only simplicity and kindness had not the frank gaze of his eyes suggested the practical sagacity of the people, the accumulated wisdom of generations.

Simon showed her all possible reverence, addressing her with utmost humility and catering to her where he could, and Miriam sensed in him the love and the devotion which the simple Jew of Galilee had for her son. She soon came to understand why Yeshua held him in such high regard. For the man was all faith, and this faith had begotten his conviction that the ways of his rabbi were those of righteousness and that his every act was performed on the word of God. It fortified his hope and assured him that no harm could come to his rabbi, that Yeshua, like Elijah before him, would avoid the narrow strait of death and ascend, undying, into heaven, there to sit on the right hand of God for the judgment of the world. In this hope Miriam found her affinity with him, for since his coming to her house, Simon had been strengthening and consoling her, saying:

"Do I not see the angels going in and out of his door as in Abraham's house? What evil can befall him, or what hurt come to him, when a host of ministering angels stand at his right and left, waiting to act at his bidding?"

This hope of Simon's for a happy issue of his rabbi's ministry brought him close to the mother and awakened her love.

With Simon in the garden were his kinsmen, the two Zebedee brothers. The elder, Jochanan, firm as diorite and with a massive head and powerful shoulders, became in her eyes the protecting wall which screened her son from every tempest.

And yet he troubled Miriam's heart. She knew him to be nearest to Yeshua. With him her son could remain closeted for many hours, initiating him into high mysteries inaccessible to others.

Prior even to Yeshua's baptism Jochanan had often come up from K'far Nahum to speak privately with her son.

His outward appearance, too, marked him off from the others. After the custom of the Essenes he never applied oil to his hair but let it tumble wild over his shoulders. He wore a stark black coat, clasped at the throat and reaching down to his bare ankles. And he was given to veiled utterances, speaking always in figures and symbols which perplexed the understanding. Nor did he ever call God by His name, but, in Essene fashion, described the Tetragrammaton by mystic synonyms as—"the Place," "the Power," or "the Presence."

As for Jacob's devotion to Yeshua, Miriam felt it sprang not only from his faith but from a higher source. It enabled him to grasp the truth that was in Yeshua, the truth that had moved the Prophets, which was one truth for all time and all men.

Miriam was anxious to know these men better. She wished to hear from them how her son fared with the people and why he was beloved of common folk but estranged from the learned, so that they could not find a place in his heart.

The three disciples answered Miriam's questions about Yeshua, where he lived and gave his sermons, and how he was received by his hearers. She sat in the threshold of her house and listened to their tale.

She learned that her son stayed the nights in Simon's house in K'far Nahum. Simon's wife looked after them, as did her mother, whom Yeshua had cured of an illness after a succession of bedridden years. Shoshannah, Zebedee's widow, also came from Bethsaida to help out in the household. And one of the wealthiest women in K'far Nahum, a certain Joanna who was the wife of an official of the king's, came there from time to time and helped them out of her own living.

By day, Miriam was told, Yeshua was with the men in the harbor. There, seated in one of the moored vessels, he spoke to the salters and the carriers and the stevedores, who, in their turn, found much pleasure listening to his speech, seeing that he brought them comfort and assurance that it was not learning but goodness of heart and humility which was pleasing in the sight of their heavenly Father.

When dusk released the people from their labors they brought their little children to him to be blessed, and their sick, variously afflicted; and the rabbi placed his hands on them and healed them of malignant spirits and dispersed their gloom. He made the lepers clean, the halt to walk, and restored sight to the blind. And the people, when they heard his words and saw his deeds of charity, lifted their hands to him, calling him "Healer," "Comforter," or "Prophet," or even "Elijah." And he blessed them all and rejoiced with them and sent them away gladdened and consoled.

Miriam heard how her son, journeying with his disciples, visited the places nearby and entered every shack and hovel. No lintel was too low for him to pass under, and no man too humble to be his companion at table. And he broke bread with the illiterate and the sinful together, allowing no difference between great and little, clean and unclean. All men were pure in his esteem, said the disciples. And if Yeshua was asked by some learned why he sat with these rabble, he returned always the same answer: "Not the healthy need healing but the sick."

Early on the morrow of the Sabbath Yeshua went with his disciples to the synagogue.

The brothers hastened to welcome him and hear his sermon, but Cleophas kept away; he foresaw a violent outburst against Yeshua and preferred not to be among its witnesses. Cleophas's wife Mariama did come to be at Miriam's side in the women's gallery, even though she heard her husband say that Yeshua's only motive in visiting Nazareth was to embarrass his family.

Jacob was still "halting between two opinions," as the saying goes. He entered the synagogue with bleak forebodings and took his place, not in the front among the scholars of the Law, but near the door in a dim corner of the aisle, and at once began to pray for a miracle, a sign to teach him where his loyalty should be. Like all the congregation, he felt certain that this Sabbath would reveal once and for all who his brother was—which would determine his own attitude and that of all Nazareth.

Jude seated himself on one of the front benches with the other Pharisees and scholars of the town.

369

The worshippers who packed the synagogue were not all Naza-renes. Many were now coming from the surrounding villages and hamlets to attend the Sabbath services, for the rabbis had by this time instituted the fusion of Sabbath limits, which enabled men to walk greater distances on the day of rest than was allowed under the original law. And many came who had not planned to attend; they came in the knowledge that the new prophet's mir-acles were commonly demonstrated by him in the synagogue. Had not most of his celebrated cures been effected in the temple of K'far Nahum, some even on the Sabbath, despite the censure of the rabbis? The synagogue of Nazareth was therefore thronged by men with ailing relatives, some possessed and some stricken with melancholy. One good man even carried his paralyzed father on his back. And there were not a few who had come in sheer curiosity to see a townsman turned magician.

For once even the women's gallery was filled. Many of them had never before been seen in a holy place—women in sheer Sidonian silks, rouged and perfumed, with painted eyes, their jaws working mechanically as they chewed aromatic herbs to sweeten their breath—a new fad this, imported from neighboring Sidon.

Still the majority of worshippers were the common citizens of Nazareth. They had come to offer their weekly Sabbatical de-votions. They too were naturally curious to see and hear again their old townsman who had been so much talked about of late. And their attitude certainly was far from hostile. On the con-trary, if a sign were forthcoming, they were very ready to be convinced that Yeshua ben Joseph was in fact what he was al-ready in reputation—a wonder-worker and a man of God. If the men of K'far Nahum, Bethsaida, and Cana were now preening themselves and basking in his glory, why should Nazareth, which had cradled and nursed the man, be more slow to acclaim him and deny itself the venial pride of having bred a prophet of its own?

But among these Nazarenes were also the sons of Pinhas, a com-pact band with Matthew at their head, all of them predisposed to raise a riot that they might bring eternal odium on the house of Hanan.

370

Of course, the old tanner was not absent. Though he regarded himself as a disciple of Yeshua's, he had too much humility to join his rabbi's immediate circle. It was an honor he left to the more favored disciples, Simon, and the sons of Zebedee. With Taddi were Bar Evion, his own son, and his foster-son Pezachi, left to his charge by the death of the boy's father Nafchi, who had suffered crucifixion in the sack of Sepphoris. Pezachi and Bar Evion were proud of Yeshua, their former playmate. Since the earliest report of his miracles, they had believed in him, partly because, in their love, they wanted to believe, and partly because Taddi was a potent influence in their thinking. Now they stood fully prepared to protect Yeshua if the need arose from the sons of Pinhas, whom they suspected of malicious design.

And in addition to its Jewish congregation the synagogue on this strange Sabbath day could point to a surprising number of Gentiles. Yekatiel, the Edomite incense-planter, was there, keeping his distance at the door, and behind him, craning her neck to see, was his swarthy wife Adamia. The Edomite had caught the universal rumor about his neighbor's miracles and his being the Messiah of the Jews who would make all the world his dominion. Now he looked forward to a fine display of sorcery that would surely outdo the magic of the Baal priests. As for his wife, though she had long relapsed into the worship of her idols, her pantheon had room also for Israel's God. It was a shame only, she thought, that she could find no sculptured likeness of Him to grace her shelf of gods. Then she could burn incense for Him to tickle His nostrils and pour out dove's blood at His feet and grease His sacred form with her best oils, as she was wont to do with practised hand for Astarte and Moloch. Jews said they did not know their God's appearance, were not allowed even to picture it in their minds. But, said the Jews, if they could not see Him, they could hear Him the better; every Sabbath morning their God spoke to them through the mouths of His Prophets in every temple of the land, even in Nazareth. But now, Adamia thought, things would be different. Her neighbor Yeshua, whom she remembered from his infancy, was the Messiah and the son of the Jewish God; his form, heaven be thanked, was known to all; so she had kindled even in her husband some faith and enthusiasm for this Messiah of the Jews.

Thus they stood in the doorway of the synagogue, with a host of other Gentiles about them, with illiterate and paupered Jews, with no end of cripples and sick. Every ailing or malingering wretch from miles around mobbed at the door of the synagogue, shaking with nervous anticipation lest he miss a view of the impending miracle within.

Inside the building the tension was almost as palpable. All eyes were on Yeshua, for even those who sat before him in the nave were continually turning their heads to throw him covert glances. And those to whom he had for years been a familiar sight glanced again and again, so different did he appear to them. It needed effort to identify him with the modest, unobtrusive joiner who had been their townsman, who had been civil and serene with young and old, with a marked predilection for small children. Whether it was the publicity that had preceded his coming, every man in the congregation felt him to be apart and unapproachable. Even his physical appearance loaded them with a novel sense of respect. The recent leanness of his body seemed to have heightened his stature and he moved with a quiet positive assurance that suggested to his watchers a conviction of infallibility. It was the deportment of a man too conscious of his power to need self-assertion and display; a bearing which was not lost on the sons of Pinhas or on those scholars who had planned to meet him with derision. Since Yeshua's entrance there had been a noticeable shift of mood among his enemies; they were still prepared to differ with him, but only as scholars differ with each other, without detriment to mutual esteem.

The scholars generally were not all hostile, most of them preserving an expectant neutrality. Yeshua's miracles and cures disposed them neither to disfavor nor enthusiasm. Such things had been heard of before and could never overwhelm a cultivated mind. To the sensitive observer, all creation was a miracle; some miracles were commonplace and regular manifestations; others, like Yeshua's alleged cures, were less frequently seen. But, in the end, all were equally inexplicable without the hand of God. The scholars therefore left the gaping to the vulgar rabble. If Yeshua ben Joseph made prophetic claims, he would have to prove his divine appointment by the divine word of the Torah. If such proof were forthcoming they would gladly and humbly incline their ears to him, as to a new Prophet. Until that time their reservations were in order. And one man in the group quoted a rabbinic saw which seemed most apposite for the occasion: "Suspect but do not disrespect him."

The service in the synagogue proceeded as usual. The reader stood before the ark, chanting the Sh'ma, to which the children answered "amen." Facing the reader on the platform sat the town rabbi, with the rich Reb Tudrus, head of the congregation, on one side, and Reb Sheshet bar Caspi on the other. Behind them sat the town's seven elders and the Pharisees—and then the people, grouped according to their trades. Yeshua ben Joseph had resumed his old seat among the carpenters, his disciples sitting to his right and left.

Overhead, in the women's gallery, Miriam stood with her sister, gazing down at her son through its wooden balustrade. She remembered the day when she had first presented the child Yeshua in this same synagogue. She remembered him standing in a line of children, chanting the "amen" and the last words of the Hymn of Praise under the preceptor's direction. She saw the rabbi, followed by the head of the congregation and the chief of the court, approaching the ark. They were lifting out the sacred scroll of the Torah and all the congregation rose to their feet and cried—"And it came to pass when the Ark was set forward, that Moses said, Rise up, Lord, and let Thine enemies be scattered." And then began the reading of the Torah.

One after another the elders of the town were called to the reading of the weekly lesson, until every section had been read but the last and the portion from the Prophets. The reading of this final section was commonly reserved for honored guests, and now the name of Reb Yeshua ben Joseph was called that he stand forth and read.

Yeshua rose, adjusted the prayer shawl across his shoulders, and ascended the platform. He read his portion of the law in a clear voice for all to hear. And when he had finished, the reader of the synagogue handed him the book of Isaiah, indicating with his

373

finger the week's chapter and verse. But Yeshua ben Joseph, turning to another place in the book, lifted the scroll up high and read:

"The Spirit of the Lord God is upon me, because the Lord hath anointed me to preach good tidings unto the meek; he hath sent me to bind up the brokenhearted, to proclaim liberty to the captives, and the opening of the prison to them that are bound. To proclaim the acceptable year of the Lord . . . ."

He halted in mid-sentence, returned the scroll to the reader, and sat down on the platform in the sight of the assembled congregation.

Everyone in the hall sat petrified at Yeshua's audacity. At first, as soon as it had become clear that he was reading the wrong passage, several of the scholars had felt the impulse to correct him. But their courage to interrupt had failed them when they realized that Yeshua's error was deliberate. Now the shock numbed their tongues and they sat still with hearts violently beating. Their faces were pale and their eyes stared at Yeshua as though they expected him to be struck down by lightning.

Gradually, as Yeshua still said nothing, the first shock ebbed away. The rabbi recovered his speech and rose quickly to reassure his congregation as much as was in his power.

"Yeshua ben Joseph," he began, "this chapter of Isaiah is not that which the rabbis have assigned to today's lesson. Reader, show him the passage for this Sabbath," he added, turning to the reader who stood at Yeshua's side, holding the scroll with trembling hands.

The reader once more offered Yeshua the scroll and pointed timidly to the week's lesson. Yeshua did not receive it from his hands but called out loudly:

"This day is the scripture fulfilled in your ears!"

As the word issued from his lips it became clear at once that the speaker was too deeply convinced of his vocation to feel any pride in it, or to offer any proof of it beyond the conviction itself. The simple and the poor among the worshippers, who waited longingly for a sign of salvation, craved to accept the words with perfect faith. The man who had uttered them had proclaimed himself the Messiah of the Jews; he could be no ordinary rabbi,

374

not even a prophet newly-risen. He must be the anointed for whom Israel waited, for whom it had long borne the yoke of God. He was the end of ends; he was the hope of man and his reward. Father in heaven, could it be that God's anointed was standing here before their very eyes? Would the heavens open now to reveal him in his glory? . . . And yet, who was this man who claimed for himself the doomful words of Isaiah? He was one of their own kind, surely, whom they knew from his childhood, who had been raised with them together. And in the shock of their astonishment, suspended between hope and disbelief, they turned each man to his neighbor, saying:

"Is not this Joseph's son?"

Oh, they were willing enough to believe. A lifelong nostalgia for the coming of the saviour had ripened them for the faith; they wanted nothing but to acquiesce and believe Yeshua's words with the same firmness with which they had been spoken. Some were on the point of stretching out their hands to him, the Hosannah on their lips. Some began to push toward the platform, pulling the crowd along. The sick and the infirm who had been hustling at the door surged forward as on a sudden signal and the cry went up:

"Good people, give me room to reach him."

"Master, heal us!"

"Show us a miracle as you showed them in K'far Nahum!"

But the old town rabbi, about whom the local scholars were now gathering in great excitement, kept off the crowd with up-raised hands and cried out at the limit of his voice:

"Children of Abraham, hold back! The words we have heard have made our hearts shudder. Such words have not been spoken in Israel since God took prophecy from us. And he who arrogates Isaiah's verse unto himself, as Yeshua ben Joseph has now done in our hearing, must offer us a sign, a proof that he speaks truth, even as we were taught by Moses our teacher. If, God forbid, he offer no such sign, then the words we have heard are words of sacrilege and blasphemy, and he who uttered them is a prophet of falsehood."

During the rabbi's warning the voices had gradually died down. Now there was a constrained hush in the crowd and the eyes of all were fastened on the white-robed figure on the platform, sitting motionless in the seat of Moses before the Ark.

And then the silence was rent by a cry that sprang at once from a hundred throats:

"A sign, give us a sign!"

"Let him show a miracle," shouted the sons of Pinhas. "He did it in K'far Nahum, let him do it in the town of his birth!"

And for a moment the crowd waited with suspended breath to see what Yeshua would do.

Miriam's hands clutched tight at the railings of the women's gallery as she looked down on her son. For one exultant moment she thought that all the souls of Jewry, living, dead, and unborn, from the beginning to the end of days, were convoked in this synagogue as they had been at the foot of Mount Sinai when Moses brought the tablets of the Law from heaven. Once more Jewry was gathered, to hear now that the pledge was redeemed, that the Messiah was come, to shout again in glorious unison the words unheard since Sinai: "Behold, we shall do and obey!" She saw a shudder running through the congregation as though it were one soul, one body. Now they would hear the blast of God's thunder, and see His lightning to outblaze the sun. . . . Below her everything was still; a tense, tempestuous stillness, pregnant with eruption, lasting the longest moment.

But she knew that there would be no thunder burst, no miracle. The miraculous sign must be preceded by the sign of faith; "we shall do and obey!" must be heard before the clarion of God's answering thunder. Grace does not descend from above save when it is invoked and desired below. But in this congregation the sign of faith was failing and Miriam knew that Yeshua would not yield to the temptation of a miracle.

She saw him rise from his seat and heard him say simply:

"No prophet is accepted in his own country. But I tell you in truth, many widows were in Israel in the days of Elijah, when the heaven was shut up three years and six months, when great famine was throughout the land. But to none of them was Elijah sent, save only to Sarepta, a city of Sidon, to a woman that was a widow. And many lepers were in Israel in the time of Elisha the Prophet; and none of them was cleansed but Naaman the Syrian."

376

It took a while before his hearers grasped the meaning of his words. Then the congregation began to stir angrily.

"What words are these? Does he mean that we Nazarenes are unworthy of the miracles he shows them in K'far Nahum?"

The carping voice of Matthew rendered a shrill answer:

"No, not we Nazarenes but we in Israel are unworthy. You heard him slander Elijah and Elisha, saying they performed miracles only for Gentiles—a Syrian scurf and a Sidonian jade!"

Matthew's cronies took up his cue:

"Are we to listen meekly while he insults us to our faces, us, the people of his town?"

"He knows that we in Nazareth cannot be taken in by his magic trickery and pious fakes! Nazarenes are not so lightly duped as the gulls of K'far Nahum!"

"Men, this is a crying blasphemy we've heard!"

"Well, let him show us a miracle, we demand a miracle! Else let him begone!"

"Not before he's had the forty stripes."

"Forty stripes, nothing! He has earned stoning! Stone the false prophet, says the Law!"

Then Miriam saw the insolent Matthew, with stiffened elbows and fists, pressing forward through the crowd and making for the platform. A force of irate citizens, the sons of Pinhas, followed at his heels, tearing through the crowd toward Yeshua's impassive figure that still stood motionless on the platform before the ark. Once more Miriam caught sight of her son's white face, eye to eye with Matthew. In another moment they had all reached him; arms clenched about his body, lifted him high, and over a heaving floor of heads and shoulders Yeshua's unresisting form was carried toward the synagogue door.

A fearful cry went up from the congregation:

"Men of Nazareth, stop! You put your souls in jeopardy!"

"This will bring down the doom on our heads!"

"What are you doing, men! You desecrate the Sabbath!"

Matthew's panting voice came back to them:

"Such a one may be split like a fish even on Atonement Day that falls on a Sabbath!"

And Miriam saw her son pitched on their violent shoulders, his

377

prayer shawl trailing behind him over their heads, as they carried him out through the doorway. She seized Mariama's hand and bounded down the stairs of the women's gallery.

Outside she realized at once that Matthew's enraged mob had no intention of unhanding their victim. Her son was borne at a great pace through the deserted streets of the town, and Miriam, following, was unable to catch up with Matthew's men. They had gained a long start, since in the general shock and confusion no one had had the presence of mind to hinder them. Even the disciples, dashing after the mad horde to save their rabbi, were a good way behind. And when at last they had caught up, they found that there was no way through Matthew's crowd, and they despaired of saving him. Jochanan, first of the three, tore into them like a bull in fury, but the brunt of his approach spent itself against their massed bodies, and a dozen powerful arms hurled him aside. And Jacob, Yeshua's brother, ran with the disciples, the fringes of his prayer shawl straining after him in the wind, and he called with desperate anguish:

"Let him go, sons of Abraham! You know not what you do!"

And not he only, but many of the scholars, headed by young Jude, had by this time rushed out of the synagogue to pursue the sons of Pinhas and stay them, if possible, from their intended crime. And with them ran the old tanner and the Edomite and others of the congregation, common citizens, Yeshua's fellow-carpenters, and such as had known him since his childhood. But the pack of Matthew's men ran before them all, bearing the still, white-cloaked body of the rabbi and not letting themselves be overtaken. To Miriam it seemed as though the angels of destruction had lent them wings, or as though Satan himself and his host of devils had come to deal with Yeshua after their pleasure.

A little way beyond the town the Nazarene hills inclined steeply toward the Jezreel plain. In several places the bluffs made dangerous walking for unwary travelers. One place in particular there was which the people of Nazareth called "the mouth of destruction." The plateau here was covered with a thicket of laurel shrubs, so that it was hard to see the brink where the surface of the ground suddenly opened on a gorge. Many sheep, straying from the herd had crashed to their grave in this "mouth of destruction."

And many an ox had his bones mauled by the razing spurs of rock that formed the walls of the ravine.

It was to this brink that Miriam saw them haul her son. In one moment of gasping horror, she saw them swing his body over the edge of the precipice; saw Yeshua's blood coloring the jagged teeth of the rockface, his flesh mangled in the fall.

Miriam's knees gave way; she collapsed on the ground and her eyes closed. She felt someone trying to support her and heard him whisper in her ear—"Mother, have faith!" She thought it was Jochanan's brother Jacob, and she shook the voice from her. Her mind rejected all but the gory vision of Yeshua's body, his human body which she had nourished, warmed with her love, and raised to manhood. No consolation could outweigh her grief, and Miriam, from the depth of her misery, cried out:

"Forsake him not, Father in heaven!"

It was several minutes before Miriam, praying in an ardent fever, dared again to open her eyes. She expected an uproar of excited voices, but everything about her was strangely silent.

Her son was walking toward her, calm and unharmed, away from the brink of the gorge. He was walking alone, with a sure quiet tread, as if he had been walking thus for many hours without break or incident. His erstwhile persecutors, the company of the men of Pinhas, with insolent Matthew at their head, were standing aside at a distance, to all appearances paralyzed with astonishment and terror. And with fear-dilated eyes they saw the man who but a moment before had been in their power, walking away from them unscathed.

Yeshua held his hand out to his mother to help her rise from the ground and said in a voice firm and even:

"Mother, the peace of the Sabbath be upon you."

He took her hand and led her home, while the disciples, a small group of awe-struck men, followed at a distance.

They were still outside the town when they met Cleophas, coming toward them in great haste. He had just heard how ignominiously Yeshua had been manhandled by the sons of Pinhas, and immediately his family blood had bounded into fury. Shelving his own resentments and complaints, he had at once set out in hot pursuit to save his brother's son.

On seeing Miriam and Yeshua together he stopped short and looked at them in wonder. He let them pass and joined with the small group of disciples who brought up the rear and in whose company he had descried his nephews. He went with them to Miriam's house, where Yeshua consented to spend the rest of the Sabbath in the company of his followers and kinsmen.

The brothers were now utterly convinced that Yeshua stood under the protection of a higher power. For the first time they began to fear their brother, and even Cleophas, when he heard their tale, came to feel a kind of awe.

The Sabbath closed, and after the coming out of the stars, Yeshua prepared to depart. Taking his mother aside, he addressed her, saying:

"Woman, you shall not see your son again, except in the day of his glory."

"Your will shall be done, Yeshua," said Miriam, letting her head fall.

Then Yeshua bade her farewell, rallied his disciples, and departed from his mother's house.

Miriam followed him a little way into the night.

CHAPTER XI

HEROD ANTIPAS, Tetrarch of Galilee, could not decide whether the savage prophet who was his prisoner in the dungeon holes of "Machaerus," his castle in the wilderness of the Dead Sea, should live or die. Jochanan had openly denounced him for living with his brother's wife; he had blackened his name with the Jews, whose goodwill Herod had done so much to court.

His wife Herodias, the foxiest shrew in the Eastern Empire, plagued him by day and night to seize the Prophet and cut off his head. So far the Tetrarch had done only half her bidding—he had ordered the rebel incarcerated in his desert hold, but he dared not order him beheaded, knowing the fanatic following Jochanan had among the Jews. He knew well, too well for his liking, that the Baptist was glorified by the people, that they called him the "wild seer," that he had innumerable adherents even among the Pharisees.

Tetrarch Herod Antipas was politician enough not to invite the enmity of the best in the nation by laying hands on their chosen prophet. But he had added reasons for deferring the man's execution. Sly as he was, Herod Antipas was a true son of the Herods; that is to say, he was profoundly superstitious and believed firmly that seers like the captive Jochanan were possessed of preternatural powers. He wondered obscurely if there might not be truth in the people's credence that the spirit of the Prophet Elijah had entered the Baptist and that he, Elijah, was once again among the living. This day or tomorrow Jochanan, the Prophet reincarnate, might renew Elijah's miracles and bring fire down from heaven. Could he, Herod, be expected to embroil himself with such a one who had the heavenly host at his beck?

But Jochanan's stark seditious ravings were no more to be endured. The prophet was hurling baleful threats at the Tetrarch and his illicit wife, whom he presented to the people in the similitude of Jezebel, a woman to be crushed like vermin underfoot. Under the prophet's lash the Tetrarch's standing, such as it was, began to crumble. It was high time to deny him liberty, if not to take his life. Indeed, Herod spared his prisoner despite the bitter taunting of his wife, despite the derision she set afoot in Rome, calling him a queasy coward who made the populace his bugaboo.

The Baptist's followers were of all classes, the learned and the orthodox as well as common artisans and farmers. Though Jochanan had called many to the kingdom of God, his doctrine flowed with the main stream of Israel's tradition. It said to the Jew: "Do penance, for the kingdom of heaven is at hand. Mortify your flesh by fasting and with self-denial, cleanse your body and your vessels, touch not that which is polluted, flee the pleasures of the world, and ready your soul for the kingdom of heaven." Such a doctrine was easily grasped and simple to put

381

into practice; it assured the captive prophet of an enthusiastic following throughout the country.

It was these followers who brought Jochanan news of the Nazarene, the man of whom Jochanan himself had said that he was not worthy so much as to unloose the latchet of his shoes. Yeshua of Nazareth, said the Baptist's disciples, called himself the Son of Man, and was performing miracles. His public conduct, they said, was without precedent. It was in head-on opposition to Jochanan's teachings, for it appeared that Yeshua of Nazareth spurned the ascetic way and repudiated neither wine nor meat; he was not clothed in camel's hair, nor were his loins weighted with a leathern belt. He walked in white and smoothed his head with oil. More, he had suffered a sinning woman to anoint his feet, since no one was too low to come into his presence and sit with him at table. Loose women and publicans could be seen in his company; the Nazarene befriended them all and chose disciples from out of their number.

From his prisoner's hole Jochanan sent his followers to the Nazarene. Approaching Yeshua, they asked: "Why do we, the disciples of Jochanan, fast often and make prayers, but yours eat and drink?" To which the Nazarene replied in a manner that left Jochanan's envoys baffled and uncomprehending. For he said to them: "Can you make the children of the bridechamber fast while the bridegroom is with them? But the days will come when the bridegroom shall be taken away from them, and then shall they fast in those days." And he gave them his parable in parting: "No man puts a piece of a new garment on an old."

To the Baptist's disciples this last parable was clear enough; the new prophet sought to indicate that he was no man's follower, that he was no patch on an old cloth but a new garment entirely; that he was not the consummation only, but his own beginning also.

The Baptist's followers, as much as the official circles of the scribes and Pharisees, were astonished at the Nazarene's conviviality with tax farmers and sinners. In the community of Israel the tax farming publicans embodied all the evils of godlessness and national betrayal; they gathered the tribute for Rome's kingdom of villainy which was afflicting Jewry. To feast oneself with such traitors was unheard of and unpardonable. But it was worse still to find a rabbi tolerating the presence of a courtesan, letting her anoint his feet and dry them with her hair, as had actually happened before witnesses in the house of a Pharisee. Accordingly, Jochanan's pupils, who were among the most pious in the nation, renounced the new seer and made no effort to hide their disapproval.

And the report, soon current in all Galilee, that the Baptist's following was hostile to the Nazarene, served to aggravate the resentment of Yeshua's townsmen, even that of his kinsfolk, some of whom counted themselves among the followers of the imprisoned prophet.

Miriam had never known such isolation. The neighbors shook their heads, and every now and then a voice of malice gibed at her with the old saw—"Like father, like son." Some treated her with genuine compassion, for she was known as a good woman who could not well be blamed for the misconduct of her son. Besides, it was only fair to remember that Miriam was the mother also of Jacob and Jude, exemplars both of piety and erudition. The full weight of the town's hostility fell upon Yeshua's brothers.

Jacob could escape the storm in the shelter of his piety, like a snail recoiling in its house. He needed no companionship beyond his mystical preoccupations. And his physical requirements were negligible; he would spend long days in fields and forests searching for the herbs and barks that went into his healing potions.

Jude could withdraw into his coterie of scholars, men too well trained in discrimination to hold him responsible for his defecting brother.

The real sufferers within the family were the two middle brothers, Joses and Simon. They had no privacy of learning or religion to offer a retreat. Sometimes they and their uncle stood all day at their work in the street of the sandal makers, hearing the random buzz of the street punctuated by aimed insults, as: "Those are the boys whose brother takes himself for the Messiah"; or—"Will he appoint you princes in his kingdom of Heaven?" Their children,

383

coming home from school, complained of being cruelly teased by their playmates. But the worst of it was that they were being edged into poverty. Since their brother had received such frightful treatment in the synagogue, few would have anything more to do with them, and their lives were made well-nigh unendurable. Yet they bore their fate with humble resignation and said little about it. Their mother, in particular, never heard them complain, for both Joses and Simon were now convinced that mighty things lay stored up for their brother.

Cleophas saw the ruin of the family hastening to its consummation. He cared nothing for the cold shoulders of his neighbors or the bitterness of any stranger. These could never turn him against Yeshua's ministry; it was his paternal care and the love he bore his own that made him so bitter a critic. When he bemoaned his failing fortune, it was because he saw in it the downfall of his family. Since Joseph's premature death he, Cleophas, had been the undisputed head of Hanan's house, the educator and the foster father of all Yeshua's brothers. Joses, Simon, and Jude were as good as his own sons, and his paternal responsibility extended also to his eldest nephew, the more so if Yeshua strayed from the right path. Not that he charged Yeshua with wantonness, as did many of his neighbors, calling him a profligate, a glutton and a toper, a renegade, seducer of the people, and more of the like. Cleophas regarded his nephew as a young man essentially honest if somewhat retarded and deranged in mind, who, in all fairness, could not be held to account for his actions and words. No, the fault lay not with him but with his mother. It was Miriam's passionate, deluded dreams that had warped his mind from earliest childhood. In her blind love for her first-born she had snared him into thinking himself no ordinary mortal; so the boy had grown up with the conviction of supernatural powers.

And as for his much-vaunted miracles—some succeeded, some miscarried, thought Cleophas. In K'far Nahum—where they did not know him so well—they bragged of him as a great wonder-worker. But unfortunately, the more folk believed in him, and the more miracles he carried off, the more dangerous it was for his mental balance, to say nothing of his personal safety and that of his family.

384

"Good news from your son, Miriam!" he called out, striding one day into Miriam's garden where she stood weeding the greens. "Have you heard the latest? Your son not only hobnobs with publicans and outright scoundrels—no, he lets an evil woman wash his feet. They say she comes from Magdala where she had quite a reputation as a woman of many lovers. Your son, do you hear, took much trouble to expel an evil spirit that was vexing her. And she? What do you think she did by way of gratitude? Why, she anointed his feet and dried them with her hair—and all this during a gathering of learned men in a Pharisee's house. A pretty way to disport oneself in public, is it not? And now she is one of his handmaidens."

"For those who are pure nothing is unclean," said Miriam softly, without looking up. "If my son admitted her she could not have been unworthy. Has he not said, 'I came not to call the righteous, but sinners to repentance'? 'They that are whole need not a physician, but they that are sick.' This is what my son said to the Pharisees."

"Woman, woman," said Cleophas with insistence, "I have told you before, it needs the father's rod to make good what a mother's love has spoiled. To our common sorrow your boy was too soon deprived of paternal correction. Ever since then your love for him has been his stumbling stone. You sowed a bad crop, Miriam, and now you reap the harvest. Even Jochanan's disciples have rejected him."

"So long as God is with him, everything is with him," said Miriam.

"Miriam," said Cleophas pleadingly. "Let us go to K'far Nahum —now—and fetch him home before it is too late. Remember, you have other children besides Yeshua."

"No, Cleophas, you and I cannot interfere with God's design. When the Prophet Jonah sought to escape his commission, the waves rose on the sea and would have swallowed up a ship full of innocent people. But we, if we were guilty of crossing God's will, should be wiped off the face of the earth."

Cleophas vehemently shook his head.

"Look, Miriam," he said, "here you tear out the weeds that

grow among the plants of your garden, but you would spare the wildness in your own family?"

"Because there, Cleophas, I am not the gardener. It was God who planted and tended. He will reap. His will shall be done."

They came each Sabbath to offer their respects to Miriam, for the Law that bade every man honor his mother was held dear by the sons.

They were sitting in the main room of Miriam's house, the dry fleshless Jacob, Joses, and Simon, and the learned Jude, courteous and secure in his black gown. Yeshua's affairs were not discussed, since no one wanted to oppress his mother's spirit on the Sabbath.

Among her younger sons the middle brothers were closest to Miriam's heart. Jacob and Jude were protected from the evils of the world, the one in hermit solitude, the other in the precise, staked-out field of learning. They had looked well to the safety of their souls; they walked the great thoroughfare, trodden out by a million feet. Simon and Joses had grown up without the advantages of education, but they had inherited their father's uprightness and zeal for justice. Not knowing what to think, Joses and Simon held their tongues and never grumbled over their ill-treatment at the hands of their neighbors. Resigned and forlorn, they suffered their new isolation and encroaching poverty. Yet Miriam was aware both of their plight and the endurance they brought to it. With all her heart she wanted to help them, but surely she could not accept Cleophas's advice and bring Yeshua home. It would be dire sin in her to interfere with Yeshua's mission; and even if she did, Yeshua would certainly cast her aside and proceed on his way.

Miriam knew well why God had made her mother to so many sons, and they so different from each other. Their differences spanned the range of human qualities; in her dealings with her own flesh and blood God was trying her compassion for all humankind.

Jacob's way was that of the painful life-denier; he fainted for communion with the Godhead; with thirsty lips he sucked into himself the essence of the infinite. Indeed, Miriam saw her son Jacob almost visibly consumed in his yearning for God.

386

She knew also the way of her third son Joses, righteous and innocent and yet perpetually bewildered for want of understanding. His arms were too short to scale the mystic ladder of her second son; thus he stood helpless and let his heart point out the way.

Simon's way was a humble fear of God. Unlike Joses he never felt lost in the world but trembled hourly in the consciousness of God's omnipresence. He stood like a blind creature in the midst of creation, alone with his terror of God.

And lastly there was the hard but certain way of the scholar. Jude had none of the nostalgia of the mystic. He had neither the faithful heart of the simple believer, nor the broken spirit of the God-fearer. His road was staked out with milestones and signposts for long distances ahead, but every step must be bought by his own exertion. There could be no short cuts for him. And yet, how certain was Jude of his trail! He knew it to be straight and cleared of the hurdles of doubt, and lighted all the way by the light of the Torah.

These were the four directions of her sons, the four divergent trails which men cut in their quest for God, all of them limited and stopped short by the shortness of their human breath.

But she was Yeshua's mother also, the child of the miracle birth. Through Yeshua she was the mother of a higher being. Yeshua's life invested her with a two-fold maternity, making her a mother in heaven as well as in this world. Should piety, righteousness, fear of God, and learning, which were but means to the end, outweigh the end itself?

And to her sons she spoke in this manner:

"Your qualities, however noble they may be, are the qualities of thirst. But your brother is the libation. Your ways are the ways of the quest, of groping in darkness. His is the way of the unerring guide. Go out therefore and cleave to him and your search shall be gloriously ended. For as all rivers tend toward the sea, so every road to God must meet in him. He is the bread of God for those that hunger after it."

To Nazareth came the fearful tidings of Jochanan's death.

Yielding at last to the nagging of his wife, Herod Antipas had ordered the wild prophet beheaded.

The news brought Cleophas to Miriam's house. He came with his wife, Miriam's sister, and with Jacob and Jude to tell her what he knew.

The death of the Baptist, lamented by all Israel, heaped praise and glory on his followers. His close disciples were now more deeply revered than in their rabbi's lifetime. The house of Hanan, too, had a family claim to some of the glory, and Cleophas found frequent occasion to mention his wife's kinship with Elisheva, the Baptist's mother. But Jochanan's death had yet a greater significance for the family; it underlined the danger in which Yeshua was placed.

Cleophas had delicacy enough not to tell Miriam outright what was on his mind, but, even so, the family was perfectly aware of the threat to Yeshua's life—and Miriam knew better than the rest.

She knew his destiny on earth was one of sufferance. And Yeshua's parting words had given her ample warning. And if her son was he whose life the Prophets had foretold, he could not hope to circumvent the road laid out for his ordeal. One half the ancient oracle had come to pass, the other could not but be fulfilled also.

But must the Scripture always be fulfilled? Could the Creator of heaven and earth be constrained to a single course of action? Was not He who had given the Scripture Lord of the Scripture? Must the glory of her son be bought inevitably at the price of his blood?

For Miriam had once again begun to weave her wishful hopes. Like Abraham at Isaac's fettering, she thought she would yet see an angel appear at the last moment to restrain the sacrificing knife.

Now, at the news of Jochanan's death, her hope ran out again. The Baptist's severed head proved compellingly that the mere willingness to sacrifice and die would not in this day of fulfillment be sufficient. Not the right intention, but the perfect rendering of the sacrifice must crown Yeshua's mission. For Miriam understood that Jochanan had been the Elijah who, according to the Prophets, had come to proclaim the Messiah. And could the har-

388

binger be higher than the Master, the disciple supersede his rabbi?

All this Miriam knew well—and had known ever since that day when, tying up his wallet of provisions, she had sent him to receive baptism from Jochanan's hand. She had thought then that her fears were conquered for all time, that she had gained her worthiness in letting him go. But in her horror of the abyss over which Yeshua had been held by the sons of Pinhas, in her mother's panic for his life, she had forfeited once more the right to share in her son's exaltation. Once more she could feel nothing but the imperiousness of her love. Her love dominated and enfeebled her will; and she saw with shame and grief that she was no longer ready to offer up her son.

No sign came to her. She saw no apparitions, heard no voices. It was for her alone to fight her battle.

In her loneliness Miriam had little left beyond the Psalms of David. At night her supplication carried from her chamber:

"A prayer of the afflicted when he is overwhelmed and pours out his complaint before the Lord: Hear my prayer, O Lord, and let my cry come unto Thee. Hide not Thy face from me in the day when I am troubled; incline Thine ear unto me; and in the day when I call, answer me speedily. . . ."

Jerusalem had caught the news of the new prophet in Galilee. A group of scribes and Pharisees was sent to K'far Nahum to consider by whose power Yeshua of Nazareth worked cures and miracles. They issued the following finding: "Beelzebub inhabits his spirit and it is by the power of the Demon prince that he bends demons to his will."

Miriam heard the report and thought in her heart: "Now is my child's life forfeit; any man may strike him down like a beast of the field."

By night she lay on the roof of her house where she was accustomed to pray. But she no longer prayed with the tongue of David.

"Father in heaven," she cried, weeping; "my child is in peril of his life, let me be with him now."

She knew that her prayer would go unanswered. In departing

from her, Yeshua had said she would not see his face again till the day of his glory. She felt his words closing about her like a prison wall. To save her soul this wall was not to be scaled. She shook the thought from her and repeated:

"Lord of the world, wherever he is, let me be also!"

A voice within her said—God will withdraw His grace from me if I cross His design. And suddenly she saw herself stripped bare, alone and cut off from the world of God. And she felt no fear but only a joyous acceptance of her banishment, and once again she cried:

"Lord, let me bear the fate of my child!"

Then suddenly she saw in a vision the "mouth of destruction" that was outside the town. She saw the juts of pointed rock that lined the precipice, the trunks of collapsed trees rotting in the hollow where skeletons of fallen animals lay bleaching. She was poised atop the brink, gazing far and deep into the hopeless concave. This, she knew, was not the valley of the shadow of death, furnished with hope for the faithful; this was the baseless pit of the wicked from which her son had returned whole and untouched. The pit had closed its lips for Yeshua; for her it flared wide. And still Miriam felt no terror, and she stretched her hands skyward and cried out:

"Father, let my bones be taken in the stead of my child!"

In that night Yeshua's mother descended into the pit to save the human life of her son. She determined to go to K'far Nahum.

CHAPTER XII

EASTWARD from Nazareth the land rolled from the cool green hills into a sun-baked plain—peat soil, violet-brown, gullied by the rains of recent spring. Beyond it, in a bowl of heat bordered by towns and villages, lay the Sea of Genesaret—so-called because its shore was figured like a harp. The Sea was Israel's favorite water. Of all the seven seas which God created,

He molded none with greater love—so said the rabbis—than this Sea of Galilee. Nor was it beloved without reason. It received Israel's river Jordan and sent it south to Judah, rich in blue lucent waters, till it ran to death in the Dead Sea. High and white above Genesaret shimmered the hoary crown of Mount Hermon, and, to its left, the green summits of Lebanon shut out the heathen cities of Phoenicia.

Genesaret divided Israel from the Gentile world. Its right bank climbed to the heights of the Decapolis, where sat the Gentiles, like grasshoppers innumerable. Greek thought flourished here under the porches of the Stoics, side by side with the excesses of the Hellenized aboriginals. Here lay Gergesa and Gadara, Hippos and Scythopolis, and the rest of the associated Grecian cities which Pompey the Great had severed from the land of Israel.

The low western shore of Genesaret was thickly sown with Jewish fishing villages and towns. Behind it stretched the famous fruit gardens of the Genesaret champaign, for despite its broiling heat the plain was one vast orchard. The figs and pomegranates, the vine and almonds of the Sea country were spoken of far beyond the borders of Israel. In the markets of Jerusalem the fruit crops of Genesaret yielded the highest prices, and no pilgrim, from what place soever he might come to offer his first fruits, could forestall the fruit-growers of the Sea. The earliest pomegranates, the first dates and grapes of the season, were brought to market by the orchardmen of Genesaret.

Of all the towns and regions in Israel, there was none more appropriate for Yeshua to launch his message than the little metropolis of K'far Nahum on the shore of the Sea.

K'far Nahum was enclosed in a chain of fishing villages whose toiling people brought their daily catch to its salteries and wharves.

These men, drawn from Bethsaida, Chorazin, K'far-achim, Gergesa, and Ayn-Taana, listened avidly to the blessed and hope-bearing words of the new seer. Their hearts were virgin soil, their daily lives not overplussed with ritual; their minds had never been subverted by the notion that they were the elect sitting at God's table. In their innocent fear of sinning against the many dictates of the rabbis, poor in merit and ignorant of the word of

God, they heard the words of the Nazarene prophet and received them as the benighted earth receives quickening dew. The Nazarene spoke to them in their own tongue. His parables mirrored their everyday lives. And the simple commands which he laid upon them were ample nourishment for their hungering souls.

Within the area, not only the villagers, but the townspeople too were of the same unsophisticated stock, the one exception here being Tiberias, Herod's new residential city which he had settled with Romans and Greeks. In Magdala most of the people plied the lowly trades of weaving and dyeing, and there were many pigeon breeders among them who supplied doves for sacrificial uses to Jerusalem. In K'far Nahum the people were fruit growers and fishermen. Many worked in the salteries where fish was crated for export to the surrounding towns and the Greek settlements beyond the Sea. Many more were employed in the harbor as shipwrights, stevedores, and skippers. As a port city it was peopled with hosts of officials and tribute gatherers for the state, in addition to a standing Roman cohort. And its market teemed with foreign merchants nosing for bargain prices among the fruit, grain, vegetables, and dyed cloth. They were Phoenicians from Tyre and Greeks from Decapolis, chaffering for the coveted produce of this fertile land which the small Jewish farmers brought into K'far Nahum.

A lively seagoing traffic connected the opposing shores of the Sea, and K'far Nahum was the center where Jews and Gentiles met commercially. Its Sea-bounded market place, however humble in its architecture, was a cosmopolis in little, bestrutted by rich Greek merchants from beyond the Sea, with retinues behind them of slave secretaries, tutors, and philosophers. Tyrean shipbuilders were here, with corps of timbermen brought down from the Labanese mountains; and Sidonian manufacturers purchasing raw wool to feed their weaving mills at home. Thick in the jostling crowd were Jewish fishermen and salters, naked to the waist, pushing to the shore to help their mates draw in the loaded nets of disembarking vessels; and Jewish women, their hair modestly concealed in heavy kerchiefs, sat by the anchored fishing smacks, mending nets or edging them with cork and stones. And, watchful of them all, the black-gowned guardians of rabbinic law went to and fro about their public business.

Jewish farmers came from far and wide, some with asses that had baskets of greens or wine straddling their bellies, others on ox-carts heaped with the newly-harvested fruit, which priests, walking alongside, checked for tithing. Here also were the publicans and tollmen, with brazen badges on their chests, with scales and measures in their hands and armed escorts at their heels, detailed for their protection and efficiency by the agoranome, the general supervisor of the market. Roman legionaries under a centurion's command kept order in the grinding babel of animals and men. The press was deepest about the taverns whose open portals exuded, with much smoke, the tangy smell of mutton roasting on the spit. Drunkards loitered thirstily about the vintners' stalls; and loose women with garish, painted eyes and oozing phials of perfume pending from their necks by golden carcanets, nudged their way through the male throngs that stood before the taverns till they found their dupes; while the more discriminating courtesans sat aside between the curtains of their private booths, their hair unloosed, their jaws chewing fragrant incense grains, their light fingers strumming over ornamented harps.

This was the town Yeshua had chosen for the beginning of his ministry.

Miriam and the brothers, bound for K'far Nahum, spurned the royal highway which Herod had built to link Sepphoris, the ancient capital of Galilee, with his own residence on the Sea. It was certainly the shortest route; but it led through Tiberias, Herod's impious city founded in consecrated burial ground. Miriam's party reached the plain of Genesaret through a series of by-ways.

Now they walked the road into K'far Nahum amid a jam of farmers' wains and donkey caravans.

With Miriam went the entire house of Hanan, going to K'far Nahum to bring their brother home and save him—and through him themselves—from certain disaster. Mariama walked at Miriam's side; a little way before went Cleophas with Yeshua's brethren and the sister Shoshannah with her husband. Their children too were in the party, for it was an experience well-tried that

393

the contumacy of a stiffneck was best melted by showing him the children whose future was in jeopardy. For surely the little ones would all become the butt of later generations as springing from a family that had bred one condemned by the rabbis for working magic with the aid of unclean powers, even Beelzebub, the prince of fiends.

There were many traveling on foot, some walking alone, some in small groups. Young men scuffed heavily with invalids or paralytics on their backs. Cripples dragged themselves along with rattling breath, doubling over crutches and sticks. A line of blind men, holding one another's skirts, were led by a young boy in a bright trailing tunic. Two youths with bare muscular arms carried an old man on a bamboo stretcher. A mother led her blind boy by the hand; the boy wore a colored shirt, a sure sign that he hailed from beyond the Sidonian border. The mother could be heard speaking softly to her son.

Before long she caught up with Yeshua's family and began walking side by side with Miriam and her sister. Miriam was walking heavily, wearied by the day's journey and the anxiety that pressed on her spirit.

"Do not worry yourself," said the blind boy's mother suddenly. "The seer to whom you go will ease and comfort your heart as he has comforted many others."

Miriam started. "How do you know that I am seeking comfort from the seer?"

"Your sorrow speaks out of your eyes."

"And are you also bound for K'far Nahum to be healed by him?" asked Mariama.

"We are; and so are all these others, for we have heard that the God of the Jews has sent a Redeemer to console broken hearts and mend our bodies. The gods have shut up my child's eyes from the day of his birth, but the God of the Jews will open them through the merciful hands of this healer."

"The gods, you say?" Mariama asked. "Are you one of the heathen?"

"I am a Canaanite by birth. I come from Tyre, which is by the great Sea. Moloch was my god and I burned incense to him and Astarte and slaughtered doves at her feet. They could not open the blind eyes of my child. But now the God of Israel will do so, for I have converted to Him."

"You have converted to the God of Israel?" asked Miriam.

"Why, yes, for I have heard of the Saviour which the God of Israel will send His people. Were not the Jews always waiting for him? For many years we laughed, thinking their waiting vain. But the God of Israel has redeemed His promise and sent a great healer to the Jews. We want a share of the salvation he can give. My child and I want to be healed before it is too late."

"But," Miriam asked, "have you been told that this healer is the Saviour of the Jews?"

"Must I wait to be told? The wind in the fields carries the word, the birds bear it through the forests. Do you see all these people wending toward him? You think they drag only their crippled bodies to him? Their ailing souls also need healing. For the tidings of this healer have gone abroad and have reached us whom you call Gentiles, and many folk from our cities went down to him to be healed in their bodies and they returned both cleansed and comforted. For this man heals the flesh and the soul together. He is the consolation of the broken-hearted and the hope of the poor."

The woman ceased speaking and for a while they walked in silence. Then Mariama said to Miriam under her breath:

"And are we going to K'far Nahum to deprive the broken-hearted of their consolation and the poor of their hope?"

Simon's house and yard where he lived with his wife and mother-in-law were a typical fisherman's establishment, built a good way outside the town on the road to Bethsaida hard by the shore of Genesaret. Several small boats, belonging to the Zebedee brothers, were moored on the strand. The brothers had sailed them to K'far Nahum and with their mother, Shoshannah, had moved into Simon's house as soon as they had made their resolve to join the company of the new rabbi.

Strung from a few withered fig trees, nets were drying in the sun, and fishing gear, with discarded oars, planks, and barrels lay strewn unattended on the beach. Here in the shade of a large palm the brothers had built a shed to hold their nets and tackle. The house itself was set a hundred or so paces inland, beyond the range of the tide which lapped fiercely in stormy weather. It was not one of the better dwellings—merely a wooden structure roofed with plaited bamboo stems and palm mats, and so low that it could not be seen from the other side of the knoll on whose slope it was built.

A multitude of people filled the yard. It needed long and patient effort before Yeshua's family, with Miriam at their head, could squeeze their way in, for the tide of people spilled over at the gate and overflowed the roadway that ran with the beach. They reached the inside of the court at last, but were immediately pinned in a corner and from that moment found it impossible to make any further move toward the house. A solid wall of bodies hemmed them in, and all faces were turned to the little house that barely showed above the heads of the multitude. The crowd stirred restlessly, against the pressure of confinement. Here and there a bier with a sick man upon it was reared high above the throng by powerful hairy arms and edged inch by inch toward the little house on the knoll. A mother with a sick child astride her shoulders clawed a passage through the crowd, succeeded a little way, and was jammed in a crush too dense to permit further progress. Miriam, too, with all her family, felt as though immured within a wall of bodies.

Suddenly an agitated murmur run through the crowd. The waiting mass unfroze and stirred; shouts rose and names were called out in a dozen languages. Then again all subsided into a hush deeper than before.

Someone must have recognized her—though it was not possible to tell where the word had first been given. But the news that had so moved the multitude was that the seer's mother had arrived in their midst and, with her, his brothers and entire family.

Miriam saw the confined crowd trying to roll away before her, and soon there was a narrow vacant swath all the way to the house.

Meanwhile the report of her presence had galloped ahead and, before Miriam's party could take more than a few steps, had reached the point to which they all were straining, the unseen point below the palm roof of the house where the prophet was known to be standing. They stopped to wait awhile, Miriam, her sister and brother-in-law, her children and grandchildren—all waiting for Yeshua to hear the news. The crowd waited with them, standing off to allow a space about Miriam's small group. The eyes of the multitude were turned alternately on them and on the little house from which now, any moment, the prophet would emerge. Forsaking his disciples he would issue in his white cloak to hail and make his mother welcome in his house. Nearest the house the lane widened to give the rabbi room, for those that stood in his vicinity had heard them say to him: "Your mother and your brothers stand without." The crowd pressed back and the shout went up to make way for the mother. . . . The cries died down and a new silence drifted back from the house. The white cloak did not appear. Instead, there was suddenly the form of Taddi, the old tanner, trying to push through to the mother. Then he too stopped and everything became still and motionless.

A low whisper went through the multitude. The message ran from man to man which no one wished to tell aloud. Yet in a trice it had been heard by all, and all looked with sorrow and compassion on the mother. For they knew that the rabbi, being told of her visit and that she was waiting to see him, had made no move but had asked his disciples:

"Who, think you, is my mother, and who my brothers and sisters?"—And with a sweep of his hand that took in all that sat with him, he rendered his own answer: "They that do the will of God are my brothers; they are my sisters and my mother."

Shocked and incredulous, the crowd repeated the prophet's words, softly at first, as though to spare the mother. But the whisper waxed and multiplied as it rolled back from the mound, and near the walls of the yard unabashed voices cried aloud:

"He will not see his mother!"

"He has renounced his brothers!"

"Only they who do the will of God, he says, shall be his family."

"And does his mother sin against the will of God?"

The crowd watched Miriam to see if she had heard the sentence that rejected her. Miriam had heard it clearly. She stood with lowered head in the forlorn circle of her family. Cleophas and the brothers looked hopelessly for reassurance to each other. The crowd still stood away, waiting to see what they would do. Would the mother nevertheless go to her son? She seemed too still, too crushed for any such intention. And neither she nor her sons said a word. The brothers, it appeared, could not believe that they had heard aright. Their unbelief spread to the crowd and once again the multitude stirred faintly, as when the wind ripples the lake, and voices said:

"Can it be that he leaves his mother outside?"

In the congestion of women and children that thronged all about, Miriam now spied the Canaanite woman with the blind boy at her side. Looking at her, Miriam raised her head and smiled and said:

"Why so pale, my daughter, and why do you look so fearful?"

And the strange woman replied:

"Shall I not be troubled seeing that the seer will not admit his own mother? How can I, who am a stranger, expect help from him for my child?"

"Have you not heard, daughter, what the rabbi said?—'All they that do the will of God shall be my sisters'? Go up to him and he will heal your child."

"I? I should go to him?" asked the Canaanite in a sudden panic.

"Yes, you," Miriam said soothingly. "You are more to him than his own mother, for you believe in him. Go to him; go. The rabbi waits for you."

And taking her gently by the shoulders, Miriam turned her round and sent her through the lane that still wound upward through the press. And when the woman had walked a few paces, down came the old tanner and took her by the hand to guide her into the rabbi's presence.

"Look!" said the voices in the crowd. "He spurns his mother but the stranger is called!"

And while still they gazed in pity at the humiliated mother and her house, they saw Miriam suddenly on her knees and heard her crying out in a loud joyful voice:

"Glory to God in the highest! For He has turned my sorrow into joy and my lowliness has He exalted. He brought me to the verge of the abyss that I might better see His light. Lord, in this child of my womb Thou hast vouchsafed a new birth unto man, to be born into Thy will. In him all must be born anew, even his mother, even his brothers and sisters. For there are no inequalities before Thee, O Lord, and all who do Thy will are kinsmen to my son. My son's family shall be mine also."—And Miriam raised her arms to the house on the mound and said humbly in a breaking voice: "Yeshua, my son, take your mother into your family as you take all these others."

Then Miriam's sister Mariama knelt at her side and called out also:

"And take me too, that I may be as one of them who do the will of God."

In the hearts of the multitude the words of Miriam and Mariama kindled a new hope. His mother had said that every man and woman of them could be of the prophet's family. They must only do the will of God to be his brothers and sisters, more than his own flesh and blood. And they were seized in a great longing, and the women who were mothers brought their children forward and thronged about the prophet's mother. They forgot what sores and grief had brought them to this place; they wept and saw only the light of the grace to come. Yearning filled their souls, and their lips trembled in the desire for the new kinship which the prophet's mother had proclaimed!

CHAPTER XIII

YESHUA's rejection of his family, and his professed adherence to the family of those who do the will of God, made a profound impression on the brothers. The fact that he had admitted an unknown Canaanite rather than his own beloved and honored mother was proof to them that their bond of flesh with the new prophet was no longer valid and that their brother's message was not the familiar lore of the rabbis but a new creed to which every man must aspire by his own merit and belief. Every man must pass through the gate which Yeshua had opened to the kingdom of heaven, and Yeshua stood on the threshold admitting only such as did the will of God. He knew no favorites; all men were equal in his sight; all had a right to pass if only they were willing to shoulder the yoke of the kingdom of heaven. And those who were not willing, though they were of his own flesh, were cast away.

At one stroke, Yeshua's unexpected conduct in K'far Nahum had lifted him above his family circle. And now the brothers wondered how they could ever have thought to influence him, or even command his return to Nazareth. Clearly, Yeshua's authority derived from higher sources than loyalty of kinship could control. He had been sent with God-framed powers to reign and judge on earth.

The first of the family who went to join his following was Mariama. She had wanted to stay behind at once and had returned to Nazareth only to bring her sister home. She now perceived that Yeshua—or Miriam's son, as she still called him—had, from some hidden motive, forbidden Miriam to be near him.

Before departing for K'far Nahum Mariama came a last time to bid Miriam farewell. And Miriam said to her:

"Go you, Mariama, and take my place at his side. Watch over him and attend to his wants as I did wish to do."

Then Miriam gave her sister Yeshua's warm coat which he had left behind and begged her to make sure that he would take it whenever he might have to sleep under the open sky.

"Mariama," she said, "I place in your hands all the tenderness I bear him. My hands will be in all you do for him, till the day he sends for his mother."

With that she kissed Mariama and they took leave of each other.

Jacob was the first of the brothers to follow Mariama's lead. He recognized now that Yeshua's boon could not be valued by the touchstone of the Law. In his eyes, too, Yeshua had ceased to be merely the first-born son of his mother; he had become the master who required total submission.

Joses and Simon followed soon after; as matters stood, there was little enough in Nazareth to hold them back. But even Jude, the learned Pharisee, was swayed. For Yeshua's fame was bounding free throughout the country, and it had come to Jude's ears that not illiterates alone, but many scholars, scribes, and Pharisees had joined his following. His teachings, widely quoted at scholarly meetings, were everywhere received with astonishment and even awe. No one could explain how the joiner's son had come by so much learning, unless one believed the popular fable that he was taught during the nights by Moses and Elijah and a host of seraphim. Jude realized that the time was past when he could remain aloof. A stand had to be taken for Yeshua or against. Jude, as the scholar of the Hanan clan, decided to join with his brother. After long wrangling hours he even prevailed on his old uncle Cleophas to close his shop and follow his wife into the new brotherhood which Yeshua had formed. He put it to him that the pride and unity of their house required his participation. For even if Yeshua had chosen to repudiate every family bond, the new "prophet" could not unmake the fact of his origin, which, as everybody knew, was this same house of Hanan. With this appeal to Cleophas's cardinal passion, Jude had his way with the old man and they set out together for K'far Nahum.

Nor were Yeshua's kinsmen alone in leaving their home town for the new congregation that was founding in K'far Nahum; there were Nazarenes from all walks of life, even some of those who had been among his bitterest opponents. It was known in the town that Yeshua had refused a welcome to his mother and that he had cut every tie with his family. And if at first this latest report fanned the resentment against him, it served at the same time to lift him above the narrow circle in which the feelings of the Nazarenes had held him confined. They had been blind to the prophet in the man because they knew him too well as one of their own. Now, with the repudiation of his family, Yeshua cut a very different figure in the view of those who had belittled him merely because they had known him as a child. No longer did they see him as the son of the late joiner. Perhaps he was indeed a prophet delegated by the Supreme Power to bring down the kingdom of heaven, even as he said himself. And he was making no favorites of kinsmen or compatriots; all men were equal in his sight, for he had come not to Nazareth only but to all Israel. And this was why the multitudes flocked to him from every Jewish province, to find in him their cure and succor. And furthermore, the Nazarenes admitted that the spate of Yeshua's miracles, witnessed by increasing thousands, could no longer be disposed of with doubt or derision. Had he not fed and satisfied five thousand with five barley loaves and two small fishes? And the people came to him not from the Jewish provinces alone, but likewise from Tyre and Sidon, from Transjordan and from beyond Genesaret, the cities of the Greeks. For they had all heard in what manner Yeshua had raised the nobleman's child that was at the point of death in K'far Nahum. And this he had done for the glory of God, forasmuch as the nobleman became a lover of the Jews and built a synagogue out of his own substance. It was whispered that even Pharisees came by stealth to dispute with him, and not a few stayed to enlist with his followers. Should Nazareth be rated a city of laggards, the last to recognize a prophet? Yeshua was, after all, a Nazarene; it was their town that had reared Israel's new prophet.

Even the men of the house of Pinhas, the most dogged haters of the house of Hanan, were making overtures of peace. Some of them were plagued in conscience. The fear of God fell on them whenever they recalled how they had mortified their townsman Yeshua and his old mother. What if he were indeed what people called him? Then they had laid hands on the elect of the Lord.

One day—Miriam was working in her vegetable garden—she saw a man circling awkwardly about the house, taking a step forward only to retract, as though he did not trust himself closer. Miriam took him for a wandering stranger, in search of food or sleeping quarters or a drink of water, and she approached to ask him into her house.

And it was when she came near him that the stranger fell upon his knees and held his arms before his face as if to ward her off, and he said in a quaking voice:

"Mother, have mercy on my soul."

Miriam stopped and gaped. The man was powerfully built, but trembling like a wind-struck reed. His hands shook as with the palsy and a gloss of cold sweat lay on his brow and cheeks.

"Arise, my son," said Miriam. "I will help you if I can. Are you hungry?"

"I am hungry for forgiveness," cried the stranger. "My entrails roar for the bread of penitence."

"Then tell me what you want of me, my son. How can I help?"

"I heard you in K'far Nahum when you proclaimed the new kinship of your son. Pray for me, mother, that I also be admitted!"

"The gate is open to all who believe," Miriam said.

"Not for me, mother!"

"Why not for you, my son?"

"You do not recognize me, then?"

"I have seen you before this," said Miriam. "Your face I know, but not your name."

"I am he who carried your son to the verge of the precipice. My name is Matthew, son of Hanah. They call me insolent."

"And you want to be of my son's family?"

"I do; did I not see the angels spread their wings to receive your son when I had brought him to the brink? It was then I was seized by the fear of the Lord, and now my arms are as useless stumps and my hands have lost their cunning. The fear of God freezes my limbs. I start at every shadow and my sleepless nights are hounded by bad visitations. I did go to K'far Nahum to throw myself at his feet and implore his pardon. For days on end I stood in the throng and could not reach him because the spirits paralyzed my tread. Then I saw you and heard your speech. Mother, forgive me and let me be among the kindred of your son."

"It is not for me to admit you. Go to him who was sent."

"But I fear him, mother. When I come the gate will clash to."

"He leaves it open for all men, my son. Your fear of God will wipe your sins away, even as my hand wipes your tears." Then, as she withdrew her hand from Matthew's face, she added: "From this day you shall be dear to me, even as my son."

For she saw in Matthew's appearance a sign from Yeshua, that he had sent the man to comfort and to strengthen her in her extremity.

Miriam remained alone in Nazareth. She lived on in her small

403

house, spending her days in prayer and anxiety and waiting for the sign that would allow her to rejoin her son.

God had not soothed her spirit, nor averted the sword that now pierced her soul. Miriam found no ease in her sacrifice but suffered the full torment of the love which bound her to her son. She could not rise above her fears for Yeshua's safety, but she understood now that her fall to earthly motherhood was her elevation. It was not the hand of Satan making her a stumbling block in the path of her son, but the highest grace with which the Lord had blessed her.

No messengers came to her and no sign appeared through the long weeks and months that followed. Miriam knew of the women who were ministering to her son. She did not envy them, not even Mariama who was so near to his table. She knew that Yeshua had left her alone so that she might prepare herself and, with love and submission, make her sacrifice a freewill offering to God.

Matthew ben Hanah was her only visitor. He who had been the most tenacious enemy of the house of Hanan, who had stirred up his comrades against Yeshua since their first day at school, had now become the staunchest friend of Yeshua's aged, lonely mother. And was not this a sign of grace, that God had appointed her a new protector among the former persecutors of her son? Matthew became her champion and her intimate while Yeshua was spreading the Messianic word in the towns of Galilee. He became as a son to her, helped her to till the ground of her field, tended her stock, conducted her business in the market, and ministered to her least wants. He came each evening without fail to bring her whatever good news of her son he had been able to pick up. And each Sabbath in the synagogue, before listeners both willing and unwilling, he told how he had seen a host of angels spread pinions to break Yeshua's fall while he, Matthew the insolent, was holding the Messiah over the "mouth of destruction." And there had been one mighty seraph whose wings had clothed him like a full panoply and he had looked at Matthew as if to scorch his soul. What wonder, then, that he recognized Yeshua as God's elect; that he protected and catered to Yeshua's mother who had borne the salvation of the world?

The neighbors could not understand how such a change had come over the man. Often, as Matthew wandered about the town, the Nazarenes shook their heads and said: "Poor Matthew Saucebox has lost his wits."

Since her return from K'far Nahum Miriam had been weaving a cloak for Yeshua. Whether she thought that it would clothe him at his entry into Jerusalem and be the dress of his glory, Miriam did not ask herself. Her labor at the loom was an expression of her need to be associated with her son in deed as well as in thought. If she could not tend him in person, she could at least weave the garments he would wear. The chest in the corner of her chamber contained many of the clothes she had made him in the years past. Now, in her solitary evenings, she sometimes raised the lid and, gazing at the various fabrics, recalled the visions and the hopes that had gone into their texture. She remembered the occasion of each garment. This was the coat he wore when he first went to school; this other, made of shining white, had covered him on his first pilgrimage with her and Joseph to the Temple in Jerusalem. She would never forget the sight of him, standing among the sages in the Temple court, disputing with them of the Law. And here was the shirt of many colors which she put on him the day he was presented in the synagogue. It still showed where it had creased and folded about his little body, and Miriam remembered his bright childish voice answering "amen" to his preceptor.

The visions of those nocturnal hours at the loom returned. Into one tunic she had woven the dream of Jacob at Bethel, and once again she saw the ladder set up on the earth and the top of it reaching to heaven, and the angels of God ascending and descending. Into this other dress she had woven Rebecca's love for her son Jacob; or her vision of the young David grazing Jesse's flock while he fingered his flute.

There were other thoughts and visions that came to her now in the weaving of this last cloak. This was the garment she would take to her son when her time came to rejoin him. She would make it of a piece, without seams, she thought; like the shirt Isaac's mother put upon her child when he went with his father

405

to Moriah to be offered up; like the coat of many colors which the sons brought torn and gory to the aged Jacob. And as she interlaced the yarns she heard the voice of Rachel rising from her grave.

Lovingly she caressed her visions in her heart and wove them into Yeshua's dress, together with the Psalms that poured from her lips: "In my distress I called upon the Lord, and cried out unto my God . . . He heard my voice out of His temple, and my cry came before Him, even into His ears . . ." And from the strength of the Psalms she drew new hope like water from a well.

In the day when Yeshua approached the gates of Jerusalem, Jochanan, son of Zebedee, appeared suddenly on her threshold.

"Woman, your time has come! Arise and go with me toward Jerusalem!"

Miriam's heart leapt in her breast and she turned sharply to Jochanan. He was barefoot, and his black coat was daggled with the dust and mire of the road. His short beard was black as pitch, and his eyes flashed with excitement.

Miriam obeyed. She took the cloak she had made for her son and went with Jochanan.

CHAPTER XIV

UNDER his black coat, so it seemed to Miriam, Jochanan concealed both wings and a sword; he was to her as the angel of judgment. But why of judgment rather than mercy? Because Miriam sensed that Jochanan waited only for the day of doom. It was strange to think that he was Yeshua's favorite disciple.

But could she be sure that her thoughts of Jochanan were not dictated by her jealousy of Yeshua's love? She had long known that of all the disciples Jochanan was closest to her son. More, the fact that Yeshua had sent him rather than one of his own brothers, that he had chosen Jochanan in preference to Zebedee's other son, the peaceable Jacob whom Miriam loved so well, was proof surely that Yeshua wanted his mother to turn her love to Jochanan, that she might learn to accept judgment and not mercy and come to cherish the sword which Jochanan bore under his cloak.

Miriam recoiled from the thought as though a snake had stung her. Must it be so? Could that which was about to pass not be averted?

Why was grace given to Sarah's son when God tempered judgment with mercy and the seed of Abraham was saved from under the knife? Why could not the same miracle occur again? Like Abraham she would lead her sacrifice to the altar, but at the ultimate moment God would send His angel to point to the scapegoat. A thousand times Miriam was convinced that Yeshua's sacrifice could not be evaded; a thousand times she hoped again for the intervention that would save him from death.

They were going forward at a brisk pace, Jochanan leading the way. His massive trunk cast a bold shadow on the road. He never spoke, Miriam thought, though he served her willingly and well. Sometimes she caught him talking to himself, and what she heard were visions spoken of in enigmatic symbols. Miriam knew him to be a habitual visionary; from his nonage he had been at ease with mysterious apparitions.

When they reached the heights of Mount Scopus, whence Jerusalem could be seen in the distance, her guide stopped. It was early morning and the sun was up over the Holy City. Far away its white façades basked in the young light, and the gold and bronzen turrets of the Temple gates gleamed on the hill of Moriah. They were both gazing at the city, and then it was Jochanan who spoke:

"Woman," he said, "see you what I see over Jerusalem?"

"What do you see, Jochanan?" asked Miriam.

"I see what Moses saw in the desert. But it is not a burning bush; it is a lamb. All the mountains of the earth strain toward Mount Moriah. But Moriah soars above them all, and on it stands the House of God, and high upon its dome I see a fiery altar, the stone of Moriah. And on the altar stands God's sacrifice and it burns and burns with fire and is not consumed."

407

Miriam paled.

"What is this sacrifice, Jochanan?"

"It is the lamb of God that burns unconsumed in perpetual fire."

Miriam lowered her head to hide her tears and said softly, as if to herself:

"Must it be sacrificed, then?"

"The word of the Prophet must be fulfilled: 'He is brought as a lamb to the slaughter.' Before the world was made, before these mountains were founded, God had readied this sacrifice for the world. His destiny was limned by God's own hand before the frontier between heaven and earth was drawn. Such was the Lord's design and it may not be changed."

"Except God change it!" Miriam exclaimed. "For there is none that can compel His hand or confine His mercy. Who can call Him to judgment? He saves the fledgling bird from the mouth of the lion; He protects the calf from the eagle's talons; He extricates the toad from the coils of the snake—shall He not send His angel to stay the sword that threatens the sacrifice? He appoints and He alters the seasons and the ways of the world, and none may cavil with Him or command His decisions. He will order the fate of my son. In the fateful hour He will send His seraphim and revoke the sentence that was fixed of old. He will take my son to sit at His right hand, as He foretold through the mouth of David the King. My son will ascend into heaven, like Elijah, on a fiery cloud."

"Think you then that he will die the death of Elijah, he of whom the Prophet said that his grave should be with the wicked and that he should be despised and rejected of men? For whose sins think you he will die? Not for his own, but for ours. It is for our transgressions that he will be wounded. And so that every man may have a share in him—and through him in our heavenly Father—he has, in love and humility, elected the death of the wicked. How can the wicked ascend into heaven like Elijah?"

"Did not God make Aaron's rod to yield blossoms and almonds? The Lord makes and unmakes; He orders and alters the course of the world. Shall He not be able to take away the sins of the world without the blood of my child?"

408

"He shall sooner command the morning star to sink into darkness; He shall reverse the course of the planets before the ordinance of His Messiah is diminished by so much as one jot. Your son dies to bring eternal life to men. Your son dies to make death perish, to disarm the angel of death and bestow on our mortal flesh the life of the spirit."

"Now, Jochanan, do I perceive your love for my son," she said. "It is the love of the spirit, the love of the strong, and I see that it is mightier than death. But mine is a mother's love for her child. I am only flesh and blood and I shall never give him up. I shall wrestle for him as Jacob wrestled with the angel. And though God swoop upon me like an eagle to wrest him from my arms, He shall cleave my heart before He reach him, and even then, with my heart cleft in twain, I shall still hold to him."

Jochanan arose briskly and called out:

"Woman, would you cross the will of God? Know you not that you are but the vessel wherein God raised the Saviour of Israel and mankind? Know you not that God can break the vessel at His pleasure?"

"Let Him break me then. But I know that my free will is part of the sacrifice. Without me there can be no offering. And I shall not surrender him but on compulsion."

"Will you hinder the salvation, woman? Know you not wherefore your son was made?"

"Son of Zebedee," said Miriam sternly, "I am the mother of this child. I bore him in my womb. I saw his glory ere it was revealed, and I do see him now; but not as a lamb prepared for the slaughter. For the skies above the Temple have opened for me also and I behold my son in the fullness of his glory, riding with the clouds of heaven. His raiment is as molten silver flashing in the sun. On his head is the crown of David, the blessings of the Patriarchs harness his body, and in his hand is the authority of God. He gathers together the nations of the world, but not with the sword and not with fire, but with the Holy Spirit as it rests on him. For me also, Jochanan, the clouds mass over Jerusalem. I see them now opening deep into a well and sending forth a mighty torrent. These are the waters of salvation. And I see my son. Salvation's cup is in his hand and he gives the nations of the world to drink."

"Blessed woman!" exclaimed Jochanan. "The Lord has shown you great mercy, for on the wings of His angels He has borne you over the pit of hell to spare you the sight of your son's agony, and He has set you down in the place of glory which is on the yonder side of the pit."

Miriam, hearing these words, whitened like the sand at her feet, and her heart grew heavy. She sank upon the ground and wept with outspread hands:

"Not this, Father in heaven, not this. Have pity on Thy hand-maid, separate me not from my child, and spare me no grief. Let me descend with him in his humiliation before Thou lettest him depart this earth. And cast me not from before Thy sight."

CHAPTER XV

MIRIAM was a woman in her early fifties when she came to Jerusalem. Throughout her years with Yeshua in Nazareth God in His mercy had preserved her beauty and the freshness of her youth. During this last year, since her son's going forth, age had struck her without ruth or warning. It was a heavy-laden Naomi that Jochanan led through the streets of the city.

The day was Thursday, before the eve of the Passover. Miriam carried a small bundle of things she was bringing her son—the cloak without seams she had been weaving these past months and a cruse of clear oil for his hair; and, in a gourd bottle tied to the bundle, wine for the consecration of the feast.

The narrow streets were dense with pilgrims and Jochanan had to jostle for every inch of passage. No feast in the past had drawn such multitudes of pilgrims to Jerusalem. A turbulent mob filled every avenue and rendered every street almost impassable. Overhead, men crowded walls and windows, hung from each balcony and cornice. Even the flat roofs were populated and decked out with sleeping mats and tents, and the porches of the rich were besieged by camping families in scores and in hundreds.

Everywhere the Galileans stood out from the crowd. Theirs was a larger contingent than in any year previous. If the hosts of foreign pilgrims from Egypt and Babylon preened themselves in the chromatic exuberance of their outlandish costumes—but added only to the general profusion of color, the Galileans were the more conspicuous for their unruly beards and coarse gray peasant sacks. Furthermore, these northern farmers began to celebrate the Passover a day before the rest of Jewry. The eve was held by them to be as good as the feast, and so one could not turn without seeing groups or families of excited Galileans going busily about their preparations for the holiday.

To Miriam, struggling behind Jochanan through the crowds, it seemed that all of this vast confluence of pilgrims was gathered here for the sake of her son. She thought the people knew what great events were pending on this feast day in the Holy City, as though angelic heralds had roused them from their homes to hasten to Jerusalem and become witnesses of her son's glory. She saw strain and tension written in every face, impelling every movement, even that of the Roman legionaries who patrolled the streets. The Procurator's forces were streaming in at every city gate, their columns thrusting like spears through the recoiling crowds, driving the people from the thoroughfares and packing them more tightly in the by-streets. And Miriam caught a glimpse of the notorious Ascalonian cohort which Pontius Pilate had brought down for the festival season to reinforce the cohorts stationed in the fastness of the Antonia.

The congestion of the pilgrims, the ceaseless tumult, and the agitation caused by armed soldiers in the crowd—all this, Miriam felt, must have a bearing on her son, and the thought made her heart beat faster.

It was in a high state of excitement that she finally reached the house of Joanna, the wife of the Herodian official, where the women who had come with Yeshua from Galilee were staying. Her sister Mariama, Shoshannah, Zebedee's widow, and several other women were waiting to welcome her. Mariama, at seeing her, burst into tears and began to kiss her hands. The others roused and bestirred themselves to wash her feet and regale her with food. And Miriam thanked them but declined to eat; she was too anxious, she explained apologetically, to hear about her son—where he resided and how he had fared in Jerusalem.

Mariama began to answer her questions. She said that Yeshua and his disciples spent their days in the Temple, where Yeshua preached to the people and apprised them of his mission. Great numbers, she said, gathered about him to drink up his message, cherishing his every word as sheer gospel. At night they retired to the Mount of Olives and slept in the house of Simon the Leper in Bethany. In this inconspicuous hamlet, among the bare Judaean hills on the fringe of the desert, they need fear no intrusion. Raids were not likely in this out-of-way spot, though it was best to be prepared since Yeshua had openly challenged the administration of the Temple and the rule of Hanan and Caiaphas when he drove the chandlers and money changers out of the Temple court. No, said Mariama, in answer to Miriam's query, the womenfolk did not often see the men, though they went from time to time to Bethany to look after the rabbi's wants and that of his group.

Then the other women joined in the telling, and the mother heard how Yeshua had entered Jerusalem riding an ass richly caparisoned, and how the people had hailed him with branches and wreaths and cries of "Hosanna" and "Son of David"; how he had cast out all them that sold and bought in the Temple and had publicly rebuked the learned and the Sadducees and the officers of the priesthood; and of the Temple itself he had said that he could destroy it and build it up again within three days— for which blasphemy the officers of the Temple sought to arrest him and bring him to trial, but would not, for fear of the populace which thronged about him as soon as ever he appeared within its courts.

It was manifest from the description of the women that the day of her son's glory was approaching at last. It could be tomorrow, or the following day, and Yeshua was making ready. He was taking leave of his disciples and preparing to depart; and he had warned them that they too would drink of his cup.

412

For the first time Miriam now saw the woman of whom she had heard so much, the woman Yeshua had cleansed of seven devils, who had repented of her former life and joined the womenfolk who served the rabbi. They called her Miriam of Magdala. Miriam was told that once, in the leper's house, the Magdalene had opened a treasured alabaster box of ointment to anoint the master's feet. One of the disciples had chided her a wastrel, seeing that the precious spikenard might have been sold for three hundred pence and the money given to the poor. But the master had upheld her, saying: "Let her alone; against the day of my burial has she anointed me."

Miriam listened silently. But at the word "burial" she winced as though a knife had been sunk into her heart.

Miriam had no sooner rested herself than she arose to go into the Temple. For her heart was filled with anxiety and she wanted to stand alone before God as she had done in former years when she was young. Leaving Joanna's house, she went unaccompanied to the Court of the Women and there knelt down in the face of the Sanctuary.

Ashamed and contrite for crossing the will of God, she saw nothing of the crowd about her. Even the excited preparations for the paschal sacrifice escaped her attention, though priests and Levites moved to and fro in their white vestments. Miriam was utterly absorbed in the world of her fears, seeing only a rose glow in her closed eyelids. She felt too heavily oppressed with guilt to call on God's name or importune Him with a sinner's prayer. She hid her head and murmured, not her own entreaty, but the words of David:

"Hide not Thy face from me, O Lord. My heart is smitten and withered like grass, so that I forget to eat my bread, because of Thy indignation and Thy wrath. For Thou hast lifted me up and cast me down. My days are like a shadow that declineth and I am withered like grass."

But even as the Psalm fell from her lips, her heart swelled with the prayer she did not dare to voice:

"Father in heaven, leave me to bear the burden Thou hast ordained for him. Spare me no trials and sever me not from my

413

child. Behold, all things are possible with Thee. Thou canst carry him safe over the precipice, even as Thou borest me when I did fall."

And she called on the holy matron of Jewry to intercede for her:

"Have pity, Rachel, mother of Israel, beloved wife of Jacob; thou who knowest the throes of birth and didst die aborning, plead for me. And plead for me, all who are mothers on earth. And beasts of the field, in whom God planted the devotion of motherhood, pray for me.

"If Thy will must be done, O Lord, and the world cannot be redeemed but by the blood of my child, I pray Thee, Father, let me stand by his altar. Stripped of Thy grace, let me be no more than his mother."

Miriam sank down exhausted on the ground. The roar of the multitude had abated. For a moment she wondered at the sudden stillness. She roused herself and looked about: the vast rectangle of the women's court was deserted.

From behind the hills of Moab the departing sun sent back its rays to strike white fire from the silver-threaded curtains that lined the stairways of the Temple. A crew of Levites was preparing to swing to the heavy bronze wings of the Beautiful Gate which, with a blinding gleam of gold, responded to the setting sun. Any moment now the Gate would be locked fast and she would be shut within the Temple court. Had she been overlooked by the watchman? There was no one abroad but her. How beautiful and holy did this place grow in silence! With reluctance in the pace of her movements she turned to pass the Gate before its bolting, and it was then that she beheld the remembered form of a woman standing near her in a veiling of black.

The figure seemed to Miriam so familiar, so much more intimate and homely than her own mother would have seemed to her at this moment of despair, that she cried out without halting:

"Rachel, Rachel, have pity! You have come in my hour of need. Pray for me, Mother Rachel!" And Miriam made no effort to check the flow of her tears while she heard the words of the dark woman:

"Be comforted, my child, for you shall be greatly blessed. This

414

is the night of temptation, the last span to Moriah where Isaac's stone lies ready for the sacrifice. For a little I will go with you, for like you I am the mother of the child. You and I were elected to taste every mother's sorrow. Are you ready, child?"

"I have prayed God to let me be only the mother of my son," said Miriam softly.

"Your prayer was heard," said the veiled woman. "You shall be spared no pain. Your heart shall be the sponge of your son's agony. Brace yourself for your holy office, child, for in your motherhood you shall be lifted above the heavens and their hosts, wearing the raiments of mercy. Come, you shall see the souls that hunger for your love."

And as the woman went before, Miriam followed her out of the sight of the first watch of priests who now issued from the Tabernacle with ram's horns and torches in their hands. For a moment Miriam thought that she was entering one of the fabled underground caverns of the Temple. But the walls of the cave yielded to her vision and she looked across a wide expanse of meadowland.

Twilight hung over the field and Miriam saw it sparkling with innumerable lights—will-o'-the-wisps, she thought, arrested and rooted like an infinity of luminous flowers. She felt the air softly fanned by their music that rose in a sweet exhalation to the sky. And the sky too was sown with singing stars whose melody descended even as the other soared. And they blended—the light of the stars of the earth even with the lights of heaven.

And it was when Rachel and Miriam set foot on the lea, that the chant of the earth lights waxed mightily and sounded with a stormy longing that tore at the heart, like the unbridled joy of a child seeing its mother return after an absence.

And the two mothers went their way over the meadow till they came to the fringe of a river. Its waters flowed limpid and clear, even as molten crystal, and made no ripples as they ran. A sweet fragrance rose up from its surface, permeated through the ether, and stole slowly into Miriam's heart, transmuting her base substance so that she thought herself ascending like a prayer disembodied into heaven.

"Speak to me, Mother," she begged, "where am I, what are

415

these lights I see; what means this chant, and what this heady fragrance which seems to wing my being so that I cannot feel the ground under my feet?"

Then Miriam's hand was taken and the woman's voice said:

"Come, child, we will sit together by this bank and you shall hear:

"The name of this place is called the green pastures whereof your father David sang. Hither God leads His righteous and His saints. The lights you see, they are the souls of the righteous, and they are brought to Him by me when their time comes to quit the flesh which they indwell for a brief span while they walk upon earth. The chant you hear is their yearning for the Holiness in the Highest to which they seek attachment. The song of the stars on high, it also is the yearning of these earthly souls, for the Holiness which is their common desire was shared out between heaven and earth and shall not meet in harmony until the King-Messiah comes. Till that day they faint for communion, and the chant of their longing which ascends and descends begets every good and noble thought that fills the space between the earth and heaven. And these still waters at our feet, they are the tears of unknown, righteous men, of all who languish after God while they are living, of all who suffer and bear tribulations or are hounded and bruised for the glory of God. They are the tears of children torn from their mothers, and of mothers weeping for their young. All these tears, gathered up by God, flow in this brook which waters the green pastures.

"And the sweet fragrance of these waters is the compassion which these tears awaken in the heights of the heavens. For the waters of this river flow into the other world and, when they reach the throne of glory, rouse the pity of the Lord who answers them with grace—and this is the fragrance which fills all the air. For whosoever has drawn breath standing by these tears, his compassion is aroused and mercy is born in his heart."

There was a silence while Miriam gazed at the still flow of the brook. Then the other continued:

"My child, I too wished to be no more than a mother. But when Jacob came to Padan-aram and, single-handed, rolled the stone from the well's mouth to water my flock, he lifted the stone that

416

lay over the mouth of the future, revealing to me all the destinies of Israel unto the end of days. And when he kissed my mouth and lifted up his voice and wept, his tears in me quickened the springs of compassion. In his tears I forefelt the agony of Israel, gored like a lamb by the beasts of the field, driven from exile to exile. In his sobs I heard Israel treading the way of its sorrows unto the day of redemption. For Jacob wept with the tears of a father and sanctified me to be the mother of Israel's grief. And thus was I made the mother of the children of Israel.

"For you also, Miriam, God has prepared a motherhood of many, for you shall be mother to the nations of the world that wait to come under the wings of the faith. God in His mercy has let salvation come to the Gentiles—through the fruit of your womb, the guerdon of your motherhood. Now, Miriam, you shall see the souls that wait for you."

And in a moment of time Miriam saw the meadowland give way to a deep valley through which clouds of heavy vapor wallowed and rolled. And when her eyes had grown accustomed to the haze, she discerned, beneath the nether sky of smoke, a multitude of human faces; some ground and furrowed by old age, with red-smouldering eyes, some young but pain-distorted; faces of women with eyes set in sunken tear-wells, and faces of children, puffs of nameless flesh; wherever Miriam cast her eye—the dappled swamp of human faces, numberless, beyond compute. No bodies could be seen, they being steeped as in a quagmire of smoke. But their eyes stared up at her, converged on her like burning shafts. My God, my God, how many eyes! As though the earth were sown with eyes! They gaped at Miriam, raw and dilated, and struck against her heart like muted cries.

"They also wait to be saved," said the dark voice at her side. "They are dumb in their tongues for they have not the word of God in their hearts, and no other language in these fields is audible. Their bodies are caught in the nets spun by their pagan gods; they stick in the dark filth of their idolatries. But the spark of God flickers in their souls and speaks out from their eyes. They await the redemption which is in your son Yeshua. Would you, daughter, deny them his grace?"

417

"God forbid!"—and Miriam fell on her face and cried: "Father in heaven, be it as Thou wilt!"

She did not know how long she lay thus on the ground. No word came from the other, and a heavy silence settled on the earth. She thought sound itself had died in a deaf world and every motion ceased, as though never to move again. Then, through the muted void, one voice lifted in prayer:

"*Abba,* Father, if it be possible, let this cup pass from me. . . ."

"It is the voice of my child!" Miriam cried. "My child is in agony. I must be with him."

"You shall be with him. You shall see and hear. Your heart shall break and your lips shall be silent."

And when Miriam next opened her eyes she found herself among the cypress trees that skirt the Gethsemane orchard at the foot of Olivet.

Miriam saw the garden through a trellis of trees. It lay softly laved under the starlight. In one corner of the garden she saw her son clothed in the white seamless cloak she had brought for the day of his glory, but it was soaked through by the sweat of agony. He was kneeling, with his head sunk on his chest. Near him, resting between clumps of bushes, the disciples sprawled on the ground—sleeping, as it seemed to Miriam. But not the disciples only—all creation seemed to her caught in the web which sleep and gloom had spread upon it. This night in Gethsemane no one was waking with the son but the heart of the mother. And through the screen of cypresses which separated Miriam from the garden, she heard Yeshua's voice fading at her ear:

"Nevertheless, not as I will, but as Thou wilt."

Which Miriam, softly, repeated after her son:

"Not as I will, but as Thou wilt."

And the ground at that moment trembling under her feet, she heard from afar the thud of men marching and the clang of spears.

Miriam turned sharply. The dark form of her guide blended with the night; only the voice sounded once more:

"Henceforth go your way alone, Miriam, daughter of Hanan. The trial of your motherhood is now."

CHAPTER XVI

GOLGOTHA was quiet again. The crowd that had followed the condemned man to his execution to see if he was indeed the Messiah, had wearied of waiting for a miracle and had dispersed at last. The sixth hour was approaching; the sun stood at its zenith and it was almost time to bring the paschal offering into the Temple.

The cross against which Yeshua was nailed was somewhat taller than the other two. Of the three bodies, Yeshua's alone still showed symptoms of life. Robbed of its garments it looked pale, almost white under the sun. It writhed briefly with a snake-like movement as Yeshua tried to straighten himself on his impaled feet. Blood ran in trickles from his scalp where plaited thorns wreathed his black hair and dried against his sharp, protruding ribs. His thin arms, transfixed to the crossbar, sagged from the weight of his body as it strained away from the cross. The soldiers, when they stripped him, had left him only the four-cornered ritual shirt whose fringes could be seen to flutter lightly, pointing the breeze.

It was all silent now. The Roman quaternion that had been detailed to this crucifixion were squatting away at some distance. They were casting lots for Yeshua's cloak that lay before them, flecked with incrusted gore. Their captain every now and then glanced at the crucified one to see if he would not produce a miracle at this late hour. The sight of the white body stirred points of anxiety in his eyes and, averting his head, he returned to his brooding.

On another part of the hill, a good distance from the site of the crosses, a woman in black lay on her face, whimpering to herself. Under Yeshua's cross stood Rabbi Nicodemon, Yeshua's childhood friend. Aged and gray before his time, he swayed back and forth in prayer, a *tallith* pulled over his head. Again and again his hands reached out toward Yeshua's body; his inflamed eyes, which had cried much, scanned Yeshua's face, and his lips murmured endlessly:

419

"Yeshua, holy man of God, give us a sign, forsake us not in our darkness. Tell us who you are."

The other Jew with Nicodemon was the rich Joseph of Arimathea. His handsome head with its dark fringe of beard was raised toward Yeshua. Sorrow and veneration lay heavy on his features, and he said:

"By the living God, they have killed him for whom we waited all our days!"

And Yeshua, as if he had heard the words, murmured in a dying voice:

"Father, forgive them, for they know not what they do."

And when Yeshua had spoken these words, behold, a somber cloud shaped like a giant fist over Jerusalem, and suddenly a midnight darkness over all the earth, and this although the day had not begun to wane.

And then it was that a small group of three was seen ascending the slope. In the middle went an old, bowed woman, draped in black, and she was upheld on one side by a woman and on the other by a tall massive man clothed in a shroud-like sheet.

It was Miriam, coming to see the dying of her son. In obedience to his word she had avoided seeing him while he fulfilled his ministry on earth. Now she was led by her sister, the faithful Mariama, who had come with Yeshua to the very foot of the cross, and by Jochanan, Yeshua's best-loved disciple, to see the visage of her son in the hour of his glory, even as he had foretold.

They approached with halting, shuffling steps till Miriam was face to face with her son. Then they retreated from her—but a little space only lest she fall, being unsupported.

Miriam's eyes remained open. She saw the body of her son convulsing with pain, and she looked unblinking with large wounded eyes. This was the body she had held in her arms, that she had bathed and aneled, often and often since the day of his birth. Now she gazed at its bruises and lacerations, and the red welts where the soldier's whips had struck.

She looked at his head. His hair which she had often smoothed with oil was dressed with his life's blood. It trickled steadily from his brow, and Miriam's eyes traced every stream to its gash. She looked up at his hands that had often lain in her own, and her glance followed the nails through his palms where the stigmata were beginning to fester.

She did not weep at the sight. The lines of her face were hard and set, as though the muscles had been arrested forever. Only her eyes were strangely dilated and the whites were shot with a red tracery of veins so that they seemed like open wounds.

At last her gaze met Yeshua's; imperceptibly, her lips began to move; lightly at first, then with a flying flutter; and, almost inaudibly, the words came with the tremor of her breath:

"Tinoki, tinoki, tinoki . . ."

The son's body winced on the cross. His ribs shifted under their skin; for one fleeting moment the muscles of his body tensed and Miriam caught his word:

"Emi!"

She swayed as if to fall. Strong arms held her from behind, and as her son's voice said, "Behold thy mother!" she fell back in Jochanan's embrace. And even then she did not close her eyes, but continued to meet the gaze of her child. She felt her life falling away, falling away like an old garment. A new life was entering her. She was no longer her own person only; she was one with her child. In his glance she was nailed with him to the rood. Her body burned with his pain, the sting of gall and vinegar was on her tongue, and as her consciousness fled into darkness, she heard these words,—

"Into Thy hands I commend my spirit"—and knew not whether he or she had spoken them.

CHAPTER XVII

T HE Sabbath eve fell quickly on Jerusalem, not as on other nights when the lingering sun loitered on the city roofs, reluctant, as it were, to part from the golden peaks of the Temple. This night the sky darkened of a sudden and Sabbath tapers were lighted in every nook and corner of the city. Near

Golgotha the narrow streets were loud with the hosannas of the pilgrims. Their mood was high; one and all felt elated by the holiness of this Sabbath which fell on the Feast of Deliverance, and groups of townsmen, as well as families and student fellowships, filled every house, street, balcony, and roof with celebration.

Passing these jovial streets, the little group of mourning women conducted Miriam from her son's grave at the foot of Golgotha to the home of Joanna. The house was but a short distance away. It had sheltered the women of Yeshua's following while Yeshua himself, with the disciples, had spent the nights in concealment on the Mount of Olives. Now his aged mother was brought here for the Sabbath. Behind her group of women went Jochanan and Simon bar Jonah, who had kept himself in hiding near Golgotha. There was no sign as yet of Cleophas, Mariama's husband, nor of Yeshua's four brothers, nor of the old tanner, none of whom had seen the Place of Skulls since the erection of Yeshua's cross.

When they came into Joanna's house the mother put away her widow's veil so that her face was revealed. There was a movement of surprise among the others when they saw her change of countenance. They saw an old face seemingly emptied of grief, almost serene, but with pitifully sunken eyes. A profound silence governed all her motions, and she said, in a low voice:

"Wash your hands and faces. Light the lamps, and may the peace of the Sabbath come over you as it comes over all the world."

The women did as they were bidden. They washed themselves and lighted the lamps. Then they spread the table, and Jochanan sanctified the Sabbath over a cup of wine, as the master would have done had he been living. And all took seats at the table to eat the repast of the Sabbath.

Throughout the day she sat motionless in a corner of Joanna's house. Her narrow hardened lips were tightly closed and her eyes stared fixedly without seeing.

Her body gave no signs of life. It crouched, closed about itself like a still bundle or the lifeless hulk of an existence she had left behind. And yet, in the bystanders it evoked neither sorrow nor compassion so much as a sense of holiness which seemed to them to place Miriam beyond approach. The women in her presence were afraid to violate her silence, trod softly, and spoke in whispers that only deepened the hush.

From time to time Miriam's eyes returned to the present; then she looked at the women with a wan smile on her lips as if to beg their pardon for having overlooked them before. And, without speaking, her eyes would invite them to come closer. Then, for a while, the women would gather about her—her sister, the good Mariama, the faithful Shoshannah, Zebedee's widow, and their stately hostess, Joanna, the wife of Herod's officer. Miriam, with a gentle smile, eased their sorrow; her hands went out to them and she caressed their heads and calmed their spirits.

One of the women kept her distance. Since the mother's arrival in Jerusalem, Miriam of Magdala had been afraid to let the sacred shadow of Yeshua's mother fall on her. She had not dared to approach her on the hill of Golgotha where she had lain apart from the others, weeping to herself. And now, in Joanna's house—the only home she had since she had been brought here by the rabbi—she cowered in a distant corner, far from the mother's presence. Alone among the women she did not minister to Miriam, and it was she alone who remained in her corner while the others came forward at Miriam's gentle invitation. Her skin showed white under the rents of her garment; her face was hidden in the copper gleam of her hair. She lay motionless but for the spasms that convulsed her body as she tried to stifle the sound of her sobbing.

She started when she heard the others cross the room to gather about Yeshua's mother. For a moment she raised her head, and her eyes, crimson-framed, looked with mute pleading.

Miriam smiled, nodding her head, and beckoned her to come near—at which the Magdalene stared back in unbelief and terror. Then, like a vagrant animal, called from the nightly street to warm itself in a strange house, she crept forward and hid her face in the wide folds of Miriam's dress.

"Dry your tears," said the mother, laying her hand lightly on the girl. "It is the Sabbath today." And she clasped the girl's head in her arms while the Magdalene wept like a child.

423

Of all Yeshua's mourners no one, with the exception of the mother, felt his loss more poignantly than Miriam of Magdala. If for all others the Nazarene had been Israel's, even the world's, Messiah, for Miriam he had been her personal redeemer.

The others, after all, were of the holy community of Israel. If their hopes in Yeshua had faded, they still had the root from which the Messianic faith had sprung. This was not the first, no, nor the last time that Israel had been deceived. Jewry loved its Messiah, sickened for his coming. Their love and their nostalgia would in time nurture the new Messianic fruit. If the Nazarene had failed them, another would arise, the true Redeemer who would rally the heavenly host and descend in the panoply of vengeance.

But for Miriam of Magdala, Yeshua and none other had been the Messiah, and with his death perished her hope. What other Messiah, or what other rabbi, would stoop to lift her kind out of the gutters, cleanse her polluted body and soul, efface what was past even as the light of day scatters the bad dreams of the night, and infuse her with a new spirit to thirst for purity and holiness? What other rabbi would turn his back on the mighty, the learned, and the elect to embrace sinners; and finding her among the most unclean, on whom sin lay like a constrictor snake, would call out to her judges, "Let him among you who is without sin cast the first stone?" What other master would admit her to his presence?

But if Yeshua was not the Messiah, then all her effort was in vain, and vain was her purgation in the fires of penance. She would relapse into the clutch of sin from which he had delivered her. With all her longing and hunger for purity, she would be thrown back to the gutter that had been her cradle.

For her no hope existed outside Yeshua, the redeemer who had come with the blessing of God in his hand to help fallen ones like herself. All things passed away with him—the love and the splendor of God, the thirst and the longing, the hope and the remission of sins. Life with him had been blessed, without him it would be perdition.

She had been striving all day to suppress the show of her sorrow, that her sighs disturb not the peace of that Sabbath which enveloped the mother.

424

With the close of the Sabbath the armor fell from Miriam, the mother. Darkness sprang upon the house like the gloom of the soul. Seated motionless in the same place, her body looked shrunken and crushed as by the heels of grief. Her lips remained closed and her weeping inaudible. Nothing moved in her face save the tears that ran in the wrinkles of her yellowed skin. By the light of the single lamp—the memorial lamp for her son—the women in the room noticed for the first time the fearful gashing depth of these wrinkles. And they watched with aching hearts as Miriam's tears flowed over her still, frozen face.

And when they saw how the tears ran without cease, they vented at last their own woe and a loud keen burst from their mouths. Beyond the house and in the yard and street was heard their wailing.

The disciples Simon and Jochanan heard it, sitting in the yard. They were not weeping, but sat dejected and forlorn, not knowing where to turn or what more was decreed for them by their master.

Indoors, Miriam of Magdala beckoned to Mariama. The two women often spoke together. Mariama had been the first to befriend the Magdalene, for she felt the wholeheartedness of her conversion and the dedication of her soul to Yeshua. In their common love for the crucified rabbi, they had become as two sisters.

Now, with lanterns in their hands, they issued from the house together, and Miriam led her friend to the market in the lower city where the incense vendors had their stalls. One of these was known to the Magdalene, for she had in former years bought balms and salves from him. The two women purchased incense and sweet spices for the anointing of Yeshua's body, since there had not been time for this sacred rite on Friday in the hour of his deposition. Then only Nicodemon had brought a bundle of spices to lay in the sepulchre, but neither had he given the ultimate unction.

Miriam of Magdala doffed her black veil and wrapped it about the incense she had chosen. They returned to Joanna's house and there, all night, the girl sat on the ground, sorting the plants according to their kinds; the scarlet heart-leaves of the rose of Engedi, which, upon pressure, yielded a most fragrant balm; the

425

berries of wild myrtle; the spikenard and club moss which is brought from the shores of the Red Sea; the strange mystic plant called "moonlight"; the cassia, galbanum, and saffron, the castus and calmus, whose smoke dresses the Temple. She ran her fingers lightly over every leaf and flower, remembering how she had embalmed her master's feet when he sat with his disciples on Mount Olivet in the week of his death, and how the master had said: "She did it for my burial." And when she pounded them in the mortar, her tears mingled with the incense.

The nights of spring are brief in Jerusalem. Before the morning star asserts its light, the scent of flowers opening to receive the sun conveys the message of dawn. And soon the wind brings the rough smell of the desert and of Jericho's date groves. Waves of brightness pass through the air; a sweeter smell floats in from the vineyards of Bethlehem where the sun reddens the sky.

Miriam of Magdala no sooner heard the earliest cheep of the birds than she gathered up the vials and caskets she had filled with her fresh unguents, and placed them tenderly in a small basket. Mariama took up a bundle of remaining incense twigs and spices and wrapped them in a linen cloth. Then, with oil lamps in their hands, the two women sortied into the dark, drowsy streets of the city, walking at a brisk pace toward the rock tomb in the grounds of Joseph of Arimathea where, on the previous Friday, they had laid Yeshua's body.

Miriam, the mother, was left alone to watch over the lamp that burned on the table for the soul of her son. The rest of the women, exhausted by prolonged waking and grieving, had at last fallen asleep.

The first hesitating shafts of morning light came through the open windows of Joanna's house. From far away came a hint of small voices, the cooing of turtle-doves awakening in the aviaries of the Temple; then a fanfare of trumpets—the priests on the Temple walls proclaiming the end of the night watch.

Now the lights struck boldly in at the windows, dispersing the shadows in the house and bringing with it the bright smell of every flower. Miriam heard the noisy chirrup of birds on the roof, the hum and buzz of insects in the air. This was the anthem of Creation, and Miriam's heart joined in the song. She thought her

426

smart was strangely soothed and felt her inward being suddenly in tune with the glad sounds that wafted in from outside. Her lips parted and she whispered faintly:

"O Lord my God, I cried unto Thee and Thou hast healed me. O Lord, Thou hast brought up my soul from the grave; Thou hast kept me alive that I should not go down to the pit. Sing unto the Lord, O ye saints, and give thanks at the remembrance of His holiness. For His anger endureth but a moment; in His favor is life; weeping may endure for a night, but joy cometh in the morning."

Once more she listened to the joyous sounds, repeating to herself the last words of the Psalm. Every creature was sending up its matin song, singing the morning's resurrection.

She started at the words her lips had been faintly forming. Her hands began to shake, and sweat broke out on her skin. But in the selfsame moment she felt her head turned giddy with happiness and her limbs kindling with new life. A long-forgotten vigor surged through her body, such as she had not felt since her young motherhood.

Suddenly her groping palms lighted on living flesh; they touched the surface of an infant's body; hers. She felt the chubby caress of his hands, dabbling at her throat and cheek, the warmth and weight of him as he rocked himself across her knees. The child was back in her arms, pressing his small form against hers, merging his soul with hers so that they blended like two flames meeting in fire.

The music outside loudened, and Miriam recognized the chant of the Levites drifting down from the stairways of the Temple. It was floating in with the blatant light of the sun and the full-throated aubade of insects and birds. And as she distinguished a word, or a phrase, she joined in the chanting:

"The Lord is high above all nations, and His glory is above the heavens. Who is like unto the Lord our God, who dwelleth on high, who humbleth himself to behold the things that are in heaven, and in the earth! He raiseth up the poor out of the dust, and lifteth the needy out of the dunghill; that He may set him with princes, even with the princes of His people. He maketh the

427

barren woman to keep house, and to be a joyful mother of children. Hallelujah!"

Then she saw Yeshua; a small boy in a white shirt of her weaving. He was out on the green hill that faced their house in Nazareth, surrounded by her small domestic flock. "Moon," his beloved lamb, was snuggling at his side, its fleece white and undaggled, a patch of snowblink in the sun. Her hands went out to him:

"*Tinoki!*"

The child heard, threw up his head so that the dark curls shook and fluttered. He leapt up on the hill and ran and, flinging out his little hands, called:

"*Emi!*"

The cry repeated and swelled, and a deafening scream struck at her ear. Footsteps clattered across the yard and Miriam turned and saw the door fly open. The girl from Magdala, with disheveled hair, and Mariama after her, burst into the room; after them Simon and Jochanan. And all looked with a wild and frightened aspect.

"Mother, they have taken away our Lord!"

"Who?"

"We do not know; the tomb was empty when we came," cried Mariama, wailing.

The mother dropped her head in silence. But Simon bar Jonah made a bound to the door and called over his shoulder:

"Follow me, Jochanan, we shall see what happened!"

Jochanan lingered a little, watching the mother. He was the first to mark the change in her face, and he marveled at her transformation; his mouth opened to speak, but then he turned on his heel and followed Simon out through the door. The girl from Magdala ran after him.

"Miriam, what can this mean?" asked Mariama, clutching at her sister's hand.

"God will let us know in His time," said the mother, and her wrinkled mouth smiled faintly.

A short walking distance separated Joanna's house in the outmost part of the city from the hill of Golgotha, which rose just behind the outer wall. It was not long, therefore, before Jochanan and Simon returned.

Jochanan's face was dark with rage. His forehead was drawn into ragged folds, the copious mass of his black hair and beard shook with agitation. He flung himself down in a corner and said nothing.

Simon entered after him. His old, lined face was damp with weeping, and in his hands was a white headcloth which he held up to the mother, saying in a broken voice:

"This we found outside the tomb. See if it is not your son's."

And Miriam took the cloth, and said:

"It is his kerchief which I wove for him before he left my house."

Meanwhile the other women who were staying in Joanna's house awoke to the excitement, and they emerged sleepily from the inner chambers to gather about Mariama and the mother.

"What has happened?" they asked anxiously. And Mariama told them how she and the Magdalene had gone to the rabbi's grave, bearing spices and incense, but, coming near, had found the entrance to the tomb unsealed and the interior vacant. And now, she said, the disciples Simon and Jochanan had returned to confirm their Job's tale, having found only a discarded shroud within the sepulchre and Yeshua's headcloth a little way outside. When Joanna and the mother of the brothers Zebedee learned what had occurred they wrung their hands and set up a loud wail.

Outside, the day was growing warmer. The sun stood at full splendor in a powerful sky. Lightbeams of wandering dust filtered in at the windows, bringing a breath of warmth, brightness and holiday. The light and airy gaiety that flowed into the room made a sharp contrast to the gloom of its tenants. For if they were not actually sobbing, they sat in dismal expectation of some new disaster. Only Miriam, the mother, stood off from the others, seeming to be at one with the joyousness of the morning. Her face wore an expression of serene contentment and she sat erect with majestic, almost youthful, poise.

Suddenly they heard a voice outside, a singing voice coming as from afar. They held their breath to listen; the voice vibrated with a soft frail tremor, so that one could not tell if it were raised

429

in joy or lamentation. And as it came closer, the company in Joanna's house roused themselves as one man, for there was in it an urgent and annunciative quality, like the toll of a bell. And then the door opened and Miriam of Magdala stood on the threshold.

And they marveled to see her so changed who had gone out weeping, for she was standing taller, prouder and erect, and her copper-hued hair flamed about her head and shoulders like torchfire, and her face shone with a radiance that overwhelmed and comforted all them that looked on her.

"I have seen my Lord!" she said in a voice of triumph.

No one answered. It was as though an angel had addressed them, for the fear of God came over them and their hearts melted for terror. The women and disciples looked from one to the other and their tongues were dumb. Then it was Jochanan who broke the silence, speaking in a hard metallic voice:

"When did you see him, and where?"

"It was when you left the master's grave. I stayed behind alone weeping for my Lord, and stooped down and looked into the sepulchre. And there I saw two angels in white sitting, the one at the head, and the other at the feet, where his body had lain. And they said to me, 'Woman, why weepest thou?' And when I had told them that my Lord had been taken away, I turned myself and behold, Yeshua standing behind me! And he said, 'Go to my brethren and say unto them, I ascend unto my Father, and your Father; and to my God, and your God.' "

"She is seeing spirits!" Jochanan cried with mounting anger. "We were with her at the sepulchre and to us, his disciples, he did not appear; shall we believe that he revealed himself to a woman?"

"I have seen my Lord," the girl repeated with firmness, meeting Jochanan's frown. "He spoke face to face with me and called me Miriam. I knew him by his voice and answered, 'Rabboni,' my rabbi."

"Here we are like sheep that have lost their shepherd," said Simon, in misery, "and we were not worthy that he should show himself to us. We did not see him, but a woman did."

"I have seen my Lord," repeated Miriam of Magdala. "My

Lord lives; he is risen from the dead to ascend to his Father and to our Father."

"I believe you, my child." And the mother rose from her seat and went over to Miriam of Magdala and took her in her arms.

Only then did the other women in the house take note of the great transformation that had come over the mother, how she seemed strengthened and younger than they had seen her in many days. And they took it as proof that her son abode no more in the land of the dead, and said to each other:

"Behold, the mother also has risen from the dead."

But the men would not believe.

CHAPTER XVIII

FOR all that waited in Joanna's house, the day was one of utmost tension and perplexity. Were they to believe that the Messiah had indeed risen? Where then was the blast of angels' trumpets to proclaim the joyful tidings of redemption?— "Lo, this is the day of the Lord, fling wide the gates of heaven for all the sufferers of the earth!"

The mother put off the black widow's veil which she had donned after the Sabbath. And she called for her belt of purple that had the Lion of Judah wrought in silver on its buckle—young Joseph's wedding gift to her, which she had kept these many years as a memorial of his loyalty. Lastly she bade them lead her to the roof, to sit there under the sun, that all might see her.

And upon the roof the sun poured, as it were, a new light, as though indeed the seraphim were sounding God's message in the brightness of the heavens. And all the roofs of Jerusalem sparkled argent and white and joyed in the Passover feast. And they seated the mother in the view of all and the spirit of God came and rested on her.

The women, when they saw her so transfigured, knew not what to say for terror and joy. They saw the old familiar face, but one from which all grief was magically drained. And they saw her spread her hands as though to embrace the world and share with it her overflowing happiness. They were infected with her spirit and clapped their hands in jubilation.

"This is the day the Lord hath made," they sang; "we will rejoice and be glad in it!"

Later in the day the others—those of the rabbi's following who had gone into hiding—came drifting back sheepishly. Like thieves they stole into Joanna's house—the brothers, Jacob, Joses, Simon, and Jude, with their uncle Cleophas and Taddi the tanner. Having weathered the storm among the anonymous mob, they now judged the danger past and were returning to take the mother home to Nazareth. They no sooner came within earshot than they heard sounds of jubilation coming from the upper chambers of Joanna's house. And when they reached the yard they caught sight of delirious women falling in each other's arms and weeping for joy.

But when they entered the house they discovered shortly that only the womenfolk were thus taken. The two men among them, on the contrary, were in a heavy mood. In one corner they found Simon bar Jonah, who, in his bitterness, was chewing the flap of a napkin, while tears trickled into his beard.

"Surely, my Lord has not found me worthy," he was saying. "I am of all his servants the most spurned. For I have sought him and have found him not."

The brothers knew not what to say; Simon was babbling like a man fallen from reason. They turned questioning eyes on Jochanan.

"She saw a spirit," said he, "and that is all. If the master had truly shown himself he would have sought out his disciples, not a girl possessed like this Magdalene."

Without waiting to hear more, the brothers clambered to the roof where the joyful women surrounded their mother.

The mother herself had altered almost beyond recognition and, in that first moment, the brothers felt paralyzed by terror and shock. Never before had Miriam appeared to them in such a light. This was not the aging woman they had left behind in Nazareth; they saw her youth renewed as in long bygone days, a phantasm,

432

they would have said, conjured by their childhood recollection, but that this woman's youth was of a majesty to defy time. The grace of heaven rested on her brow and shone in the dark kindly wisdom of her eyes. Though her mouth smiled in greeting, yet could they not move forward in this first rapture of their awe. And then the mother opened her lips and said joyfully:

"God has done great things unto us, for the Lord has returned into our midst."

They paled with terror at these words and looked helplessly from one to the other. Was it the crucified Yeshua—and his own mother called him "the Lord"? They dared not move, nor speak a word for fear. Then Joses and Simon fell upon their faces and wept bitterly, while Jacob, the eldest, stood by, trembling head to foot. Jude alone retained a measure of his poise and was the first to recover his tongue, addressing himself, not to the mother, nor to any woman present, but to the disciples who had followed the brothers on the roof.

"Have any of the disciples," he asked, "seen the master?"

"No," came the reply. "We found only his shroud in the tomb, but saw nothing of him. And what reliance is in the word of a woman?"

As the day progressed more of the disciples returned, each from his own coign of safety, and each with his own hearsay offering. No one could tell how the tidings had spread, whether the wind or the angels of heaven had cast them abroad. Nor was any man fairly convinced of his own version, certain only that something great and noteworthy had befallen the body of their master. His body, they knew, had gone from its tomb, for the report was all over Jerusalem. It flew from mouth to mouth in every street and bazaar of the great city. Yeshua of Nazareth, it was declared, nailed to the cross on Friday last, the man bruited by the Galileans to have been the King-Messiah, had mysteriously vanished from the sepulchre of the rich Joseph of Arimathea. Some said that the body, by order of the court, had been taken from the tomb for re-interment in the martyrs' cemetery, so that its disappearance accorded both with the laws of nature and the Mosaic code. Others again insisted on invoking supernatural agencies. In short, no one could escape the rumors, least of all the disciples, who in their trepidation kept their ears cocked for every news of their rabbi.

Knowing that the eldest of the disciples, Simon bar Jonah and the beloved Jochanan, could both be found in Joanna's house, they crept back, by turns hopeful and despondent. Faith in the healing rabbi flared again in their hearts. Perhaps, after all, God had redeemed his pledge and sent, in Yeshua of Nazareth, a Saviour for the Jews. Perhaps, this day, an ancient prophecy had been fulfilled and the Messiah, though entombed—like Jonah in the belly of the whale—had risen in glory with hosts of angels waiting on his word. If this was the case, why then should they keep silent and hide their faces in dark corners? Rather should they proclaim the news with a loud tongue, for now the heavens would open and all men behold the glory of the Lord resting on him whom they had been the first to recognize. They recalled now how the rabbi, in his life, had spoken enigmatically of the sign of Jonah, and so they came, some sanguine in expectation, some more in dread of disappointment. "He who shall lose his life for me shall save his life," they thought, remembering the master's promise. Then let them come, the soldiers of Pilate; let them bring all their arsenal of thongs and swords, and bring them to trial, for the rabbi had foretold that they should suffer for his name.

But they had no sooner set foot in Joanna's house and seen the faces of Simon and Jochanan, than their spirits fell. Their terror returned and their hearts became as water.

"What has happened, speak!"

"We do not know," replied Jochanan. "The master has vanished from his tomb."

"But saw you the master?"

"No," replied Jochanan, and added with slow emphasis—"the master was not seen."

"Why then do the women rejoice?"

"Because of the Magdalene; she says the master appeared to her and spoke."

At which Simon shook his head sadly, saying again:

"I have followed my Lord from the first day, since he was baptized in Jordan. But I have not merited to see him, nor to hear his voice. My Lord has not found me worthy."

"Oh, for shame!" said Jochanan impatiently. "That the whims of a possessed girl should find men so credulous! Hear me, brothers: if the master had returned, he would have shown himself to his disciples, to them that love him, whom he elected in his life—not to a woman who is possessed by spirits!"

"You speak true, Jochanan," said one of the latecomers. "In matters of such weight a woman's evidence cannot be trusted."

"And we know that the rabbi's body was moved to the martyrs' field on orders from the High Priest," said Cleophas.

"How do you know?"

"How do I know? Why, everybody knows; it is told in every market!"

"And they will come for us next and drag us all to court," said another.

"But what I cannot understand is why the women make such jubilation. They will only bring the High Priest's agents down on our heads. Just listen to . . ." The speaker stopped, for the mother had come down from the roof and entered their circle. She must have sensed the topic of their discourse, or read it in their faces, for she addressed herself at once to Jochanan:

"Jochanan, son of Zebedee," said she firmly, "can you not see that the Lord revealed himself first to them that needed him the most, even the humblest, as he did in his life—and not to them who are proud and confident of his love?"

"For us the master has already come and has given us the way," replied Jochanan. "It is all one whether we see him again with our eyes or no. For our master is spirit and he is in us. Therefore, I say, it is bootless to sit idle and wait for the master's return. The Lord is in us and we, in his spirit, shall determine what we have to do."

"For me, Jochanan, the master must come back," said Simon bar Jonah. "He will return and set us on the road, for we are like sheep strayed upon the rocks. And though I was not chosen to see his return with my own eyes, yet I rejoice in his resurrection. For now he tries the limit of our faith for the salvation of our souls. Therefore, I say, we shall wait here for our Lord, and, I tell you,

435

he will come not once but day after day to tell us what we have to do. Like the good shepherd who leads his flock into green pastures we shall follow without fear, though he lead us through the valley of the shadow of death."

The mother went to him.

"Simon bar Jonah," she said, "you shall point the way for us. In your footsteps will we follow, for the Lord has spoken through the mouth of faith."

But Simon shook his head in bewilderment and exclaimed:

"Who am I to lead his flock? Only a lowly servant to Yeshua-Messiah! Without the master's guidance I know not what to do." And he threw himself on the ground and cried: "Lord, Lord, where art thou? Come thou to us, for behold, without thy guiding staff we are as straying sheep. Thou who broughtest us the everlasting life, leave us not in darkness. See, thy flock stands forlorn since their shepherd was taken. Come, thou good shepherd, come to us. . . ." And Simon remained long on his knees, hiding his tear-stained face in his hands. No one spoke, not the disciples, nor the brothers. They lowered their heads and heard the stricken man sobbing on the floor, and some shivered as the remnant of their hope faded in silence. They stood still and waited.

And suddenly the mother's body shuddered. They saw her eyes directed at a point in space, her lips open and mute. They followed her glance—seeing nothing—and looked back to the mother. They saw her pale suddenly, a violent gasp wrenching her mouth; then saw her smile, her eyes filling with tears. Her hands reached out, trembling, and from her smiling lips, softly and tenderly, fell the familiar words:

"*Tinoki, tinoki. . . .*"

The disciples turned again. Before them stood He whom they sought, white, His pierced hands spread in an infinite embrace, and they heard the voice they knew so well:

"*Shalom aleichem*—Peace be unto you."